WHERE
SECRETS
LIE

WHERE SECRETS LIE

D.S. BUTLER

 THOMAS & MERCER

Text copyright © 2019 by D. S. Butler
All rights reserved.

Published by Thomas & Mercer, Seattle

www.apub.com

Amazon, the Amazon logo, and Thomas & Mercer are trademarks of Amazon.com, Inc., or its affiliates.

ISBN-13: 9781503905016
ISBN-10: 1503905012

Cover design by @blacksheep-uk.com

Printed in the United States of America

WHERE SECRETS LIE

PROLOGUE

James Hunter was drunk.

Tonight he'd flown past the happy, confident, slightly tipsy stage, straight into the depressive, miserable phase. He poured another measure of vodka, splashing some on the coffee table.

At one of his first AA meetings, he'd stood up in front of the group and told them he drank to forget, but that was a lie. Alcohol didn't help him forget. It numbed the pain a little bit, but it also turned him into a melancholy, blubbering mess.

He wiped away the fat tears rolling down his cheeks with the back of his hand.

From the outside, most of his acquaintances saw James as a successful forty-three-year-old man who ran a thriving website-design business. He was happily married. His mortgage was paid off. He was financially secure. On the surface, he was one of life's winners. Only his drinking hinted at his dark secret.

AA had seemed to be the answer for a while. Of course, it didn't solve all his problems. The reason he'd turned to drink in the first place hadn't disappeared, but AA gave him enough support to avoid the seductive lure of alcohol most of the time.

Vodka had always been his drink of choice. Clear and discreet, it could be poured into a water bottle and carried around all day without arousing too much suspicion. It wasn't completely odourless, but it didn't smell as strong as other alcohols, and, most important of all, it was effective and got him drunk fast.

'How long has it been since you fell off the wagon?' his friend asked, looking concerned.

James felt a wave of unrelenting shame. Why was he so weak?

'Two years,' he said quietly, looking at the almost-empty bottle of vodka on the table next to the small glass tumbler. James sat on the sofa, and his friend sat opposite him in an armchair with his fingers interlinked, hands resting lightly on his lap as he looked at James reproachfully.

'Two years is pretty good going. We all have setbacks sometimes. The trick is to get back on the wagon.'

James nodded. 'You're right. I'll pour the rest down the sink.'

He didn't want to, though. He wanted to finish the bottle. Once you started, it was so hard to stop. His fingers itched to reach out and grab the bottle. Could he pretend to pour it down the sink and then stash it somewhere, so he could finish it after his guest had left?

'No need to do that,' he said. 'It's open, so you may as well finish it.'

James blinked in surprise. That wasn't the response he'd anticipated.

'I shouldn't really,' James said. 'Not now. I'm feeling better. Just talking about it has helped. I should have come clean years ago. I'm already feeling stronger. The guilt was eating away at me.'

'I'm not surprised. It must have been a horrible thing to go through, and keeping it to yourself must have been unbearable.'

James sniffed, his gaze fixed on the bottle of vodka.

'Go ahead,' his friend said. 'You can start afresh tomorrow.'

James shook his head and stood up. Unsteady on his feet, he reached out to grasp the arm of the sofa before staggering forward towards the balcony doors. 'No, I'd better not. I just need to sober up a bit. Fresh air will help. I'm sorry for unloading all this on you.'

He'd not been keen on buying a flat. That had been his wife's idea. James would have preferred a house with a garden. They couldn't have animals in the flat either, and he'd always imagined himself having a dog to take for walks and to greet him enthusiastically when he came home.

His wife worked away a lot, and he got lonely. He didn't like his own company. When he was alone he had time to think. He didn't like that at all.

He pushed open the balcony doors and felt the cold night air wash over him. The breeze was bracing and felt good. They'd had a mild start to the autumn, but the weather had shifted, and James found the evening air cooler than he'd expected. He leaned heavily on the painted railings and looked down.

Their flat didn't have the best view. Lincoln had lovely old buildings, and some of the other apartments looked out on the castle or cathedral. Their apartment had been sold as having a view of the river, but you could only see it if you stuck your head out of the bathroom window. The apartments with appealing vistas were more expensive, so they'd opted for this one because it meant they could afford an extra bedroom for James to use as an office.

He gripped the railings and swayed a little as he looked across the road at the multistorey car park. Not the most attractive sight.

James saw someone moving near the entrance. He squinted, leaning forward. It was the homeless girl; he saw her most days. He sighed. Life could be very unfair. She was only a youngster. His wife often carried a cup of coffee down to the girl before she went to work. James had given her a slice of his birthday cake last month. She was a sweet kid.

He couldn't see her clearly because it was dark, but he could make out the outline of her sleeping bag and the couple of bags she always seemed to have with her.

She was an addict, of course. He'd seen the marks on her arms, but who was he to judge? He was an addict, too. He might be functioning well enough to hold down a job and keep a roof over his head, but an addict was an addict.

James heard a noise and turned to smile as his friend stepped out on to the balcony beside him.

'I feel like a weight has been lifted,' James said. 'I should have come clean ages ago. They say a problem shared is a problem halved, but I'd never believed that until today.'

His friend said nothing but stepped closer and glanced over the railings.

James shivered and looked down. 'It's quite a drop, isn't it? I wasn't sure about being on the eighth floor, but Diana insisted. She liked the views better higher up. I'm not sure being higher makes the car park look any better, but I suppose we get more light up here.'

He turned to his friend, who was still silent, and wondered if he'd shocked him with his confession. 'I hope you don't mind me telling you all this tonight. I've been carrying it around with me for so long. It was making me ill.' James looked away. 'I hope you don't think too badly of me.'

This time when James turned back to him, his friend had a strange look in his eyes.

He almost looked angry.

James blinked. His alcohol-muddled brain was trying to tell him something, trying to warn him something wasn't right, but he couldn't process his thoughts fast enough.

It wasn't until he felt the man's hand beneath his armpit and another hand on his belt that he realised something was terribly wrong.

Even then, when his mind finally recognised the danger, when he realised he needed to run, his body wouldn't obey his commands. Instead of springing into action from the flood of adrenaline, his muscles refused to respond. Trembling, all James could do was let out a little whimper as he was hoisted into the air and over the railings.

At the last minute, his body jerked into action, and he bucked and twisted, desperately trying to free himself and get back to the safety of the balcony. His body rested on the railings, and he felt a dull pain in his hip as he squirmed against them, and then in the next moment he was given another shove that sent him hurtling to the ground.

In the short time it took James to plummet from the eighth floor, one thought ran through his mind: *What have I done?*

CHAPTER ONE

PC Sanderson and PC Montgomery arrived at 92 Old Road, Skellingthorpe, just after nine a.m. The woman who had called the emergency services for help stood at the front of the house, waving at them as they exited their police vehicle.

'Thank goodness,' she said, pressing one hand against her chest and flapping the other one at them to try to hurry them along.

'Are you the neighbour who called the police? Mrs Maud Kennedy?' PC Sanderson asked.

The woman replied in short, staccato sentences, each word punctuated by a gasping breath. 'Yes. I knew something was wrong. We hadn't seen him on his bike this morning, you see. And he always cycles to the shop for his paper. I should have checked on him before now.'

She quickly walked along the garden path towards the front door, and the officers followed her.

'Are you sure he hasn't gone away?' PC Montgomery asked. 'Perhaps he's gone to visit relatives.'

The woman turned on him scornfully. 'I've lived opposite him for twenty years, and I have never known him to visit family since his wife died. Or, for that matter, family to visit him. Besides, I thought I heard him groaning.'

PC Sanderson looked at the dilapidated exterior of the house. The old wooden window frames were half rotted away. The front door was also wooden, with thin cracks criss-crossing the weather-damaged blue paint.

'It's all right, Mrs Kennedy,' Sanderson said. 'We'll check up on him and make sure he's all right.'

Mrs Kennedy shook her head. 'But he's not all right. I told you, I can hear moaning. If you put your ear against the door, you should be able to hear it.'

Sanderson gave his colleague a nod, and PC Montgomery pressed his ear against the front door before peering through the letterbox. 'I can hear something. But I can't see him.'

He continued staring through the letterbox, and after a short pause, he let out a yelp and fell on to his backside.

Sanderson rushed to his side, grabbing his elbow and pulling him to his feet. 'What was it?'

PC Montgomery shook his head, looking abashed. 'Nothing. It was just a cat. It gave me a fright.'

Sanderson resisted making a sarcastic comment. He turned to Mrs Kennedy, who was looking at both of them, no doubt wondering at the state of the police these days.

Sanderson tried to exert a little control over the situation. 'Let's go round to the back, shall we? We may be able to gain entry a little easier there.'

Mrs Kennedy nodded. 'The back door is old and has glass panels. You should be able to break one of those.'

They walked around the side of the house and saw Mrs Kennedy was right. An old-fashioned door with glass panels and a brass handle stood before them like a burglar's dream. Sanderson didn't bother returning to the car to get any tools or request backup. Instead, he picked up a large decorative stone, one of many that lined the flower-bed, and broke the small pane of glass beside the handle.

In the distance, they heard the wail of a siren.

'That'll be the ambulance,' PC Montgomery said to Mrs Kennedy with a confident smile.

If his aim was to reassure her, it didn't work. She turned her back on him, clasping the small gold cross that hung from her neck, and watched PC Sanderson slip his hand carefully through the broken pane of glass to grasp the door handle from the inside. When the door didn't open, he felt down a little lower, locating the bolt, and a moment later he gave a satisfied grin as he slid the bolt across and opened the back door.

As they heard the ambulance pull up outside the house, PC Montgomery turned to Mrs Kennedy and asked her to remain outside.

She looked most put out. 'He won't like it,' she warned. 'Bert doesn't like strangers, and he doesn't like anybody in his house.'

PC Sanderson thought she was exaggerating. 'If he needs help, we need to go inside. If you could stand back a little, please.' He pointed to the spot where he wanted Mrs Kennedy to stand, but she just took one tiny step backwards. She was beginning to irritate him. It was one thing to be concerned about her neighbour, but she seemed almost to be revelling in the excitement.

'What's his name?'

'It's Bert. Albert Johnson. He's in his eighties and a little bit doddery on his feet these days. I've offered him help time and time again, but he's too proud to accept it.'

PC Sanderson left his colleague outside to greet the paramedics and keep an eye on Mrs Kennedy and stepped inside the property.

He called out, 'Police! We're here to help, Bert. Where are you?'

There was no answer.

The air smelled damp and old. The kitchen was dirty. It wasn't that there were unwashed pots and pans lying around, but the counters were filthy. A thick layer of dust covered the windowsills. Sanderson looked around at the neglected, rundown kitchen and felt a pang of sympathy for the poor old bloke who lived here. Maybe he didn't notice the state of the place. Maybe his old eyes couldn't see the dust and grime properly anymore. Sanderson sighed. Maybe the man's old body was too tired for cleaning.

The decor hadn't been updated since the seventies, he noticed as he left the kitchen and headed along the hallway.

He called out again. 'Bert? We're the police, we've come to help you. Where are you?'

But PC Sanderson didn't have to wait for an answer. As soon as he turned the corner he saw a pair of legs at the bottom of the stairs. One of them was folded at an awkward angle.

'Bert, my name is PC Sanderson of the Lincolnshire Police. We have an ambulance outside, and we're going to get you to the hospital and fixed up. Okay?'

He approached the elderly man and knelt down beside him, reaching out to take his hand. That wasn't protocol, but it felt like the right thing to do. He wanted to offer the old man some comfort.

The man turned to him, but as Sanderson looked down into his rheumy eyes, he didn't see gratitude or relief, he saw fear.

That was understandable, he supposed. The poor man must be terrified. Goodness knows how long he'd been crumpled at the bottom of the stairs, injured and unable to move. The dark patch on the front of his trousers made Sanderson suspect it had been quite some time.

'You're going to be all right, Bert. Everything's going to be just fine.'

The staircase was steep and each step was narrow. It wasn't surprising the old man had taken a tumble.

Bert's fingers tightened around his hand just as PC Montgomery entered the house with the paramedics.

Before Sanderson could say anything to the paramedics and explain the circumstances, the old man's face twisted in anger as he rasped, 'I never let you in.'

Sanderson hadn't chosen this job for the compliments. He'd come across plenty of people who didn't appreciate his help or assistance, but the man's reaction surprised him. From the state of him, he guessed Bert had been flat on his back for hours, in agony and unable to get up. Now that the emergency services had turned up to help, Sanderson had expected a little more gratitude. Maybe the poor old boy was delirious.

As the female paramedic knelt down beside Bert and leaned over to examine his injuries, he batted her hands away. 'Go away. I don't need your help.'

She exchanged a look with Sanderson. 'He's overwrought. Not surprising.'

Bert tightened his hold on Sanderson's hand, causing the officer to wince. The old man still had a surprisingly strong grip.

Bert's watery blue eyes locked with Sanderson's. 'You are not to go upstairs. Do you hear me? It's private. Do not go upstairs!' He paled dramatically and began gasping for breath.

Both paramedics sprang into action, and Sanderson pulled his hand away. He got to his feet and took a step back, giving them room to work. It wasn't long before they had an oxygen mask over the old man's face, and a few moments later, they wheeled him out of the house on a trolley.

PC Montgomery widened his eyes and blew out a breath, puffing out his cheeks. 'Well, he wasn't exactly pleased to see us.'

Sanderson shrugged. 'He was probably delirious from lying here for so long.'

He was trying to convince himself, but he had to admit there was something about the old man's reaction that set off alarm bells.

Montgomery grinned at him. 'So what do we do now?'

Distracted, Sanderson frowned. 'What do you mean? We secure the premises and then talk to Mrs Kennedy before writing up our report.'

'Yes, of course, but before we do that we're going to look upstairs, right?'

Sanderson's gaze was drawn to the steep staircase. There was no reason for them to go up there. It was a domestic accident. They needed to secure the broken window, write their report and head back to the station.

'Come on,' PC Montgomery said. 'It won't take long. It's worth a look. That old bloke really didn't want us to go upstairs.'

He started to climb the stairs, his big heavy boots crushing the paisley carpet beneath his feet.

Sanderson objected. 'This is someone's home. You can't just trample all over it without good reason.'

'You stay there, then,' Montgomery called over his shoulder. 'I'm going upstairs to find what he didn't want us to see.'

Sanderson hesitated at the foot of the stairs for a moment or two before huffing under his breath and following. The steps creaked beneath his feet as he walked past the peeling wallpaper, and he noticed that the handrail was a little loose.

He tugged on it but decided that couldn't have been the cause of the accident. Poor old Bert must've just slipped. It was easy enough to do on these narrow steps, and at his age, the old man's reactions weren't quick enough to break his fall or save himself.

When he reached the hallway at the top of the stairs, he saw PC Montgomery staring at a padlocked door. He pointed at the lock. 'Now tell me that old man isn't hiding something.'

Sanderson shuffled around to get a better look at the door. It appeared to be the kind of padlock you'd see outside, on a garden shed. It was not the type of lock anyone would usually attach to an internal door.

He shrugged. 'That's it, then. I guess we'll never know what he's hiding.'

'What do you mean, *that's it*? We can't go now, not without finding out what's behind this door.'

'It's padlocked. We are *not* going to force the lock. We'll include it in our report, and if the inspector thinks we need to find out what's inside, then we'll come back.'

PC Montgomery looked at him incredulously. He moved closer to the door, bending down to inspect the padlock. Then he laughed. 'The silly old coot left the key in the bottom.'

He grinned broadly as he turned the key, removed the padlock and pushed open the door before Sanderson could object.

Although the curtains were drawn, the bedroom was surprisingly bright. The sun shone through the thin yellow curtains. Like the rest of the house, every surface was covered in a layer of dust. Sanderson stepped into the room. A neatly made single bed was pushed back against the wall, and a picture of a Spitfire was hung on the wall above the nightstand. He thought it looked like a normal spare bedroom and couldn't understand why Bert had gone to the trouble of putting a padlock on the door.

The only odd thing in the room was a large, navy-blue suitcase sitting in the middle of the peach carpet. It was covered with dust and old cobwebs and looked as though it had recently been brought down from the loft. The rest of the room was dusty, but not as bad as the case.

PC Montgomery made a beeline for the case. 'What have we got here, then?' he muttered, grabbing the handle and attempting to pick it up. 'Good grief! It weighs a ton.'

His eyes glinted with excitement as he unfastened the leather strap and reached for the zip.

'You can't open it,' Sanderson said, well aware that PC Montgomery was paying him no attention.

'Of course we have to open it! It's our duty. There could be stolen goods inside, or weapons or . . . Jesus Christ!'

Montgomery squealed and dropped the suitcase on the floor, scurrying away from it.

'What is it?' Sanderson asked, starting to suspect he was the victim of a prank. Montgomery was well known as a practical joker at the station.

But if this was a joke, he was putting on a good act. His face was pale, and he couldn't take his eyes off the suitcase.

'There's a body in that case.'

At that moment, the cat Montgomery had seen earlier walked up to him, rubbing against his leg and meowing loudly. Startled, Montgomery jumped.

Wide-eyed and looking a little green, he turned to Sanderson and said, 'I'm calling the inspector.'

Sanderson watched him rush out of the room. If he hadn't worked with Montgomery before, he probably would have fallen for the windup. He leaned down to stroke the cat. Poor thing was probably hungry. He made a mental note to check in the kitchen for cat food after he'd dealt with the current situation.

He turned back to the case. Montgomery had to be pulling his leg. He'd been called out to enter properties containing dead bodies on two previous occasions, and both times the whole property had been permeated by the most awful smell. The smell of death wasn't something you forgot in a hurry.

The room smelled musty, but it didn't smell of death. The thought gave Sanderson confidence. He straightened up and approached the case. The zip was open, but the lid of the case had fallen shut when Montgomery dropped it.

The cat meowed again.

'All right, I'll get you some food in a minute.' He hesitated, then gritted his teeth. This was ridiculous. Montgomery had to be winding him up.

He glanced over his shoulder, expecting to see Montgomery smirking in the doorway, but there was no sign of him.

He looked at the cat. 'It's no big deal. I just have to check the case.'

The cat watched him with curious green eyes.

Sanderson took a deep breath and flung back the lid of the case.

Blood rushed in his ears, and his stomach churned as he stared down in disbelief at the contents of the case. Montgomery had been right. Curled up in the foetal position, decayed to just leathery skin and bones, was a human corpse.

CHAPTER TWO

DI Scott Morgan hung up the phone and stared down at his hastily written notes. A skeleton in a suitcase was certainly a first for him. He ripped the top sheet of paper from the pad and carried it out into the open-plan office area. His team looked up as he approached.

'We've got a new case,' he said, handing the notes he'd made to DC Rick Cooper. 'It's an interesting one. A body has been found inside a suitcase at a house in Skellingthorpe.'

He looked at Rick, who was quickly scanning the notes. 'Can you and Sophie collect background information while Karen and I go to the scene? We'll need to find out everything we can about the house and its owner. The officers who found the body say it's very old, practically a skeleton. The house belongs to Albert Johnson, an elderly man who suffered a fall. Police and paramedics were called to the scene, and it was while the officers were securing his house that they found the body.'

DS Karen Hart stood up, grabbing her jacket from the back of her chair. 'I bet that gave them a shock.'

'I imagine so. Both officers are going to stay at the house so we can have a chat with them when we get there. The crime scene unit are already on their way, and so is the pathologist.'

Rick looked up and passed the notes to DC Sophie Jones. 'We'll look into his background, sir. Do we know if anyone else shares the house with him?'

DI Morgan shook his head. 'No, we don't know much about him at all, so that's one of the first things you'll need to determine.' He turned to look at Karen. 'Ready?'

'Lead the way.'

They reached the detached property in Skellingthorpe just after eleven a.m. The spring sunshine was finally burning off the persistent mist, but it lingered in the open fields around the property, giving the area a strange, otherworldly appearance.

It was March, but the weather this morning felt more like autumn, Karen thought as she pulled on the handbrake. The remnants of the mist made her feel gloomy and cold.

'It's pretty isolated around here,' DI Morgan said as he unfastened his seatbelt.

Karen nodded. There was a small house on the other side of the road, but apart from that, the next nearest house had to be over a mile away.

'The perfect place for a murder to be carried out without anyone noticing or hearing anything,' Karen said.

'That's a morbid thought.'

They both got out of the car and walked towards the uniformed officer standing beside the crumbling stone wall at the front of the property.

'Morning, ma'am, sir,' the officer said as he held out the logbook for them to sign.

'Where are the officers who found the body?' DI Morgan asked.

The uniformed officer pointed in the direction of a squad car. 'They're sitting in the back of that car, sir. They were pretty shaken up.'

Karen felt her stomach tighten. She hated attending crime scenes, but it was a necessary part of the job. It was hard to investigate a case without seeing where the crime had been committed. The scene usually held many clues. Maybe the one in this case would be less disturbing than others she'd attended. If the body was very old, she hoped that meant the smell wouldn't be too bad this time.

'Good, the pathologist is here already,' Karen said, scanning the logbook before signing it.

'Yes, he arrived about ten minutes ago, ma'am.' The officer lifted the crime scene tape.

Karen ducked beneath the tape, and DI Morgan followed.

She carefully picked her way along the garden path. It was only the beginning of spring, but green weeds were already poking through cracks between the paving slabs. The front garden, although small, was mature and full of a mixture of evergreen plants and stick-like perennials that hadn't yet been cut back.

Mr Johnson, or whoever else had lived here with him, was certainly green-fingered, but it seemed like the garden was getting too much for him. The narrow path led around the side of the house, and markers had been laid out to indicate the route they should take so that the scene would be disturbed as little as possible. At the back door, Karen saw a pane of glass had been broken and guessed that was how the officers had gained entry to the house.

A box full of protective shoe coverings sat at the side of the back door. Karen selected a pair and slid them over her shoes. DI Morgan did the same, then they put on protective gloves and entered the house.

Karen nodded a greeting to one of the crime scene photographers who was taking photographs of the kitchen.

'Raj is upstairs. First bedroom on the right,' the photographer said, then turned back to her work.

Karen thanked her and walked ahead towards the stairs.

'This is where Albert Johnson was found,' DI Morgan said as they reached the base of the steps.

Karen felt a pang of sympathy for the old man, who'd been hurt and stranded at the bottom of the stairs, but quickly pushed the feeling away. The old man could be a murderer. In fact, it was extremely likely that he was. She supposed murderers got old and frail just like everyone else.

They climbed the stairs and made their way to the first bedroom. Inside, the pathologist was already hard at work peering into the suitcase.

Karen had never seen a body like it. It wasn't completely skeletonised. There was some shrivelled brown skin hanging on to the brown and yellow limb bones. It looked like a shrunken shell of a person.

She stepped forward and said hello to Raj, but her eyes didn't leave the collection of leathery skin and bones inside the suitcase.

'Good morning,' Raj said, straightening up. 'I can't examine the body properly here, so I'm going to move the whole lot back to the lab.'

Karen tore her gaze away from the body to look at Raj.

Rajinder Kumar reminded her of an Indian Poirot. He was short, overweight and had a fine moustache. Considering his line of work, Karen had found him consistently cheerful and always helpful. She liked working with him.

'Can you give us some idea of how long ago she or he died?' DI Morgan said as he stared at the body with the same intensity Karen had a few moments earlier.

Raj pursed his lips and then said, 'I can't give you an accurate answer, but I'd say at least twenty years, probably no more than forty.'

He pointed out some fabric draped over what Karen assumed was a leg bone. 'Our victim was wearing some manmade fabric, which might help us with identification. I'd guess from the size of the bones and the width of the pelvis that our victim is a man, but don't hold me to it.'

Karen leaned forward, intrigued by the fabric. It was vivid blue, stained with splotches of yellow and brown. No doubt the colour had been dulled by the passage of time and by decomposing fluids seeping into it, which would mean it had been an even brighter blue when the fabric was new. 'It looks a bit like one of those tracksuit tops. You know, they were all the rage in the eighties.'

'Like a shell suit?' DI Morgan asked, standing further back from the body than Karen, but still studying it intently.

'Yes, and they were all manmade fibres, weren't they? That would explain why it lasted all this time, and the bright colour.' Karen looked at the pathologist.

Raj nodded. 'Quite likely. The cotton and other natural fibres seem to have degraded. I might be able to recover something once we get the body back to the lab.'

DI Morgan slowly circled the case. 'It's strange,' he said finally.

That was the understatement of the century. A body in a suitcase was more than strange in Karen's book.

'The suitcase is very dusty,' DI Morgan continued. 'It's covered with cobwebs all around the base, but the rest of the room isn't too bad.' He looked around. 'It is dusty in here, but I can't see any cobwebs.'

They both looked up at the same time and saw the hatch to access the roof above them. 'Do you think the old man brought the suitcase down from the loft?' Karen suggested. 'The exertion may have brought on a dizzy spell or made him feel light-headed, which led to his fall.'

'It's a good theory,' DI Morgan said, looking up at the hatch above them. 'Shall we take a look?'

At that moment Darren Webb, the crime scene manager, appeared in the doorway. 'I'm sorry, DI Morgan. I'll have to ask you to wait until the team have photographed the loft before you go up there.'

DI Morgan held up his hands. 'Of course, sorry. I wasn't thinking. How are you getting on with the rest of the house? Anything interesting?'

Darren motioned towards the stairs. 'Yes, we've found something in the kitchen that I think you'll both be very interested in.'

DI Morgan followed him out of the room, and Karen turned to say goodbye to Raj.

'Thanks, Raj. When do you think you'll have more answers for us?'

Raj pulled a face. 'It's not going to be an easy one, Karen. I'm going to need to take my time and make sure I don't ruin any evidence. The body has been curled up in this position for a long time. I'm not even sure I'm going to be able to give you a cause of death. But, luckily for you, my caseload is light at the moment.'

Karen smiled. 'If you find anything, don't wait to file the full report. Just give me a call, okay?'

Raj nodded, and then his gaze flickered back to the body.

Downstairs, Karen joined DI Morgan and Darren Webb in the kitchen. They both wore serious expressions and were studying something on the kitchen counter.

Karen stepped forward, peering around DI Morgan. It was a note printed in a large font on a plain sheet of A4 printer paper. The paper was creased in three places where it had been previously folded. That was innocuous enough, but the message made Karen catch her breath.

It read:

It's time to pay for your crime.

CHAPTER THREE

It was midday by the time Karen and DI Morgan left Albert Johnson's house and crossed the road to speak to his nearest neighbours. They had attempted to talk to the officers who had found the body, but the two men had already returned to the station. Apparently, they were still very shaken up. DI Morgan looked displeased with the news, and the poor uniformed officer beside the crime scene tape had been very apologetic, even though it wasn't his fault. He told them PC Montgomery had already been sick twice, and, finally, DI Morgan softened a little and agreed to find them at Nettleham headquarters later.

The mist had finally disappeared, and it was starting to feel like spring. Blackbirds and wrens sounded alarm calls as they darted in and out of the hedgerows. No other buildings could be seen around the two properties. There was nothing but fields, and an occasional ash tree dotting the landscape.

'I'm surprised it's so isolated,' DI Morgan commented. 'We're not that far from the centre of Skellingthorpe.'

Karen nodded, but she was deep in thought. The note found in Albert Johnson's kitchen had set her nerves on edge. She'd come to the scene working on the assumption that this was an old case, possibly an accidental death or a murder that had been covered up for decades.

The most likely perpetrator, Albert Johnson, was an old man who was now in Lincoln County Hospital, no threat to anyone, but what they'd discovered suggested a different perspective.

The note hadn't looked old. The paper was pristine and white, with no signs of yellowing with age. She wondered if this case was really as cold as she'd thought. Had Albert fallen, or had he been pushed?

'If we work on the assumption that Albert Johnson recently brought the case down from the loft, do you think he was trying to move the body?' she asked.

DI Morgan considered that, then said, 'Maybe he panicked when he got the note and wanted to hide the body somewhere less incriminating.'

'It must have smelled really bad a few years back,' Karen said, wrinkling her nose. 'How could he have lived with the stink?'

DI Morgan stopped by the garden gate and paused. 'From the state of the suitcase, it looked like it had been in the loft for a while, but not necessarily since the victim's death. He could have kept the body elsewhere or even buried it for a time. Hopefully, Raj will be able to give us a better idea when he's done with the post-mortem.'

Karen thought for a moment. 'The note . . . It must mean someone else knows about the body.'

'That's if the note was referring to the body. *It's time to pay for your crime* could be directed at something else entirely.'

It could also mean that Albert Johnson's life was in danger. If he had been attacked or pushed down the stairs, the perpetrator could try again. They'd need to organise an officer to keep watch over the old man in hospital.

Karen looked up at the neighbour's house. It was a small detached property, very similar in style to Albert Johnson's house. The front door was at the side, and at the front of the house were two large bay windows. The garden was well maintained, and there was a pretty lilac tree that would be coming into blossom in a month or so. All the flowerbeds were neatly tended. The spent daffodil leaves had been tied up neatly, and it made Karen think of her own garden that had been woefully neglected over the past few months.

'How do we play this one, sir?' Karen asked.

'We'll tell them the bare minimum. We don't want anything getting out if we can help it. The last thing we want is the press getting wind of the story. It's just the type of news item that would run and run.'

Karen shrugged. 'We might need their help. As the murder was committed a long time ago, the press running a few stories could jog people's memories and generate some leads.'

'Hopefully it won't come to that. Today's visit is all about gathering background. We need to find out if he had a wife and family, and if so, what happened to them. We'll just tell the neighbours he had a fall and we're making sure it was an accident. And if it wasn't an accident, we don't want to let on how much we know this early in the investigation.'

'Right,' Karen said as she raised her hand to press the doorbell. It made sense to ask after Albert's family.

The door was opened by a short woman with dark, grey-streaked hair. She'd had it cut in a chin-length style, but it seemed to have a natural kink. It wasn't quite curly but flicked up at an awkward angle around her jawline. Her eyes were wide, and she gave them a nervous smile.

Karen judged her to be in her late fifties or early sixties.

'Good morning, sorry to disturb you. I'm DI Morgan, and this is my colleague, DS Karen Hart. We'd like to ask you a few questions about Albert Johnson.'

'Of course, come in. I'm Maud, Maud Kennedy,' the woman said, stepping back.

The hallway was narrow and dark, not helped by the densely patterned wallpaper. A marmalade cat meowed plaintively and zigzagged in front of Maud as she walked.

'It's Bert's cat,' she explained. 'I'm keeping an eye on her for him.'

She led them into the kitchen, her dress swinging about her legs as she marched on. 'Stop eating, Harold,' she called into the kitchen as they passed. 'The police are here. They need to talk to us.'

Karen peered into the kitchen and saw a balding man wearing spectacles, trying to stuff the last remnants of a sandwich into his mouth.

'Apologies,' he spluttered, trying to talk with his mouth full.

Maud led them into the front room. It was a compact little living room, with a large three-piece suite arranged around an open fireplace that was unlit but decorated with dried flowers.

'Please, take a seat,' she said formally, pointing to the armchairs.

Karen and DI Morgan both sat down and accepted her offer of a cup of tea.

She bustled off to the kitchen, and her husband shyly walked into the room. He gave them a small smile and shuffled from foot to foot, as though not quite sure what to do next.

'Thank you for talking to us today, Mr Kennedy.'

'Oh, no trouble at all. Such a terrible business. Poor old Bert. Do you know if he's going to pull through?'

'I'm afraid we haven't been updated on his condition yet,' Karen said. 'I do know he was taken straight to Lincoln County Hospital.'

The man blew out a long breath through pursed lips, making a whistling sound. 'I feared something like this might happen. He's been living on his own for far too long, and the stairs in these properties are so steep. All it takes is one missed footstep, and there you go.' He slapped his hands together, making Karen jump.

'How long has Albert lived on his own?' DI Morgan asked.

'Oh, years. His wife died about ten years ago, and since then it's just been Bert. He does well, though. He maintains that garden all on his own.' He sighed heavily. 'I suppose even if he does get better he won't be able to move back here. The house will be too much for him, let alone the garden. I suppose it happens to us all in the end.'

Maud walked back into the room carrying a tea tray, and she looked sharply at her husband. 'Oh, for goodness' sake, do sit down. You're making the place look untidy.'

'Yes, dear,' he said meekly, and perched on the edge of the sofa.

Maud set the tray down on the small coffee table and began to pour the tea. She handed a cup to Karen first, then DI Morgan.

'So, how can we help you?' Maud asked.

'I believe you were the one who phoned the emergency services this morning?' DI Morgan said.

Maud inclined her head. 'That's right. I do my knitting in that chair there.' She pointed to a wingback chair beside the window. 'Every morning, come rain or shine, Bert gets on his bike and cycles to the local shop. It's about a mile and a half away, and he's a little doddery these days, so I do like to keep an eye out to make sure he gets back okay. But this morning, he didn't even set off. I thought perhaps he was ill, so I decided to go and check on him. He didn't answer the front door, so I walked around the back, and that's when I thought I heard him moaning. Honestly, I was terrified it was too late. But the ambulance rushed off with him, and I took that as a good sign. They wouldn't have been in such a hurry if they thought he couldn't make it, would they?'

'I'm sure the paramedics did everything they could for Albert,' Karen said. 'I think he'll be very thankful when he recovers.'

'I do hope he's okay. He's a good neighbour, and we've lived opposite him for twenty years. He doesn't socialise really but always says good morning, and he gives me some of his apples in September so I can make him an apple pie.' Maud blinked, and sniffed loudly.

'We were just asking your husband about Albert's wife,' Karen said.

'She died over ten years ago. Bert was devastated – he didn't want to leave the house even though there are some lovely bungalows in Skellingthorpe now that would be more suitable, but he said he didn't want to leave his home. It had so many good memories for him, you see.'

Karen took a sip of the hot tea. She suspected Albert had more reasons for staying at the property than he'd let on. The major one being the dead body he'd stashed in a suitcase. But she could understand Albert's reluctance to leave his memories behind, too. After her husband and daughter had passed away, she hadn't wanted to leave their family home. Karen couldn't imagine leaving the house where they'd shared so many times together.

'What was Albert's wife's name?' DI Morgan asked.

'Veronica,' Maud said.

'Did Albert and Veronica have any children?'

Maud shook her head. 'No, they didn't have children of their own. Bert was the head of the local secondary school for a while. It's called the Academy now, but in his day, it was Greenhill Secondary School. He liked to joke he had enough children in his life, with his job.' Maud smiled.

DI Morgan and Karen asked a few more questions, trying to get an idea of the type of man Albert Johnson was, but according to the Kennedys, Albert had been a very ordinary old man. He enjoyed gardening and reading, and had been an upstanding member of the community for years.

'I must say,' Maud commented with a smile, 'it's refreshing to find the police so interested in a case like this. So often you read about the police not caring anymore.'

'You don't think it was anything other than an accident, do you?' Harold said suddenly.

Karen had almost forgotten he was sitting there. She shook her head. 'There were no signs of a break-in. But we like to be thorough and look into things, just to be on the safe side.'

'Honestly, what a question! We appreciate everything you do, officer. Thank you very much,' Maud said, shooting a disparaging look at her husband.

◆ ◆ ◆

When they got back into the fleet vehicle, DI Morgan said he'd drive, giving Karen the chance to phone the station and catch up with Rick. She gave him a quick update.

'We've spoken to the neighbours, and by all accounts Albert Johnson was a well-respected man. He used to be the headmaster at Greenhill Secondary School, and his wife, Veronica, died of natural causes ten years ago. I'd like you to look up the death certificate on that though, Rick.'

'Already done it, Sarge, and I have an electronic copy. It all looks above board. And records show his wife was cremated.'

'Right, so the body in the suitcase isn't her.'

'Doesn't look like it. Is it true the body was wrapped up like a mummy?'

Karen frowned. 'Who told you that?' Police stations were terrible places for spreading unreliable gossip and rumours.

'I just went to get a sandwich from the canteen, and a group of officers were talking about it.'

'Well, it's not a mummy. The body is probably decades old, but it's mostly skeletal. There are a few clothing fragments, hair and some leathery skin remaining, but that's about it. There are no mummy wrappings, that's for sure. Now, can you dig up more information on Albert Johnson, particularly focusing on what he was doing twenty to forty years ago?'

'Absolutely, Sarge. I'll get right on it.'

'If Albert Johnson won't tell us what happened, we need to put the pieces of this puzzle together ourselves.'

Karen pressed her fingers against her temples. This case was already giving her a headache. If they weren't able to get the answers they needed from Albert Johnson, they'd need to dig deep to find the link between the body in the suitcase and the note they'd found in the old man's kitchen.

The body was old, but the note was not. They needed to find out who'd sent that ominous message to Albert as soon as possible.

CHAPTER FOUR

DI Morgan dropped Karen off at Lincoln County Hospital, so she could check on Albert Johnson's condition while he headed back to Nettleham to brief the team and talk to Superintendent Michelle Murray.

Karen entered into the hospital through the main entrance. It was busy and confusing. She'd been there only a few months ago, working on another case, but she was sure they'd changed things around. She put her hands in her pockets and waited for her turn by the reception desk.

She gave her name and held up her warrant card, and asked where she could find Albert Johnson. The woman behind the counter gave Karen directions to the intensive care unit. It didn't take her long to find it.

At the entrance to the ward, she followed the instructions, using a squirt of the alcohol hand sanitiser and pressing the green button.

The staff nurse who came to the door smiled. 'Can I help?'

Karen showed her warrant card again. 'My name is DS Hart. I'd like to talk to the person in charge of treatment for Albert Johnson. He was brought in this morning.'

The nurse pointed to the row of chairs behind Karen. 'If you'd like to take a seat in the waiting area, I'll try to find the doctor for you.'

'Thank you.'

There were a few magazines on the low table beside the plastic chairs, but Karen ignored them. She'd read an article recently detailing how bacteria and viruses could linger on the pages of magazines in doctors' waiting rooms, and she imagined the same was true of a hospital.

The walls were covered with posters, displaying slogans such as 'Caring isn't sharing' alongside pictures of various horrible bugs.

She had to wait for about ten minutes before a harassed-looking man in a white coat walked into the waiting area. He was short with dark-brown hair and bushy eyebrows, which knitted together in a frown as he approached Karen. He stuck out his hand. 'I'm Dr Clark. Are you DS Hart?'

Karen shook his hand. 'Yes. Are you the doctor treating Albert Johnson?'

'I am. But I can tell you now he's not going to be talking to anyone for a while. He's been in and out of consciousness since he arrived. He suffered a nasty blow to the head from his fall and had a heart attack in the ambulance.'

'Do you think he'll recover?'

'Difficult to say at his age. I suppose you want to talk to him to find out who did this. We had an old lady in last week. Two men had broken into her house and roughed her up.' Dr Clark glared at Karen as though she were personally responsible.

'We don't know if anyone else was involved in Albert Johnson's fall.'

The doctor's frown deepened. 'Then why do you want to talk to him?'

'It's important to the case I'm working on. He has vital information.'

Dr Clark huffed. 'Well, give him a few days to recover, at least. He's not up to questioning yet.'

She'd experienced some hostility from doctors and nurses in the past. Only because they were very protective of their patients, which was a good thing. People were vulnerable in hospital and often needed someone on their side, looking out for their interests, and in this case, the doctor had no idea what they'd found in Albert's house.

'Do you know if Albert has communicated with anyone since he's been admitted?'

'I wouldn't know. He hasn't said anything in my presence; you'd have to speak to the nurses. I'll ask them to come out and talk to you.'

'Thank you,' Karen said, and sat back down to wait.

It was another ten minutes before someone came out. It was the same staff nurse who'd opened the door to Karen earlier, but now she wasn't smiling. Her pretty features were contorted into a scowl.

Karen smiled and stood up, hoping to get the nurse on side. 'I'm sorry to bother you, I know you're busy. I just wondered whether Albert Johnson has spoken to anyone since he's been here. Has he said anything to you?'

'What kind of thing?'

'Anything at all. I'd be interested in anything you heard him say.'

'Sorry, I can't help you. He was muttering a few things here and there.' The nurse paused. 'He was in a panic when he first came in, screaming for help and shouting at the team treating him. Since then he's been sedated and hasn't said a word.'

'Right. Thanks for your help.'

She turned to leave, and the nurse said, 'You know, it's not very nice, what you're doing.'

Karen turned back. 'What I'm doing?'

'He's an old man. He's going to need time to recuperate. Surely your questions could wait until he's recovered.'

Karen took a deep breath. 'I'm afraid it can't wait. We're going to need to talk to Albert as soon as he wakes up.'

The nurse crossed her arms over her chest and shook her head.

She saw Karen as the bad guy in this situation. Of course she had no idea the sweet old man she was caring for had kept a dead body in his house for decades.

◆ ◆ ◆

By the time DI Morgan got back to Nettleham headquarters, it was almost one p.m. He briefed Sophie and Rick, making sure they understood the tasks assigned to them. They updated him on how they were progressing in digging into Albert Johnson's background.

Satisfied with how they were getting on, he left Rick on the phone to the council and Sophie trawling through various pictures of suitcases in an online database, and headed upstairs to update Superintendent Murray.

'I don't want this getting out to the press,' she said before DI Morgan had even sat down.

'Absolutely, ma'am. We'll keep it as quiet as possible.'

'So where are we with this investigation?'

'The body is old. Raj thinks our victim has been dead at least twenty years.'

'So we're dealing with a cold case?'

'Sort of. The body was found in an upstairs bedroom, in a suitcase. But we suspect it was recently moved, probably by Albert Johnson, the exertion then causing him to fall and injure himself. A printed note was found in the kitchen with the words *It's time to pay for your crime.* The concerning element is the fact the note looks new. At least, it didn't look decades old to me.'

The superintendent held the bridge of her nose between her thumb and forefinger. 'I'm not liking the sound of this.'

'It's an unusual one,' DI Morgan said. 'Right now, we don't have much to work with.'

'Was Albert Johnson married?'

DI Morgan nodded. 'That was our first thought, too. We wondered if it was the spouse or a family member and he'd managed to keep it covered up all this time, but his wife died ten years ago, so it's unlikely to be her body. Plus, there was a death certificate issued, and all the details seem to be in order. She was cremated. They have no children, so we need to expand our scope of potential victims.'

Superintendent Murray frowned. 'Yes, we do. Has he lived in the area all his life?'

'I've got DC Cooper and DC Jones both working hard looking into his background. As far as we know, he's lived in Skellingthorpe for a very long time. We're looking at the deeds to see when he purchased the house. He used to be the headmaster of Greenhill Secondary School.'

The superintendent's eyebrows lifted. 'A headmaster. Are we sure the victim is an adult?'

'Raj thinks so. There's always a chance that when he looks closer, he might get a different answer. But he believed that the skeleton belonged to a fully grown adult male.'

'Right, well, thanks for the update. Let me know as soon as Raj is finished with the post-mortem.'

'Of course, ma'am. You'll be copied in on all the reports.' DI Morgan stood up. 'I have a feeling this case is going to be a complicated one.'

His boss sighed and said, 'Let's hope you're wrong and we get some answers quickly. This is the last thing we need at the moment. I've got the assistant commissioner visiting us next week. I'd prefer to show him cases we've put to bed rather than one like this.'

DI Morgan gave her a sympathetic smile. Sometimes he was very glad he was only a detective inspector. It seemed the higher you got in the police, the more you had to say the right thing at the right time to the right people. He wouldn't be very good at that.

He didn't envy Superintendent Murray her job at all.

The duty sergeant was happy to point out PC Sanderson and PC Montgomery in the cafeteria for DI Morgan. The two officers were sitting at a large table, surrounded by their colleagues, who were listening avidly to Montgomery describe his grisly discovery. He was relishing the attention and seemed to have completely recovered after his bout of sickness.

Sanderson, in contrast, was clearly not enjoying being the centre of attention and hung his head, looking thoroughly fed up.

DI Morgan's presence put an immediate stop to the conversation.

Montgomery looked up nervously. 'Ah, DI Morgan, we were going to come and find you.'

DI Morgan looked at the trays on the table, which were littered with empty crisp packets and sandwich wrappings. 'I'm glad you managed to eat lunch. I was informed you were very unwell at the scene this morning.'

The officer's colleagues chuckled until DI Morgan sent them a warning look and they all scuttled away.

'Sorry, sir,' Sanderson said. 'We really were going to come and see you after lunch.'

'Firstly, you will not tell anybody else about this morning. We need to keep this out of the press, and thanks to you that task has just got a lot harder.'

Both officers bowed their heads as DI Morgan slid into a seat opposite them. 'Right, tell me what happened.'

Sanderson did the talking, describing the events of that morning, clearly and accurately.

'What puzzles me,' DI Morgan said, 'is why you went upstairs and looked in the suitcase?'

Sanderson and Montgomery exchanged guilty glances.

Finally, Montgomery said, 'That was my fault. The old man told us not to go upstairs, and because he was so adamant, I knew he was hiding something.'

DI Morgan leaned back in his seat and scrutinised the two officers. They looked contrite, and without PC Montgomery's inquisitiveness, the body may have gone undiscovered for another decade.

'I want your reports written up and on my desk by the end of the day. And don't forget, tell no one about this.'

'Yes, sir,' they said in unison.

When Karen arrived back at the station, she updated Rick and Sophie on Albert Johnson's condition. 'It doesn't look good. He's heavily sedated at the moment.'

'So Albert isn't actually in a coma,' Rick asked. 'They're keeping him sedated with drugs?'

Karen nodded. 'Yes, that's right. The medical staff seem very protective of him and aren't happy with us questioning him anytime soon. But, of course, we don't want to tell them the real reason we want to speak to him yet. The longer we have to get our ducks in a row before the press get wind of this, the better.'

As soon as the body in the suitcase became public knowledge, they'd need extra officers on the case just to cope with the flood of concerned calls from members of the public.

Sophie, who was sitting at her desk, spoke up. 'They just see him as a harmless old man, I suppose.'

'Well, to be fair, we don't know for sure that he's killed anyone,' Rick said, leaning back against his workstation.

Sophie swivelled around on her office chair to face him. 'Well, the skeleton hardly climbed in the case itself, did it? He can't be completely innocent.'

'Anyway,' Karen said, interrupting the squabble before it got started, 'we're still waiting to hear back from Raj on the post-mortem. It looks like it could take a while to perform all the necessary tests. One thing I did notice at the scene was some bright-blue material with the body. I assumed it was something like a shell suit. They used to be popular back in the eighties. My sister and I had matching ones.'

'Very stylish,' Sophie said.

'Don't knock it. One day you'll look back on your youthful fashion mistakes and feel the same sense of shame.'

Sophie laughed. 'I'm sure I didn't wear anything as bad as a shell suit.'

'No, you probably didn't. They were pretty hideous. Comfy, though. We wanted them for ages and were thrilled when we got them for Christmas along with our matching L.A. Gear trainers.'

Karen had forgotten all about the Christmas she and her sister, Emma, had unwrapped the shell suits, but now memories came flooding back. The crinkly material that rustled with every movement. Kiwi lip balm from The Body Shop, Exclamation perfume, and Bananarama on the radio.

'So around the time you and your sister were feeling very trendy in your shell suits, someone was shoving our victim's body into a suitcase,' Rick said.

It was a sobering thought. 'We don't know for sure when our victim died,' Karen said. 'Those suits were popular in the late eighties and into the nineties, but our victim may have carried on wearing his for years.'

Sophie gave Karen a sceptical look.

DI Morgan came out of his office and walked towards the team just in time to hear Rick crack a joke about skeletons in the cupboard.

'Perhaps you'd like to go to the hospital, Rick,' DI Morgan said. 'You can wait there until Albert Johnson wakes up and is able to answer some questions.'

Rick groaned. 'That's a punishment for the skeleton joke, isn't it?'

The detective inspector simply raised an eyebrow.

Rick sighed and began to pack up his stuff. 'Fair enough.'

DI Morgan crossed his arms and leaned against Rick's desk. 'We can't miss an opportunity to talk to him. If he's as frail as the doctors suggest, we could lose our primary suspect. Keep a look out for any suspicious characters hanging around. The note we found at the scene suggests Albert's fall may not have been an accident.'

'Will do.' Rick shrugged on his coat.

'What do we know about Albert Johnson's private life so far?' Karen asked.

'He lives alone,' Sophie said. 'He's owned the house and lived in it for fifty years. His wife lived with him until she died ten years ago. He went to Cambridge University, then became a teacher. He taught at Greenhill Secondary School from 1970 and retired from his position of headmaster twenty years ago.' Sophie shrugged. 'That's about it so far. Although, I should add that all signs point to him and his wife having a happy marriage.'

'Okay, good. We're going to need to expand Albert's family tree. Can you follow up on that, Sophie, as Rick is heading to the hospital?' Karen asked.

Sophie bit her lip. 'I will, just as soon as I get back from my appointment, if that's okay.'

'Appointment?' DI Morgan frowned.

'Yes, remember I told you I had an appointment with a mortgage adviser? I'm going to find out today whether I can afford the house I want.'

'Oh, yes, of course,' DI Morgan said. 'Good luck.'

'Yes, good luck. I'll get started on the background, and you can take over when you get back,' Karen said.

After Sophie and Rick had left, Karen and DI Morgan went over their notes, brainstorming and making sure they hadn't missed anything. Karen was scribbling down a quick reminder to contact Greenhill Academy when the phone on her desk rang.

She picked it up. 'DS Hart.'

'Karen, it's Raj. Could you come down to the lab?'

'Absolutely. I'll be straight down.'

She hung up and smiled at DI Morgan. 'That was Raj. They've found something.'

CHAPTER FIVE

Karen and DI Morgan found Raj downstairs in the main lab. The air smelled of antiseptic, and the air conditioning unit buzzed in the corner.

'That was quick, Raj. This has to be a record, even for you,' Karen said. 'What have you got for us?'

The pathologist looked up and smiled. 'Don't get too excited. I haven't even performed the post-mortem yet. But we thought you'd be interested in this.'

It was brighter in the lab than elsewhere in the police station. The work surfaces seemed to reflect and intensify the light. All the benches were made of stainless steel, for ease of wiping down and to minimise the possibility of contamination. Raj stood in front of a light box that was nestled between a rack of pipettes and a small, bench-top centrifuge.

On top of the light box was what looked like a very old, disintegrated piece of leather and some stained papers.

'It's an old driver's licence,' Raj said, using a pair of tweezers to straighten a fragment of paper. 'It was partially encased in a protective plastic sleeve.'

Both Karen and DI Morgan stepped closer to the light box, intrigued.

'Can we get an ID from it?' DI Morgan asked.

'Not yet.' Raj set the tweezers down on the bench. 'We've scanned the licence, and with a bit of luck, we should be able to enhance the text using a computer program. We might not be able to read it all, but I hope we'll have enough to provide some clues to our victim's identity.'

DI Morgan stared intently at the fragments of paper. 'That's excellent work, Raj. It looks indecipherable to me. If you can get a name from that, I'll owe you a pint.'

Karen found it hard to believe they would be able to extract any information from the tattered paper. It didn't have the usual greenish hue of a driver's licence. Instead, it was stained with yellow and brown splotches. Karen felt her stomach churn as she realised the colour change would be due to the cadaver's bodily fluids soaking into the paper as the body slowly decomposed.

'Who's running the computer program?' DI Morgan asked.

'Harinder. If anyone can get a result from this, it's him,' Raj said, taking a pen from his lab coat pocket and making a note in an A5 pad. 'I was in the pathology lab at the hospital when I discovered the licence, and brought it straight here myself. I haven't started a full examination of the body yet.'

'It's a shame you didn't find any bank cards,' Karen commented.

Raj slipped the pen back into the breast pocket of his lab coat. 'That would have made life easier because the plastic wouldn't decompose as easily.'

DI Morgan turned to Raj. 'Do you still think we're looking at twenty to forty years ago for our time of death?'

Raj nodded. 'Yes, I should have more for you by the end of the afternoon. I'm going to get back to the pathology lab now and Harinder will update you when he's got a result on the licence. As I extracted the body from the suitcase, I did notice a fracture on the left side of the skull. That could have been what killed him, but it's not easy to identify a definite cause of death when the body is in such a state.'

Karen felt a little dizzy. The lights were too bright, and the reflections on the stainless steel had a dazzling effect. It was horrible to think that a selection of bones, fabric from a garish tracksuit, and this stained, tattered driver's licence were all that remained of a person's life.

'We're assuming it was the victim's licence . . .' Karen said.

'It's pretty likely, don't you think?' Raj asked, raising an eyebrow.

'I suppose, but we can't say for sure. Do you still believe the victim was male?'

Raj pulled a face, showing his reluctance to answer the question. 'I'm not willing to go on record yet, but I'd say our victim was a man between the age of thirty and his mid-fifties. But that's it for now. I really need to examine the bones further before I can tell you any more. If we can get an ID from the driver's licence, then we should be able to confirm identity with dental records, or even DNA if it came to it.'

'Do you think you'd be able to extract DNA from the victim?'

Raj smiled and his moustache lifted. 'Yes. Of course.' His smile disappeared. 'The problem will be trying to find a match in the database.'

'Thanks, Raj,' DI Morgan said. 'We should let you get back to the pathology lab. I don't suppose you have any idea how long this program of Harinder's takes to run?'

Raj smiled as he began to meticulously remove the fragments from the light box and transfer them to an evidence storage box. Karen thought he looked more like Poirot than ever.

'It should be finished within the hour,' he said, and switched off the light box.

Sophie glanced at her watch and tried to hide her irritation. Her meeting with the mortgage adviser was meant to have started ten minutes ago. The delay was especially annoying today, as she needed to get back to the station as soon as possible. She crossed her legs and tapped her fingers on the arm of the chair.

All her paperwork, including the multitude of forms the bank required to be filled in, was in a single file resting on her lap. Sophie was not one to come unprepared. She had all her bank statements as well as a selection of utility bills, and a budget and expenses accounting sheet. By her own calculations, she could afford to buy the house she desperately wanted. Of course, it would mean cutting back here and there and tightening her belt, but it would be worth it.

The house she'd fallen in love with was in Washingborough, near the Washingborough Hall manor house, and was built from beautiful sandy-coloured stone. It needed some work, but most of the alterations Sophie had in mind were cosmetic.

The house had been purchased and renovated by a couple a few years ago, but they'd either got fed up with the project or run out of money, and hadn't finished off the interior decoration. It could do with a new kitchen, but both bathrooms had already been replaced. The whole house had been rewired, and as far as she could tell the plumbing seemed sound. It was a three-bedroom house with two reception rooms. She loved the size of the rooms, which were so much bigger than in modern houses. It had a pretty front garden and parking spaces for two cars. The mature back garden had a large magnolia tree, and the beautiful flowers had been budding the first time Sophie visited the property. She'd fallen in love with the place straightaway.

She'd gone to view the house with her father, who had sucked in a breath through his teeth at the sight of the windows, which he declared needed replacing. And he looked horrified by the seventies-style wallpaper. But Sophie could see past all that. She could picture the interior decorated in warm tones and modern colours, and, most importantly, she could see herself relaxing there and enjoying her very own place.

It wasn't that she didn't love her parents or appreciate them. It was just that she hadn't ever envisaged still living in her parents' house when she was in her mid-twenties. All the articles published in the papers recently about people living with their parents when they were still in their forties had horrified her. She didn't want to end up like that, but it was so hard to get on the housing ladder these days.

She'd been saving desperately since she joined the police, and had managed to secure a decent deposit. Many of her friends had their own houses, but most of them had been helped out by their parents or had an inheritance from grandparents. These days, buying a house was tough if your family couldn't help you out.

She looked at her watch again. Now the meeting was fifteen minutes late. This was getting ridiculous. She reached for her handbag and was preparing to leave when she saw a tall woman rushing towards her with her hand outstretched. 'Sophie Jones? I'm so sorry to keep you waiting. Nobody told me you'd arrived.'

The woman introduced herself as Pippa Kearny and babbled on, blaming her colleagues for the mix-up. Sophie felt like replying with a smart remark, but instead she smiled and shook the woman's hand. 'Nice to meet you.'

Pippa led the way into her office, which was really just a partitioned cubicle. Inside, there was barely enough room for her to squeeze around the desk.

Sophie managed to slip into one of the seats, put the folder on the desk in front of her, and tried to look more confident than she felt.

The mortgage adviser tapped a few keys on her keyboard and looked at her computer screen. 'Right, so you're looking for a mortgage. Have you seen a property you like?'

'I have,' Sophie said, and gave the details.

'Okay, let's see how we can help you.'

The next half an hour passed interminably slowly. Even though Sophie had already worked out her own finances with carefully allocated amounts for what she spent on her social life, food and other outgoings, the mortgage adviser wanted to do it her way, filling in yet another form, which was slightly different to Sophie's format.

It was frustrating, but it would be worth it if she managed to get the house. Pippa tapped away on the keyboard, turning to Sophie and asking her questions every now and again. Finally, after pressing the enter button, her face fell.

'Oh, I'm afraid that, according to our calculations, you won't be able to afford that much of a mortgage. In fact, all we could offer you, if you're buying it alone, based on your deposit, would be one hundred and twenty thousand.'

Sophie felt a sharp stab of disappointment. She'd been through her own finances and knew she could afford it. All right, her calculations didn't leave much room for error, but this was ridiculous.

'Are you sure? Maybe we should try the questionnaire thingy again.'

Pippa shook her head and gave Sophie a tight smile. 'I'm afraid not. The computer doesn't get it wrong.'

'So you're saying I can't afford that house.'

'Well, I couldn't say that exactly, but we wouldn't be able to lend you any more than one hundred and twenty thousand based on your current circumstances. Of course, you could try another bank, but I don't think you'd be successful.'

'I see.' Sophie began to stuff all her papers back into her file.

'I'm sorry we couldn't be more help. But a young woman like you would probably be better off looking at something a bit cheaper to get you on the ladder. Maybe a flat or something, in the city.'

Sophie gave the woman a curt nod. She couldn't believe this. She was disappointed they hadn't agreed to lend her the money she needed, but most of all, she was irritated that she had been made to wait for ages only to be told they couldn't help her.

She stood up and squeezed past the desk to get out of the cubicle, muttering, 'Thank you for your time.'

Sophie collected her car from Lucy Tower Street car park and headed back to the station. She fought the urge to go back to Washingborough for one last look at her house. She still kept thinking of it as *her* house, which was ridiculous. She couldn't afford it now, and by the time she could, it would be sold.

She hit the top of the steering wheel after she pulled out into a long line of traffic. Great. Now it would take ages to get back to the station.

It wasn't fair. She'd always worked so hard. She'd been top of her class at school and achieved all A's for her A levels. She could have gone to university like most of her friends, but she'd joined the police instead. Even when she finished school, her studies weren't over. She took courses and read all the policing textbooks she could get her hands on, because she wanted to climb the career ladder as quickly as possible.

It had all started with getting lost at the park when she was six – a policeman had found her crying and returned her to her mum and dad. Since then, Sophie had always wanted to be a police officer. She had even done her school work experience at a police station. Of course, it had been admin work rather than witnessing any arrests, but she'd loved it. It was the job she'd always wanted, but right now she couldn't shake the feeling she was standing still in her career.

She'd reached the rank of detective constable, but it felt like she was missing something – the experience she needed to progress. And that was frustrating. She was slowly coming to realise that you couldn't learn everything from books and courses.

Finally clear of the traffic, she lightly pressed the accelerator and sighed. It wasn't the end of the world. She'd be able to afford a home of her own soon. It would just take a little longer than she'd expected.

CHAPTER SIX

When Rick arrived at the hospital, he was on his best behaviour. DS Hart had warned him to be pleasant and as unobtrusive as possible. They needed the medical staff on their side. He'd followed Karen's instructions, tiptoeing around the medical staff, trying to be amenable and to avoid offending anyone.

One of the staff nurses looking after Albert Johnson had introduced herself as Nadine, and although she'd viewed him with suspicion when he'd first introduced himself, she seemed to be warming to him.

Rick gave her a friendly smile as she passed him. 'I hope I'm not getting in the way, sitting here.'

She paused beside the row of chairs outside ICU. 'You're fine there. I know you're only doing your job.'

'I'm only here because I really need to talk to Albert Johnson when he wakes up. I'll stay out of your way, though. You won't even know I'm here.'

Nadine rearranged the patient files she was holding. 'We were expecting you. We had a visit from one of your colleagues earlier.'

Rick nodded and said in his most charming voice, 'That would have been my boss, DS Hart. I know it's an inconvenience, but it really is important we talk to him. If he wakes up, would you let me know?'

Nadine considered his request. 'We've reduced the amount of sedation in the hope he'll wake up on his own soon. There is still a little swelling around his brain, so he's not going to be able to communicate well when he does wake up. But his condition has improved enough to move him to the cardiac care unit soon.'

'Oh, that's great news,' Rick said.

Nadine smiled warmly at him. 'He'll probably be moved in the next hour or so. But once he wakes up, I'll let you know.'

'Thanks very much, Nadine,' Rick said, wondering what on earth Karen had been talking about. She'd implied that the medical staff had been quite difficult and obstinate, but Nadine was incredibly friendly and helpful.

Nadine turned to walk away and then stopped. 'He's not in any trouble, is he?'

Rick shook his head. He didn't want to lie, but he couldn't let anything slip about this case. 'I just want to ask him some questions about his fall.'

Nadine's smile returned. 'I'll get you a cup of coffee, if you like. The stuff in the machine isn't too good.'

'That would be lovely.'

As he was waiting for Nadine to return, he noticed an old man shuffling along the corridor to the ICU ward. The man scratched his head, staring at the various posters and signs on the door, tried to open it and failed.

'You need to press the green button, sir,' Rick called out. 'Then one of the nurses will come and let you in.'

The man turned around and held up a hand. 'Oh, thank you.'

He held what looked like a bunch of grapes under his arm. He pressed the green button and, after a short wait, a nurse let him in.

After the old man disappeared inside the ward, Nadine approached and held out a mug of coffee for Rick.

'I hope that's all right. I've added a splash of milk, and here's a packet of sugar if you need it. I forgot to ask how you took your coffee.'

'That's smashing. Perfect.'

Nadine blushed. 'Well, I better get back to work. I'll let you know when Mr Johnson wakes up.'

As Rick sipped his coffee, he wondered how Priya, his mother's new carer, was getting on. She'd been helping Rick out by staying overnight three nights a week. But this was the first time she'd be alone with his mother all day.

His sister used to stay with their mother while Rick was at work. Because their mother had early-onset dementia, and her condition had worsened recently, she couldn't be left on her own. But caring for someone in her condition wasn't easy, and his sister had found it extremely difficult.

She still visited most days, but she'd taken a part-time job to help out with the costs of the carer. Today was a full training day at her new job, so she wouldn't even be popping in.

Rick traced the outline of his mobile phone in his pocket and wondered whether he should call home and check up on Priya. He had just pulled his phone out when he heard someone call out.

He looked up and saw Nadine beckoning him over. Rick put his coffee mug down and slid his mobile back into his pocket, then walked towards her.

'Any news?'

Nadine smiled. 'Yes, he's woken up.'

Karen checked her watch for the third time in five minutes. She and DI Morgan were going over some paperwork, but Karen was finding it hard to keep her mind on the task. They were still waiting to hear from Harinder.

'Do you think it's a bad sign we haven't heard from him yet?' Karen asked, putting her pen down on the desk.

'It's not even been an hour yet, Karen,' DI Morgan said.

'It's been fifty-seven minutes.'

'Patience isn't your strong point, is it?'

Karen was about to argue but decided against it. He was right. She hated waiting for answers.

DI Morgan was walking over to the LaserJet to grab some printouts of their morning report when his mobile rang.

He said a few words to the caller and then pressed mute. 'It's my solicitor calling about the house sale. Go and see Harinder without me. If he hasn't got any answers by now, maybe you can persuade him to work faster.'

DI Morgan was currently in the process of buying a house in Heighington after renting in the area since his move to Lincolnshire from the Thames Valley Police. Despite the pretty gruesome crime they had investigated in the village not long ago, DI Morgan had fallen in love with the location and decided it would be the perfect place to live.

Karen went downstairs to see Harinder alone. He was in the main computer room beside the laboratory. She stuck her head through the doorway. 'So, Harry, what have you got for me?'

The room was small and crowded with electronic equipment. Harinder turned from the computer screen and gave Karen a wide smile.

He was young, good-looking, fiercely intelligent and made some of the female staff go weak at the knees, especially Sophie, who was always first to volunteer to liaise with the handsome technical analyst.

Karen didn't understand the swooning over Harinder. He was too smooth and too young to be her type, but she still had a lot of time for him. He was extremely talented. Some of the technical staff could be stuffy and intimidating, but Harinder always had a ready smile when Karen visited the lab. She'd come to him with numerous problems in the past, and he'd always found a way to help. He had a strong work ethic and enjoyed solving problems.

'Please tell me you have an ID for me,' Karen said as she slipped into the computer chair beside him.

He smiled again. 'When have I ever let you down, Karen?'

There were multiple windows open on his computer, and he quickly tapped on the keyboard, his fingers moving like lightning.

A fuzzy scanned image appeared on the monitor, and Karen felt her stomach sink. There was no way they could get anything from that.

'I had to do a manual adjustment to really get the name and text to pop. It just involved tuning up the contrast and lighting. Here, let me zoom in.'

He used the mouse to select an area of the fuzzy driver's licence, and an expanded view of the document appeared on the screen.

Karen stared in amazement. The name was clearly visible. She couldn't believe he'd managed to get text from that stained piece of paper. It was magic.

'Oliver Fox,' she said quietly, reading from the screen. 'So now we have a name for our victim. Brilliant. Do you have an address, too? Driver number?'

Harinder chuckled. 'You're never satisfied.'

Karen shrugged. 'If you don't ask, you don't get.'

'The driver number is here, and that area is particularly stained and degraded,' Harinder said, opening up another file, which displayed a larger fragment of the licence. 'I need to work on it some more, but I may be able to get you the address, or at least part of it. God knows what's leaked on to this driver's licence. It's definitely been stained with some kind of liquid.'

Karen pulled a face and wondered how much Raj had told Harinder. Did he know where the licence had been found? She knew the stains were likely to be putrefying fluids, which wasn't the nicest thing to dwell on. She decided not to mention it.

'Right,' she said, getting to her feet. 'Excellent work, Harry. Please do your best to get us an address. It'll make our life a lot easier. I'll send Sophie down later to see how you're getting on.'

'Mm-hmm,' Harinder mumbled, but his attention was focused on the screen.

'Thanks again,' Karen said.

Karen rushed back to the main office, eager to give DI Morgan the good news. Now they had a name, they could get their teeth into this investigation. The victim's ID had opened up a wealth of information.

She saw DI Morgan walking towards her as she entered the office.

'I was just coming to find you,' he said. 'I'm guessing from the beaming smile on your face that Harinder has come through for us?'

Karen grinned. 'He certainly did come through. He's still working on the driver number and address, but he's given us a name. Oliver Fox.'

DI Morgan followed her over to her desk.

'Does the name ring a bell?' he asked.

Karen nudged the mouse on her desk, bringing the computer screen to life, and then quickly typed in her password. 'No, his name isn't familiar to me, but if this crime happened decades ago, it would be long before my time.'

She logged into the system. 'I'm going to see what I can find about Oliver Fox. He could be entered in our database. If not, I'll try press archives, and if Harinder gets another good result, we might be able to use the driver number to check with the DVLA.'

'I'm amazed he got anything from that tatty old licence,' DI Morgan said. 'Let's hope someone filed a missing persons report on Oliver Fox, at the very least.'

Karen nodded as she typed the name into the search bar.

'I'll leave you to it and go and update the superintendent.' He looked at his watch. 'Sophie should be back soon. With three of us going through the records we should get a quick result. Have you heard anything from Rick?'

Karen shook her head but kept her eyes fixed on the screen. 'Not yet. The hospital could be giving him the runaround. They just see Albert Johnson as a frail, elderly man that the police are harassing.'

'Rick is quite capable of turning on the charm when he wants to,' DI Morgan said. 'Let's hope that works to our advantage this time.'

After DI Morgan left, Karen completed the search and waited for the results to populate on her screen.

'Come on,' she muttered. 'Tell me your secrets. It's been decades, but we're finally going to find out what happened to you.'

She leaned forward, resting her elbows on the desk, and held her breath when she saw the top result on the screen.

It had to be him. A forty-five-year-old Oliver Fox from Skellingthorpe had gone missing in 1988. A missing persons report had been filed, and an officer was assigned to the case to investigate his disappearance.

Karen exhaled a long breath and clicked on the link to open the report.

Nineteen eighty-eight would be in the right time period. It would fit with what Raj had told them. There was a very good chance that this missing person would turn out to be the body in the suitcase.

She gritted her teeth when she realised that the report was only a covering page, which consisted of a few typed lines of information and a case reference number. The record hadn't been fully digitised yet.

Great. This was a complication they could do without. It would take time to acquire the original report, and the clock was ticking. They couldn't talk to their main suspect until he regained consciousness, they had no idea who'd sent Albert Johnson the threatening note, and to top it off, she couldn't even access the files she needed.

Still, she now had an address and a date of birth, so that was a start. She made a note of the case reference number and checked her watch. Sophie would be heading back now from her appointment, so perhaps she could pick up the records on her way.

Karen only hoped they were still at the local police station and had not yet been taken to the main depository.

She picked up the phone on her desk and dialled Sophie's number.

Sophie answered on the second ring. 'Hello, Sarge, I'm just in the car park.'

'Sorry, Sophie, I'm going to need you to get back in the car and head over to Skellingthorpe.'

There was a pause on the other end of the line, and then Sophie said, 'Okay, why?'

'We've had a development. A good one. We now have a name for our victim – Oliver Fox – and there's a missing persons report filed for him. I have the reference number here, but it's not been digitised, which means we need to get the paperwork from Skellingthorpe. I'll email you the reference number, okay?'

'All right. I'll head there now.'

'Thanks, Sophie. I'll give the station a ring and let them know you're on the way. Hopefully, they'll get the files ready for you.'

After she hung up, Karen stared at the screen. This man, Oliver Fox, had to be their victim, didn't he? She bit down on her lower lip. Should they go and talk to the family before the full results from the lab were in? Or should they wait for the dental records? There was a minuscule chance the man could have been carrying somebody else's wallet and driver's licence.

Karen sighed and leaned back in her chair. How on earth had forty-five-year-old Oliver Fox ended up in Albert Johnson's house in a suitcase?

She scribbled the names *Oliver Fox* and *Albert Johnson* on the note-pad beside her keyboard, and drew an arrow linking the two.

She then put in a call to Skellingthorpe station and gave the reference number, telling them that DC Sophie Jones would be by shortly to pick up the records. Karen hung up and picked up her pen again. There was something about having a pen in her hand that helped her to think.

It was different now, for younger generations. They'd grown up with screens and computers and typed everything. But when Karen was at school, everything had been written by hand, and she still found the writing process more natural than typing.

She tapped the pen against her notepad. How was Albert Johnson involved? Was he a killer? Had he covered up the death of Oliver Fox after an accident? But that didn't make any sense. If Oliver had died of natural causes or by accident, then surely Albert would have reported it to the police.

The phone on her desk rang, and she snatched it up. 'DS Hart.'

'Karen, it's Darren Webb. We've finished looking around the loft at Albert Johnson's property. I thought you'd want to know it looks like things had been moved around up there. It's my opinion that the suitcase was brought down from the loft very recently.'

That was interesting. 'Do you think Albert Johnson could have brought it down from the loft on his own?'

'Possibly. I wouldn't like to say for sure. It would have been some effort if he did. There are some marks on the side of the hatch, so it looks like the case was dragged out of the loft. We'll have the full results soon, and you'll get a copy of the report.'

'Thanks, Darren. I appreciate the heads-up.'

After ending the call, she mulled things over. It was possible that Albert had just found the suitcase in his loft . . . That would be enough to give anyone a heart attack, but the officers at the scene said he hadn't wanted them to go upstairs. If he'd innocently stumbled across the body, he would have wanted the police to help.

Besides, the idea that someone else had placed Oliver Fox's body in Albert Johnson's loft wasn't feasible. Albert had owned the property for fifty years, which meant a previous owner couldn't have hidden the body.

She made a note on the right side of the pad and drew a box around her comment.

The simplest explanation was often the right one, which meant Albert Johnson had killed Oliver Fox, put him in a suitcase and hidden the body. But why? There had to be a link between the two men.

Karen opened up another screen on her computer and looked up news reports, searching for Oliver Fox and Skellingthorpe. One of the top hits from the search was from a local paper called the *Skellingthorpe Advertiser*. Old copies had been scanned and uploaded on to a website, but the printed version of the newspaper was now defunct. The old articles were freely available on the internet.

Unfortunately, the article was very brief.

She clicked to enlarge the scanned page. It said Oliver Fox, forty-five, of Lincoln Road, Skellingthorpe had now been missing for three days. His family, friends and colleagues at Greenhill Secondary School were asking for anyone with information to contact the local police.

Well, there it was, Karen thought, leaning back in her chair, smiling. Oliver Fox had been a teacher at the same school as Albert Johnson.

There was a relationship between the two men. They had a link. Now all Karen had to do was connect the dots.

CHAPTER SEVEN

When Sophie got back with the records, she entered the office, staggering under the weight of all the files. She was carrying two boxes, one perched on top of the other.

As soon as Karen spotted her, she rushed over to take the top box from under Sophie's chin. 'You should have told me you were back. I would have come down to help you.'

Sophie gave a half-hearted shrug in response and carried the other box to her desk.

Karen noticed the shallow crease between the other woman's eyebrows. Sophie looked thoroughly fed up as she flopped into her chair with a sigh.

'How did your appointment go?' Karen asked, pulling out one of the files from the box she'd taken from Sophie.

'Not great,' Sophie said. 'But I don't really want to talk about it.'

'Fair enough. Thanks for picking up the files. I've just found an article online about an Oliver Fox who is a similar age to our victim. He went missing in Skellingthorpe in 1988. The newspaper article says he lived on Lincoln Road.'

Sophie seemed to perk up at this news. 'Do you think his family could still live in Skellingthorpe? They could be at the same address.'

Karen nodded as she flicked through the missing persons report. 'Well, there's only one way to find out.'

Sophie smiled, and Karen was pleased to see she looked a little bit more excited about the case.

'Can I be the one who talks to the family? Find out what they know?'

Karen picked out another file and agreed to Sophie's request. She found the young officer's eagerness endearing, but a little too much at times. 'I don't see a problem with that. We'll have to wait until DI Morgan gets back from talking to the superintendent before we plan a visit to the family, though. Right now, we don't have much information to give them, and they're going to want some answers. We need to go in there with a plan, and we need to deal with this matter as sensitively as we can.' Karen put the file back in the box and selected another. 'Oliver Fox went missing decades ago, but to his family this is still going to be incredibly painful.'

Sophie let out a little huff. 'I know that.' She turned away from Karen and began flipping through another of the files.

Karen had no idea what had happened at Sophie's appointment, but it definitely hadn't gone well. She'd said she didn't want to talk about it, though, so Karen carried a selection of files back to her own desk and started to make her way through them.

When DI Morgan came back to the office, he announced that the superintendent was pleased with their progress so far, but still very keen to keep the case out of the press.

'Sophie picked up the files from the original investigation into Oliver Fox's disappearance.' Karen handed DI Morgan the missing persons report. 'I found a newspaper article that says Oliver Fox was a teacher at the same school as Albert Johnson. I'm sure the original report must mention his employment history.'

DI Morgan looked up sharply. 'That's our link, then. The two men knew each other.'

Karen nodded. 'Sophie's only just got back with the files, so we've not had a chance to look through them properly, but after we've done that perhaps we should think about talking to the family. Sophie was keen to be involved.'

DI Morgan was too focused on flipping through the report to look up and notice Sophie's eager expression. 'I don't think that's a good idea. I should be the one to talk to the family, and you should come with me, Karen.'

'But it would be really good experience for me,' Sophie said.

'Not this time.' DI Morgan didn't notice how downhearted she looked in response.

'Why don't you go to the computer lab and talk to Harinder?' Karen suggested to Sophie. 'He could be close to getting the address or driver number, and then we can contact the DVLA to double-check the details.'

Sophie got to her feet with a sigh. 'Okay.'

Karen watched her go. Usually, Sophie jumped at the chance to speak to Harinder.

When Sophie left them, DI Morgan asked, 'Have you heard of DI Goodfield? He was the SIO on this missing persons case.'

Karen shook her head. 'No, but I imagine he's retired by now.'

She focused on the computer, typing in Oliver Fox's old address and smiling at the result of the search. 'Fox's widow, Elizabeth, still lives at the same address, according to the electoral roll.'

'Good. I think we have enough to approach the family. We'll have to tread carefully, but I suggest we tell them we've found a body that could be Oliver Fox.'

'You don't think we need to wait for dental records?'

DI Morgan shook his head. 'We might not be able to tell the family much, especially not where we discovered the body, but they've been waiting for answers for thirty years. All this time, they must have been wondering if he was still alive. Not knowing must have been torture for them.'

He took one of the files with him to his office. Karen watched him through the glass pane as he picked up the phone to call Oliver Fox's widow.

Delivering any kind of death message was always a terribly difficult job. It was one part of being a police officer she really didn't like. Thankfully, she hadn't had to inform relatives of deaths too often.

She knew what it was like to be on the receiving end of a death message, too. It had been late afternoon when the officers turned up at her front door. She'd been working nights that week, so she'd stayed home while Josh and Tilly went to the local Tesco at the bottom of Canwick Hill.

She'd noticed they hadn't come back but thought perhaps Josh had needed to stop for petrol. She hadn't bothered to try to call him. He would never answer his phone while driving anyway. So when the knock at the door came, it had been a shock.

Despite the fact Karen had seen the same sombre expression on police officers' faces many times, she hadn't believed it was really happening to her at first. But they'd given her the look. The look that told her they were here to deliver bad news, before they even opened their mouths. But she'd told them there had been a mistake. They must have been sent to the wrong house. It had to be a mistake. Things like that didn't happen to her.

Except, of course, they did. And just like that, her happy little family, her life, her reason for getting up in the morning had gone.

After the visit from those officers, things had become a blur. DI Freeman had come to offer his condolences personally and said not to worry about coming back to work for a while. That she could take as much time as she needed.

Christine had been there for the worst of it. Karen's next-door neighbour had been a tower of strength. The days, weeks and months that followed had been a hazy nightmare.

At least her news had come suddenly. How would she have felt if Josh and Tilly just hadn't come home that day? If she'd never had any answers, would she have been able to cope? How would she have been able to carry on living, not knowing whether they were alive or dead?

Karen took a deep breath and forced the memories away. Turning back to the case files, she began to read.

Sophie's blood was boiling as she trudged down the stairs. She couldn't believe DI Morgan had just dismissed her like that. How was she supposed to get experience on cases when she was banned from doing the important things like talking to the family of the victim? The only jobs they gave her involved sitting behind a computer screen or acting as a messenger, running errands and picking up files.

She was better than that, and she could show them how good she could be if they'd only give her a chance. The last big case they'd been on had gone quite well. She'd worked really hard, and so she thought she'd earned a bit of trust. She certainly didn't want to be a DC for any longer than necessary. Rick seemed perfectly happy as a detective constable, but Sophie had set her sights higher. She had goals.

She continued to walk down the corridor towards the computer lab, unable to shake off her irritable mood.

When she reached the door, she paused. They weren't giving her a chance. Why? Because they wanted to do the interesting work themselves? Or was it because they didn't think she was up to the job?

Sophie swallowed the lump in her throat. She'd never considered that before. She'd always believed that as long as she put the work in, she could achieve anything she wanted. That was the line her parents had fed her since she was small. She'd worked really hard at this job, but perhaps she just wasn't suited to this career.

As if today wasn't already bad enough. Her mortgage application had been declined, and now she'd been shown that the senior officers in the team had no confidence in her abilities.

Feeling wretched, Sophie rapped on the door and then entered the computer lab.

'Hi, Harry.'

'Hi, Sophie. Good news. I've managed to get most of the driver number and the address for you.' He winked at her. 'They don't call me Harry for nothing.'

But Sophie didn't even raise a smile, even though she was one of the officers who called him Harry due to his tech wizardry.

'Is everything all right?' he asked.

Sophie nodded. It must be nice to be like Harinder. Everyone knew he was brilliant at his job. He worked minor miracles on a daily basis and had earned the respect of everyone in the department, unlike her.

'I've emailed the report to DS Hart, but I can print out a copy for you if you'd like.'

'That would be great,' Sophie said, trying and failing to muster up some enthusiasm.

Harinder gave her a funny look and then pressed print. The printer hummed into life, and after a moment he picked up the paper and handed it to her.

'Thanks very much,' Sophie said and walked out of the room, leaving Harinder wondering what was wrong.

Rick followed the porter who was taking Albert Johnson to the cardiac unit. The porter pushed the large, wheeled bed carefully along the wide hospital corridors.

Rick was feeling optimistic. He'd seen Albert Johnson awake and sipping water after his breathing tube had been removed. He didn't look well at all, but Rick supposed that was hardly surprising.

He glanced at his watch. It was half past four. With any luck, he'd get the truth from Albert and be home in time for his mother's carer to leave at her allotted time of seven p.m.

But it took longer than expected. When they reached the cardiac unit, the bed had to be manoeuvred into position, and all sorts of wires and machinery had to be connected up to the old man again. They'd given him a private room, separate from the rest of the ward, and Rick wasn't quite sure whether that was because the police were interested in Albert or because there was a medical reason for doing so. He couldn't think why having a fall and a heart attack meant a patient got a private room, but at least it made it easier for him to keep an eye on Albert without annoying any other patients.

The nurses' station was just outside Albert's room. And as Rick waited for the medical staff to do all their technical stuff, he took a look around the unit, trying to be discreet.

In the main area of the ward there were twelve beds, all occupied and surrounded by beeping electronic displays and drips.

'Can I help you?' The sharp voice came from behind him.

Rick turned around and saw a short woman with fierce eyes and a cropped hairstyle. 'I'm sorry. I'm DC Cooper. I'm waiting to speak to the gentleman who has just been admitted into that room there.' Rick pointed at the room Albert was in.

The woman looked over her shoulder. She was dressed in a white tunic and navy-blue trousers, so Rick put her down as some kind of medical staff.

'Oh, they've put him in the isolation room.'

'Why is that?'

'It isn't being used at the moment, so as all the other beds are full, he gets a private room.'

'It takes a while to get the patients set up, doesn't it?' Rick grinned.

The woman didn't return his smile. 'It's probably better if you wait over there,' she said sternly, pointing to a line of four chairs beside the nurses' station.

Rick did as he was told. He didn't want to get on the wrong side of anyone before he'd had a chance to talk to Albert Johnson.

After what seemed like an age, a nurse came out of the room and smiled at him. 'He's settled now. A bit tired, but I think you should be able to talk to him. I've told him you have a few questions.'

Rick quickly got to his feet. 'Thank you very much.'

He pushed open the door and slipped inside the small room. It was quiet, apart from Albert's hoarse breathing and the occasional beep from the machinery.

Rick walked over to his bedside. 'Hello, Mr Johnson. I'm DC Rick Cooper, and I'm here to ask you a few questions.'

The old man didn't respond or even open his eyes. Rick frowned. Perhaps he was worn out from the rigmarole of moving to a new ward and had fallen asleep.

The thought Rick had been trying to push out of his mind since he'd arrived at the hospital kept niggling at him. He'd be waiting by another hospital bed before long. His mother was ill, and she was only going to get worse. They could keep her at home now, but there would come a day when Rick would stand by her hospital bed just as he was doing today with Albert.

He turned away from Albert, taking a deep breath to compose himself – not that the old bloke could see him, but Rick was at work. He needed to keep it together.

He tried not to think about the future. It didn't help. He couldn't change it. But here in the hospital, he couldn't stop thinking about the eventualities of his mother's illness. Maybe it was selfish, but he wished Sophie had been assigned the task of waiting for Albert Johnson to come around.

There was a chair next to the bed, so Rick sat down. He kept his eyes on Albert, and that was when he noticed something very odd.

When they slept, most people had their eyelids closed, but they didn't have them squeezed shut like Albert Johnson. It was as though the man was stubbornly resisting opening his eyes because he knew Rick was there.

After a few minutes, Rick tried again. 'I just wanted to ask you a few questions, Mr Johnson. When you feel up to it . . .'

The only response was Albert Johnson's hands clutching the bed sheets.

Rick frowned. This wasn't working. He suspected Albert knew exactly why he was here and was pretending to be asleep.

'No rush, I can stay all day until you're ready to talk.'

Albert's whole body seemed tense, and that made Rick feel guilty. The man on the bed in front of him could be a murderer, but it was hard to see him as anything other than a weak old man, and Rick was starting to feel like a bully.

He waited for half an hour and then slipped out of the room and approached the nurses' station.

Both nurses looked up from their paperwork.

'Sorry to bother you,' Rick said, keeping his voice quiet so as not to disturb the other patients. 'The nurse I spoke to in ICU told me that Albert Johnson had woken up and would be able to talk to me soon, but he seems to be asleep. He's not opening his eyes. Is he still sedated?'

The nurse on Rick's left frowned as she leaned back in her chair. 'No, he isn't. I'm sorry, but it seems to me that Albert Johnson just doesn't want to talk to you.'

CHAPTER EIGHT

They made it to Skellingthorpe in under fifteen minutes. DI Morgan was driving, and Karen had punched the Fox family's Lincoln Road address into the GPS. The female voice, which Karen thought always sounded a little smug, announced they were nearing their destination.

It was hard to see the house numbers along the stretch of road. The first section was surrounded by open fields and hedgerows, but a cluster of houses appeared as they got closer to their destination.

Skellingthorpe was a small village, three miles outside Lincoln city centre. There had recently been a proposal for 280 new homes to be built on Lincoln Road, along with other amenities to serve the new community, but it had been met with considerable opposition, and as far as Karen knew, the plans had been shelved.

DI Morgan slowed the car so they had a better chance of spotting the house they were looking for. Luckily, there was no traffic behind them.

'It's that one,' Karen said, pointing out a narrow detached house set back from the road. It wasn't built from the type of stone that was popular around here. Instead, the house looked dark, grey and quite sombre.

DI Morgan pulled into the gravel driveway and drove slowly towards the house. The plot was surrounded by tall Himalayan cedar trees. Karen had one in her own garden, which was the only reason she recognised them. She tended to think they looked like overgrown Christmas trees, but she supposed they had a kind of dark, majestic appearance.

As DI Morgan parked outside the house, beside a silver Volvo that had seen better days, Karen quickly called Sophie. When they went in, she wanted to have the latest details to hand.

'Have you got anything more for us, Sophie? We're just about to go and speak to the family.'

'I've confirmed the driver number with the DVLA, and it definitely belongs to Oliver Fox.'

'Okay, Sophie. Thanks, I'll let you know how it goes.'

'Right,' said Sophie morosely.

Karen guessed she'd had her nose put out of joint by DI Morgan saying she couldn't come along, but that was the way things went on big cases. Sophie was ambitious, but the case came first and DI Morgan was right. In situations like this, it was better to have a more senior officer talk to the family. She would need to find some time to chat to Sophie later, though. The younger woman seemed a bit down. Her mind wasn't focused on the job.

After Karen hung up, she turned to DI Morgan.

'Ready?' he asked.

Karen nodded firmly and then looked at the house. A curtain twitched downstairs.

Because DI Morgan had phoned ahead, Elizabeth Fox was expecting them, and she knew their visit concerned her husband's disappearance. She had to be imagining bad news, and Karen didn't want to keep her waiting any longer. Both officers got out of the car and walked across the driveway, their feet crunching the gravel.

Above the doorway, the year *1886* was carved in stone. It was an unusual house. The other houses along the same road were more modern, built from red brick and with uPVC windows. This one seemed strangely fixed in time, and out of place.

The door was opened by a petite woman with dark-red hair. For a moment she said nothing, but kept her green eyes fixed on them.

'I'm Detective Inspector Scott Morgan, and this is my colleague Detective Sergeant Karen Hart. Are you Mrs Fox?'

The woman stepped back. 'Yes, you'd better come in.'

As she opened the door wider, Karen noticed that there was another woman inside watching them. She stood in the hall at the foot of the stairs beside a grandfather clock. She had the same petite build, and although she had darker hair, the family resemblance was clear.

'This is my sister, Laura. I asked her to come after I got your phone call,' Elizabeth Fox explained.

'Laura Nicholson.' She held out her hand rather regally, and Karen and DI Morgan both shook it in turn.

Elizabeth led them into an old-fashioned drawing room. The ceilings were very high, and the windows were single-paned glass with wooden frames. Despite the fact it was mild outside, the house felt draughty and cold. A small fire burned in the grate but didn't seem to be giving off much heat.

'Please, have a seat.'

Elizabeth sat in a high-backed winged chair beside the fire, and her sister sat in the seat opposite.

DI Morgan and Karen took the sofa, which was hard and uncomfortable.

The room reminded Karen of something out of Victorian times, when parlours were supposed to be for show rather than comfort. Her own sofa had floppy cushions that constantly sagged and needed to be fluffed up, but at least it was comfortable.

'You said on the phone you think you've found Oliver . . .' Elizabeth said. Her hands were tightly clutched in her lap as she looked at DI Morgan.

'We have found a body, and we have reason to believe it's Oliver. His driver's licence was found with the body.'

Elizabeth pressed a hand to her stomach and took a shaky breath. Laura got up from her seat and perched on the arm of her sister's chair.

Karen thought she was going to pull her in for a hug and tell her everything was going to be okay, but instead she just patted Elizabeth's shoulder perfunctorily and said, 'Are you sure it's him?'

Elizabeth shot her sister a sharp look. 'Don't crowd me, Laura.'

Laura muttered something under her breath, then stood up and returned her own seat.

'Do you need me to identify him, Inspector?' Elizabeth asked in a tremulous voice.

DI Morgan cleared his throat and shifted uncomfortably on the sofa. 'I'm afraid, due to the length of time your husband—'

Elizabeth's hands flew to her face. 'Of course. Sorry, I'm not thinking straight. There won't be anything left for me to identify, will there? There will just be bones.'

'You wouldn't be able to recognise him,' Karen said. 'But when we've finished our investigation, you will be able to give him a proper burial and hold a service for him.'

Elizabeth blinked at Karen as though only just remembering she was there. 'How long do you think the investigation will take?'

'I'm afraid that's very difficult to say at this stage. We want to complete the investigation as quickly as possible, so you're able to get closure and lay Oliver to rest, but at the same time, we need to make sure we don't miss anything.'

Elizabeth's glance flickered to the window. 'I've told my sons. I knew they'd want to hear the news as soon as possible. They should be here soon.'

'Do they both still live nearby?' Karen asked.

'Yes,' Elizabeth said, 'they both live in Lincoln. They were only young when Oliver went missing. Stephen was ten and Martin only eight.'

'It must have been incredibly difficult for them,' Karen said.

'How do you think he died?' Laura asked. 'Was it an accident or . . .' She broke off, not finishing her sentence, and glanced at her sister.

'We're not sure at this stage. That's something we're looking into.'

'Where did you find him?'

It seemed cruel not to tell them all the details, but they didn't want to give away too much information at this point. Elizabeth Fox looked very much the grieving widow, and Karen guessed by the size of her she was unlikely to have killed her husband, put him in a suitcase and hidden the case in Albert Johnson's loft, but that didn't mean she wasn't working in cahoots with someone. For all they knew, Elizabeth could have had some kind of a relationship with Albert. Someone had sent that threatening letter. It could well have been someone in the Fox family.

DI Morgan saved her from having to answer. 'I'm afraid we need to keep the details confidential at this stage. We'll be able to give you the full story once the investigation is completed.'

'So you can't even tell me where you found him?'

DI Morgan shook his head. 'I'm very sorry, but no, we can't tell you that yet.'

'That's ridiculous,' Laura said sharply, leaning forward in her seat and glaring at DI Morgan. 'Don't you think our family has been through enough? The very least you could do is tell us what happened.'

'We don't know what happened yet, Laura. When we do, and when we have the whole story, the family will be the first to know.'

'Can you at least tell me if he was found nearby, or had he gone somewhere . . .' Elizabeth asked in a small voice.

Karen understood what she was asking. She'd probably spent the last thirty years wondering whether Oliver had abandoned her and their two young sons.

'Once we have more information, Mrs Fox, we'll pass it on.'

Elizabeth closed her eyes briefly, then turned to look at the fire.

'What can you tell us about the day Oliver went missing?' Karen asked.

Most of this was already in the missing persons report, but there could be something that was overlooked or not recorded at the time.

'It was a normal Thursday. He was supervising after-school football training, so I wasn't surprised when he was a little late, but he never came home. I called everyone we knew in the village. I even went to the school, but there was no sign of him. I reported him missing. The police didn't take me seriously at first. They said he was a grown man and maybe he'd turn up tomorrow. I tried to explain it wasn't like Oliver to go missing, but . . .' She shrugged. 'I think I knew that day that something awful had happened to him.'

There was a noise behind them in the hall and they heard the front door open, letting in a draught which almost put the fire out.

Elizabeth got to her feet. 'That will be one of the boys. We're in here,' she called out.

A tall, thin man appeared in the doorway. He had dark eyes and closely cropped dark hair. Karen and DI Morgan stood up to shake his hand and introduced themselves.

'I'm Stephen Fox,' was all he managed.

Karen noticed his hands were shaking.

He strode across the room to hug his mother. 'Are you okay?' he whispered.

Elizabeth took a step back and blinked away tears. 'Yes. They've found him.'

Stephen rubbed his hands over his face and then turned to Karen and DI Morgan. 'Where did you find him?'

'As we were just explaining to your mother, this is very early days in the investigation, and we can't reveal too much at this stage. As we find out more, we'll keep you updated.'

Stephen looked a little startled. 'You can't reveal too much? You think he was murdered, then?'

'We're not ruling anything out at this stage, Stephen. We're treating this investigation like any other unexplained death.'

Stephen nodded slowly and then pulled over a chair and sat down.

'Do you have a photograph of Oliver?' Karen asked. She wanted to shift the subject away from the fact they were unable to give the family any information about where they'd found the body. Karen knew if it was her, she would be fuming at this point and demanding answers.

Elizabeth cleared her throat. 'There's one in the bedroom. Would you get it, Stephen?'

Stephen left the room, and when he came back he was holding a silver-framed photograph. It was a family shot, and Karen guessed it was probably one of the last ones they'd had taken of them all.

'It was taken on our last holiday together,' Stephen said. His mouth tilted up in a half-smile as he gazed at the photograph, then he passed it to Karen.

Elizabeth was in the photograph and hadn't changed much at all. She even had the same hairstyle, a short choppy bob with a heavy fringe. Oliver stood with his hands on the shoulders of both boys. He had been a slim, tall man with dark hair, and she could see the resemblance to Stephen.

Stephen, the older boy, was looking at whoever was behind the camera with a big beaming smile and holding an ice cream.

His brother, on the other hand, didn't look so happy. He had the same dark hair and tanned skin, but he was scowling at the camera.

'Did your husband have any problems around the time he went missing?' DI Morgan asked.

'Problems?'

'Perhaps money worries, or had he fallen out with friends? Issues at work?'

Elizabeth's face tightened. 'No, nothing of the sort. Everything was absolutely fine. He just didn't come home one night.'

Laura shook her head slowly, and Karen switched her attention to the sister. There was something unusual about this family. Some unspoken secret was hanging heavily over the room. She'd expected grief and sadness but not sullen looks and guarded expressions. She made a mental note to talk to Laura alone at some point.

'Yes, I can't remember anything out of the ordinary. He seemed perfectly happy to me, but I was only ten when he went missing,' Stephen said. 'So, I'm afraid I'm not going to be much help. Why don't I make us some tea, Mum?'

Elizabeth blinked. 'Oh, yes, of course. I didn't think to offer you anything. I'm sorry.'

'Not at all,' Karen said as she got to her feet. 'I'll give you a hand, Stephen.'

CHAPTER NINE

After seeing the front room, Karen had been expecting the kitchen to be drab and old-fashioned, so she was surprised when Stephen led her into a modern black-and-white kitchen with an open-plan dining area. The units were white and shiny, with chrome handles, and all the appliances were built-in. A large granite-topped island sat proudly in the middle of the room. The kitchen was spotless.

Stephen filled the kettle at the sink.

'Can I help?' Karen offered.

'Yes, the cups are in that cupboard there.' Stephen gestured to a cabinet above the microwave, and Karen took out five white mugs.

Stephen switched the kettle on and then looked up at the ceiling, shaking his head. 'I knew this day was coming, so it shouldn't be a surprise, but it's really hit me for six.'

'It's understandable. It must be a terrible shock.'

'I've had thirty years to prepare for it but it's just horrible. I can't stand to think that he's been dead all this time and we didn't know.'

Karen grabbed the milk out of the large chrome fridge and shot him a sympathetic smile.

'Can you at least tell us when he died?'

'I'm afraid we can't say that for sure yet.'

'But you suspect he died around the time he went missing?'

Karen nodded. 'It looks that way.'

Stephen raked his fingers through his hair. 'I remember so much about the day he went missing. We had fish fingers, waffles and peas for dinner.' He gave another half-smile and shook his head. 'My brother, Martin, was going through a phase and refused to eat any other vegetables. It was just after the Easter holidays. We'd spent a week at a caravan in Mablethorpe.'

'Was that where the photograph was taken?'

Stephen's face softened. 'Yes, it was a happy holiday.'

He had looked happy in the photograph, but his younger brother hadn't. Of course, a photograph only captured a split second in time and didn't necessarily mean anything. But Karen couldn't help wondering whether Martin held some of the answers. Could he have seen or overheard something? Perhaps Martin had seen something that upset him. Perhaps his father had asked him to keep a secret. An affair? Or had Oliver discovered an affair between Albert Johnson and his wife . . .

Stephen held his hand out for the milk and Karen passed him the plastic container. 'Do you know a man called Albert Johnson?'

Stephen poured the hot water into the teapot and shook his head. 'No, I don't think so. Why?'

'He used to work with your father.'

'Oh, yes. Mr Johnson, the old headmaster. Yes, actually, he was the head at Greenhill Secondary when I was there. I started at the school the year after Dad went missing. That wasn't easy. After a while, I got used to people pointing and making comments, but it's a hard thing to go through when you're only eleven.'

'Was Mr Johnson close to your father? Did they socialise together?'

Stephen paused and turned to Karen. 'Not really. Why are you interested in him? Do you think he had something to do with my father's death?'

Karen shook her head. She didn't want to lie outright, but she didn't want to give too much away at this stage. Stephen's hands were shaking, and he spilled some tea on the counter.

'Here, let me help you,' Karen said, reaching for the roll of kitchen towel and wiping up the mess. 'You weren't aware of any problems he had, or financial worries?'

'He wasn't really the type to talk about problems. But as far as financial worries go, I don't know. I was only ten, so I wouldn't have picked up on anything like that.'

Suddenly, there was a loud crash, and Stephen looked up sharply as Karen went to the kitchen door. A man was standing in the hall. He had the same dark hair as Stephen, but his was receding and cut even shorter.

'Who are you?' the man demanded, striding towards the kitchen.

'I'm DS Hart. Are you Martin?'

'Yes. So, you've finally found him, have you? After all this time, you've finally got your finger out and discovered what happened to him.'

'Martin . . .' Stephen's voice carried a warning.

Karen took a deep breath. 'I'm very sorry to tell you this, Martin. But we have found a body alongside your father's driver's licence. We still need to confirm it's him.'

Martin let out a bark of a laugh, which was a strange response under the circumstances.

Stephen walked forward, forgetting about making the tea, and put his arm around his brother's shoulders. 'Come on, Martin. Come through to the front room and talk to Mum. She needs you to be strong right now.'

Martin started to resist, but in the end he let Stephen lead him away. 'I knew he hadn't walked out and left us.' He practically snarled the words at his brother. But Stephen didn't react.

Karen contemplated finishing the tea, but she didn't want to miss anything. Martin seemed to be a whirlwind of furious energy, and when people were angry, they often let slip small details that could provide clues. She followed them along the hall and paused by the doorway to see what happened.

'I bet you all feel a bit stupid now, don't you,' Martin said.

'Please, Martin, don't do this now,' Elizabeth Fox said in a weak voice. She was slumped in her chair, as though she couldn't find the energy to get up and greet her youngest son.

'Why didn't you stick up for him at the time?' Martin demanded. 'Why were you so quick to believe that he would walk out on us?'

Nobody answered Martin's questions. He strode forward, shaking off Stephen's arm, and stopped beside the cabinet in the corner of the room, grabbing a crystal decanter and pouring himself a large measure of amber liquid. He swallowed it down in one go.

'Really, Martin. That is very thoughtless of you,' Elizabeth said.

When Martin set down the glass, Stephen walked over to him, linked his arm in his brother's and pulled him towards the door. 'Let's talk outside.'

They passed Karen and walked back along the hall. DI Morgan gave Karen a pointed look, and she guessed he wanted her to follow and listen in. It seemed incredibly intrusive to eavesdrop on a grieving family, but when you were investigating a potential murder, manners and politeness had to take a back seat at times. She followed and saw they had walked through the kitchen and used the back door to get into the garden. Karen decided now was the perfect time to finish making the tea. Thanks to the thin, draughty windows, she could hear every word they said.

'Pull yourself together,' Stephen said. 'Mum doesn't need this now.'

'I don't care what she needs. She never worried about what *we* needed.'

'Don't be ridiculous. Of course she did. She brought us up single-handedly after Dad . . .' There was a pause.

'See, you were going to say *left*, weren't you? Even now, you're putting the blame on him.'

'I'm not, Martin. It's all just such a shock.'

'Not for me. I always knew he hadn't left us. He would never have walked out on us.'

Karen was putting the cups on to a tray when Stephen asked, 'Have you been taking your medication?'

'That's none of your bloody business.'

Karen put the milk back in the fridge. That was interesting. Maybe something they could look into later.

Stephen came back into the kitchen and saw Karen loading up the tea tray.

'Oh, I'm sorry,' he said. 'Here, let me carry it in.' He picked up the tray and took it into the front room.

Karen held back, and then went over to the door to see if Martin was all right.

'Are you coming back inside, Martin?'

She knew Martin was thirty-eight years old, but right now he looked younger, like a lost little boy. The anger had disappeared. A tear trickled down his cheek, and he wiped it away.

'I knew he hadn't left us,' he said quietly.

'I'm very sorry we were the bearers of this news, but once the investigation is finished, you'll be able to give him a proper burial.'

Martin sniffed and nodded. 'You must think I'm stupid. You must deliver this news to people every day. It's probably no big deal to you.'

Karen felt her stomach clench. It was very much a big deal. The day it started to be a normal, everyday occurrence was the day she would leave this job. She'd been on the other side. Her experience wasn't the same as what Martin was going through. He'd had thirty years of not knowing what had happened to his father, but Karen knew what it was like to deal with loss. She knew what it was like to have someone turn up at the door and tell you your worst nightmare had come true.

'I was eight when he disappeared. I blamed myself,' Martin said. 'It's such a cliché, isn't it?'

Karen said nothing but stepped outside, closing the door behind her, and stood beside Martin. She sensed he wanted to talk.

'The day before it happened, I'd been naughty. I can't even remember what I'd done, but Dad had sent me to bed without any supper. I'm thirty-eight years old, and yet, deep down, I still think it's my fault he left.'

'I can't imagine how hard that must have been for you,' Karen said gently.

Martin's face hardened. 'It didn't help that they kept saying he'd left us. I'm glad you found him. I know that sounds horrible, but I'm glad I now know that he would have come back to us if he could. This proves we weren't abandoned.'

Karen nodded.

'How did he die?'

'We don't know that yet. We'll have a better idea once the post-mortem has been carried out.'

'It was an accident, though? Or do you think he was murdered?'

'We're still figuring that out. As soon as we have some concrete facts, we'll let you know. The family will be first to find out, I promise you that. Shall we go back inside?'

Martin rubbed his hands over his face and followed Karen into the kitchen. They were about to walk back into the front room when DI Morgan stepped out into the hallway. He held up his mobile phone. 'Karen, we need to get back to the station. The superintendent wants to talk to us.'

They said their goodbyes and promised to stay in touch with the family and keep them updated with any developments.

As soon as they got outside the house, Karen turned to DI Morgan. 'What's so urgent she needs us to get back to the station straightaway?'

'Apparently there's someone she wants us to talk to about the case.'

Karen opened the passenger door and got into the car. 'Who?'

'She wouldn't say. I have the feeling someone was in her office while she was talking.'

'I wonder who that could be.'

'I guess we'll find out soon enough.'

When they reached the station, DI Morgan and Karen headed straight for the superintendent's office. It was six thirty p.m. and already dark.

Pamela, Superintendent Murray's assistant, sat in the small reception area outside her office.

'Oh, good,' she said, getting up from her desk and smiling at them. 'She's been waiting for you.'

She gave them a meaningful look that Karen couldn't quite interpret. Then Pamela rapped on the door and announced them.

This was unusually formal. The superintendent tended to leave her office door open unless she was making a private call or conducting a performance review. Pamela was normally happy for them to knock on the door themselves if it was closed. The formality made Karen even more curious. Who did the superintendent have in her office?

Karen followed DI Morgan into the large office and saw that Superintendent Murray was standing beside the window next to a tall man with dark hair. They both turned as Karen and DI Morgan entered the room.

'Ah, DI Morgan and DS Hart, I'd like you to meet retired Detective Superintendent Robert Fox.'

Karen's eyes scanned the man's face and features. She judged him to be in his mid-sixties, and he had to be a relative of Oliver Fox . . . His hair was neatly combed in a side parting and was grey at the temples. He wore a dark, well-cut suit and a navy-blue tie. Karen guessed he was the type of man who didn't like to dress casually even though he was retired.

The man smiled and held out his hand. 'Oliver Fox was my brother.' He had a strong, confident handshake, and looked Karen in the eye as he spoke.

After he dropped her hand, Karen shot a look at DI Morgan. His expression was neutral, but he had to be as surprised by this development as she was.

Robert Fox turned back to the superintendent. 'I am devastated, of course, but I can't say this is an unexpected outcome.' Taking charge, he added, 'Perhaps we should all sit down.'

CHAPTER TEN

Superintendent Michelle Murray sat in her usual seat, and Karen, DI Morgan and Robert Fox took chairs in front of her desk.

'We are very lucky that Detective Superintendent Fox is able to assist us with our enquiry,' Superintendent Murray said pleasantly, but her expression looked strained.

The last thing she'd want was a retired officer interfering with her investigation. No matter how polite and friendly Robert Fox seemed now, in Karen's experience these things didn't end well.

'I am sure Superintendent Fox will be very helpful. Do you have any questions you'd like to ask him?' Murray continued, sending a pointed look at DI Morgan.

DI Morgan hesitated, then said, 'Perhaps you could tell us in your own words how much you remember of the events surrounding your brother's disappearance.'

'Of course.'

As Robert Fox began to talk, Karen couldn't help wondering why Elizabeth and her sons hadn't mentioned the fact that Oliver's brother had been a high-ranking officer. Surely he would have had some sway over the investigation at the time and would probably have been their contact point with the police.

'I was only a DCI in 1988,' Robert Fox said. 'I spent most of my career in Lincolnshire but moved to Nottingham after my brother's disappearance. I threw myself into the job and progressed through the ranks. I tried to keep in touch with Elizabeth and the boys. I felt like I owed it to Oliver to play a role in their upbringing, to be a male influence, if you like. But they didn't make it easy for me. I can't blame the boys, of course, but I suspect I reminded Elizabeth of what had happened. After I moved to Nottingham, I didn't see so much of them. We still exchange Christmas cards, but other than that, we've grown apart, I'm afraid.'

He shifted slightly in his seat. 'Elizabeth called me the day Oliver disappeared. She was in a terrible state because the local police weren't taking the missing persons report seriously. There was no indication anything terrible had happened to him at that point. If I remember correctly, she called me about ten p.m. I went over to talk to her and the boys and tried to act as a liaison with the local force. I was based out of Lincoln, but she'd reported Oliver missing to the local force in Skellingthorpe. It was only a small police station, and they weren't exactly going to work through the night looking for Oliver. To be honest, I wasn't greatly concerned at first. I thought perhaps he'd made plans to go out and forgotten to tell Elizabeth. But because she was so worried, I stayed with her. Then, when he didn't come home that night, I knew something was definitely wrong . . .' He broke off and looked at DI Morgan. 'What can you tell me so far, officer to officer? How was he killed?'

Superintendent Murray cleared her throat, and Karen caught a quick glance between her and DI Morgan.

'There's not much we can tell you so far, sir,' DI Morgan said. 'The post-mortem has not yet been carried out. We'll update you as soon as possible, of course. Can you give us your contact details?'

'Yes, not a problem.' Robert Fox put his hand in his jacket pocket and pulled out a wallet, then removed a business card and handed it to

DI Morgan. 'I'll help in any way I can. Don't hesitate to get in touch if there's something you want to ask.'

'Thank you, sir. If you don't mind me asking now, what were your initial thoughts after he went missing? Did you suspect foul play?'

Robert Fox took a deep breath. 'Well, to be honest, I wondered whether he'd had a bit of a breakdown. His marriage wasn't a happy one.'

Karen frowned. That wasn't consistent with what Elizabeth Fox had told them less than an hour ago.

'We've spoken to Elizabeth,' DI Morgan said. 'But she can't think of any reason Oliver would have been unhappy at the time.'

'I don't suppose she mentioned Oliver's affair with her sister Laura, did she?'

Karen tried to hide her surprise but failed. She'd sensed an undercurrent between the sisters, but Oliver having an affair with Laura hadn't topped her list of suspicions.

'Did Elizabeth know about the affair?' Karen asked.

'I don't know for sure, but I don't see how she could have missed it. Though I certainly never mentioned it after Oliver went missing. I'm pretty sure the boys don't know either, so I would prefer to keep it that way. He disappeared when they were very young, and they were at that age where they idolised him.'

'We'll do our best to keep that information to ourselves, sir,' DI Morgan said. 'Have you been in contact with Stephen and Martin recently?'

'No, to my regret, I haven't. It's sad, really. As I said, I did make an effort immediately after Oliver's disappearance. But things were difficult with Elizabeth. Don't get me wrong, she never went off the rails or put the boys in any danger. She was just very shut down emotionally and accused me of hiding things from her. She made it very difficult to keep in touch. I tried to see the boys at Christmases and birthdays, but gradually that fizzled out over the years.' He turned so that he was directly facing DI Morgan. 'Can I ask where you found his body?'

DI Morgan shifted uncomfortably in his seat, pausing and waiting to see what Superintendent Murray said. Under normal circumstances, in a case like this, information would be kept secret even from the family. The fact that the man sitting next to them was a retired detective superintendent made it quite a tricky situation to handle.

DI Morgan stayed silent, and Karen didn't blame him. As far as she was concerned, this kind of politics was above their pay grade.

'As soon as we have gathered all the facts, you'll be the first to know, Robert,' Superintendent Murray said with a tight smile. 'You know we have to follow procedure. You're a highly regarded officer, but you are still a member of the victim's family, and we need to treat you as such.'

Robert Fox's expression changed. 'You can hardly suspect I had anything to do with it?'

'That's not the point, Robert. I'm sure you understand my position. You'd do the same in my shoes.'

'I'd like to think I would have a touch more compassion,' he said sharply.

Karen and DI Morgan watched the exchange like it was a game of ping-pong. It was a battle of wills, but Superintendent Murray wasn't about to be pressured into revealing details about the case.

'I promise we will give you an update as soon as we can, Robert. I hope you understand.'

'Well, I suppose I'll have to. I don't have much choice,' Robert Fox said, getting to his feet. 'I'm sure you're very busy, so I'll leave you to it. I would appreciate an update on the case tomorrow.'

'Of course, sir. I'll call you personally,' DI Morgan said.

After Robert Fox left the room, Karen turned to look at Superintendent Murray. 'This could be a complication.'

The superintendent nodded. 'You don't know the half of it. Apparently, he's golfing buddies with the assistant commissioner. Just when I thought my job couldn't get any more difficult.'

'How far do you want to keep him in the loop, ma'am?'

Murray pursed her lips and linked her fingers beneath her chin, thinking. 'I don't want you to tell him anything. Not yet. Not until we know what we're dealing with. Have you managed to get through all the reports on Oliver Fox's disappearance, the contemporary records?'

'Not yet, ma'am,' Karen said. 'Sophie's been looking through them this afternoon. And it looks like DI Morgan and I have some evening reading.'

Superintendent Murray thought for a moment and then said, 'I think you should talk to the original investigator, too. I imagine Robert Fox tried to put some pressure on him. He seems like that type of officer to me. So the investigating officer's opinion might be useful.'

After they were dismissed, Karen and DI Morgan went back down to the main office area.

'What did you make of him?' DI Morgan asked.

Karen shrugged. 'I think he could be difficult. Let's hope he stays out of our investigation. A concerned brother is one thing, but if he's used to throwing his weight around and getting his own way, we could have trouble ahead.'

'The affair came out of left field,' DI Morgan said. 'Though I'm not surprised Elizabeth and Laura didn't mention it, especially with both sons there today.'

'It's strange, though. There was definitely some tension between the sisters, but when she heard we'd found Oliver's body, Laura was the first person Elizabeth called.'

'Thirty years is a long time. It's a lot of water under the bridge, and perhaps she's learned to forgive and forget.'

'Perhaps.'

Karen frowned. Had Elizabeth found out about the affair before Oliver disappeared? Or did it come out during the aftermath? They'd have to look into Laura now. They didn't know yet if she was married or had a partner. A jealous husband could top their list of suspects.

'Laura did seem a little on edge. I got the impression there was something she wanted to say to us,' Karen said.

'Interesting. Perhaps we should talk to her alone.'

Karen pushed through the double doors, and DI Morgan followed. The office's day-shift workers were slowly thinning out. The night shift had arrived, and Karen's thoughts turned to Rick, who was still at the hospital.

'I'm going to give Rick a call and see if he's had any luck with Albert Johnson.'

'Good idea,' said DI Morgan. 'I'll see if Sophie's managed to find anything interesting from the original reports on Oliver's disappearance.'

Karen sat down at her workstation, reached for the phone and dialled Rick's mobile number.

He answered quickly but spoke in a whisper. 'Hello, Sarge.'

'Rick, any luck with Albert Johnson?'

'No, I'm afraid not. The nurses say he's not under sedation, but he's keeping his eyes shut when I'm in the room. I think he might be pretending to be asleep to avoid my questions.'

Karen sighed.

'What do you want me to do, Sarge? Shall I stick around?'

'Yes – sorry, Rick. I know it's not the most exciting task.' She glanced at her watch. 'After I've finished up here, I'll come over to the hospital. Is there anything pressing you need to get back for tonight?'

Rick hesitated and then said, 'Actually, Sarge, it's Priya's first day looking after Mum on her own. I'm sure she'll be perfectly fine. She is fully trained, and she's used to Mum now, but . . .'

'Of course, Rick, I'm sorry. Don't worry. I'll be there in half an hour so you can get off home.'

'Thanks, Sarge, I'd appreciate that. Normally I wouldn't worry, but it's just because it's her first full day alone with Mum.'

'Not at all, I should have remembered. I'm sorry. See you soon.'

Karen hung up, grabbed the paperwork on her desk and headed over to Sophie's cubicle. DI Morgan was asking Sophie whether she'd had any luck tracking down the manufacturer of the suitcase.

Sophie shook her head. 'Not yet. I've been flicking through pictures of cases all afternoon.'

She still looked miserable, and Karen thought she'd better have a private word with Sophie tomorrow to find out what was bothering her.

'Any luck?' DI Morgan asked, looking up at Karen.

'Rick says he's still not talking. He's pretty sure the old man is pretending to be asleep. The medical staff told him Albert is not sedated.'

'Suspicious,' DI Morgan said.

'Yes. Rick needs to get home, so I said I'd head down to the hospital.' She pulled up a chair and sat beside Sophie. 'Though if Albert Johnson is pretending to sleep that means he probably hasn't eaten all day. That can't be good for him in his condition. Perhaps we should leave him alone tonight so he actually eats something.'

'Maybe,' DI Morgan said, but he looked doubtful. 'Although, right now, he's the only one who can tell us why he had a body hidden in his home.'

'It's not like he's going anywhere in a hurry. Maybe he'll be more responsive tomorrow.'

DI Morgan agreed. 'All right. I'll ask Rick to go to the hospital again tomorrow. If Albert does wake up this evening, the nursing staff can tell us, then we'll know for sure if he's faking sleep to avoid questioning.'

Karen nodded. But if Albert Johnson was faking sleep, she didn't know what they could do about it. It wasn't like they could shake the old boy awake.

If they weren't able to get the answers they needed from Albert or the Fox family, they were going to have to look elsewhere. Perhaps questioning Oliver Fox's old colleagues should be their next step.

Investigating old cases could be complicated. It was hard to track witnesses down, as people tended to move away from the area over time.

Karen stood up, intending to grab her coat and bag, when Superintendent Murray marched into the office area. DI Morgan and Sophie looked up as she approached.

'I've had the assistant commissioner on the phone,' she said. 'Apparently, the only decent thing to do is keep DSI Fox updated with every latest development in the case. He's got a handicap of four, don't you know?' She gritted her teeth. 'I've always disliked golf.'

Karen had never seen the superintendent so angry. Two bright red spots burned in the centres of her cheeks as she paced in front of them, shaking with rage.

'So what do you want us to do, ma'am?' Karen asked. 'How much should we tell him?'

The superintendent turned her intense eyes on Karen. 'How long have you known me, DS Hart?'

Karen was taken aback at the question. 'Um, seven years, I think.'

'And do you think I'm the type of officer to bow to the pressure of the old boys' network?'

'No, ma'am, I don't.'

'So my original instructions remain. Don't give anything away. Ex-Detective Superintendent Fox may be friends with the assistant commissioner, but we don't know who we're dealing with. Be polite, make him feel like he's involved, but keep your cards close to your chest. Don't tell him any details about the body's condition or where it was found. Is that understood?'

DI Morgan, Sophie and Karen all nodded, and said in unison, 'Yes, ma'am.'

'Good. I thought I'd better let you know that Robert Fox will be coming by for a chat tomorrow morning.'

DI Morgan and Karen exchanged a look.

'I know what you're thinking. You could do without this sort of thing getting in the way of your work, but you just need to give him ten minutes of your time. Give him a tour around the labs, make him feel important.'

'Yes, ma'am,' DI Morgan said.

'Good. I'll see you all tomorrow.' Then Superintendent Murray turned on her heel and marched out of the office.

Sophie leaned back in her chair. 'I'm not getting anywhere with this search for the suitcase. I'm just going to go home. It's seven thirty, and it's not going to make any difference if I finish this tonight. He's already been dead for thirty years.'

Karen was too shocked to say anything. But DI Morgan wasn't. 'That's not a good attitude to have when you're investigating a death, Sophie.'

Oliver Fox had been dead for thirty years, but the note found at Albert Johnson's house was a threat – a very immediate one. Karen frowned. Sophie was struggling with her motivation on this case, which was very unlike her.

Sophie's cheeks flushed, and she straightened up in her chair. 'I know, I'm sorry. It's just been a hell of a day.'

But DI Morgan wasn't about to let it rest there. 'Just because he's been dead a long time doesn't mean that we don't need to take this case seriously. It gets investigated just like any other case. Do you understand?'

Sophie lowered her head and muttered, 'Yes, sir.'

Karen decided to walk with Sophie as she left and have a quick word. But before she could leave, DI Morgan asked if she could locate the file from the original Senior Investigating Officer.

It took a few minutes to do so, and by the time she'd made it downstairs, Sophie was long gone.

CHAPTER ELEVEN

Sophie walked up Steep Hill, wishing she'd worn flat shoes. She'd picked the spiky red heels because she wanted to look good tonight. Her friend, Angela, who she'd known since school, had a way of making her feel competitive.

Sophie had always been top of the class. She'd excelled in every subject. They'd met up frequently in the years since they'd left sixth form, and Sophie usually enjoyed going out with Angela. But tonight she was nervous, uncertain. For the first time in her life, Sophie felt like a failure, and she didn't like that feeling at all.

She entered the tapas restaurant, which was heaving with people. The air was thick with the smell of onions and sizzling garlic, and every table was full. The noise of the chatter was quite overwhelming after the relative quiet of Steep Hill.

Sophie took a moment to get her bearings and then spotted Angela sitting at a corner table by the window. She hadn't looked up or spotted Sophie. Staring intently at her phone, she was tapping away at the screen.

Sophie took a moment to study her friend. Angela had changed since their school days. In fact, she'd undergone a pretty dramatic transformation. Her hair used to be brown and rather frizzy. Angela had joked that she kept Frizz-Ease afloat, but now she'd had her hair dyed blonde and professionally straightened, and it hung glossily around her shoulders.

She'd had a nose job a couple of years ago too, and that had really changed her appearance. It was amazing the difference it had made. She looked like a new woman.

Finally, Angela raised her head and saw Sophie. She smiled widely and waved.

Sophie took a deep breath and tried to wind her way past the tables without nudging any of the patrons. She knocked a handbag to the floor. It had been hanging on the back of a chair. Not a good idea, Sophie thought, as she picked it up and apologised to the owner. The restaurant was popular, and they really liked to pack them in. Didn't people realise how many opportunistic thefts occurred in Lincoln every day?

Finally through the obstacle course, she sat down opposite Angela with a sinking feeling in her stomach. Angela was a success, and Sophie was not. If people were being kind, they might say Sophie was a work in progress. The trouble was, the progress wasn't quick enough for Sophie's liking.

'What are you having to drink?' Angela asked. 'I ordered a glass of red because I wasn't sure if you were drinking.'

'Oh, I am definitely drinking,' Sophie said. 'Let's get a bottle.'

The waiter magically appeared at their table and offered the wine list. Sophie was about to opt for the house red when Angela picked out one of the most expensive wines on the menu.

Sophie blanched. That was a ridiculous amount of money for one bottle. When the waiter left, Sophie said, 'Angela, that was a bit pricey.'

'Oh, don't worry about it. I'm getting dinner tonight. My treat.' Her phone buzzed. 'Sorry, Soph, I just need to get this. It's work. You don't mind, do you?'

Sophie smiled and shook her head as Angela got up from the table and took her phone outside. She'd left her handbag perched on the chair, and Sophie studied it. Prada, she realised enviously. Typical.

She tapped her fingers on the table and stared out of the window at the cobbled street outside.

She was still smarting from not getting her mortgage. And the fact she'd been tracking down suitcase suppliers who'd been operating in 1988 and photocopying all afternoon hadn't exactly put her in a better mood.

She knew she wasn't being fair. Her job could be exciting and it was important, and the team had achieved some good results in the last couple of months. But she wondered whether she'd played much of a role in their successful cases. Would it have made a difference if she hadn't been on the team?

She smiled up at the waiter as he arrived at the table with the bottle and poured her a small amount of wine to taste. She took a quick sip, even though she wouldn't know the difference between an amazing vintage wine and one stocked by the local Co-op. She gave him an approving nod, and he filled the rest of her glass.

Angela was working in PR. She had been since she left school, and at first Sophie had thought it was an odd career. She had to attend parties and clubs and advertising events. Cosying up to people, laughing at boring jokes and making sure people's parties went off without a hitch was her job.

But Sophie had to give credit where it was due – Angela had worked hard and suddenly appeared to have the world at her feet. She was always jetting off on business trips to exotic places that Sophie had only ever seen in magazines or on the TV.

When Angela arrived back at the table, Sophie raised her glass. Angela slid into her seat and chinked her glass against Sophie's. 'Here's to us. It's been ages since we last met up. What have you been up to? How's work?'

Sophie didn't really feel like talking about work at the moment. She shrugged. 'Work's just work. Okay, I suppose.'

'I was always so envious of you, Soph. You knew exactly what you wanted to do when you left school, but I didn't have a clue. You're happy with your job, aren't you?'

If she'd been asked that question a week ago, Sophie would have said yes, but today she just wasn't feeling very positive. She reminded herself that her job wasn't terrible. She had monotonous tasks to do, but that was the same with most careers. She was just having a tough day because her mortgage application had failed.

She struggled to raise a smile. 'Yes, it's great. I'll be applying for a promotion next year if all goes well.'

'That's brilliant. I'm really pleased for you.'

'I'm feeling a bit sorry for myself today, though,' Sophie said, taking a sip of her wine. 'I found a house I really wanted to buy, but the bank wouldn't give me a big enough mortgage.'

'Oh, what a shame. I've got the opposite problem. I have the money to buy a property but keep missing out because it's hard to find time for the viewings. The estate agent I'm using now is pretty good, though. I've been living in serviced apartments in Manchester for the past few months. It's not ideal. It doesn't feel like home, know what I mean?'

Sophie nodded, but she was actually thinking she'd prefer to live in a serviced apartment than stay in the same bedroom she'd had since childhood. 'I'm starting to think I should have picked a different job – one that earned better money for a start.'

Angela raised an eyebrow. 'Well, if you're serious about a career change, you could always work with me. I could get you an interview. There's loads of money in it. God, they're just throwing bonuses at me these days. Do you want me to put in a word for you? I'm sure they'd snatch you up. You could make a killing, Soph.'

'Thanks, but I don't think I'm ready for a career change just yet. I do like my job. I just get . . .' Sophie paused as the waiter stopped by their table, pad in hand, to take their orders.

They ordered a selection of tapas dishes to share – garlic mushrooms, chorizo and *patatas bravas*.

When the waiter left, Sophie smiled apologetically. 'Sorry, I probably should have cancelled tonight. I'm just in a bad mood. I'll be fine tomorrow.'

Angela's phone beeped, and she looked down at the screen. 'The estate agent must be working late.'

'So you're seriously looking?'

'Yes, I'm sick of living in those apartments. I need a proper base, somewhere to call home. I wanted somewhere near Mum and Dad, so I was looking in Washingborough, and the estate agent says she has the perfect property for me. She said it needs some work, but I'm looking for a good investment.'

Sophie's stomach lurched. Surely Angela couldn't be talking about the same house Sophie had wanted to buy in Washingborough? Her fingers tightened around the stem of the wine glass.

'At least I can hire decorators and fitters to work while I'm away,' Angela continued, reading the message on her phone. 'It sounds like most of the renovations have been done, but it needs a new kitchen. Shouldn't cost too much, and I need to do something with this money I'm earning.'

'Where's the house?' Sophie asked quietly.

'It's on St Clements Street. Near Washingborough Hall.'

Sophie's jaw dropped open. After a moment, she said, 'That's a coincidence!' She tried to laugh it off but couldn't. 'That's the house I wanted to buy.'

The smile fell from Angela's face. 'Oh, really? I had no idea. I can tell the agent not to bother booking a viewing.'

Sophie shook her head. 'No, don't do that. It's fine. It's just a house. We always did have similar taste.'

She started babbling about the ideas she'd had for the house. Maybe Angela would benefit from the hours she'd spent poring over decorating ideas on the internet. Sophie didn't know whether to laugh or cry.

To be still living at home with her parents in her mid-twenties was not how she'd imagined her future. She'd always been an overachiever, and yet Sophie had to sit in front of a computer, searching for suitcases, while Angela was jet-setting around the world. Is this really what she wanted out of her life? It wouldn't be so bad if she felt she was making a difference, but anyone could do the boring admin tasks.

Angela leaned forward and met Sophie's gaze. 'Well, if you're absolutely sure . . .'

Sophie gulped her wine. 'I am. Honestly. It's a bargain, and I'm sure the house will be lovely when you're done fixing it up.'

The waiter arrived with their dishes. The garlic mushrooms sizzled. Normally, Sophie would have wolfed down the tapas, but today she just wasn't feeling hungry.

Sophie spooned two mushrooms on to her plate as Angela said, 'So, tell me more about your job. It must be so exciting.'

Sophie drained her wine glass and pointed at the bottle. 'I think I'll need another drink first.'

CHAPTER TWELVE

It was almost eight p.m. by the time Karen arrived at Lincoln County Hospital. The car park was nearly empty. She slid the parking ticket into her back pocket and walked quickly to the main entrance.

The bright lights in the hospital reception area made her squint. Rick told her they'd moved Albert Johnson to the cardiac care unit, so she headed straight there and spotted Rick sitting on an orange plastic chair near the nurses' station.

When Rick saw her walking along the corridor, he got to his feet and massaged the small of his back. 'I don't think I've ever sat in such an uncomfortable chair,' he grumbled.

'Sorry to keep you waiting,' Karen said.

One of the nurses, sitting at the nurses' station, sent an angry look in their direction.

Rick gestured to the double doors at the end of the corridor. 'Let's talk out there.'

He yawned as they walked through the doors and paused on the other side.

'I take it Albert Johnson didn't start singing like a canary in the last half an hour?' Karen asked.

'I'm afraid not, Sarge. He's still asleep, or pretending to be. The nurses are a little concerned.'

Karen sighed. 'I think it's best if we leave it for tonight. Maybe he'll wake up tomorrow. I've arranged for a uniform to guard his room overnight just in case. Do you still think he's faking it to avoid talking to you?'

'Maybe. He seems tense. It's almost as if he's screwing his eyes shut. He must know we've found the body and that, as soon as he opens his eyes, we're going to have a lot of questions for him.'

'All right. Let's hope we have more luck tomorrow. You get off home now.'

'Thanks, Sarge.'

After Rick left, Karen walked back into the cardiac care unit and looked through the glass door at Albert Johnson. Even from a few feet away, she could see what Rick meant. Albert's face wasn't as relaxed as it should be if he was asleep. It looked like they had a waiting game on their hands. He would have to wake up and face the music eventually. Surely he wouldn't be able to fake sleep for more than a day or two.

She thanked the nurses on the ward and then headed back to her car. After she left the hospital building, she pulled out her mobile and saw she had a missed call from her sister, Emma. She hit redial, and her sister answered on the first ring.

'Hey you,' Emma said.

'Hey yourself. I was thinking about you today.'

'You were?'

'Yes. I'm working a case where the subject of shell suits came up. Do you remember those? We used to have matching ones. We thought we were the business wearing those suits with our fancy white trainers. We got them the same Christmas we discovered Exclamation perfume.'

'Oh God, yes. I remember that. Do you know they still sell that perfume? I smelled it in Boots the other day, and I was taken right back to 1990.'

Karen laughed.

'I did have a reason for calling, Karen.'

'What's wrong? Is Mallory all right?'

'She's fine. It's not bad news. In fact, I think it's good news. Mike met a chap through work last week and brought him around for dinner. He's just started work at the University of Lincoln, and he's lovely. I think you'll like him.'

Karen shivered. She knew where this was going. 'I'm going to stop you there. I'm not going on a date with someone Mike has just met, no matter how lovely he is.'

'Oh, come on, Karen. You'd like him. Besides, you can't live like a hermit for the rest of your life.'

'Why not?' Karen asked, shoving a hand in her pocket to locate her car keys. 'I quite like living like a hermit.'

'I could send you his picture. You could take a look at his Facebook profile.'

Karen groaned. 'For goodness' sake. Now I feel like I'm back in 1990 and you're trying to fix me up with the brother of that boy who used to work at the petrol station.'

Emma laughed. 'I'd forgotten about that.'

'You may have forgotten, but I haven't. It was awful. And this will be awful, too.'

'No, it won't. It's different now, and I promise he doesn't have braces and acne.'

Karen used the key fob to unlock her car. 'Absolutely not.'

'All right, no pressure. Just promise me you'll think about it.'

Karen shook her head. Emma was nothing if not persistent. 'Fine,' she said, sliding into the driver's seat, 'I'll think about it.'

She had no intention of thinking about it. She'd already made up her mind, but she needed to get Emma off the phone.

After she hung up, Karen gave DI Morgan a quick call to tell him that Rick was going home and they'd had no joy with Albert Johnson but would try again tomorrow.

'Are you at home now?' she asked.

'Yes, surrounded by boxes. Remind me why I thought it was a good idea to move?'

'Oh, I'd forgotten about the move. Have you had any news?'

'Yes, I should complete tomorrow.'

Wow, Karen thought. The sale had certainly moved fast. DI Morgan had mentioned he liked Heighington when they were investigating the disappearance of two young girls from the local primary school a few months ago, but she hadn't expected him to buy a house there. It was a pretty village with a couple of pubs and a good bus service. The drawback was, it was on the opposite side of Lincoln to the police headquarters. It wasn't far from where Karen lived herself, in Branston. Still, when the new bypass was built, it might make the journey easier.

'That's it, then,' Karen said. 'No going back now. You'll be a proper yellowbelly. You've put down roots.'

'Looks like it,' DI Morgan said.

'No regrets?'

'Not yet. Ask me again after I've met the neighbours.'

Karen couldn't help laughing. 'I'll see you tomorrow.'

Rick was back home by half past eight. It felt a little strange to be going home knowing that someone outside the family would be there. He was used to his sister taking care of their mum during the day, but this was different. Over the past couple of weeks, he'd got to know Priya and liked her, but it still felt odd to have someone in his house. Priya had grown up in the UAE, but she'd lived in England for the past ten years. Rick had been so relieved when his mother had warmed to her.

On the drive home he'd tried to put morbid thoughts of the future out of his mind. Spending so much time at the hospital today had been a harsh reminder of the inevitable. After the hours spent watching over Albert Johnson, he felt like going to the pub and having a few drinks instead of coming home to look after his mother. The temptation to shake off his responsibilities for a few hours was powerful, but he pushed the thought away immediately. That was selfish.

He found them in the living room. His mother was in her favourite armchair with the small folding table set up in front of her. Priya sat on the floor with her legs tucked beneath her. They were playing a game of cards.

He said hello to Priya and then kissed his mother on the cheek. 'Sorry I'm late. I've been waiting around at the hospital all day.'

'Oh, I hope it wasn't anything serious,' Priya said with concern.

'I was waiting to question a suspect, but he didn't wake up. How have you two been getting on?'

'We've been playing gin rummy,' his mother said with a smile. 'I think Priya's been letting me win.'

Priya shook her head, her dark hair swinging around her face. 'I haven't! You're a bit of a card shark I think, Mrs Cooper.'

His mother chuckled.

After his mother's minor surgery, Priya had helped out with her overnight care, but because Rick had been home every night, and his sister was there every day, he hadn't worried at all. Today he'd been uneasy, scared something would go wrong. It seemed his nerves had been unfounded. His mother was perfectly happy in Priya's company. He had to admit it was nice having some help, and it took the pressure off him and his sister.

'I can take over now, Priya. Why don't you get off home?' Rick said, shrugging off his jacket.

'You must be joking,' Priya said with a grin. 'I need to win a game to get my money back.'

Rick raised his eyebrows. 'You're playing for money?'

Priya looked down at the pile of copper coins by his mother's slippers, and Rick smiled.

'All right, I'll put the kettle on and you can deal me in.'

The following morning, Sophie woke with a crushing headache. The fact it was self-inflicted made it worse. The sunlight sliced into her bedroom through a gap in the curtains and felt like a razor blade stabbing at her eyes. She tried, unsuccessfully, to drag the curtain closed with her foot. But it was too much effort. She pushed the duvet back and struggled to sit up. The room spun.

She couldn't remember the last time she'd felt this bad after a night out. They'd polished off two bottles of wine over the tapas and then decided it was a good idea to head out for cocktails. Angela was probably used to drinking quite a lot, in her line of work, but Sophie certainly wasn't.

She shakily got to her feet, leaning hard on the desk beside her bed. Her bedroom was the same one she'd had since she was a girl. She'd removed some of the childish posters from the wall and replaced them with grown-up artwork, but there was no disguising the fact it was still a kid's bedroom in her parents' house. She only had a single bed – that's all there was room for with the large wardrobe and the shelves crammed with books on police procedure and forensics.

Sophie was a bookworm and enjoyed a challenge, but as she looked around her small bedroom and tried to rub the sleep from her eyes, she couldn't help wondering if the job was worth all the effort she put in. Even if she wanted to do this job for the rest of her career, she didn't know if she was any good at it. Both DI Morgan and DS Hart had been annoyed with her yesterday, and she'd deserved it.

Her comment about Oliver Fox being dead for thirty years and not needing them to rush had been callous and uncalled for. Maybe she really wasn't cut out for the job.

She'd tried so hard, but perhaps this was one career where book learning and studying weren't the be all and end all.

She could hear her parents moving about downstairs and was glad she didn't have to wait for the bathroom this morning.

She thought of Angela in her serviced apartments and the fact her friend would soon have her own place in Washingborough. That stung. Sophie had daydreamed about renovating that house. She'd pictured herself reading a book in the seat beneath the bay window in the living room.

She shouldn't dwell on it. It wouldn't help. It was only making her feel more depressed.

In the bathroom, she winced at her pale cheeks and the dark circles under her eyes. She put some toothpaste on her toothbrush and tried not to gag as she brushed her teeth, promising herself she wouldn't drink margaritas ever again.

When she was showered, dressed and on the way out, her dad called her into the kitchen.

'Are you all right, sweetheart? You don't look very well,' he said, his face a mask of concern.

She felt guilty then. She was hungover. She didn't deserve any sympathy.

'I'm fine,' she said. 'I just shouldn't drink during the week. See you later.'

She went outside, blinking at the bright spring sunshine, hoping she'd have a better day than yesterday.

It couldn't get much worse.

CHAPTER THIRTEEN

By eight thirty, all members of the team were back at work. Karen, DI Morgan and Sophie were at their desks at Nettleham headquarters, while Rick had resumed his watch over Albert Johnson at the hospital.

Karen was nursing her second cup of coffee of the day when she heard a groan from Sophie.

'What is it?' she asked, looking up from a pile of reports.

'I've just been sent some notes about the original investigation. They were made by DI Goodfield, the investigating officer.'

Karen got up and walked to Sophie's desk so she could see the notes on the screen.

'Sarah, the woman who gave me the files yesterday, discovered them this morning. For some reason they weren't with the other files I collected from Skellingthorpe. She scanned in the notes to save me another trip.'

'That was good of her.'

Sophie rested her forearms on the desk and used the mouse to scroll through the folder of scanned images. 'There's quite a lot of them. It'll take me a while to get through everything.'

'Do your best to get through as much as possible. I'd like to fit in a visit to DI Goodfield today.'

Sophie double-clicked on one of the images, enlarging it, and let out a low whistle.

Karen leaned closer to the screen, narrowing her eyes. 'That hand-writing is going to take some skill to decipher.'

Sophie sighed. 'I thought they used typewriters back in 1988.'

Karen grinned. Sophie was part of the generation where everything was done on a computer. It surprised the younger woman to find that some people preferred handwritten notes. Official reports at the time would have had to be typed. But they might be able to dig out some interesting information from these handwritten notes. Perhaps something that hadn't made it into the report because it wasn't thought to be important at the time.

'You can send me some of the notes, if you like,' Karen said, then drained the last of her coffee and glanced at her watch. They'd been told Detective Superintendent Fox would be arriving soon, and she wasn't looking forward to dealing with him. She sensed he wouldn't be able to resist trying to pull rank despite being retired. Somehow, they had to make him feel like he was being kept in the loop, but not actually tell him anything about the investigation. That wasn't going to be easy.

Just then, DI Morgan strode out of his office and gave a smile that looked more like a grimace. 'Karen, DSI Fox is waiting for us in reception.'

Karen put her mug on the desk and followed him out of the office. He sounded about as enthusiastic as she felt.

Detective Superintendent Fox was sitting in reception, flicking through a magazine on home security. His dark hair was neatly combed, and he wore an expensive-looking navy-blue suit and dark-blue tie.

'Good morning, sir,' DI Morgan said, holding out a hand.

Robert Fox stood up, shook DI Morgan's hand and smiled. He seemed less strained today. Perhaps they'd seen the worst side of him yesterday, which was hardly surprising. He'd been waiting for the news for thirty years, but being told his brother's body had been found must have come as a shock.

'I apologise for taking up some of your time this morning. I know you're busy,' he said, looking at DI Morgan and then Karen. 'I know what it's like to have to pander to a senior officer. You must think I'm an old fuddy-duddy, who should be at home with his slippers and pipe.'

Karen smiled, feeling awkward. 'Not at all, sir.'

'Superintendent Murray thought you might like a quick tour of the station and then perhaps to look around the laboratories to see the work we're doing on this case,' DI Morgan said.

Robert Fox smiled graciously. 'I would like that very much.'

DI Morgan swiped his pass card and held the door open for the ex-superintendent. Karen followed them into the corridor, looking at the broad back of DI Morgan next to the narrow shoulders of Robert Fox.

Was he going to give them a hard time on this case, or did he simply want to be involved? She could understand his need to find answers. Karen had been desperate for information after the road accident that killed Josh and Tilly.

She should have been able to accept that their deaths were simply the result of Josh's late braking and distracted driving. After all, she'd spent months compiling evidence, picking up on every little hint the officers working in traffic would give her. There was a vague mention of another set of tyre marks on the road, so Karen had immediately leapt to the conclusion that another car had to be involved. But the accident report determined the other tyre marks had been old and not relevant to the accident.

Karen hadn't accepted the verdict easily, and she'd spoken to everyone involved in the investigation. They must have seen her the same way she was viewing Robert Fox now – as a nuisance. It wasn't that they hadn't been sympathetic; she had seen the pity in their eyes. They'd felt sorry for her, but she was a thorn in their side. They were doing their job, and she was getting in the way.

It had fallen to DI Freeman, who was good friends with the head of traffic at the time, to try to make Karen see sense. She hadn't. At least not then. Instead, she'd just stopped talking to people about it. She kept all the reports she could get her hands on in a blue folder at home and pored over them every night. She'd just kept it secret.

It was only a few months ago that she'd finally felt ready to move on and had burned the folder. She had to admit it felt like a weight had been lifted.

For five years, she'd been consumed by theories about what must have happened that day. It was better now, though. At least she was dealing with it. Occasionally, her mind wandered back and she found herself wondering whether Tilly had been upset, distracting Josh . . . Maybe he'd turned, looked away from the road, or maybe he'd mistakenly pressed the accelerator rather than the brake . . .

She'd slowly come to accept that she would never find out the truth. She would never know what had caused the accident, only that it had happened and it had ruined her life. Now she needed to let go.

But Oliver Fox's family hadn't had the option of putting it behind them until now. They'd lived for thirty years without answers, and Karen couldn't even imagine what that was like.

DI Morgan slowed as they approached the laboratories. 'This is one of the labs where we examine evidence. Post-mortems are carried out at Lincoln County Hospital. But most of the other evidence is examined here. If Harinder is about, he'll be able to explain how we got the details from the driver's licence.'

'I was wondering about that last night,' Robert Fox said. 'It must have been in a terrible state after thirty years.'

DI Morgan gave him a sympathetic smile. 'I'm afraid so.'

He led the way into the lab, and Karen stepped in after them. There was a faint smell of disinfectant in the air, and as usual Karen found the lights made the lab sterile and too bright. She wouldn't like to work there all the time.

Harinder was sitting in front of one of the many computers that lined the right-hand side of the lab.

He turned to smile at them. 'Morning.'

'Good morning, Harinder,' DI Morgan said. 'I'd like you to meet retired Detective Superintendent Robert Fox. He's Oliver Fox's brother.'

The smile slid from Harinder's face. 'I'm very sorry for your loss, sir,' he said stiffly.

He wasn't used to dealing with members of the public, especially not the victims of crimes. He was more comfortable behind a computer screen, working his magic there.

'Harinder ran the program to sharpen and extract the text. It's thanks to him we got Oliver's name and address from the licence.'

'Thank you very much for your hard work. I'm grateful you're working so hard on this case. I have to admit I was worried that after thirty years the evidence would only be given a cursory glance before being stuffed at the back of a storage room.'

'We intend to find out what happened to Oliver, sir. You have my word on that,' DI Morgan said.

Robert Fox's eyes were glassy with tears. Karen wished she could offer some words of comfort, but she came up blank. She felt guilty for viewing the man as a problem rather than a distraught family member. Detective superintendent or not, the victim was his brother.

'I could show you the image of the original driver's licence and then the final version, where we were able to see the text, if you like?' Harinder volunteered.

Robert Fox blinked away his tears and then said, 'Oh, yes, I'd love to see that.'

As Harinder scrolled through the files on the computer, enlarging images, the older man said, 'Oh, that is impressive. We didn't have anything like this in my day. Computers really are marvellous, aren't they?'

Karen was thankful for Harinder's help. They only needed to spend a few more minutes with the former DSI and then they would be able to get on with the job of finding out what had happened to Oliver Fox.

As they left the lab, Detective Superintendent Fox turned to them. 'I know you must resent me for this. I've used my sway with the assistant commissioner, and I'm not proud of it. It's something I never imagined myself doing, but maybe you can understand if you imagine this was a member of your family.'

Karen smiled at him. 'I think we all would do everything in our power to get answers. It's absolutely understandable.'

He returned her smile. 'I really do appreciate all the hard work you're putting into this.'

They took him back to the main office and introduced him to Sophie, who was going through the handwritten reports. He chuckled and made a joke about deciphering the handwriting.

'Has the post-mortem been completed yet?' he asked.

DI Morgan shook his head. 'No, in older cases like this, it takes a little longer.'

Robert Fox glanced around the office. Karen was glad she'd thought ahead and moved the whiteboard with the case notes into one of the empty interview rooms.

'I suppose you still can't tell me where the body was found?'

Karen shook her head. 'No, but we'll provide you with an update on the post-mortem as soon as we can.'

His features tightened, the skin around his eyes crinkling at the corners. 'And the reason you think it was Oliver's body is the driver's licence? After all this time, his remains must have been unrecognisable.'

Karen answered. 'Yes, and the evidence indicates the man was in the same age range as Oliver. We'll be carrying out a dental record comparison to make sure. And, of course, we have DNA these days to double-check we've identified the right person.'

Robert Fox took a deep breath. 'I don't envy the pathologist's job.' He turned to look at Karen. 'Will I be able to see him? I mean, I understand there won't be much left of him to see, but . . .'

Karen observed him carefully. 'You'll be able to see him as soon as the pathologist has concluded the post-mortem. I'll let you know as soon as that happens.'

'Right, of course. Thank you for being so open with me.'

'Not at all,' DI Morgan said. 'We'll walk back to reception with you.'

'There is something you might be able to help us with,' Karen said. 'Do you remember any names of your brother's work colleagues? We'd like to talk to them.'

Detective Superintendent Fox thought for a moment and shook his head. 'I'm sorry, but names escape me at the moment. I'll have a think and get back to you.'

'Thank you,' Karen said. 'We should be talking to the original SIO on the investigation later today.'

'DI Goodfield?' Robert Fox raised an eyebrow.

'Yes.'

'Good luck. I'm not sure you'll get much out of him. I wasn't happy with him at the time.'

'No? Why was that?' Karen asked.

She noticed DI Morgan staring intently at the detective superintendent.

'He was a drinker. I was disappointed. I wanted someone who would really put a good effort into looking for Oliver. In fact, I'd be surprised if DI Goodfield is still alive. He was a very heavy drinker.'

As they reached reception, Karen opened the door. 'Thanks for the heads-up.'

They said their goodbyes, and Karen and DI Morgan both paused by the door to watch him leave.

'What did you make of that?' DI Morgan said.

'Detective Superintendent Fox seems to be open about things on the surface, but then I get the impression he's holding back. What about you?'

DI Morgan grinned. 'You want to know what my instincts are telling me?'

Karen rolled her eyes. It was a running joke between them. Karen tended to rely on her gut when she was evaluating people, but DI Morgan dismissed that as vague nonsense. He insisted he only liked to deal with facts.

'I'm not sure about him,' DI Morgan said. 'Yesterday I thought he was going to be a pain in the backside, but today I felt sorry for him.'

They turned and started to walk back towards the stairs, and Karen said, 'I agree. It can't be easy. He must want to get involved and lead the investigation, so us not telling him much must be frustrating.'

DI Morgan frowned. 'Yes, but he seems to be dealing with it quite well. It's a shame he couldn't remember more about his brother's colleagues. I think our best bet is to ask Elizabeth Fox about that directly. She might be more relaxed and able to remember things today. Yesterday must have been a hell of a shock.'

'I'm very keen to talk to DI Goodfield now,' Karen said.

'Agreed,' DI Morgan said as he pushed open the door to the office. 'And as right now our only link between Albert Johnson and Oliver Fox is Greenhill Secondary, it's worth checking in with the school and asking to view their staff records.'

'Right, good idea. I'll pay them a visit after I talk to Elizabeth Fox this morning. Should I mention Oliver's affair with her sister?'

DI Morgan thought for a moment, then shook his head. 'No, don't bring it up. Try to get her on side. We need her to be as cooperative as possible.' He gave a wry smile. 'I have a feeling this case is about to get complicated.'

CHAPTER FOURTEEN

When Karen visited Elizabeth Fox later that morning, the woman was alone. There was no sign of her sister or her sons.

She led Karen into a large glass orangery at the back of the house. It was a sunny morning, but there had been a chill in the air outside, and Karen was surprised it was so hot in the orangery.

She settled down in a rattan armchair as Elizabeth served tea using a blue-and-white china tea service, which looked expensive. There were plants covering every surface, and the smell of compost hung in the air, mixed with the scent of green herbs.

In the corner of the room there was a large electric heater. So that was what was pumping out the heat and making Karen feel so uncomfortable. She shrugged off her jacket after balancing her teacup and saucer on the arm of the chair.

'How are you doing?' Karen asked.

Elizabeth bowed her head, looking at her hands and twisting her wedding band. 'I'm all right. The news did leave me shaken. To be honest, I didn't think when the news came I would feel so upset. I mean, I knew something had happened to Oliver, so . . .'

'What did you think had happened to him?'

'As far as I could see, there were three options. One, he'd run off and left us; two, there'd been some kind of accident and he'd died, but for some reason, his body was never recovered; and three, someone had killed him.'

'Was there any reason to suggest he might leave you and the boys? Was he under stress at the time?'

Elizabeth shook her head. 'Not really. We had our ups and downs as any couple does, but we were happy. He adored the boys. You do hear about that sort of thing happening, and for a while, I wanted to believe he'd run off. At least that way there was a chance of him coming home.' She looked up, her bright green eyes trained on Karen's face. 'Can you understand that, or does it seem silly?'

'It doesn't seem silly at all. It must have been incredibly difficult to go through that and bring up two young sons on your own.'

Elizabeth lowered her head. 'It certainly wasn't easy, especially with Martin . . .' She trailed off.

'Especially with Martin . . . ?' Karen prompted, wondering what she had been about to say.

'Oh, it's nothing. Martin was just a little more demanding.'

Karen sensed there was something Elizabeth wasn't telling her, but now wasn't the time to press the matter.

'I was hoping you could give me some names of people who worked with your husband at the school.'

'Oh, why?'

'We just want to gather as much background information as we can about Oliver, and it's possible his ex-colleagues might be able to remember something important.'

'Right, well, we didn't have much to do with them, to be honest. We didn't socialise with them. There was Mr Moss, who was the religious education teacher. The head teacher was Mr Johnson. Albert, I think his name was. Then there was Mr Grant. His first name was Wilfrid or William. I believe he was the English teacher. Stephen or

Martin might know more about the teachers. I could ask them, if you'd like?'

Karen smiled. 'Thank you. That would be very helpful.'

She finished her tea and placed the cup on the saucer, studying the intricate pattern. She knew her next request might get Elizabeth's back up. 'Would you be able to give me your sister's address?'

There was an instant change in Elizabeth's demeanour. 'And why would you want to talk to her?'

Karen hesitated for a moment and then said, 'For the same reason we want to talk to his old colleagues. We want to build an in-depth picture of Oliver's life.'

Elizabeth's eyes narrowed, and she gave a cold chuckle. 'Don't worry, dear. I know you've found out my sister was having an affair with my husband.'

Karen didn't say anything. She wanted to see how much Elizabeth would give away. The fragility Karen had seen in her eyes was now replaced with steel.

Elizabeth smoothed her skirt with one hand. 'But their affair isn't relevant. It was over long before Oliver died. It wasn't the first time she'd done something like that. She was always jealous of me, always wanted what I had, even when we were little girls.'

'But you're still close? Laura came here as soon as you heard from us yesterday.'

'It's complicated,' Elizabeth said. 'Laura is a troubled woman. I look after her. If she didn't have me, I don't know what she would do.'

Elizabeth didn't seem vulnerable anymore. She interlaced her fingers, resting her hands in her lap, and smiled.

A chill ran up Karen's spine. She had a feeling they'd underestimated Oliver Fox's widow yesterday.

After she left Elizabeth Fox, Karen called to check in with Rick to see if Albert Johnson was ready to talk.

'I'm afraid not, Sarge,' Rick said, sounding thoroughly fed up.

'I should have expected as much.'

'According to the nurse I spoke with this morning, he was awake last night, eating and drinking, and they're happy his condition is improving. I got here just after eight o'clock this morning, and he's remained stubbornly asleep the whole time. He didn't even stir when they brought the tea trolley around.'

'All right, Rick. I know it's a tedious job but keep with it. Maybe sit beside him and have a bit of a chat.'

'I think it'll be a very one-sided chat, Sarge.'

'You never know. If you just chatter away about normal, everyday things, it might convince him you're not a threat and he'll decide to talk.'

'All right, I'll do my best.'

After she'd hung up on Rick, Karen called Sophie.

'Any developments?' Karen asked.

'I called Greenhill Academy and made you an appointment for eleven o'clock. Do you think you can make it there by then?'

Karen glanced at the clock on the dashboard and saw it was only ten thirty. 'That shouldn't be a problem. Thanks.'

'The current head teacher is Terence Smith. I only spoke to the school secretary, but she said they were happy to provide any information they can to help.'

'How much did you tell them?'

'Don't worry. I told them we're investigating a cold case. I didn't mention the fact we've discovered Oliver Fox's body. I just said we were looking into his disappearance again.'

'Great. Look, Sophie, is everything okay? You seem a bit down at the moment.' Karen didn't really want to have this conversation on the phone, but she'd never known Sophie to be so negative and it worried her. She was coping with the tasks assigned to her, but her attitude was off.

'I'm fine, just tired,' Sophie said after a moment's pause, then continued in a businesslike manner. 'I found a Facebook group for old students of Greenhill Secondary School, and some of the members have posted their memories of the staff. So I've made a list.'

'Great. Can you email it to me?'

'Already done.'

'Thanks. Have we had any news back from Raj about the post-mortem? I thought we might have some preliminary results by now.'

'He spoke to DI Morgan about half an hour ago, I think. He's going to get an external expert to take a look at the bones. Apparently, he knows a specialist at Lincoln University. He believes Oliver Fox died from a blow to the head, but he wants an expert to take a look to see if they can give us any insight into how the injury was inflicted.'

'Right, sounds promising, but I think it's unlikely we'll find the murder weapon after thirty years.'

After Karen thanked Sophie and hung up, she checked her emails and opened the message from Sophie with the list of staff. It didn't give employment dates, and in many cases they just had a surname to go on. But it would give her a starting point when she spoke to Terence Smith.

Greenhill Academy was less than five minutes' drive from Elizabeth Fox's Skellingthorpe home, so Karen arrived early for her appointment with the headmaster.

In one of the old newspaper articles describing Oliver Fox's disappearance, there'd been a photograph of the old secondary school. The new academy had been extensively expanded and modernised, so it was barely recognisable.

A long, sweeping drive led up to the main building, which was a square brick-and-glass construction that, according to Sophie's research, had been remodelled in the nineties.

She didn't need to show any ID to get on to the school grounds, and just followed the driveway to the car park at the rear of the Academy. After getting out of the car, she looked around. There were playing fields at the back of the school and tennis courts beside the car park. It was clear a fair amount of money had been invested in the Academy.

A large sign at the entrance declared the school had been rated excellent in a recent Ofsted report. Despite the fact she was still ten minutes early for her appointment with Terence Smith, Karen walked in through the swinging glass doors. She guessed lessons were underway, as all the corridors were quiet. To her right, she saw a sign for reception and walked along the hallway until she saw the reception area.

Set behind a white, kidney-shaped desk were white bookshelves. There weren't any books on them, but they were used to display pieces of modern art. Karen wondered whether the artwork had been produced by the students.

The Academy didn't look anything like Karen's old school. It reminded her of one of those high-tech start-up companies. Everything was modern and sleek, and moulded plastic seemed to be the material of choice for everything from the bookshelves to the desks and chairs.

Karen's school had smelled of polished wood floors, but here there were plain white, shiny tiles, and everything was light and bright. There was no wood to be seen anywhere, and even the doors looked plastic.

A woman in a red suit sat behind the desk. A large glass bowl of sweets sat at one edge of the desk, and the receptionist reached up, plunging her hand in the sweet bowl, not bothering to look up.

When Karen cleared her throat, the woman jumped and snatched her hand back, as though she'd been caught stealing sweets. Then she pushed up the sleeves of her jacket and sniffed. 'Can I help you?'

Karen showed her warrant card. 'DS Karen Hart. I have an appointment to see Mr Terence Smith, although I'm a little early.'

'Ah, I think he's in a meeting at the moment, but you shouldn't have to wait too long. Perhaps you'd like to take a seat.'

'Thanks.'

The reception area wasn't a proper office; it was more of an alcove attached to the main corridor. There was a line of four white chairs that looked comfortable enough, but instead of sitting down, Karen walked over to the bookshelves to look at the artwork. Most of it was pottery, and as she got closer, she saw a student's name next to each piece. The bright colours of the pottery brightened up the place, as the only splash of colour in the otherwise white and sterile surroundings.

She scrolled through the emails on her phone and saw a message from Raj, which just repeated the information Sophie had already relayed.

By the time she had sorted her new emails into various folders, she heard the woman at the reception desk say, 'If you'd like to come with me, DS Hart, Mr Smith is ready to see you now.'

She followed the receptionist along the corridor. They passed a number of classrooms, and Karen peered through the windows as they walked.

They reached a white door with a chrome plate which read *Mr Smith*, and underneath was printed the word *Head*.

Not head teacher or headmaster, just head. Karen thought that was a bit strange. That, together with the sleek modern look of the Academy, almost made her expect to see a disembodied head floating around in the office, like something out of a sci-fi programme.

But when they entered the room, she saw that Terence Smith looked very ordinary. He was a small man with messy brown hair streaked with grey. His wire-rimmed glasses suited his round face. Karen judged him to be in his fifties.

'DS Hart, please have a seat. Thank you, Denise,' he said. He waved a hand at the receptionist, dismissing her.

Denise turned and left, closing the door behind her.

The room was decorated in a different style to the communal areas Karen had seen. For one thing, the large desk was made of real wood. There were wooden shelves on either side of the room, but no student artwork sitting on them. Instead, a variety of model cars were on display.

Terence Smith sat directly in front of the window. Bright sunlight shone through the blinds, making Karen squint.

'How can I help you, DS Hart?' he asked, interlinking his fingers and smiling at her.

'As my colleague mentioned when she called, we're investigating a cold case. The disappearance of a man called Oliver Fox who used to work at the school.'

Terence gave her a tight-lipped smile. 'That was before my time, I'm afraid, but I will help in any way I can.'

'Were any of the current teachers here at the Academy when Oliver Fox was a member of staff?'

Terence shook his head. 'I'm afraid not. The last teacher who worked with Oliver Fox left a good seven years ago now. That was William Grant. I worked with him for a year or two before he retired. And, of course, there's Bert Johnson. He was the headmaster here for many years. That was before it became an academy, of course.'

Karen didn't react to Albert Johnson's name. Terence Smith didn't show any concern for the former headmaster's welfare, so Karen guessed he hadn't heard about the fall.

'Both William Grant and Albert Johnson still live in the area, as far as I know. I'll see if I can get their addresses for you.'

'Thank you. That would be very helpful. I do have a list of other teachers' names, so if you have any records or contact details for them, I'd appreciate those, too.' Karen pulled out her mobile phone and navigated to the list Sophie had sent her, and showed it to Terence Smith.

He made a note on a yellow pad. 'We should be able to help. We do keep old records, so I we can compile a list of teachers who worked here at the same time as Oliver Fox. We may not have current addresses for them, but it should be a starting point.'

'That would be very useful,' Karen said, and gave him her email address.

'It's all on the computer system, but I'm not great at using it,' he said, grinning at Karen. 'They certainly haven't made our system idiot-friendly. I'll pass the list on to Maggie Reynolds, she's head of the sixth form and is fantastic with the system. She's on a free lesson at the moment, so I'm sure she'd be happy to help. I'll ask her to email you as soon as she's done. Is that okay?'

'Yes, thank you. I know you didn't work with Oliver Fox, but did you ever hear any stories about him?'

Terence Smith's expression grew guarded. 'I'm not sure what you mean. I don't give the time of day to rumours. I'm shocked a police officer would pay any attention to them.'

Karen was surprised by his reaction. He'd immediately assumed she was referring to something negative. Interesting. Sometimes rumours were all they had, and with a little digging and background research, they turned into solid leads.

'I meant stories about his time here. His wife told us he coached the football team in his spare time,' Karen said. 'But rumours, speculation, I want to hear it all. I can't afford to ignore anything.'

Terence looked down at the desk. He twisted his fingers nervously. 'Well, like I said, it was well before my time, but I did hear that there was some tension between Oliver Fox and some of the other teachers, including Bert Johnson.'

'Do you know what caused that tension?'

Terence shook his head quickly. 'I have no idea. Bert Johnson did have a reputation for being quite old-fashioned and a bit of a curmudgeon. He was well liked by the students, but he certainly didn't stand for any bad behaviour. He was strict. Stricter than would be acceptable these days.'

'In what way?'

Terence looked extremely uncomfortable. He ran his hands through his hair so it looked even messier.

'Well, I think when he started out as a teacher, they still used to give kids a whack on the back of the hand with a ruler.'

'Are you saying that Mr Johnson physically reprimanded the students?'

Terence shook his head vigorously. 'No, I said nothing of the sort. You see, this is why I don't like to speculate. He was a good teacher, but I'm just trying to explain why he and Oliver Fox may have had a difference of opinion. Maybe they had different teaching styles. I don't know. I never even met Oliver Fox.'

Karen raised an eyebrow. 'I see.'

'I hope you're not going to put that on the record. It could smear the man's reputation.'

It couldn't smear his reputation any worse than the police finding a skeleton in his house, Karen thought.

'We're just looking for leads. We don't intend to smear anybody's reputation, Mr Smith.'

Terence Smith appeared mollified. 'Good. I'm pleased to hear it. Now, I do have another meeting . . . unless there's something else you want to ask me?'

'No. Thank you, Mr Smith, you've been very helpful,' Karen said, getting to her feet and shaking the man's hand.

Her chat with the head teacher had been enlightening. There had been some tension between Albert Johnson and Oliver Fox. Now all they had to do was find out why.

CHAPTER FIFTEEN

Karen checked her messages as she left the school, and rolled her eyes when she saw she had another message from her sister.

It will be good for you. Take a chance. He's nice, I promise.

Emma was still going on about that blind date. It was the last thing Karen wanted to do. She ignored the message and put her mobile phone back in her pocket before climbing into the car.

It took her less than fifteen minutes to drive back to Nettleham. When she got to the office, she said hello to the officers she passed, but Sophie didn't respond. She was resting her chin on her hand and staring at the computer screen.

Karen decided her colleague's recent attitude was worth mentioning to DI Morgan. Sophie was a hard worker, but this job could get to anyone at times. She needed encouragement, and as her senior officers it was Karen and DI Morgan's responsibility to make sure she was coping with the demands of the case.

Karen headed straight to DI Morgan's office, but before she could knock on the door, it opened.

He stood there, grinning. 'Well, it's done. I am now an official resident of Heighington.'

Karen smiled. 'Congratulations. That's great news.'

'Yes, it is. I'm surprised at how quickly I've settled here. It already feels like home. Well, it will feel like home once I get everything unpacked. I might start moving some boxes to the new place tonight.'

Karen looked over her shoulder at Sophie and saw that she was still slumped in her chair. 'Have you noticed Sophie seems a bit down recently?'

DI Morgan frowned and said, 'Oh, what's the matter with her?'

'I'm not sure. I thought I'd have a chat with her later. I just wondered if she'd mentioned anything to you.'

'No, she hasn't said anything to me. How did you get on at the school?'

'Okay. The place has changed a lot since Oliver Fox worked there. As we predicted, after thirty years none of his old colleagues are still at the school. The current head teacher, Terence Smith, mentioned Albert Johnson. He also mentioned a man called William Grant who he thinks is still local. A teacher called Maggie Reynolds is compiling a list of Fox's contemporaries, and she's going to send it to me later today.'

'Good. Have we unearthed anything else?'

'Apparently there was some tension between Albert Johnson and Oliver Fox, but Smith didn't want to speculate. He was a bit touchy about the whole thing. It sounds like Albert and Oliver had a disagreement at some point, so that's worth looking into.'

'Definitely. Somehow, Oliver Fox ended up dead in a suitcase in Albert Johnson's house. The most likely scenario is that they had an argument, Albert killed him and managed to hide it from everyone for over thirty years.'

'There's no forensic evidence to suggest anything violent happened at Albert's house,' Karen pointed out.

'No, but carpets and wallpaper could have been changed over the years. It would be hard to say for certain he wasn't killed there.'

'Well, our link between Albert Johnson and Oliver Fox is the school, so when we get some more details about his old colleagues, we can ask the appropriate questions and find out if there was a major bust-up between the pair of them. We've also got that odd dynamic between Elizabeth Fox and her sister to look into. I didn't bring up the affair, but Elizabeth mentioned it herself. She said Laura had always been jealous of her and the affair didn't mean anything.'

DI Morgan raised his eyebrows. 'I wonder what Laura has to say about that.'

'That's exactly what I was thinking. I thought I might pay her a visit. I asked Elizabeth for her address this morning.'

Before they could say anything else, Sophie approached, holding out a piece of paper. 'I've managed to get in touch with DI Goodfield, who headed up the original investigation. He's living in Bassingham and is happy to talk to us this afternoon.'

Karen smiled. 'Great. If I go and talk to him, do you want to come with me?'

Sophie's gaze shifted from Karen to DI Morgan and back again. 'If you think I can handle it, Sarge.'

Karen frowned, but DI Morgan didn't seem to notice anything was amiss. He slapped his hands together. 'Excellent, although how much he'll remember about the case if he's a heavy drinker is anyone's guess.'

Karen looked at her watch. 'Okay. I'll be back in time to drive us to Bassingham this afternoon. I'll go and see Laura first.'

'And I'll try to track down William Grant,' DI Morgan said. 'If he's still local, that shouldn't be too hard.'

DI Morgan turned and went back into his office, and Karen watched Sophie walk back to her desk with her shoulders slumped and her head bowed. She didn't have time to talk to her now, because she really wanted to fit in a visit to Laura before they went to talk to DI

Goodfield. But on the way to Bassingham, it would be just her and Sophie in the car, and maybe then she would be able to get the young officer to open up and talk about what was bothering her.

It was after midday when Karen arrived at Laura Nicholson's home on Saxilby Road, just outside Skellingthorpe. It was a detached house with a pebble-dashed exterior, and apart from two farm buildings and associated storage units, there wasn't much else around. In the distance, there was a long line of tall poplar trees, and a pleasant view of the surrounding farmland.

Karen pulled into the driveway. The house was shaded thanks to high leylandii hedges surrounding the property. The front door was painted a cheerful pillar-box red. Karen got out of the car and noticed how peaceful it seemed, despite the traffic from the busy road.

When Laura opened the door, Karen noted again how similar she looked to her sister, despite the difference in hair colour. She had high cheekbones, a long, narrow nose and pinched lips. Karen wondered if that was due to the fact she was constantly pressing them together.

She wore heavy gold jewellery, including three bangles on one of her small wrists. She had thin, spidery lines around her mouth, and Karen wondered if she smoked. But as Karen stepped inside the house, she didn't detect the smell of cigarettes.

Laura led her into a small sitting room. The furniture looked old and a little tired, but everything was clean and tidy. Karen sat down on a faded armchair, and a tabby cat wandered haughtily into the room before jumping on to Laura's lap, curling up and making itself comfortable.

She didn't offer Karen tea or coffee but got straight down to business. 'What can I do for you, Detective?'

'I hoped you could tell me a little more about your relationship with Oliver.'

Laura narrowed her eyes. 'I see. You didn't waste your time digging up dirt.'

Karen didn't respond. She wasn't asking these questions because she was interested in gossip. She only wanted the truth.

Laura stroked the cat. 'I'd like to know who told you about my relationship with Oliver.'

It was Laura's guilty conscience talking; Karen hadn't mentioned the affair. When she'd used the word 'relationship', most people would have taken that to mean how they got along with the other person. They wouldn't have leapt to the conclusion that Karen was referring to an extramarital affair.

She didn't want to answer Laura's question. That wasn't how this worked. She was the one who needed to ask questions and control the direction of the conversation. 'We need to gather all the background information we can so we can fully understand Oliver's situation at the time of his death.'

'I don't see why it's important. It happened so long ago.'

'Because you were close to him at one point. Maybe Oliver mentioned something to you that could be useful in our investigation.'

Laura gave a little huff under her breath, but she didn't object further.

'Were you seeing him at the time he disappeared?'

Laura looked up sharply. 'Are you sure this is important?'

Karen nodded.

'Yes, I was still seeing him. I fell for him in a big way. I was naive.'

'Were you in a relationship with anyone else at the time?'

Laura bit her lip and then shrugged. 'I was married. To Maurice.'

'Did your husband find out about the affair?'

Laura gave a mirthless laugh. 'Do you think Maurice lost his temper and decided to murder Oliver? Is that your theory?'

Karen raised an eyebrow. 'We're considering all options at the moment.'

'Well, I can tell you there's no way it was Maurice. He was a quiet, mild-mannered man, and didn't care what I did as long as it didn't interfere with his fishing.'

'And are you still married to Maurice?' Karen asked.

'No.'

'Do you have contact details for him? I'd like to speak to him.'

'He died, four years ago . . . cancer.'

'I'm sorry.'

'I miss him. We never had a great relationship, but when he was gone, I realised how much I took his company for granted.' The cat purred on Laura's lap as she continued to stroke its fur.

'I want to ask you a question, and it might be difficult for you to answer. I don't want to hurt your feelings, Laura.'

Laura pursed her lips.

'Were you the only woman Oliver Fox was seeing?'

Her cheeks reddened. 'Do you mean was he having an affair with another woman?'

'Yes.'

Laura's gaze dropped to her lap again. 'I don't think so.' Raising her head, she looked at Karen defiantly. 'And even if he was, it wouldn't have been serious. He loved me. The only reason he wouldn't leave Elizabeth for me was the children. It wasn't just an affair. We fell in love. Of course, my sister didn't believe that. She likes to tell everybody that I'm jealous of her and that I can't stand to see her happy.'

Karen listened as Laura talked, mostly about her strange relationship with her sister. Laura had insisted she'd been in love with Oliver, yet she didn't offer much information on the man himself. She didn't tell Karen what he was like. She couldn't tell her anything personal about him.

When Laura had finished her tirade, Karen asked, 'Did Oliver confide in you?'

'What about?'

'Was he having trouble at work, any issues with co-workers or his boss?'

'No, he never mentioned anything about that. He was a respected member of the community, and everybody admired him. He coached the boys' football team in his own personal time and didn't get paid for it. Those children were lucky to have a teacher like him.'

Karen smiled encouragingly, then asked if she could remember the names of any of his colleagues.

Laura looked blankly at her. 'To be honest, we didn't talk about his work much.'

'What *did* you talk about?'

'Oh, all sorts of things. We had so much in common.'

Laura wouldn't offer any specific facts, and Karen started to wonder whether her relationship with Oliver had been mostly in her head.

She couldn't picture Elizabeth or Laura physically overpowering Oliver Fox, but there was an underlying current of jealousy and unhappiness that made the back of Karen's neck prickle. DI Morgan would probably laugh at her, but her instincts were telling her something was wrong here. Something was very wrong indeed.

CHAPTER SIXTEEN

Karen reached Nettleham just after one p.m., intending to grab a sandwich from the canteen and make some notes before she and Sophie set off to talk to DI Goodfield. She was listening to the local news as she turned into Deepdale Lane. There was nothing being reported about the discovery of Oliver Fox's body. For now, they could get on with their investigation without worrying about journalists getting in the way.

She parked in a spot near the marked cars. Rummaging in her handbag, she pulled out her purse and walked towards the main entrance of the station. She smiled at the duty sergeant, swiped her card to enter the secure area and headed straight to the canteen. It was busy, and she had to queue, but there were still some sandwiches left. DI Goodfield said he'd be home all afternoon, so Karen had an hour or two before she had to head to Bassingham. She put her lunch on her desk, hung her jacket over the back of the chair and sat down with her notepad.

She wrote: *Laura Nicholson – delusional? Odd relationship with her sister?*

She was about to unwrap her sandwich when DI Morgan noticed she was back.

He walked over to her desk. 'How did it go at Laura Nicholson's?'

'All right. She believes the relationship she had with Oliver Fox was something special. I get the impression she thinks he was her soulmate. It's hard to get the full picture when you're dealing with two different versions of a relationship. Laura describes it one way and her sister another.'

'Was there any lingering anger or resentment? Any reason the affair could have led to Oliver Fox's death?'

'Laura was married at the time she had the affair. It's possible her husband could have been jealous, although she did say he wasn't really the type to get in a red-hot rage over it. Unfortunately, we won't be able to follow up that angle easily because he died four years ago.'

DI Morgan sighed. 'That's the trouble with cold cases. Witnesses and suspects have either moved away or died. I've managed to track down an address for William Grant, though. I called him and said we would pay him a visit. Are you up for another trip before you go to see DI Goodfield in Bassingham?'

'Give me five minutes, and I'll be with you.'

Karen ate the cheese and ham roll at her desk as she checked her messages. There was nothing from Rick, so Albert Johnson must still be asleep, or pretending to be. And there was no sign of Sophie, so Karen assumed she'd gone to get some lunch.

After gulping down the last of the orange juice, Karen logged off the system and went to find DI Morgan. 'Ready?' she said.

He grabbed his coat.

William Grant lived in North Greetwell. Karen was grateful it didn't take them long to get there from the station. DI Morgan drove, following the instructions from the satnav. He turned right into Westfield Approach, and then stopped beside a bungalow on Westfield Drive.

'There are a few mentions of William Grant in the original inter-view notes, but only cursory details, nothing major,' DI Morgan said as he parked beside the curb.

Karen unbuckled her seatbelt. 'Let's hope he has a good memory.'

They got out of the car and walked along a paved drive towards the small bungalow. The doorbell rang out a cheerful tune that seemed to go on and on, and then finally the door was opened by a short, grey-haired man who blinked at them nervously.

DI Morgan held out his warrant card. 'Mr Grant, I'm DI Morgan, we spoke on the phone, and this is my colleague, DS Hart.'

'Yes, come in,' William Grant said, giving them a tentative smile and opening the door wide.

The hallway was spacious and brightly lit; the decor was old-fashioned. A thick, pink patterned carpet was partially covered by a rug, and the flow-ery wallpaper was dated, but it felt welcoming and homely.

'I'm really not sure how I can help you,' William said. 'As I men-tioned on the phone, I wasn't very close to Oliver.'

Karen and DI Morgan followed him along the hallway.

'Can I get you something to drink?' he asked.

Both Karen and DI Morgan turned down the offer. William led them into a large living room, with big windows that let in plenty of sunlight.

He made his way over to a comfortable-looking recliner. It was one of those chairs that tilted upwards when you needed to stand up. He settled down in it, and Karen and DI Morgan took the other two chairs. The bungalow was certainly larger than it looked from the out-side. Above the fireplace, there were numerous photographs of happy, smiling faces.

'Are they your grandchildren?' Karen asked, nodding at the framed photos.

'Yes,' William said, smiling proudly. 'I'm lucky they live close by. My daughter's been a sweetheart since my wife passed away. She brings the grandkids to see me at least once a week. I moved here from Skellingthorpe to be closer to them.'

There was a gas fire opposite them that had one bar alight.

William noticed Karen looking at it. 'If you're too hot, I can turn it off.'

Karen shook her head. 'I'm fine.'

'I feel the cold these days. That's the trouble with getting old. That and the insomnia. I haven't slept any later than five a.m. in years – and to think I used to look forward to retirement so I could get more sleep.'

'How long did you work with Oliver Fox?' DI Morgan asked, kicking off the questioning.

He was starting slowly, and Karen understood why. Despite cheering up when they spoke about his grandchildren, William Grant looked nervous. She put that down to the fact that he was a law-abiding citizen who didn't know what it was like to be questioned by the police.

'About fifteen years, I think. I was the English teacher, and Oliver took mathematics.'

'He also coached the boys' football team, didn't he?' Karen asked.

William frowned. 'Yes, I believe he did.'

'Did you organise any extracurricular clubs for the students?'

William shook his head. 'No, I had enough to do with marking homework and looking after my own children.'

'Do you remember Oliver acting any differently before he disappeared?'

William shook his head. 'No, I'm sorry. I didn't know him terribly well. We didn't mix socially. I wouldn't say we were friends.'

Despite William Grant saying he felt the cold, Karen noticed his cheeks were flushed and his skin looked a little dewy.

'Do you know Albert Johnson? He would have been the headmaster at Greenhill Secondary School when you worked there,' DI Morgan asked.

William swallowed and cleared his throat. 'I do. I worked with Bert for some time. We're good friends. Do you mind if I ask why there is this new interest in Oliver Fox's disappearance? He's been missing a very long time.'

'His case is up for review. We do this with cold cases from time to time to see if any new evidence has come to light,' DI Morgan explained smoothly.

William looked down at his lap. 'I see.'

'Did you hear Albert Johnson had a fall at home?' Karen asked, watching William carefully for his response. If he was a good friend, she expected to see immediate concern.

William's face creased, and he shook his head slowly. 'I did. It's a terrible business. His neighbour telephoned yesterday to tell me. I've been meaning to get up to the hospital to see him.'

'How did you find Oliver Fox?' DI Morgan asked, switching the subject, a technique they liked to use to keep the person they were questioning on their toes.

'How did I find him?'

'Yes. Was he kind? Compassionate? Difficult to get along with?'

William rubbed a hand over his forehead. 'Well, let me see, I'll try to remember. It was ever such a long time ago.'

Karen smiled. 'Take your time.'

'I'd say he was a bit difficult. He could rub people up the wrong way, I suppose.'

'How did he get along with the headmaster?'

'Bert? Fine, as far as I know. Why do you ask?'

'We're just trying to get some idea of what Oliver was like – who he got along with, and who he didn't. You're not going to get anyone in any trouble, William. You seem nervous.'

'Sorry, I'm just not used to being questioned by the police. I feel a bit shaken up after what happened to Bert. I told him he'd be better off living in a bungalow.'

'How was Oliver's family life? Did he ever mention trouble at home?'

William shook his head. 'No – as I said, we didn't really discuss things like that because we weren't very close.'

'Right.' DI Morgan leaned back in the armchair and studied William. 'You worked together for a long time . . . fifteen years. You must have found out things about him during that time. Maybe even things he liked to keep from his family.'

William shook his head. 'Honestly, I really didn't know much about him at all. Like I said . . .'

Karen finished his sentence for him. 'You didn't really know him very well.'

William shrugged and gave a sheepish smile. 'What do you think happened to him?' He glanced at DI Morgan and then Karen. 'There were rumours he'd done a runner and gone off to France.'

DI Morgan raised an eyebrow. 'There were? That's the first I've heard of it. Tell us more.'

'It was just talk in the staffroom, really. We all had theories about what happened to him. Most people's ideas focused on him running off with some woman. I don't think he was the faithful type.'

Karen leaned forward. 'That's exactly the sort of thing we want to know, Mr Grant. You probably know more than you think.'

William gave a half-hearted smile. 'It's really only from the talk in the staffroom. It was nothing I got directly from Oliver Fox himself.'

Karen and DI Morgan spoke to William Grant a little longer, trying to dig deeper and get him to open up, but he was unable to relax and confide in them. Karen wasn't sure whether that was because he truly didn't know anything, or because he didn't trust them enough to tell them what he did know.

When they'd first started talking to William, Karen had put his nervousness down to the fact he'd had limited dealings with the police, but now she had to wonder if there was something more to it. If he was a good friend to Albert Johnson, did he know more than he was letting on?

DI Morgan wrapped up the questioning and they said goodbye to William. As Karen handed him a card with her contact details on it, she focused intently on the man's face. His gaze refused to meet hers, and a muscle in his temple twitched.

By the time they'd left, Karen was sure William Grant knew more about Oliver Fox than he was letting on.

CHAPTER SEVENTEEN

Rick stood up and stretched. He was getting bored. He didn't know how the old bloke could pretend to be asleep for so long. It was a battle of wills, and Rick was losing.

He'd sat beside the hospital bed waffling away about nothing in particular, and Albert Johnson hadn't reacted once. Rick was starting to doubt himself. Maybe the old fellow really was asleep.

There wasn't much else he could do. He'd taken to strolling to the window, and up and down the waiting area once an hour, just to get the blood pumping again and to save his backside from getting numb.

It was one thirty, and they'd soon be bringing Albert's lunch. Rick was hoping the smell of cottage pie, or whatever it was they had on the menu, would spark some life into Albert. But Rick's own stomach was rumbling, and he was desperate for a shot of caffeine, so when he saw a smiling DC Shah walking towards him holding a paper coffee cup in her hand, Rick decided she was his new best friend.

'Please tell me that's for me,' he said as she reached his side.

Farzana Shah chuckled as she handed him the coffee. 'Yes, it is for you. I told Sophie we were bringing in a suspect, and she asked me to look in on you. She said this was the second day you've been waiting at the hospital.'

Rick took a sip of coffee and nodded. 'Yes, I'm waiting for a chap to wake up, but he's a very deep sleeper, apparently.'

They shuffled to one side, trying to get out of the way as a porter wheeled a bed containing an elderly lady towards the ward. Unfortunately, Farzana took a step just at the wrong time and nudged Rick's elbow. The entire contents of the cup spilled down his white shirt.

Rick took in a sharp breath, because the coffee was still really hot and now he'd be wearing stained clothes for the rest of the day.

'Oh, Rick, I'm so sorry,' Farzana said, pressing her hands against her cheeks as she looked down at the dark-brown coffee stain.

'It's not your fault. It was an accident.'

'Look, why don't I wait here in case the gentleman wakes up? You can go home and change. I'll call you if he wakes up.'

Rick hesitated. He really didn't want to sit there for the rest of the afternoon in coffee-stained clothes, but could he chance it? Albert might wake up. It would be Sod's law that as soon as he left, Albert would wake up and Rick wouldn't be there to question him. But Farzana would let him know as soon as Albert woke up, so where was the harm?

'Have you got time to wait?' Rick asked. 'I'll be about an hour and a half getting home, changed and then back here.'

'Not a problem.'

Rick smiled. 'You're an angel.'

'Not really. It's my fault you're wearing coffee at the moment.'

Rick chuckled. 'I won't be long. Thanks.'

He strode quickly out of the cardiac care unit and along the corridor, pulling out his mobile phone as he walked. He dialled Karen's number.

'Sarge? It's Rick. How are things going?'

'We've just spoken to William Grant, an old colleague of Oliver Fox's and an apparent friend of Albert Johnson. Any news? Has he woken up yet?'

'He's still playing the sleeping game,' Rick said. 'Actually, I was calling just to let you know that I'm popping home. DC Shah is here. She's going to keep an eye on Albert for me and let me know if he wakes up while I'm gone. I've poured a load of coffee over myself, and I need to get changed.'

'Ouch, that sounds painful.'

'It wasn't too bad. Just a little on the warm side,' Rick replied. 'But I look a state.'

After he ended the call, Rick made his way to the pay point for the car park.

'How much?' he exclaimed after he inserted the ticket and saw the amount on the screen. 'Daylight robbery,' he mumbled under his breath as he fed pound coins into the slot.

In less than a minute, he was in his car, driving towards the barrier at the exit. He really hoped Albert didn't wake up while he was gone. But with Rick's luck, he probably would.

Sophie stood by the communal scanner feeding in documents. Her task was to ensure everybody working on the case had scanned copies of all the reports.

The screen on the scanner flashed up with an error, and Sophie gritted her teeth. She wasn't in the mood for it to play up today.

Swearing under her breath, she punched in some numbers, trying to get the stupid machine to work. Finally, it hummed into action. She leaned heavily against the bench and pulled out her mobile phone. Why on earth had she spent so many years studying hard so she could be what amounted to an admin assistant?

She was even working through lunch. She pulled up the Facebook app on her iPhone, not feeling guilty in the least because technically she should be on a break. The first update she saw was a set of pictures posted by Angela. A glass of champagne in the first-class lounge, a photograph taken from an aeroplane window . . . Angela was off to Monaco.

Sophie gazed at the warm blue sky in the photograph and sighed. She could really do with a holiday.

When the machine had finally finished scanning, she gathered up the original documents and removed the USB stick from the side of the scanner. For some reason, Sophie's computer would never connect to the network, so she had to put the JPEG files on to a USB and then convert them to PDFs when she got back to her workstation. Another monotonous task to look forward to. She trudged out of the printer room, back towards the main office.

She was almost at her desk when DI Morgan called out from his office.

Arms still full of paperwork, she shuffled over to the door. 'Yes, sir?'

'How did the lab get on with the note left at Albert Johnson's house?'

'Oh, not good news, I'm afraid,' Sophie said with a sigh.

A note saying *It's time to pay for your crime* was something straight out of a crime novel. But if it had really been in a crime novel, then it would have been printed on a typewriter with a dodgy key or a malfunctioning ribbon or some other definitive clue that would lead them directly to the mastermind behind the crime. Unfortunately, real cases didn't work that way.

'The technician said it was printed on an inkjet machine – a very basic, common one, apparently,' Sophie said. 'They think it was probably a HP mono printer.'

'Fingerprints?'

Sophie shifted the paperwork in her arms and shook her head. 'Nope, only one set, which we are assuming are Albert Johnson's. We'll be able to rule them out if we can get him processed.'

'Any more news on the pathology report?'

Sophie shook her head again. 'Raj is still waiting for the bone expert to weigh in on the matter.'

'Okay, thanks, Sophie,' DI Morgan said and lowered his head, focusing on the papers on his desk, furiously making notes.

Sophie took a deep breath. She guessed that meant she was dismissed.

Karen had booked one of the fleet cars for the trip to DI Goodfield's home in Bassingham. It was about a twenty-five-minute drive from Nettleham, depending on traffic, and now she was alone with Sophie she had the perfect opportunity to find out what was bothering the young officer.

She'd spent a lot of time with Sophie and had never known her to be so quiet. Karen had taken her bubbly, go-getting personality for granted, and now she found she missed Sophie's usual enthusiasm.

'I've noticed you've been a bit quiet recently,' Karen said as she started the car, reaching over and turning down the volume on the radio. The local Lincolnshire station was playing Billy Ocean.

Sophie sat in the passenger seat, staring glumly out of the window as a soft rain began to splatter the windshield.

Karen had pulled out of the parking space and was heading out of the car park before Sophie answered.

'I've just been a bit tired,' Sophie said. 'It's nothing major.'

Karen frowned as she turned into Deepdale Lane. 'You can talk to me, you know. Especially about work. I know this job is difficult sometimes. Or if there's something bothering you at home, I can be a good sounding board.' She shot Sophie what she hoped was a reassuring smile.

Sophie turned away from the window and managed a smile in return. 'I don't know. It's silly, really.'

'What is?'

Sophie shook her head. 'I've been feeling a bit down about the job.'

'This case, you mean?'

Sophie shrugged. 'Not really. It's the job in general.' She tugged on her seatbelt and twisted in the passenger seat so she was facing Karen. 'Do you think I'm any good at this job?'

Karen blinked. Where had that come from? Was Sophie having a crisis of confidence?

'Of course I do. You've done some excellent work this year. Really good, solid police work, Sophie. You should be proud of yourself.'

Sophie pulled a face. 'I'm not sure. I'm starting to think I'm not cut out for this job.'

'Have you had your performance review with DI Morgan yet?'

She grimaced and plucked a stray thread from the sleeve of her jacket. 'Not yet. I can't imagine it'll be much good.'

'What makes you say that?'

'Well, he didn't want me to go and talk to Oliver Fox's family, did he? You were happy for me to go, but he pulled rank.'

'It was an important stage of the enquiry, and he wanted to be there to talk to the family members. It wasn't anything to do with how he views your ability to do the job, Sophie.'

'It felt like it was. It felt like he didn't trust me.'

Karen hesitated. She had a speech prepared that she'd used on junior officers in the past, which went on about having to earn trust and respect by putting in the hours and covering all the basics, but she had a feeling Sophie wouldn't appreciate that particular lecture at the moment. What she needed was an encouraging pep talk.

'I think you're reading too much into it, Sophie. It's my fault. I should have cleared it with DI Morgan before saying you could come along to visit the Fox family. But you need a thicker skin. You can't take things like this personally.'

Sophie shot her a glance, and Karen detected the hint of a pout.

'There's no need to mope. I think you're going to go far in this job, Sophie, but I can't help feeling you want everything to happen yesterday. It doesn't work like that. You need to start small and build your career step by step. It doesn't happen overnight.'

Sophie sighed. 'I know you're right, but sometimes I feel like I'm just standing still and not getting anywhere.'

Karen smiled at the younger woman's impatience. It was good to see her showing enthusiasm for her career again. Karen preferred to see this side of Sophie than her earlier sullenness. She was only in her mid-twenties and had a long career ahead of her.

Karen flicked the switch for the windscreen wipers as the rain increased and the splashback from other cars on the road made it hard to see through the glass.

'You've got a good, solid foundation, and now you need to build on it with experience.'

'Maybe I should do a few more training courses,' Sophie said.

'You could. But you need more on-the-job experience. Nothing can compete with that.'

'I suppose you're right, but it just feels like the experience is slow in coming. Over the last two days, I've spent all my time scanning, photocopying and searching for a suitcase manufacturer. It's not really what I expected when I dreamed of being a police officer.'

Karen grinned. 'It could be worse.'

'It could?'

'Yes, you could have Rick's job. He's been stuck at the hospital for the past two days, and I don't think he's finding Albert Johnson's company particularly stimulating.'

Sophie managed to raise a smile, but Karen sensed she still hadn't got through to the young officer yet. She tried a new approach.

'You think you're having a bad week? You should try living my life for a while. My sister is trying to set me up on a blind date.'

Sophie perked up. 'Really? Are you going to go?'

Karen wrinkled her nose. 'I'm not sure yet. It's not really my cup of tea.'

'You should do it. It could be fun, and besides, it's only a date, nothing serious. If it's terrible, you can leave.'

'Maybe.'

'Yes,' Sophie said, brightening further as she warmed to her theme. 'If you're having an awful time, send me a quick text and I'll call you. You can pretend it's a major emergency and you have to leave straightaway.'

'I may just take you up on that.'

By the time they reached Bassingham, Sophie seemed almost back to her normal, jovial self.

Karen had explained the direction she wanted to take with the interview, but a lot of it would have to be determined when they got there. There was a limit to how much could be planned in advance. Some interviews required officers to think on their feet. In this case, they weren't sure how reliable DI Goodfield would be. If Robert Fox had been correct about his drinking habit, his memory could be very bad. And Karen was concerned he would try to hide things from them if he suspected they were evaluating his old case. If his drinking had resulted in shoddy police work, he would probably do his best to cover it up.

'Is this the house?' Karen asked, sounding surprised.

'That's what the satnav says, and look, it says Riverdean – that's the address I've got here,' Sophie said, checking her phone.

Riverdean was large. It was constructed from sandy stone, and although Karen didn't know much about architecture, even she could see the house had been there for a very long time. It fitted perfectly into its surroundings. The roof had a strong curve, and the walls seemed to rise up from the earth as though they had grown there rather than been built. There was a long, sloping driveway leading up to the house. As they got closer, Karen realised the house was even bigger than she'd first thought. It was absolutely massive.

She'd imagined DI Goodfield would be living in a rundown little cottage – she certainly hadn't been expecting something like this.

'Looks like he's got a few bob,' Sophie commented as she unfastened her seatbelt.

Outside the front of the house were various wooden planters containing pansies and cyclamens, which gave the garden a cheerful splash of colour. A large oak tree, surrounded by daffodils, towered over the left side of the house near the detached double garage, and Karen could make out the long, sweeping branches of a weeping willow behind the garage.

Pausing after she shut the car door, she drank it all in. She could hear the sound of water and guessed there was a brook or stream behind the house.

'Wow,' Sophie said, looking around. 'This is exactly the type of house I think of when I think about living in the country. It's big, but it's still got a kind of cottage feel, hasn't it?'

Karen nodded. It was peaceful – tranquil, even.

The knotted branches of a lilac caught her attention. It would be flowering before long, and would look beautiful in a month or two. Karen pressed the key fob to lock the car, and then turned when she heard footsteps on the gravel.

A man dressed in a cream knit jumper, faded jeans and a pair of green Wellington boots trudged towards them. He had a ruddy face, greying hair and a healthy, outdoorsy look to him.

'DS Hart?' he asked, approaching Karen with his hand outstretched.

'Yes, and this is my colleague, DC Sophie Jones.'

His large hand enclosed Karen's, and his eyes crinkled as he smiled. 'Retired Detective Inspector Goodfield. You can call me Derek. Come with me. We'll walk around and go in the back door.'

Karen and Sophie followed DI Goodfield along a paved garden path that ran beside the house. The garden was beautiful, and was clearly where he spent a lot of time now that he was retired.

He gathered some of the garden tools he'd clearly just abandoned, and glanced up. 'I'd hoped I'd get more done before the next shower, but I think I'd better put my tools away for the day.'

The sky was a bruised grey, threatening more rain. They waited patiently for him to lock up the shed. Karen noticed his hands shook as he reached for the spade, fork and trowel, but she hadn't smelled alcohol on his breath.

He brushed his hands together and smiled at them both. 'Right, let's get inside and have a cup of tea.'

He marched ahead and led them through the bi-folding doors into a large conservatory, which looked like it had been added on to the kitchen recently. As they entered the house, they were immediately struck by the warmth and the smell of baking. DI Goodfield paused inside the door, struggling to take off his boots, and then finally walked into the kitchen and stopped by the sink to wash his hands.

There was a large sponge cake cooling on a rack by the cream Aga. It looked delicious.

'I'm not sure how much more I can tell you about the case,' he said, scrubbing his hands. 'I kept notes, of course. But I left them all at the station. We're not supposed to keep stuff at home, and to be honest, I didn't want any reminders.'

'We've been going through them,' Karen said. 'They've been very helpful. We wanted to ask you about your feelings on the case, and what you thought of Oliver Fox. We want your opinion, the sort of thing that doesn't get filed in a report. As the SIO, you had an insight nobody else did.'

DI Goodfield's face hardened, and he wiped his hands on a tea towel. 'Well, first let me tell you that the missing persons case wasn't the first dealing I had with Oliver Fox.'

CHAPTER EIGHTEEN

After DI Goodfield finished washing his hands, he led them out of the kitchen and into the hallway. A tall woman was shrugging on her coat beside the front door.

She looked up, and DI Goodfield introduced her as his wife, Sandra.

She smiled at them. 'Nice to meet you. Sorry I have to rush off. I'm manning the cake stall at the village hall today.' She turned to her husband. 'I've left you a Victoria sponge.' She raised a finger and looked sternly at him. 'Make sure you only have one slice.'

DI Goodfield grinned and kissed his wife on the cheek. 'See you later, dear.'

Karen noticed he didn't agree to the one-slice limit. Crafty. She couldn't blame him. The cake smelled amazing.

After Sandra left, he led them into the living room, which was large but comfortably furnished. It had a low ceiling with beams, and the large fireplace was the centrepiece of the room. The mantelpiece was covered with photographs. Karen took a closer look, recognising DI Goodfield and Sandra in some of them and guessing the rest were of their children or grandchildren.

'The cake smells so good,' Sophie said. 'I wish I lived with someone who could bake like that.'

DI Goodfield smiled. 'Is that a hint? Then I'd better head to the kitchen and cut you a piece.'

Sophie's cheeks flushed. 'Sorry, I didn't mean I expected a slice.'

'You'd be crazy if you turned down the opportunity to sample some of Sandra's baking. I fell on my feet when I married her. I'll go and make a pot of tea. Make yourselves comfortable.'

When DI Goodfield left them alone in the room, Karen sunk into the plump sofa cushions beside Sophie.

'Sorry, Sarge,' Sophie whispered. 'I was just commenting on the smell. I know we're not here to have afternoon tea.'

Karen shook her head. 'Don't worry about it. It smells absolutely delicious.'

While DI Goodfield was out of the room, Karen took the time to study her surroundings and to try to work out what sort of man he really was. Detective Superintendent Robert Fox had told them the man was a drunkard and had been terrible at his job, but Derek Goodfield seemed to live in domestic bliss, spending his time gardening while his wife baked cakes. The house was attractively decorated and had to be worth a lot of money, so the couple had obviously done well for themselves. She guessed Sandra was retired now, too, and wondered what she'd done for a living while she was working. Perhaps she was the one who'd earned the money to pay for this huge house.

When DI Goodfield came back into the room, proudly carrying three slices of cake on a tray, along with teacups and saucers, Karen stood up. 'Can I help you with that?'

He put the tray down on the coffee table. 'Nope, I'll just pop back into the kitchen and grab the teapot. You two tuck into that cake. I guarantee it's the best you've ever tasted.'

Karen and Sophie helped themselves. He was right. The crumbly, buttery sponge melted in Karen's mouth, and she imagined the calories going straight to her hips. But it was worth it.

Sophie closed her eyes after the first bite. 'Oh, wow. I think I could eat the whole cake.'

DI Goodfield returned, carrying the teapot in one hand and a little jug of milk in the other.

He set out the cups and poured the tea. 'Like I said, I fell on my feet when I met Sandra. Her family had money, too. That's how we could afford this place. It certainly wasn't from my salary!' He smiled and passed Karen her tea. 'I got stuck at DI. You probably think that's due to the drink, don't you?'

He raised an eyebrow and looked at Sophie.

She flushed again and began to stammer. 'Well, no . . . I mean . . .'

'Don't be embarrassed. I bet DCI Fox made you aware of my drinking problem. In fact, I'm pretty sure he made sure you had that information sharpish, didn't he?'

Karen hesitated. There was obviously some history between the two men. She didn't know the full story, so she opted for a non-committal remark. 'He's retired now, but he reached the rank of detective superintendent.'

DI Goodfield made a tutting sound and shook his head, passing a cup of tea to Sophie. 'I shouldn't be surprised. He was always good at climbing the greasy pole, that one.'

Neither Karen nor Sophie replied.

'I see you're not going to partake in gossip,' DCI Goodfield said, chuckling. He carried his own cup of tea to a chair near the fireplace, moving a few cushions before sitting down. 'It's sensible of you, but the truth is, Oliver Fox was a horrible man, and I won't pretend I wasn't happy when he disappeared off the face of the earth. I didn't think much of his brother, either.'

Karen, who had been about to take a sip of her tea, froze and looked steadily at DI Goodfield.

Sophie began to cough and splutter. 'Sorry, a bit of cake went down the wrong way,' she said, before taking a large gulp of her tea.

'That's a very interesting comment, DI Goodfield,' Karen said. 'Why do you say that? What made you think badly of Oliver Fox?'

He took a deep breath. 'I'm sure his brother would prefer I didn't mention it.'

'I'm sure you're right, but you're going to tell us anyway, aren't you?'

A broad grin spread across DI Goodfield's face. 'Yes, I think if you're looking into his disappearance, you need to know the whole story. There is a tendency to put people up on a pedestal when they've been gone for a while. But I never went in for that. I don't care what connections people have, how much money they earn, that's not important to me. At the end of the day, we're all people struggling to get by. Some of us are bad, and some of us are good, but most of us lie somewhere in between. Oliver Fox was one of the bad ones.'

'What did he do?' Sophie asked, unable to bear the suspense.

Karen had the measure of DI Goodfield now. He liked to tell a story. And he liked to do it in in his own time. But Sophie was impatient.

Karen knew if they gave him the chance to explain in his own way, rather than getting him to answer a set of questions, they'd get a lot more from him. Nuances and details that might otherwise be left out could tell them a great deal.

'Tell us in your own words everything you can remember, DI Goodfield,' Karen said. 'We need to know as much about Oliver Fox as possible.'

The smile slid from DI Goodfield's face as he reached for his cup of tea, and Karen noticed his hands shaking. She wondered whether it was due to nerves or a craving for alcohol.

'Before all this happened, I worked on a bad case. We all have them. The case that works its way inside you. The one you really want to solve but can't. It centred around a boy called Mark Bell. His mother came to me, to report one of Mark's teachers. I spoke to the boy about it. He was embarrassed but told me his maths teacher held an after-school football club. After the boys had finished training, he would do things in the changing room that made them feel uncomfortable. On one occasion, Mark said he'd been made to strip naked and do push-ups when he was alone with the teacher. I was sure there was more to it, but Mark was scared and embarrassed. He wanted to forget all about it, and who could blame him? He was angry with his mother for coming forward in the first place. I did what I could to make Mark aware he wasn't the one at fault, but I'm not sure I did enough.'

He paused to take another sip of tea. 'I was angry enough to take it further. In those days, things were different. You certainly needed a lot of evidence before you brought charges, and Mark swore blind that he'd been made to feel uncomfortable but nothing else had happened. I wanted to investigate and talk to the other children who attended the football club. I spoke to my boss about it, but he ordered me to drop it. I've never been happy following orders without an explanation, so I confronted him. I said unless this teacher was investigated, I was going to go over his head.'

He looked down at the cup in his hands and shook his head. 'I was naive. It turned out his boss was best buddies with DCI Fox, so of course it was in their interest to cover it up.'

He looked up to see both Karen and Sophie watching him intently. 'I spoke to DCI Fox. I confronted him and told him exactly what I thought of his brother. He told me I was imagining things, making it all up, and if I didn't drop it, he was going to get me fired.'

'Did you drop it?' Sophie asked.

DI Goodfield shook his head. 'No. I went to see Oliver Fox. I waited until after football training on a Thursday and confronted him.'

'He admitted to abusing Mark Bell?' Karen asked.

'Of course not, but I know guilt when I see it. I warned him off. Told him I'd be on his case permanently from that point on and told him to watch his back. I couldn't do anything officially, so I threatened him. I'm not proud of that, but I felt powerless to do anything else. I kept in touch with Mark's mum and tried to help out, but I didn't do enough. Mark's dad had walked out on them a couple of years before, so the boy was vulnerable. I told her and Mark to come to me if anything else happened to make the boy feel uncomfortable.'

DI Goodfield turned to look at the rain streaking down the window. 'Nothing happened, and for a while I thought my little visit had worked. I'd assumed I'd scared some sense into him. I'd let him know in no uncertain terms that I would be watching him like a hawk.'

He swallowed hard and turned away from the window to look down at his lap. 'But then, I got a phone call from Mark's mother. I'll always remember it. It was the day of that big storm, do you remember? October fifteenth, 1987. She was calling to tell me that Mark had hung himself in the garage after school. And when the hurricane descended, it felt like the heavens were angry at what had happened to the boy. I'll be the first to admit the drink got the better of me after that, but I never drank when I was on duty.'

The room was quiet. The brass clock on the mantelpiece ticked as the seconds passed. Even Sophie stayed silent.

After a moment, Karen asked, 'What did Mark's mother say? Did she blame the incident with Oliver Fox for her son's suicide?'

This could certainly be a new lead. A devastated mother, blaming the teacher for her son's death. It was a powerful motive for murder. Karen thought it unlikely the woman would have been able to carry

Oliver Fox's body in a suitcase and hide it in Albert Johnson's loft, but perhaps she'd had help.

'She was devastated. I went to the funeral and tried to talk to her a couple of times afterwards, but she didn't want to discuss it. She had nothing left to keep her in the area after Mark died. She sold the house and moved to Nottingham, I think.' He looked up at Karen, one fist clenched in his lap. 'The worst part was, she thanked me for trying to help him. I did nothing. I let the boy down.'

'It sounds like you were fighting a losing battle,' Karen said. 'But you tried.'

'I didn't try hard enough though, did I?' Without waiting for an answer, he continued. 'When Oliver Fox disappeared the following year, I wanted that case. I cajoled, wheedled and basically made myself a thorn in my DCI's side until he agreed to make me the lead investigating officer on the case.'

'But you never got close to finding out what happened to Oliver Fox?'

DI Goodfield shook his head. Karen watched his expression carefully, trying to read him. Was he telling the truth? Was this a cover-up? She had to wonder what he would have done if he'd discovered Mark's mother or perhaps the parent of another abused child had killed Oliver Fox. Would he have protected them? Their meeting today had shown Karen he had a strong sense of duty and justice, but she didn't know how far he'd go. He'd certainly taken the death of Mark Bell personally.

She waited to see if he would offer more information and explain why he thought his search for Oliver Fox had been unsuccessful. But he stayed silent, staring at the floor.

'What do you think happened to Oliver Fox? What's your gut feeling?' Karen asked.

'I'd like to think he was overcome with remorse and topped himself, but that seems too convenient for me.'

'What about an angry parent? Or even an ex-student?'

DI Goodfield shrugged and leaned across to pick up his cup of tea again. 'I considered it. To be perfectly honest, I think he got what he deserved.'

CHAPTER NINETEEN

Karen and Sophie walked back to the car in silence. Once they were close to the vehicle, Sophie swore and bent down. 'Just a sec, Sarge. I've got a stone in my shoe.'

While Sophie leaned on the car and dumped the offending stone back on to the gravel driveway, Karen pulled out her mobile and typed a text to her sister.

All right. You win. I'll go on the date.

It was just one evening and it would get her sister off her back for a while. She was just fine on her own, but hearing DI Goodfield talk affectionately about his wife had made Karen consider her own future. Who would be there for her when she retired? Her thumb hesitated above the screen.

Sophie straightened up. 'All ready now, Sarge.'

Karen hit send and put the phone back in her pocket.

'What did you make of DI Goodfield?' Karen asked as she executed a three-point turn on the driveway.

'He certainly provided some *unexpected* information,' Sophie said. 'He was honest with us. I think the incident with Mark Bell and his mother has really eaten away at him over the years.'

Karen nodded as she drove slowly over the gravel, wincing as some of the stones were kicked up by the wheels and hit the bodywork.

'What did you think of him, Sarge?'

Karen was still trying to work that out. She'd come here this afternoon expecting DI Goodfield to have forgotten the decades-old case, and had imagined they'd be meeting an officer who hadn't taken his job as seriously as he should. That's what they'd been led to believe by Detective Superintendent Robert Fox. But after meeting him, Karen felt DI Goodfield had been very dedicated to his job. The question was, how far had that dedication taken him?

Certain cases got to you more than others, but when it came down to it, a police officer's job was to investigate the bad guys. It wasn't their place to act as judge, jury and executioner. Had DI Goodfield taken the case too far? Had he decided to take justice into his own hands?

She glanced at Sophie. The young officer didn't seem at all concerned about their chat with the ex-policeman. In fact, she seemed invigorated by the meeting. For the first time that week, Sophie was interested and involved in the case.

'You do realise our conversation with DI Goodfield has opened a whole can of worms?' Karen said as she turned right into Croft Lane.

'What do you mean? He's given us a new angle.'

'He's done more than that, Sophie. If Oliver Fox was abusing boys at Greenhill Secondary School, we have a lot of suspects to investigate. His killer could be any one of the students, or a furious parent.'

Sophie mulled that over. 'True. If he was targeting Mark Bell, then the chances are he was doing it to other boys, too.'

'It's likely, don't you think?'

Sophie was silent for a moment. 'What are we going to do? Will we have to track down everybody who attended the school thirty years ago? That's going to be practically impossible. And who's to say they're going to want to talk to us after all this time. If it was a student who killed him, they're not going to admit they were abused, because that would just point the finger at them.'

Karen let Sophie talk through the problem, trying to come at it from different angles. This was the type of experience books were unable to teach.

Karen didn't doubt Sophie felt overwhelmed, because she certainly did. She felt sick. A heaviness sat at the bottom of her stomach, and it had done since DI Goodfield had told them of his experience dealing with Oliver Fox.

'Of course, we need to speak to Albert Johnson now more than ever,' Sophie said. She turned to Karen. 'What if Albert Johnson caught him with one of the children and decided to deal out his own punishment? Maybe he found him with a young boy and lost his temper?'

Karen nodded slowly. 'It's possible. But a lot of people seem to have motives for wanting Oliver Fox dead.'

The next stage in this case was going to take a lot of work. And it wouldn't be the exciting police work Sophie longed for. For the next few hours, and possibly days, they wouldn't be visiting suspects and drilling the truth out of them with clever questions. Instead, most of their time would be spent online, tracking down people who had attended the school decades ago and looking for families who had left the area.

This suddenly seemed to dawn on Sophie. 'I have a feeling I'm going to be doing a lot more paperwork, aren't I?'

'I'm afraid so,' Karen said. 'The scope of this investigation just got a whole lot bigger.'

At home in Skellingthorpe, Elizabeth Fox picked up the telephone. Her hand was shaking as she dialled her eldest son's mobile number.

'Stephen?' she asked breathlessly when he picked up.

'Mum, what is it?'

'I need you to come home straightaway.'

'I'm at work. We've just got a new contract to handle the sale of an office building. I'm in the middle of a meeting. They're important clients. I can't just leave.'

'Please, Stephen.'

She heard him moving at the other end of the phone. Probably leaving the meeting room to get some privacy. 'What is it? What's wrong?'

Elizabeth gripped the cordless handset and walked along the hall towards the kitchen. Her eyes filled with tears as she stood and stared out of the back door.

'You need to come home, Stephen. I can't cope.'

'Now? What if I come by after work?'

'No, you don't understand. You need to come now. It's your brother . . .'

There was a heavy silence, then Stephen said, 'What's he done?'

'Nothing yet.'

Stephen sighed. 'All right. I'll get away as soon as I can. I just need to wrap things up here.'

Elizabeth watched her youngest son pacing back and forth on the lawn, talking to thin air. She didn't like to admit it to anyone, not even herself, but he frightened her.

'He turned up twenty minutes ago. I couldn't calm him down. He's in the garden. You know he doesn't listen to anybody but you. Please, come now.'

Martin terrified her. The tablets usually kept him on an even keel, but he hadn't been taking them. He'd lied about it when she'd asked him. He told her he'd taken his usual dose that morning, but from his wild expression, she'd known it wasn't true.

He had that sinister look in his eyes again. The look that struck the fear of God into her.

Martin made a loop in the garden, his movements lumbering and slow, until suddenly he whipped around and stared straight at his mother. She wanted to look away, but his gaze locked with hers and she felt an icy trickle of sweat making its way down her spine.

A smile stretched across his face, but it wasn't a normal smile. It wasn't a happy smile. She hated herself for thinking it of her own son, but the thought came anyway.

It was an evil smile.

Rick yanked on the handbrake, turned off the engine, jumped out of the car and strode to his front door. The spilled coffee was now cold, and the wet shirt clung to his skin. He checked his watch to see how he was doing for time. He didn't want to keep Farzana waiting for too long. She was already giving up her lunch break, and he didn't want to get her in trouble for being late back to her shift as well.

He opened the door and prepared to call out as he usually did when he got home, but something made him stop. There were two coats Rick didn't recognise hanging on the rack by the front door. Then he heard voices.

He kicked off his shoes, a habit his mother had instilled in him when he was young. The carpet had seen better days, but he always took his shoes off when he came inside.

He walked down the hallway slowly, feeling awkward. Did Priya have friends visiting? He wasn't sure how he felt about that. She was supposed to be working, concentrating on looking after his mother. That's what she was being paid for.

He wondered whether he was going to find out that she kept his mother locked in her room all day while she used the house as her own to entertain her friends.

But Priya wasn't like that, was she? She seemed a genuinely kind person. Rick didn't like to think he was having the wool pulled over his eyes.

The voices were coming from the living room. Rick paused by the door, feeling oddly out of place in his own home.

It was ridiculous.

When he stepped into the living room, he stopped and looked at the visitors with surprise. They weren't Priya's friends, after all. They were old friends of his mother's.

Mrs Mackintosh, who used to be the office manager where his mother had worked, and Jenny Limer, whom his mother had known since her schooldays. He hadn't seen them in donkey's years, and neither had his mother. Aware he looked gormless, but unable to stop himself, Rick just stood there gawping at them.

His mother's friends sat side by side on the sofa. His mother was in her wheelchair, and Priya was kneeling in front of the coffee table pouring tea.

They'd all turned to look up at him, smiling and saying hello, and were waiting for him to say something in return.

But he was finding it hard to process the situation. Early on, after his mother's diagnosis, she'd continued to see her friends and even stayed at work for a time, but as she got worse, she'd taken Rick to one side and made him promise something.

'Whatever happens, Ricky, I don't want people to see me like this. Not people I've known all my life. It's bad enough you and your sister have to see me changing into someone I'm not. I want to keep my problems private.'

His mother was a very proud woman. The diagnosis had terrified her, but the thing she hated more than anything was changing and losing her identity. She hadn't wanted to tell people, not straightaway, and Rick had gone along with it. It was his mother's condition to deal with, after all.

After she started going downhill, there were still times when she was perfectly lucid, but that almost made it worse because she was aware of what was happening to her. She knew she was losing that essential sense of self and she hated it. She didn't want anyone else to see her like that, and so it had been her choice to cut people off.

She didn't make a big song and dance about it. She just stopped returning telephone calls. She didn't meet her friends for lunch and stopped going to her local book club. Slowly but surely, she cut herself off, but now two of the women she had deliberately stayed away from were sitting in the living room.

His mother didn't seem bothered in the least, but Rick wasn't sure if she even remembered them.

'Rick? Is everything okay?' Priya was looking up at him with a frown on her face.

He gave her a tight smile. 'I had to come home to change my shirt.'

'Was that tea or coffee?' Mrs Mackintosh asked from her perch on the sofa.

'Err . . . um, coffee,' Rick said.

He knew he sounded distracted but he was looking at his mother, watching for any signs of discomfort or distress, but right now she seemed to be perfectly happy. For some reason, that niggled at Rick.

He continued to watch his mother as the two women on the sofa offered up laundry tips and techniques to get the stain out of his previously pristine white shirt.

'Do you have time for a cup of tea?' Priya asked.

Rick shook his head. 'No, sorry, I'd better go and get changed.'

He backed out of the room and tried to swallow the bitter taste in his mouth. He took the stairs two at a time and attempted to push away the anger that was encroaching on him. It wasn't Priya's fault. She didn't know that his mum was proud and didn't want her old friends to see her this way. He felt caught between two people. The woman his mum used to be and the woman she was now.

His mother was downstairs, now perfectly happy in the presence of her visitors, but the woman she used to be would be horrified that they'd seen her while she was ill. It wasn't that Rick believed she should be cut off from her friends – after all, they had been good friends to his mum for years – but he felt like he was going against his mother's wishes, and the very thought made him sick.

He threw his dirty shirt in the laundry basket and selected another from his wardrobe. Once he'd buttoned it and replaced his tie, he made his way reluctantly downstairs.

What should he do? What would his mother want him to do? Asking them to leave would be very rude indeed.

He stuck his head back into the living room to say goodbye, but before he could leave, Mrs Mackintosh heaved herself up from the sofa, walked towards him and grasped his hand. She looked at him, staring into his eyes. 'I had no idea she was this bad, Rick. I'm so sorry.'

He could see the pity in her eyes, and though he knew Mrs Mackintosh's heart was in the right place, he was angry.

His mother hadn't wanted this. It was so unfair. Not only did she have to suffer from this awful disease, but she couldn't even keep her suffering private.

People would talk.

They wouldn't say anything nasty, of course. No, they would be compassionate and concerned.

'Did you hear about Mrs Cooper?' they would say. 'Oh, it's awful. The poor woman! I don't know what I'd do if it happened to me.'

Rick didn't want his mother diminished to nothing more than a sad story a group of women talked about over lunch, but there was nothing he could do about it.

He looked again at his mother, who was sipping her tea, looking perfectly content.

He removed his hand from Mrs Mackintosh's grip, said thank you and then walked towards his mother. He knelt down by her chair, kissed her on the cheek and whispered, 'Is everything all right, Mum?'

She gave him a smile. 'Everything is smashing, love.'

'I've got to get back to work now.'

'All right, I'll see you later. Don't be late. We've got steak for tea.'

He kissed her once more on the cheek and stood up. He nodded at Priya and the two visitors. 'Lovely to see you. Sorry I have to rush off. I need to get back to work.'

'If there's anything you need, Rick,' Mrs Mackintosh said, grabbing on to his sleeve as he passed, 'you only have to ask.'

'I appreciate that. But we're doing okay, thanks.'

He meant it. He did appreciate the offer of help. There had to be something wrong with him for resenting them coming to visit his mum. They were being kind, and they weren't there to gawp at someone less fortunate than themselves.

But still, he couldn't shake the sense he was betraying his mother.

He tried to swallow the lump in his throat but failed. Unable to talk, he raised a hand to wave goodbye and quickly left the house.

CHAPTER TWENTY

Rick made it back to the hospital by three o'clock. He dashed along the corridor towards the cardiac care unit and was relieved to see DC Farzana Shah was exactly where he'd left her.

'He didn't wake up?' Rick asked as he walked towards her.

She put down the magazine she'd been flicking through and picked up her handbag before standing up. 'I'm afraid not. I looked in on him every five minutes or so, but he hasn't stirred.'

'Thanks for covering for me. I appreciate it.'

'It's the least I could do after throwing coffee all over you. I am sorry about that.' She pulled a face. 'I was trying to be helpful, not boil you alive.'

'It's the thought that counts,' Rick said with a smile, but he was distracted. He couldn't stop thinking about the pitying look he'd seen in Mrs Mackintosh's eyes.

After DC Shah left, Rick had a quick word with the nurse on duty and then entered Albert Johnson's hospital room.

He sat in the visitor's chair beside the bed, taking care to avoid the drips and wires that connected Albert to all the machines.

'I'm back,' he said to Albert. 'I hope you didn't miss me too much. I had to go home and change after a mishap with some coffee.'

Rick saw the old man's eyes flutter, and he was more convinced than ever that Albert was faking sleep.

'You know, I'm going to stay here until you wake up. I don't mind, I'm getting paid for it. But surely there's a limit to how long you can keep your eyes shut.'

Nothing.

Rick pushed on. 'It's only a few questions, nothing to worry about.'

Still nothing.

'I'm not going anywhere, so maybe you should just get the questions over and done with.'

Maybe he should keep nattering on until Albert Johnson couldn't bear it anymore and told him to shut up.

It was worth a try. Waiting patiently didn't seem to be getting him anywhere.

So Rick made himself comfortable and proceeded to tell Albert all about his trip home. He told him all about his mother's early-onset dementia and how the disease had changed her.

'I'd always thought it was a mental thing,' Rick said. 'I'm surprised at how physical the disease is as well. She's gone from a healthy woman who used to walk two miles to work every day, to someone who needs to use a wheelchair even for short distances. Luckily we had a room downstairs that we could use for a bedroom, because there's no way she could manage the stairs these days.' He paused and looked at Albert's face.

The old man had a little bit of colour back in his cheeks. He didn't look quite as bad as when Rick had first seen him, but he still had a greyish tinge.

'I did think about getting a stairlift installed so she could get upstairs, but I suppose there's not really any point. The bathroom is downstairs and so is the kitchen and her bedroom, and that's all she needs, really. Maybe you should think of getting a stairlift installed, Mr Johnson.'

Rick paused when he noticed a tiny tremor in Albert's little finger, but then the old man stilled, and Rick began to think he must have imagined it.

'You'll be looking for a new place when you get out of here,' Rick said. 'It's not safe for you to be back in your house with those steep stairs. I didn't see them, but the officers I spoke to said they were ever so steep. It's no surprise you fell. I suppose it was an accident waiting to happen.'

This time there was a definite movement. Albert's fists clenched, gripping the sheet, and he opened his eyes and raised himself up on his elbows. 'I'm not a doddering old man,' he growled in a hoarse voice. 'I'm quite capable of looking after myself. I didn't fall, I was pushed.'

Startled, Rick leaned forward in his chair. 'Who pushed you? Who sent you that threatening note?'

Albert narrowed his eyes. 'How do I know you're really a . . . policeman?'

His voice was rough and gravelly, but he was talking. That was the main thing. Now, maybe they'd finally get to the bottom of this.

'I've got my warrant card here. Look.' Rick held out his ID.

Albert peered at it suspiciously. His eyebrows came together, wrinkling his pale, papery skin.

'I don't know who sent the note.' He paused to draw in a raspy breath. 'And I don't know who pushed me.'

'You must have some idea. If you don't tell me, how can we protect you? Talk to me, and we can make sure whoever pushed you doesn't come back to finish the job.'

Albert hesitated.

Rick was desperate to ask him about the body in the suitcase but wanted to get him on side first.

Albert licked his thin, cracked lips. 'First, you have to promise me no one is allowed in my house without my say-so.' He clutched at his stomach and grimaced. 'Can I have some . . . water?'

Rick stood, reached for the pitcher of water and poured some in a paper cup before passing it to Albert.

The old man's hand trembled and he dropped the cup. The water soaked the sheets, and the cup tumbled to the floor.

Rick bent down to pick it up, then saw Albert was struggling for air. His face began to turn purple as he desperately tried to suck in a breath.

No. This could not be happening. Not now. He hadn't even asked him about the body yet.

The machine started beeping.

Rick rushed to the door to call for help, but a nurse was already heading towards him.

He turned back to Albert. 'Did you kill Oliver Fox? Did you see who pushed you, Mr Johnson?'

But Albert had fallen back against his pillows. Rick watched his chest, praying it would rise and fall with a breath, but there was no movement. Albert lay motionless.

He couldn't believe this was happening. Not now, when he'd been so close to getting answers.

He moved back and watched the doctors and nurses desperately work on Albert before a nurse ushered him out of the room.

Rick stood outside as the team tried to resuscitate the old man.

'Is he going to be all right?' Rick asked when a nurse he recognised from the day before left Albert's room. It was a silly question. He could tell from the look on her face that Albert certainly wasn't all right.

She shook her head. 'I'm afraid not. He had another heart attack.'

'He's dead?'

The nurse lowered her head. 'Yes,' she said quietly. 'I'm sorry you didn't get a chance to ask your questions.'

Rick ran a hand through his hair. Was it his fault? He'd known that Albert Johnson was very ill. The man had already had one heart attack. Rick shouldn't have been pestering him like that.

'I was in there,' Rick said. 'I was talking to him. I asked him some questions, which seemed to upset him . . . Do you think it was my fault?'

The nurse shook her head. 'No, don't think like that. He'd already had one major heart attack, so the chances of him having a follow-up were very high. At his age, it was too much for his body to recover from.' She smiled at Rick. 'You mustn't blame yourself. You were just doing your job.'

Rick thanked her, but he couldn't help feeling as though he'd seriously messed up.

How horrible that there were none of Albert's family or friends around him when he died; just Rick demanding answers. Albert may have had a skeleton stashed away in a suitcase in his house, but Rick still felt it was sad there was no one there for him at the end.

He closed his eyes and leaned back against the wall, sighing heavily. What now? He'd blown their only chance of getting answers.

Now, it was looking more and more likely they'd never find the reason the skeleton had been hidden in that house. Albert's secrets had died with him.

Karen was back at the station when she got the phone call from Rick.

'Sarge, I'm afraid we're not going to get anything from Albert Johnson now,' Rick said. 'He passed away a few minutes ago.'

Karen slumped in her chair. After finding out a huge number of people could have a motive for killing Oliver Fox, Karen had been hoping to get some answers from Albert Johnson, but now they would never get any help from their number-one suspect.

'This investigation is getting more complicated by the minute,' Karen said. 'Are you okay?'

'Yes. I was talking to him at the end, just nattering on about stuff, and he woke up. He said he didn't fall downstairs. He told me he was pushed, and when I asked him who pushed him . . . well, that's when the machine started going crazy, and all hell broke loose.'

'So he didn't give you a name?'

'No, nothing. He just said he was pushed, and that was it really.'

'He woke up, told you that and then had a heart attack?'

'That about sums it up, yes.'

Karen's phone began to vibrate on the desk, but she ignored it. 'We need our luck to turn around on this case. We went to speak to DI Goodfield, the SIO on the original investigation. He told me about a boy who accused Oliver Fox of abuse back in the late eighties. One theory we're considering is maybe Albert Johnson stumbled across Oliver Fox with a student and decided to administer his own justice.'

'I'm not sure how we'll find out what happened now, boss,' Rick said. 'Any clues Albert could have given us have died with him.'

Karen leaned forward and rested her hand on her forehead. She'd really been holding out hope that Albert Johnson would cooperate when he woke up.

'I'm heading back to the station now, Sarge.'

'All right, I'll see you soon.'

She hung up and then picked up her mobile as it beeped and scrolled through the multiple messages from her sister. Mostly a set of 'yippee!' and celebration GIFs. Karen shook her head and put her phone back on the desk. She had to be crazy to consider going out on a date in the middle of all this.

Sophie walked past Karen's desk on the way to the photocopier. 'Was that about your date?' she asked, nodding at Karen's mobile.

'Yes, it was a message from my sister.'

Sophie's eyes lit up. 'You've decided to go, then?'

'Yes. I must be mad. But enough about my social life. Rick just called. We've had a serious setback. Albert Johnson died a few minutes ago.'

'Oh, crap.'

'My sentiments exactly.'

CHAPTER TWENTY-ONE

'The post-mortem report is back, Sarge,' Sophie said, looking over the top of her computer monitor.

Karen checked her email and saw Raj had sent the post-mortem and copied in the whole team. She double-clicked on the attachment to open the report, and then quickly scanned the contents. There were no big surprises. The cause of death was likely to be the blow to the left side of Oliver Fox's skull.

Sophie walked across to Karen's desk. 'The dental records have confirmed the victim was Oliver Fox.'

'The post-mortem is the only thing that's given us the expected result,' Karen said. 'Everything else about this case is confusing. Just when I think I know where the investigation is heading, we find more information that turns everything upside down.'

Karen read the report in more detail, with Sophie looking over her shoulder.

Although the post-mortem identified the most likely cause of death was a blow to the head, extra notes had been added, which stated the blow to the head could have been caused by a blunt instrument or a fall. If they couldn't rule out a fall, it was still possible Oliver Fox's death had been an accident. Although the fact his body had been hidden for thirty years made Karen think that was unlikely.

'I guess Raj's bone expert couldn't help much. The report just backs up Raj's original theory,' Sophie said, leaning against Karen's desk.

'It looks that way,' Karen said, and glanced at the clock on the corner of her computer screen. 'Now I have to go and tell Superintendent Murray that our main suspect in the case has passed away.'

Sophie pulled a face. 'The superintendent is not going to be very happy.'

That was an understatement. She would be fuming. Luckily, she wasn't the type of boss to take out her frustrations on the team, but the assistant commissioner was piling on the pressure to get this case solved because he was mates with the victim's brother. She was not going to take the news well.

Since they'd come back from DI Goodfield's, Karen had buried herself in paperwork, thankful that the superintendent was busy with meetings all afternoon. But her last meeting should have finished by now, and Karen couldn't put it off much longer.

She and DI Morgan had agreed to put on a united front when they told the superintendent that there was a strong possibility Oliver Fox had abused schoolboys under his care in the eighties. Superintendent Murray would be frustrated to hear Albert Johnson had died, but being told their victim in the suitcase could be a child abuser took things to a whole new level.

She would want to know how much Robert Fox knew about the accusations levelled against his brother. It was a good question. DI Goodfield's account suggested he was well aware of his brother's behaviour. As Fox had been working for Lincolnshire Police at the time, he could have used his influence to cover up his brother's crime and prevent a thorough investigation into Mark Bell's allegations.

'I'd better go and speak to the superintendent now. I can't put it off forever. Is DI Morgan still in his office?' Karen asked Sophie.

Karen couldn't quite see into the office from where she was sat behind her computer.

Sophie, who was sitting on the edge of the desk, said, 'Yep. He doesn't look happy, though. In fact, it seems like he's looking forward to speaking to the superintendent almost as much as you.'

Karen left Sophie going through the finer details of the post-mortem report and stuck her head around the door of DI Morgan's office.

'Ready to go upstairs?'

He glanced at his watch. 'Is it that time already? I'm not looking forward to this.'

They walked together along the corridor and up the stairs to the superintendent's office. Her secretary was just about to leave for the day and was picking up her handbag as they arrived.

'She's been expecting you,' Pamela said. 'Go straight in.'

DI Morgan rapped on the door and then opened it, and Karen followed him inside.

'What have you got for me?' Superintendent Murray looked up from her desk. She was frowning already, which Karen took to be a bad sign.

As they slid into the seats in front of the superintendent's desk, DI Morgan began to describe what they had uncovered. The superintendent's expression darkened as he explained the situation.

When he'd finished, she said, 'So, to summarise, you're telling me our main suspect is dead, and on top of that, our victim is a suspected child abuser?'

'Yes, ma'am,' DI Morgan said.

She exhaled a long breath and put her head in her hands. 'I spoke to the assistant commissioner not half an hour ago and assured him we are making progress.'

'To be fair, we have made some progress, ma'am,' DI Morgan said. 'The fact that Oliver Fox could have been abusing students gives us a lot of potential suspects.'

Superintendent Murray lifted her head and steepled her fingers beneath her chin. 'We've got too many suspects. The investigation has suddenly multiplied in scope.'

Karen couldn't argue with that.

'How reliable do you think DI Goodfield's information is?' the superintendent asked her.

'He certainly wasn't the drunk, unreliable ex-copper I was expecting after what Robert Fox told us, ma'am. He was obviously deeply affected by what happened to Mark Bell, the young lad who'd come forward with the allegations and later hanged himself. I believe he told us the truth. How do you want us to handle this? Detective Superintendent Fox is bound to be in touch soon, and . . .' Karen trailed off.

'This isn't 1988 anymore,' Superintendent Murray replied. 'Oliver Fox and his brother do not have the old boys' network protecting them now. At the same time, we can't jump to conclusions. Right now we have DI Goodfield's version of events, in which he levels extremely serious allegations against our victim. We have no evidence that Detective Superintendent Fox knew about his brother's actions.'

She broke off, shook her head, and then got to her feet and began pacing behind her desk.

'If the allegations are true, ma'am, it's very likely that Mark Bell wasn't the only boy involved,' Karen said. 'If we widen the investigation and talk to the other boys in his classes and the football club, we'd have more to go on.'

The superintendent pinched the bridge of her nose between her thumb and forefinger. 'Yes, and you should talk to Mark Bell's mother. We can't speak to Mark himself, but we can corroborate DI Goodfield's version of events by talking to the mother.'

'Sophie is trying to track her down, ma'am. According to DI Goodfield, she moved out of the area shortly after her son died.'

Superintendent Murray put her hands on the back of her chair and looked at DI Morgan and Karen in turn. 'I wanted to keep this investigation as quiet as possible, but as the nature of this case has changed, I really don't see how we can keep things quiet much longer. As soon as you start questioning former staff and students of the school, rumours are going to start.'

'I don't see how we can help that, ma'am,' DI Morgan said.

She sighed heavily. 'No, neither can I. The assistant commissioner is not going to be pleased.'

Karen didn't really care what the assistant commissioner thought. For her, it was far more important to get to the bottom of this dark crime. They'd started this case thinking they had one victim – a body in a suitcase. But now it seemed there could be many more.

With Albert Johnson dead, the chances of them finding out who killed Oliver Fox were rapidly diminishing. The only evidence they had to go on was the child abuse allegations. Karen found it hard to believe that Mark Bell was Oliver's only victim. If they could track down other boys Oliver Fox had abused, maybe then they could get some answers, or at least some solid suspects.

As they left Superintendent Murray's office, she was picking up the phone, ready to call the assistant commissioner.

'That wasn't quite as bad as I'd expected,' Karen said as she shut the office door behind them.

'It's days like these when I want to stay a detective inspector. I don't envy Superintendent Murray the call she's making.'

Karen agreed. She preferred to be actively investigating a case rather than overseeing it. Dealing with politics and paperwork was not what she'd joined up for.

When they reached the main office downstairs, Karen's mobile phone started to buzz in her pocket. DI Morgan went back to his office, and Karen walked over to her desk, pulling her mobile from her pocket. It was her sister.

She tapped the answer icon. 'Emma, is everything all right? I'm still at work.'

'Yes, everything's fine. I just wanted to call and tell you I've arranged the date for tomorrow night.'

'Tomorrow? That's a bit soon!'

'I don't want to give you a chance to change your mind.'

'Very funny. I need time to think about it, to get in the right frame of mind.'

'No, you don't. You'll just end up building it up into something bigger than it is. It's a night out with a nice man, and you'll have fun.'

'If you say so,' Karen mumbled, suddenly feeling nervous.

'All right, I'll let you go. But don't forget. Seven thirty tomorrow at the White Hart.'

'Right, great.'

'You could sound more enthusiastic.'

But Karen couldn't summon up any enthusiasm right now. 'Sorry, Emma, I've got to go.'

'All right, but don't forget to text me to let me know how it goes tomorrow.'

'Okay, will do.'

Karen ended the call and stared at the phone. She was starting to regret agreeing to this. And when she sat down at her desk, Sophie approached with more bad news.

'Sorry, Sarge, we're not going to be able to talk to Mark Bell's mother. She passed away two years ago in Nottingham.'

Karen leaned back in her chair and stared at the ceiling. When were they going to catch a break?

The Fox family seemed to have put Oliver on some kind of pedestal. None of them had mentioned the child abuse allegations, and surely they would have known about them. Maybe not his sons, they'd have been too young, but Elizabeth must have known, and Laura – and so must Detective Superintendent Fox.

So far, they only had the word of DI Goodfield to go on regarding the allegations. A man who, by his own admission, had turned to drink.

Despite that, Karen thought he was the most reliable person they'd spoken to so far about Oliver Fox's disappearance.

'Thanks, Sophie. Well done for tracking her down so quickly.'

'Where on earth do we go from here, Sarge?'

Karen shrugged. That was a very good question.

CHAPTER TWENTY-TWO

Sophie and Rick had left for home an hour ago, but Karen and DI Morgan were still at the station, collating information and trawling through the old paperwork. Karen was trying to make some headway on DI Goodfield's notes. They'd been removed from the original notepad to be scanned in, and it was hard to follow the order of the pages. Karen had a sneaking suspicion that some of the pages could be missing. She could find no mention of the alleged abuse in Oliver Fox's missing persons file. She thought that was strange.

DI Morgan left his office, yawning. 'I'm going to call it a day. I've got a house full of boxes I need to unpack, and my brain could do with a break. We can come at this fresh in the morning.'

Karen looked up and stretched. She'd been sitting in front of her computer in the same position for too long, and her neck was starting to ache. 'You're right, we can't do anything else tonight. Tomorrow we can contact the students from Greenhill Secondary School we've traced, and ask Oliver Fox's old colleagues if any of them knew about the abuse allegations.'

After DI Morgan had collected his jacket from his office, Karen asked, 'Do you need a hand tonight? I could probably keep my eyes open for another hour or so if you want some help unpacking.'

'No, you should get some rest. I'll manage.'

'I really don't mind. Besides, it'll give me an excuse to see your new house.' She grinned.

'Well, if you're sure, that would be great. Thanks.'

They left the station together, but drove to Heighington in separate cars.

Karen picked up a bottle of Shiraz on the way, and then headed to DI Morgan's new house in the heart of the village. He'd opted for one of the older properties, near the stream that ran through the centre. It was a terraced cottage, with a small driveway just big enough for two cars, and Karen managed to squeeze her Honda Civic in beside DI Morgan's car.

She held out the wine as he opened the door. 'Housewarming gift.'

'Cheers, I'll get some glasses.' He led the way through the house and into the kitchen. It had been remodelled at some point – a wall had been knocked through to make a spacious kitchen-diner. Every counter was covered with cardboard boxes.

'Don't feel you have to open it now on my account. I'll be sticking to water because I've got to drive home,' Karen said. 'Are we unpacking the kitchen stuff first?'

DI Morgan nodded. 'If you don't mind. That box there is cups and glasses, and the one next to it is plates. At least, I *think* it is. I should have used a better labelling system.'

'When's the rest of your stuff coming?'

'I didn't bother with a removal firm. I've not got that much furniture, but I hired a couple of guys with a van to give me a hand on Saturday with the bed, sofa and dining table.'

'So you're not sleeping here tonight, then?'

'I am. I've got one of those blow-up mattresses in the bedroom. That'll do me for tonight.'

Karen got to work unwrapping the glasses and stacking them in the cupboard above the sink. It took her an hour to fill the cupboards and drawers in the kitchen with plates, cutlery, glasses and cups. 'I can tell you're not a minimalist!' Karen said.

'It's only when you move that you realise how much stuff you've got,' DI Morgan said. 'I'm surprised how much I'd managed to accumulate over the last few months. Thanks for your help. I'm nearly finished here. I've just got to unload two more boxes, and then I'll buy you dinner if you like. We can go to my local.'

Karen smothered a yawn. 'Sounds good.'

'Don't sound too enthusiastic,' DI Morgan said dryly. 'Here, can you unpack that box and put the CDs in that cabinet?'

He pointed to a cabinet close to the television unit. Karen knelt down on the floor and began to delve into the box of CDs.

She held one up. 'Oh, so you're a Bowie fan. You must have every single one of his albums here.' She pulled them all out, inspecting the covers, then turned to put them in the cabinet.

'I have. I've even got the Tin Machine stuff. Only a true fan listens to that.'

Karen chuckled and started to inspect the rest of his CDs. He had quite the collection, a mixture of classical and popular artists from the seventies and eighties. He didn't have much modern stuff.

'Are you going to put those CDs away, or just read the titles?' he asked as he finished putting books on to one of the bookshelves and then opened the final box.

Karen smirked. 'You're just getting touchy because you know I'm about to discover your secret love for One Direction or Boyzone.'

DI Morgan laughed. 'I think you're confusing my taste with yours.'

She slid a couple more CDs on the shelf and said, 'Actually, I've hardly got any CDs left. I got rid of most of them when I was having a clear-out a couple of years ago. I'm nearly all digital these days. I have to admit, I did find New Kids on the Block in my collection, though.' She smiled at the memory. 'I don't know why I suddenly thought of them. I think it's this case. It's making me remember the late eighties. Things were so different then. I was only a kid, but it's funny the things you remember. It's not just computers and technology that's changed, but attitudes and the way things are handled by the police. I keep thinking about that poor boy.'

'Mark Bell?'

'Yes. Imagine building up the courage to tell somebody, and then nothing being done to help you. I just . . .' Karen trailed off and shook her head. 'It must have been horrendous for him. I can't imagine how frustrated DI Goodfield felt when he couldn't help through official channels.'

Karen caught DI Morgan's gaze. Neither of them said it, but both were wondering whether DI Goodfield had done anything through *unofficial* channels.

As Karen slid the last of the CDs on to the shelf, DI Morgan flattened the empty boxes. 'Right, let's leave it for tonight. Come on, I'll buy you dinner at the Butcher and the Beast. It's the least I can do for all your hard work reading the covers of my CDs.'

The pub was busy when they got there, but fortunately for them it was still serving food. They were sat at a table and chatting when Karen noticed Dennis Dean walking towards them. He was the father of one of the girls who'd been kidnapped from Heighington a few months ago. He was unpredictable, and Karen shot a look at DI Morgan to communicate that trouble could be on its way. Dean was holding a pint of bitter and a glass of Coke.

'Dennis, how are you?' Karen asked as he reached their table.

'Fine, thanks.' He set the drinks down. 'These are for you.'

DI Morgan said, 'Cheers, Dennis. How is Emily?'

'She's doing all right, considering everything that happened.' He smiled at them, patted Karen on the shoulder and then turned to go back to the bar.

That was a turn up for the books, Karen thought. She'd been expecting a few harsh words, not a drink. It was certainly a surprise considering Dennis Dean's chequered history with law enforcement. He liked to play the hard man, but now he'd shown that underneath he was a father who was extremely grateful they'd managed to get his daughter back home.

One of the waiting staff brought over their food, and over dinner they discussed the case again. Karen realised it was weighing on DI Morgan just as heavily as it weighed on her. He also had to worry about the superintendent putting more pressure on the team after the events of the day.

When the body had first been discovered, it had been a perplexing case, but now the investigation had twisted and turned into something very sinister. Who had sent the note? Who, after all this time, wanted Albert Johnson to pay for his crime? And what, precisely, was that crime? Karen was starting to think they would never get to the bottom of it.

Once Karen had driven home, DI Morgan returned to the kitchen. His gaze lingered on the spirits he hadn't yet put away. Gin, whisky and brandy. He was tempted, but turned away and switched on the kettle. They had a big day ahead of them, potentially with hundreds of people to talk to about Oliver Fox and the allegations against him. He needed a clear head.

He'd just spooned some instant coffee into a mug when there was a knock at the front door.

Odd, he thought. It was late. Too late for a neighbour to call by to welcome him to the village.

When he'd got back from work earlier he'd found a little card from his next-door neighbours, welcoming him to his new home. Heighington was a small, sociable village and the people were friendly, although his first introduction to the area hadn't been particularly pleasant. His first major case in Lincolnshire had been a tough one.

When DI Morgan opened the front door, he saw a face he recognised but couldn't quite place. 'Can I help you?'

The man stepped closer to the light coming from the hallway, and DI Morgan's stomach sank.

'Hello, Scott. Long time no see, mate,' he said.

For a while, DI Morgan simply stared at him. Then he finally managed to choke out, 'How did you find out where I lived?'

He'd moved here today. It didn't make any sense. How could he have tracked him here?

'I'm a copper, aren't I? Finding out things like that is what I'm good at. Aren't you going to ask me in?'

DI Morgan was tempted to shut the door in his face, but on reflection he thought that wasn't a good idea. He stood back and opened the door wide.

'Thanks. It's a nice place you've got here.'

DI Morgan followed his visitor into the living room and folded his arms over his chest. 'What are you doing here?'

'That's no way to greet an old friend.'

But the man standing in front of DI Morgan wasn't a friend. He was Rob Miller, head of his old unit at Thames Valley Police.

DI Morgan didn't respond, and just waited for Rob to tell him what he was doing there. He would have a reason for the visit. He always had an ulterior motive.

DI Morgan had managed to bring three of the matching dining-room chairs over in his car, figuring he would get the rest on Saturday. Rob pulled one of the chairs towards him and sat down.

'I can see you're busy,' Rob said, gesturing to the folded boxes on the living room floor. 'So I'll get to my point straightaway. I need a favour.'

DI Morgan stared at him blankly.

'It's not much. I wouldn't want you to put yourself out, but I've done you favours in the past, and I kept my mouth shut. I saw you in the pub earlier. Was that a colleague you were with?'

DI Morgan nodded once, furious he hadn't noticed Rob was there, watching. He had let his guard down because he felt comfortable, safe.

'She seemed nice. I could tell she was an officer straight off. You always can, can't you?'

DI Morgan said nothing.

'You probably wouldn't want her or any of your other colleagues finding out what happened before you left us, would you?'

DI Morgan tensed. 'I don't have any secrets, Rob. You can't black-mail me.'

'So you've already told them what happened, have you?'

He gritted his teeth and stared at the ground.

'I thought not.'

'If they want to find out what happened, they can. There's no way I can stop that.'

'True, but they probably don't know what they're looking for, do they? I suppose I could give them a heads-up, but I didn't think you would like that very much.' He laughed. 'Don't look at me like that! I'm not going to tell anyone. We're friends.'

He settled himself in the chair, crossing one leg over the other and resting his right ankle on his left knee. 'All I need from you is one little favour. It's not much to ask of a friend, is it?'

'Get to the point. What do you want, Rob?'

He'd never liked his old unit leader. Rob Miller was an officer who liked to cut corners. He'd chosen a career in the police because it made him feel powerful, not because he wanted to help people.

'It's about a woman,' Rob said. 'Isn't that a cliché? But you know what it's like. Your ex-wife cheated on you, didn't she? For better or worse, don't make me laugh! Your missus ran off at the first sign of things getting tough, didn't she?'

DI Morgan stared at him with intense dislike.

'Anyway, let's not get into that. I can see it's a touchy subject for you. Let's focus on my problem. It's my girlfriend. We've been going through a rough patch, and she decided to take a job up here with your lot. She's on civilian staff but works out of Nettleham station. Her name is Louise Jackson. Do you know her? She only started there a couple of weeks ago.'

DI Morgan shook his head. 'I've never heard of her.'

'Well, I need you to keep an eye on her for me. I just don't want her making a fool of me, and you know what that's like, eh?'

'What exactly do you expect me to do?'

Rob took out his phone and pulled up a photo, turning the screen and showing it to DI Morgan. The photo had been taken at night, and the flash made Louise Jackson look startled. He thought she would be shocked if she knew what Rob was up to right now.

'I want you to use your considerable detective skills.' Rob smirked. 'You won't find it difficult. All I want to know is where she lives and if she's seeing anyone else. Just find out those two things and your colleagues won't hear a dicky bird from me. Have we got a deal?'

He stood up and held out his hand for DI Morgan to shake.

DI Morgan kept his arms folded. 'Why can't you do it?'

'Me? She wouldn't like that. It would be creepy.'

'It's not any less creepy if you get someone else to do it for you. Does she know you're up here spying on her?'

Rob laughed and put his hands in his pockets. 'But I'm not the one who'll be doing the spying. You will.' Still laughing, he walked past DI Morgan, into the hallway and out of the front door. 'See you later, Scotty.'

After Rob left, DI Morgan went back to the kitchen, ignored the coffee mug and instead poured himself a large measure of Glenmorangie. As he sipped his drink, he looked out of the window into the dark back garden.

No matter how far he moved, he couldn't escape the past.

CHAPTER TWENTY-THREE

When the alarm went off the following morning, Karen groaned and buried her head in the pillow. A long day stretched ahead of her, and she expected to spend most of it at her desk on the phone, chasing up leads.

She reached for her mobile to silence the alarm and she saw she'd missed a call last night. Sitting up in bed, she looked at the call history. She didn't recognise the most recent number; it began with the area code for Lincoln. Perhaps it was a telemarketer? It couldn't be the station. The switchboard had her home number.

Karen rolled her eyes when she saw she'd somehow pressed the button on the side of the phone to put it on silent. Fortunately, although that button muted calls, it didn't mute her alarm. She needed to get an early start today and couldn't afford to oversleep.

She left her phone on the nightstand and headed to the bathroom. Whoever had called would have to wait. It was too early to call back now. Most people would still be sleeping.

Karen finished showering and getting ready, but the missed call niggled at her. By the time she was ready to leave for work, it was just after seven.

She googled the number, expecting the search to come back with a business name, but got nothing. She picked up her mobile and pressed redial. If it was a telemarketer, she would soon find out. There would probably be some kind of recorded message.

The phone rang six or seven times, then an answerphone kicked in.

'This is William Grant. I can't take your call right now, but if you leave a message, I'll get back to you.'

Karen left a brief message explaining she was returning his call, and then hung up. She had a bad feeling. It was still early, and if she'd tried to call anyone else, Karen would simply have assumed they were still in bed. But William Grant had made a point of saying he was up by five a.m. every morning. Was this morning an exception, for some reason? Had he slept in? Or had he gone out? But where would he go this time of the morning?

Maybe he hadn't heard the phone, or perhaps he'd gone out to get the paper.

Karen worked through the possibilities in her mind as she searched for her keys, but she couldn't put her worries to rest. She located the keys, grabbed her bag, looped her jacket over her arm and called DI Morgan's number.

He answered just as she was locking the front door.

'I missed a call last night from William Grant. He phoned me about ten, but my phone was on silent.'

'Did he leave a message?'

'No, and I just called him back and got the answering service. It was quite late for him to phone me. I'm concerned. I was thinking of popping in to see him on my way to work.'

'Good idea. Maybe he's thought of something that could help us.'

DI Morgan was probably right, Karen thought as she hung up. William Grant could have remembered something relevant to their investigation and decided to call while it was fresh in his mind. Ten p.m. wasn't that late really, and she had left him her card and told him to call at any time.

Despite that, Karen couldn't shake her sense of unease as she drove towards North Greetwell.

When she pulled up outside William's bungalow, Karen saw his car in the driveway. The curtains were open, but there were no lights on.

She locked the car and walked towards the bungalow slowly. As she got closer to the front door, she saw it was slightly ajar.

Her skin tingled, and she felt a spike of adrenaline run through her body.

This wasn't good.

She looked around, taking in her surroundings, and then pushed open the door. The hallway looked exactly the same as it had when they'd first visited. The telephone table sat in the same position, and all the photographs were still hanging on the wall. Nothing looked out of the ordinary.

Karen called out, 'Mr Grant? This is DS Hart, Lincolnshire Police.'

There was no answer.

She looked around the sleepy collection of bungalows surrounding William's, but there was no one to be seen. She typed a quick message to DI Morgan and said she was going inside. She wasn't averse to taking risks, but it made sense to let someone on the team know what she was doing.

She took a deep breath and stepped over the threshold before pausing in the hall and listening for any sounds of life.

'Mr Grant? Is everything okay?' Karen tried again, but was met with the same silence.

She moved forward methodically, checking each room as she passed and looking for any signs of a struggle. But everything seemed neat and tidy, and there was nothing to indicate anything untoward had taken place.

She checked both the bedrooms last, and was greeted by the sight of neatly made beds.

Where had he gone? It was only seven thirty. People just didn't wander off and leave their doors open these days.

She walked back towards the front door, and as she approached, a shadow fell across the driveway.

Karen's heart jumped, and then she let out a sigh of relief when she saw it was William Grant. He was holding two tubs of brightly coloured pansies and looking at her in amazement.

'What are you doing in there?' he asked. He didn't sound put out or annoyed, just surprised.

'Mr Grant, you called me last night. I tried to return your call this morning but got no answer. When I arrived, your front door was open, and I thought you might be in trouble.'

'Oh, I see. I just popped round to the back garden to bring these out to the front.' He held up the pots of pansies.

Karen felt oddly light-headed and shaky now that the adrenaline was leaving her system. 'Right, well, since I'm here, perhaps you could tell me why you called me last night?'

William set the pots of pansies down next to the flowerbed and brushed his hands together.

He nodded firmly, but his face looked sad. 'Yes, I needed to talk to you. Come through to the kitchen. There's something I need to show you.'

She followed William to the small kitchen at the back of the bungalow. From a letter rack, he plucked a sheet of paper that had been folded in half and held it out to Karen.

Before she touched it, she saw the message.

'Can you put the letter down on the kitchen counter please, Mr Grant?'

She didn't want her fingerprints contaminating the evidence. The letter was typed, and it was identical to the one they'd found at Albert Johnson's house.

It's time to pay for your crime.

'When did you get this?'

'Six months ago.'

'Why didn't you tell us about this when we came to visit?'

William linked his hands together and stared contritely down at his feet.

Karen didn't understand. Surely receiving a letter like this would be one of the first things to tell the police?

'I should have told you, I'm sorry. It's just Albert . . .' He trailed off, rubbing a hand over his forehead.

Karen bit her lip. He probably hadn't yet heard the news about his friend. Despite her frustration with him for not mentioning the letter, it was up to her to break it to him as gently as she could.

'I'm very sorry to tell you the news like this, William, but Albert died yesterday,' Karen said.

William didn't look up. His shoulders were slumped as he replied, 'I know.'

Karen couldn't help feeling sorry for him when she saw his eyes were glistening with tears. 'I need to take this letter to the station. It's important evidence, William. I'll get my kit from the car.'

Karen turned, preparing to go back to her car to grab a pair of gloves and an evidence bag for the letter, and William muttered something so quietly she couldn't make it out.

'What was that?'

William looked up. His eyelashes were wet as he blinked at her. 'I didn't tell you because it was our secret. Albert never wanted anyone to know, but now he's dead.' He took a deep breath. 'I need to talk to my solicitor. I want to do this officially down at the station.'

After Karen had William Grant settled in interview room three with a cup of tea, she went to the main office to update the rest of the team. William's solicitor was on her way, which was a good thing because, despite Karen's many questions, William was refusing to talk until his lawyer arrived.

'So he received the same letter as Albert Johnson?' DI Morgan asked, looking as puzzled as Karen felt.

She nodded. 'Yes, I've just admitted it to evidence, but it looks exactly the same to me. Same wording. *It's time to pay for your crime.*'

'What did William say on the drive to the station?' Sophie asked.

'Not a lot. He said something about it not being his secret to share, but now that Albert was dead he's ready to talk.'

'Very mysterious,' Rick said.

'He was a teacher at Greenhill Secondary School when Albert was the headmaster. It's possible they found out what Oliver Fox was up to, had an altercation with him and then tried to cover up what happened.'

DI Morgan looked at his watch. 'I hope the solicitor hurries up. It's hard to plan an interview strategy when you have no idea what he's going to say.'

'I agree,' Karen said. 'I think we should keep an open mind going in, let him get whatever it is off his chest and then break for a bit to plan our next move.'

'I think that's our only option,' DI Morgan said.

The phone on Karen's desk rang, and she picked it up. It was the desk sergeant telling her that William Grant's solicitor had arrived.

'The solicitor's here,' Karen said after hanging up. 'I'll go downstairs and bring her up.'

'Great, I'll get things started in the interview room,' DI Morgan said, and then turned to Rick and Sophie. 'You two concentrate on tracking down the other students in Oliver Fox's classes, particularly focusing on any who also attended football training. Hopefully, William

Grant is about to give us some answers, but if not, we're going to need student testimony to fall back on.'

Waiting for Karen downstairs was William Grant's solicitor, a middle-aged woman with tanned skin and a slightly startled expression. She introduced herself as Megan Evans. As she shook her hand, Karen wondered how much she'd been told about the case.

'Can I ask what this is about?' she asked as Karen led her up the stairs to the interview room.

'Mr Grant would like to make a statement.' Karen said.

From the anxious questions the solicitor shot at her as they went, Karen realised her client hadn't told her anything yet.

Megan blinked a couple of times and opened her mouth to ask another question, but before she could, Karen opened the door to interview room three.

William sat on one side of the table, his hands wrapped around a paper cup filled with what must now be stone-cold tea. He half-stood as Karen and the solicitor entered the room.

'Thank you for coming, Megan,' he said, adding, 'Megan is the daughter of one of my old friends.'

The solicitor took the seat beside William, and Karen sat opposite them, beside DI Morgan. They started the recording, and once formalities were out of the way, Karen said, 'You wanted to make a statement, William?'

William was trembling, looking like he'd made the worst mistake of his life. 'I don't really know where to begin,' he said in a quiet voice.

'Perhaps you could tell us about the letter,' DI Morgan said.

William clasped his shaking hands. 'Right. I got my letter at the same time as Bert, about six months ago. It scared the life out of us. I don't mind telling you that. We weren't expecting it, you see. It had been so long since it happened . . . It didn't seem real, in a way.'

William's face was pale, and he twisted his fingers together as he rested his hands on the table in front of him.

'Do you know who sent the letters?'

William shook his head, and his bloodshot eyes lifted to meet Karen's. 'I've no idea. Bert and I talked about it, but it was a mystery. We couldn't work out who sent them. The only explanation we came up with was that after all this time, someone had uncovered our secret.'

CHAPTER TWENTY-FOUR

William Grant rubbed his face with his hands. 'When you came to talk to me, I knew you'd found the body.' He took a deep breath. 'We'd kept him in Bert's loft for the past eight years. Before that, he was kept under the floor of the outbuilding in his garden. We'd thought it would be safe out there, and it was for years, but someone pinched some garden equipment so Bert decided to move the body inside. His wife had died by then, so we thought it would be safe.'

William raked a hand through his thin, grey hair. 'I suppose you must have looked in Bert's loft and found the body in the suitcase . . . I'm right, aren't I? That's why you came to talk to me about Oliver Fox.'

He had it half-right. They'd found the body in Albert's home, although it had been in the spare room, not the loft. Perhaps Albert had decided to move the case, and the exertion was what caused his fall. The crime scene team had reported evidence that some items in the loft had been moved recently.

Neither Karen nor DI Morgan said anything, so William continued. 'It happened so long ago, so when we got the letters, it was a shock. Bert said it was some silly joke, but I was nervous. The letters were bad enough, but then a few weeks ago Bert started to get phone calls. When he answered, no one spoke, but he could hear the sound of someone breathing, and I was convinced it was linked to the letters. Eventually I persuaded him we needed to move the body again. So I hired a boat. The idea was to dump the case out at sea somewhere.' William raised his eyes to the ceiling and said, 'We weren't criminal masterminds, but after the phone calls, we felt like we didn't have a choice. I was supposed to be going round to help him, but my grand-daughter was taken ill – appendicitis – and I didn't expect him to try to move the body alone. The next day, I heard Bert had been rushed to hospital.'

'How did Oliver Fox's body get into the suitcase in the first place?' Karen asked, feeling thoroughly confused. She wished he'd started at the beginning of the story.

William's whole body began to shake, and his solicitor put her hand on his arm. 'Are you okay to continue, William?'

Karen poured him a drink from the bottle of mineral water on the bench behind them. She pushed the plastic cup across the table to him.

He took it gratefully. 'Thank you. It happened thirty years ago, so my memory is not the best. I'll try to tell you everything, though. I think it was 1987 that I first heard whispers about Oliver Fox. At first, I thought they were just malicious, unsubstantiated rumours. He was a funny man and kept to himself, and people did like to gossip if they felt others didn't fit in. It was a tight-knit village in those days, and outsiders were always viewed with suspicion. He'd lived in Skellingthorpe for years, but didn't get too involved in village life, which was unusual for a teacher in those days.

'I first realised people were taking the rumours seriously when Bert, who was the headmaster at the time, asked me to go along to the football training sessions after school on Thursdays. I got the distinct impression he wanted somebody to keep an eye on Oliver. That was in May 1987, I think.

'I did my best. But I had my own family and I couldn't make it every Thursday, and he never did anything untoward when I was around, so I started to think the rumours had been wrong. I gave him the benefit of the doubt, I suppose. Something I'd later regret.

'It was just after Easter in 1988 when it happened. I'd stayed late to mark some homework and prepare my lessons for the next week, when three young boys came into the classroom. I was about to tell them off because they weren't allowed to be wandering around the school after hours, but then I saw the blood. The first boy, James, was covered in it. It was even in his hair, and the other two had it all over their hands and shirts. They were in shock, babbling incoherently, so I took them along to the headmaster.

'When I realised what had happened, I wanted to go straight to the police, but Bert took charge. He told me we wouldn't be going to the police. I have to admit I lost my temper with him. I thought he was trying to protect the school's reputation or something daft like that, but then he explained there was a strong possibility the boys would get the blame and no one would listen to their side of the story because nobody had believed a similar allegation made the year before.

'That's when I remembered the officer who'd come round asking questions a year before. He'd wanted to know all about Oliver Fox and his relationship with the students. I'd been as honest as I could be with him, but I'd never seen Oliver do anything to make any of the boys uncomfortable, and they'd never come to me with any problems.'

His voice broke, and he took another sip of water. The events may have happened thirty years ago, but William Grant's emotions were still raw.

'Bert told me that Oliver Fox's brother was in the police force, and he'd quashed the last investigation. It knocked me for six. I'd known about Mark Bell's suicide, of course, but I hadn't known what was behind it. I suppose I was in shock. We went into the changing room and found Oliver Fox's body just lying there. His blood was all over the floor. Bert checked for a pulse and couldn't find one. I found the boys some clothes from lost property and told them to get changed after washing off the blood. I said they must tell their families that they'd managed to spill paint on their clothes and they were ruined. I burned the uniforms later.

'While I was doing that, Bert managed to get Oliver's body on to a mat from the games hall and rolled him up in it.' William shuddered. 'There was so much blood. Bert and I loaded the body into the back of his old Volvo. Then we sent the boys home, instructing them not to tell anyone what had happened, and Bert and I moved the body into the outbuilding in his garden.

'I still can't believe we got away with it. His wife was in the kitchen. We told her Bert was going to store some gardening things in the outbuilding for me. She didn't suspect anything. She didn't even look out of the window. Some blood had soaked into the carpet in the boot of the car, so we took it back to the school and gave the fabric a good scrub. Then we went home as if nothing had happened, and tried to behave as though it was a normal evening.'

When William stopped talking, there was heavy silence in the room, and Karen guessed DI Morgan, like her, was struggling to process the information.

'So you found Oliver Fox's body in the changing room?' Karen asked, wanting to clarify the scene of the crime.

'Yes, that's right.'

'And he was dead when you found him?'

William lowered his head and took a deep breath. 'Yes, Bert spent quite some time looking for a pulse and checked if he was breathing. There was no doubt about it. Oliver was definitely dead when we got there.'

'And you think the boys attacked him?' DI Morgan asked. 'You assume they were fighting back?'

William nodded slowly. 'They were only thirteen. So young, and they were terrified. One of the lads wouldn't stop crying, and one boy didn't speak at all. It was the third boy, James Hunter, who managed to lead me to the changing room, to Oliver's body.'

'Which one of the boys killed Oliver? Was it an accident?'

William took a deep breath and then said, 'I never asked. I know that sounds silly, but it wouldn't change anything, and the boys were so upset. We told them that we would deal with everything, but they couldn't mention what had happened to anyone. As far as I know, they never did.'

'Can you give us the full names of all three boys please, Mr Grant?' DI Morgan asked.

He blinked and put his palms flat on the table. 'Yes, James Hunter, Michael Simpson and Stuart Bennett. All three boys were thirteen. Whatever happened, it wasn't their fault.'

'And they were all part of this football club?'

'Yes.' He rubbed the back of his neck. 'I did wonder if Oliver was on his best behaviour when he knew he was being watched, and made arrangements to see the boys later, when no one else was around.'

DI Morgan asked a few more questions, pinning down the date and time of the murder. He asked for the registration number of Albert Johnson's car at the time, but William understandably had no idea. They'd need to contact the DVLA to find out what vehicles had been registered to Albert Johnson in 1988. It was a long shot, but if the car hadn't been scrapped, they could examine it for evidence. With advanced DNA technology, it seemed anything was possible these days.

'I think we'll pause here, William,' Karen said. She wanted to get the names of the boys to Rick and Sophie so they could track them down as soon as possible.

She also wanted to discuss with DI Morgan how they were going to proceed, because while William Grant may not have killed Oliver Fox, he'd still concealed the body, and that was a crime.

'Can I get you another cup of tea?' Karen asked. 'We're going to have a few more questions for you after a quick break.'

William nodded but didn't look up. He looked pale and exhausted, and it was clear he was finding it hard to relive the events of that afternoon.

Karen went to organise tea for him and the solicitor, and DI Morgan headed off to give the names of the three boys to Rick and Sophie. They'd need to see if they could trace the mysterious calls Albert Johnson had received, too.

They were a lot closer to finding out what had really happened to Oliver Fox, thanks to William Grant's confession, but they still didn't know who'd killed him and who had sent the notes. James Hunter, Stuart Bennett and Michael Simpson would be in their forties now but would have been minors at the time, and Karen didn't really know what the Crown Prosecution Service would do with the information. What would be the point in charging them now? Especially after all they'd been through, if the child abuse allegations were true.

As the kettle boiled, she decided to tell William he'd be better off staying with family for a few days. He'd received the same letter as Albert Johnson, and if Albert really had been pushed down the stairs, then William's life could be in danger.

Today's questioning would go on for some time, but they wouldn't be able to hold him indefinitely. At some point, he would need to leave the police station, and then he would be vulnerable.

CHAPTER TWENTY-FIVE

DI Morgan and Karen emerged from the interview room after the third round of questioning. For the past hour, they'd been needling William Grant for the details and trying to get some clarity on what had really happened on that late afternoon in 1988.

'He's getting tired,' Karen commented.

DI Morgan sighed. 'He is. But we need answers. We have to get all the details.'

'We're not going to hold him for the murder, are we?'

'I'll clear it with the superintendent, but I don't think so. He's certainly not innocent. William covered up a murder and concealed evidence, but though that's still serious, I don't think he's likely to do a runner.'

'I thought it might be a good idea for him to stay away from home for a few days,' Karen said. 'If Albert really was pushed and both men got threatening letters, he's probably better off staying somewhere else, maybe at a hotel or with family.'

'Good point. I know for a fact the budget won't stretch to putting a unit outside his home, but changing his normal routine might be a good idea for his safety.'

'Why do you think the letters were sent six months ago? I mean, Oliver Fox has been dead for thirty years. Why now?'

DI Morgan shrugged. 'We're assuming those letters are related to this case. I don't know, it doesn't make sense, unless something happened six months ago to trigger the person who sent them.'

Karen thought for a moment. 'Is it possible someone broke into Albert Johnson's house and pushed him down the stairs? Or was he just delusional when he spoke to Rick?'

'There was no evidence of a break-in,' DI Morgan said matter-of-factly. 'The attending officers had to break a pane of glass in the back door to gain entry. But the door and windows were intact when they got there.'

'Maybe he let them in.'

'Possibly. Or maybe Albert thinking he was pushed was down to his imagination working overtime.'

'I'd still feel better if William stayed somewhere else for a few days. There's something sly and nasty about those letters.'

When they returned to the main office, Rick looked up from his desk. 'I think I've got something for you.' He pointed at his monitor. 'I'm pretty sure this is the James Hunter we're looking for.' Rick had the records from the DVLA on the screen.

DI Morgan put a hand on his shoulder. 'Great work. And he lives in Lincoln?'

'He did,' Rick said.

'He did? Do you mean he's moved now?' DI Morgan frowned.

'I'm afraid it's worse than that,' Rick said, pushing his chair back from the desk to look up at Karen and DI Morgan. 'James Hunter died six months ago.'

Karen looked at him in disbelief as DI Morgan sighed.

'People associated with this case are dropping like flies,' Sophie said with a shake of her head.

'How did he die?' DI Morgan asked.

'The verdict was suicide. His blood alcohol level was very high, and he either jumped or fell from his balcony.'

'And this happened six months ago, around the same time Albert Johnson and William Grant got those letters . . .'

Rick squinted at the screen. 'He died on the twenty-fifth of September.'

Karen and DI Morgan exchanged a look. William couldn't remember exactly when he and Albert had received the letters, but he'd said the letters came in the post in the last week of September or first week of October. William hadn't kept the envelope, and there was no sign of the envelope at Albert Johnson's house either.

'Was a letter found at James Hunter's house? Perhaps that was enough to drive him to suicide,' Sophie suggested.

Rick shook his head. 'There's nothing recorded about a letter. He didn't even leave a suicide note.'

'The timing of his death is very interesting,' Karen said. 'It's possible he destroyed the letter and then committed suicide.'

'True,' DI Morgan agreed, looking down at Rick. 'Have you had any luck tracking down the other two men? We need to find out exactly what happened that afternoon.'

'I haven't yet, but I'm working on it. Sophie is looking into James Hunter's family tree, and we're going to request a warrant for his phone records.'

'Okay. Good work.'

They still had another ten minutes before their next round of questioning, but before they could discuss the case any further, William Grant's solicitor walked into the main office, escorted by DC Shah. Karen went to see what she wanted while DI Morgan carried on talking to Rick and Sophie.

'I'm requesting a delay,' Megan said to Karen. 'My client is an old man, and this whole experience has been very draining. He realises what he did thirty years ago was wrong, and he's prepared to cooperate fully with the police in this enquiry. I just ask that we continue the interview tomorrow morning.'

He had looked extremely tired, so this development didn't come as a surprise.

'I'll see what I can do,' Karen said. 'I'll need to clear it with the superintendent. If you go back to the interview room, I'll come and find you in a few minutes.'

Megan gave Karen a curt nod and left the office.

Karen went to inform the superintendent and DI Morgan of the solicitor's request. She had sympathy for William. If she'd been in his position, she wouldn't have hidden the body, but she could understand his motives weren't evil.

After the superintendent and DI Morgan agreed, Karen went to tell William and his solicitor that they should be back at the station tomorrow morning at nine a.m. As they were gathering their belongings, she added, 'I think it's a good idea if William stays away from home for the next few days. After what happened to Albert, we're concerned for his safety.'

William's jaw dropped.

Megan's face tightened. 'Do you really think he's in danger?'

Karen hesitated, but decided she needed to tell the truth. 'We're working on a theory that Albert Johnson was pushed down the stairs rather than just fell. If that's the case, after the letter William received, we think it's better to be cautious.'

The solicitor swallowed hard. 'Right, I can give you a lift to your daughter's house if you like, William.'

William nodded but said nothing.

Megan picked up her briefcase. 'Thank you, DS Hart. I'll see you tomorrow.'

Karen watched her walk away, wondering if this was the first time she'd represented a client in such unusual circumstances. If the CPS did press charges against William, he would need experienced representation with considerable expertise in criminal defence.

Karen turned and walked back along the corridor. As they wouldn't be able to talk to William again until tomorrow morning, her time would be best spent digging into the old allegations to see what she could unearth.

Rick was busy tracing Stuart Bennett and Michael Simpson, and Sophie was contacting the council and the members of the school board, to request their records. They needed to find any official documentation of Mark Bell's allegations, as well as any other complaints lodged against Oliver Fox.

Karen grabbed a coffee from the vending machine and carried it to her desk. She took a sip as she logged on to the system and then focused on the screen. One way or another, they had to find out why an old case had suddenly become active again after all these years.

At midday, DI Morgan headed down to the cafeteria to grab a sandwich. William Grant's questioning had only lasted a morning, but it felt like longer. Questioning a suspect could be intense, both for the suspects and the officers involved. Focus and concentration were needed at every moment. They couldn't allow anything to slip by unnoticed. DI Morgan didn't blame William for feeling drained. He felt pretty exhausted himself.

He picked a ham and salad sandwich from the chilled cabinet and waited in line.

The cafeteria was already pretty full, and DI Morgan's gaze drifted around the room as he waited to pay. Two tables away from the window sat a woman he recognised from the photo Rob Miller had shown him.

So that was Louise Jackson.

She was sitting alone. It would be easy for him to pay for his sandwich and take a seat at her table under the pretence of being sociable. He could draw her into a conversation and find out everything Rob wanted to know.

After moving to Lincolnshire, DI Morgan had finally felt he could let his guard down. It had been a welcome change. He'd forgotten what it was like to interact with colleagues without wondering how much they knew about him. He didn't want to lose that.

Keeping Rob sweet would be easy. If DI Morgan did as he asked, life would carry on as before, and no one would find out what had happened while he was working at Thames Valley.

He forced himself to turn away and looked at his watch. They might not be able to question William Grant this afternoon, but he had plans to go and talk to Elizabeth Fox. DI Morgan found it hard to believe she knew nothing about the slurs against her husband.

He paid for his sandwich, studiously ignoring the woman sitting at the table near the window. Rob Miller could do his own dirty work.

Thanks to a tractor causing a tailback along Lincoln Road, it took DI Morgan longer than usual to get to Skellingthorpe. Elizabeth Fox's grey stone house looked even darker and drearier in the rain. He turned his collar up and walked briskly to the door.

He hadn't warned Elizabeth he was on the way this time. He didn't want to give her a chance to prepare a story. He wanted to see her reaction to the allegations in person. Pressing the doorbell, he sheltered beneath the covered porch as the rain hit the ground and splashed back up, soaking the bottom of his trousers.

After a few moments, Elizabeth opened the door, keeping the security chain on.

Her eyes widened when she saw DI Morgan on her doorstep. 'Is there any news?'

'I wanted to give you an update,' he said.

She pushed the door closed, removed the chain and then stood back, allowing him to enter.

He stepped into the dark hallway, and Elizabeth shut the door and then led the way into the same small living room they'd sat in the first time he and DS Hart had visited the house.

The light was better in here, and DI Morgan noticed Elizabeth looked haggard. She'd lost weight off her small frame in just a couple of days.

A fire was burning in the hearth. Elizabeth shut the door to keep the warmth in. 'Can I offer you a cup of tea?'

'No, thank you.'

She held out a hand to indicate he should take a seat, so he sat in the wingback chair opposite hers beside the fire.

It wasn't that cold outside today. Despite an icy, snowy start to March, it seemed spring was finally here. But there was something about this house that made him want to keep his jacket on. A chill seemed to permeate the walls.

'First, I need to tell you we have confirmed through dental records that the body we found is definitely that of your husband, Oliver. I'm very sorry for your loss,' DI Morgan said.

Elizabeth raised her hands to her face, her gold bracelets slipping down her thin wrists.

He gave her a moment.

'It shouldn't come as a shock,' she sniffed. 'I knew when you first came here that it was him. Have you discovered how he died?'

'We're still investigating,' DI Morgan said. 'It looks like Oliver died around the time he went missing. You should know we're still treating this case as a high priority.'

Elizabeth gripped the arms of her chair.

'Mrs Fox, I do have some more questions about your husband. We've been talking to people who used to work with him, and our investigations have unearthed some worrying information.' He paused to watch her reaction.

She'd been looking down at her lap, but as he spoke, her gaze lifted to meet his. 'What are you talking about?'

'There were allegations made against your husband, back in 1987. They concerned a boy under his care at Greenhill Secondary School. His name was Mark Bell.' Again, DI Morgan paused to study the woman's expression. How would she react to Mark Bell's name?

Elizabeth raised her head regally. 'That was utter nonsense. Some silly story the boy made up. Nobody gave it any credence at all. And you should be ashamed of yourself for bringing it up now. You're slurring the name of a dead man who can't defend himself. It's really not fair.'

So she did know about Mark Bell.

'The last thing we want to do is upset you or your family, Mrs Fox. But we do need to know everything about these allegations.'

'I really don't see why,' Elizabeth said. 'It's a disgrace. You should be looking into how he died . . . You shouldn't be bringing all this up again and relying on gossip.'

'Exactly,' DI Morgan said, and noted the look of surprise on her face. 'We can't rely on gossip, which is why we need to talk to people who knew what was happening at the time. That's why I'm coming to you. I want to hear your side of the story.'

'Well, all I can tell you is that it was an outright lie. Oliver was a good man. I told him he needed to be more careful, and not spend any time alone with the students after the boy made up those lies. But he loved being the football coach, and he said he wasn't going to let one silly little boy get in the way of him helping other students.' Elizabeth paused and looked down at her hands in her lap. 'The boy was obviously troubled. His father had walked out on him and his mother, and he was looking for attention. These days I think he would have been recognised as having some mental issues, and, well, things might have turned out differently. Perhaps he would have got some counselling or something. As it was, the poor boy ended up killing himself just a few months later.'

She was utterly convinced of her husband's innocence, DI Morgan thought – or she was putting on a very good act.

'Were there any problems with any of the other students?'

Elizabeth hesitated, and then shook her head rapidly. 'No, it was just the one boy.'

'Did you ever speak to anybody else about the matter?'

Elizabeth frowned. 'No, why would I? We didn't want anyone to know. You know how these things have a habit of getting around, even when they're not true. And I certainly didn't want the boys finding out.' Elizabeth's eyes widened as she looked at DI Morgan. 'You don't have to tell them about this, do you?'

DI Morgan didn't reply straightaway, so Elizabeth carried on. 'Oh, please. It would devastate them. You can't tell them about these wretched lies. They worshipped their father. It would be unbearably cruel of you to tell them.'

'We may have to ask them if they remember anything, Mrs Fox.'

Elizabeth glared at him with intense dislike. 'It's ridiculous. Why are you bringing this up now? It can't have anything to do with his death, can it? Do you think somebody believed those lies and attacked Oliver?'

'It's a possibility,' DI Morgan said. 'We really don't know what happened to him yet. Were there any threats issued to your husband after the incident with Mark Bell?'

Elizabeth looked horrified. She rested an elbow on the arm of her chair and covered her eyes with her hand. 'I can't believe this. You think somebody murdered him over that boy's lies.'

'It's my job to consider all possibilities, Mrs Fox. Now, anything you tell me could help. Did anyone issue threats to your husband?'

Elizabeth bit down on her lower lip. DI Morgan waited, and eventually she spoke again. 'Well, there was that horrible DI Goodson . . . or Goodfield, I think it was. He had some kind of vendetta against Oliver. He came around here one night shouting the odds, threatening Oliver. Oliver called his brother Robert. He outranked the horrible little man. Thankfully, Robert managed to get rid of him, and we didn't hear from him after that. Or, at least, he didn't come back to the house.'

'That's helpful,' DI Morgan said. 'Did anyone else know about the allegations?'

'Not as far as I know.'

'I suppose other teachers at the school must've known,' DI Morgan said. 'The headmaster, for example?'

'Yes, I suppose he must have known. He would have had to deal with the situation at school. That's why you were asking me about Oliver's relationship with Albert Johnson, wasn't it? Do you think he was involved in Oliver's death?'

They were still keeping the fact that Oliver Fox's body had been discovered in Albert Johnson's house from the family, and DI Morgan felt guilty as he looked at Elizabeth's distraught face.

'I'm afraid I don't have any answers for you yet. We do need to talk to your sons, though. We've contacted Stephen, but I'd appreciate it if you could give me Martin's telephone number. The number we have for him hasn't been answered.'

'Oh.' Elizabeth turned away to look at the fire. After a moment, she turned back to DI Morgan. 'Martin's been a bit out of sorts lately. He doesn't always answer his phone.'

'I see.'

DI Morgan checked that the telephone numbers and addresses he had for Martin Fox were current. Elizabeth confirmed that they were correct and then wrung her hands. 'Please promise me you won't talk to them about the allegations unless you have to. I really don't want them getting involved in all this.'

DI Morgan could understand Elizabeth's protective instinct towards her sons, but the boys had been eight and ten when their father went missing. It was possible they'd heard conversations, either between other children or by overhearing adults talking about the situation and Mark Bell. He didn't want to upset the two men unnecessarily, but he couldn't rule out the need to talk to them in the course of the investigation.

'We won't mention the allegations to your sons unless we have no other choice.'

Elizabeth didn't look particularly reassured, but she nodded and stared into the flames. 'Poor Oliver,' she murmured. 'He did so many good things with his life, but now this is how people are going to remember him.'

CHAPTER TWENTY-SIX

Back at the station, Karen was still looking through files when her phone beeped. She picked it up, checked the screen and groaned. It was a cheerful message from her sister reminding her about her date that evening.

Don't forget, seven thirty tonight at the White Hart!

'Bad news, Sarge?' Rick asked as he walked towards Karen's desk holding a pile of paperwork.

'It's nothing,' Karen said, locking the screen and putting the phone in her pocket. 'What have you got?'

'I think we've identified all three boys,' Rick said. 'They're men now, of course. All older than me.' He handed Karen a file. 'This is the report on James Hunter's death.'

As she opened the file and flicked through it, Rick described what had happened. 'He'd been alone, drinking heavily, and at just after ten p.m., he fell from his eighth-floor balcony. His body was discovered by a neighbour. He shared the apartment with his wife, but she was away on a business trip in London at the time.'

'And there was no sign of foul play at the scene? No signs of a struggle?'

Rick shook his head. 'No – no signs anyone else was there.'

'What did his wife say?' Karen asked. 'Was he suicidal?'

'She told the investigating officers he'd suffered from periods of depression in the past, but he'd never talked about suicide.'

'Do you have her current address?'

Rick handed Karen another piece of paper. 'As far as I know, she's still living in the same apartment. It's registered in her name and she's on the electoral roll. The apartment building is right in the centre of Lincoln, by the wharf. She hasn't responded to my call, but her office said she's working from home today.'

Karen looked at her watch. 'I think we should talk to her now.'

'I'll come with you, shall I?'

Karen nodded. 'What about the other two boys?'

'I'm pretty sure we've identified the right men. One still lives in Skellingthorpe, and the other lives in Hykeham. Sophie's waiting for a phone call from Greenhill Academy to confirm the details. They keep records of all previous students, so we can crossmatch their dates of birth.'

'Excellent. Hopefully that won't take too long.' Karen smiled. It looked like the case was slowly coming together.

Before they left the station, Karen caught up with Sophie. She pulled over a chair and sat down beside the young officer at her desk. 'How's everything going?' She was asking about the case, but also wanted to find out how Sophie had been coping since their chat.

'Good,' Sophie said, pausing with her fingers above the keyboard.

'Rick told me you're tracking down home addresses for Stuart Bennett and Michael Simpson?'

'Yes. I have addresses already, but I'm just waiting to crosscheck our information with Greenhill Academy.'

'Great work,' Karen said. 'Rick and I are going to go and talk to James Hunter's widow. Are you okay here?'

'I'm fine. Once I have confirmation from the school, do you want me to contact Stuart Bennett and Michael Simpson?'

'Yes. We need to speak to them as soon as possible.'

As Karen walked out of the office with Rick, she turned back to see Sophie furiously typing away. She definitely seemed to have more energy now, and Karen hoped she was feeling more positive about the job.

James Hunter's widow, Diana, lived on the eighth floor of Mercury Apartments, a tall, modern block set back from the river. When Rick and Karen pulled up outside, Karen was surprised to see that the view of the river was almost completely blocked by a multistorey car park.

'That sprung up out of nowhere,' Karen commented. She'd always found Lincoln a pain for parking.

She drove into the car park, took a ticket from the machine and picked a spot on the first floor. After they'd walked down the stairs, Karen noticed a homeless girl sitting cross-legged on the concrete floor. She was bundled up, wearing a huge blue fleece jacket and a scarf. Propped up against her legs, next to a folded pink blanket, was a cardboard sign which read: *Fifteen pounds will get me a safe bed for the night.*

Rick pulled out some coins from his pocket and put them on the blanket.

'Thanks very much,' she said, smiling up at him.

It was a prime spot, right by the pay machine. She'd chosen it well. People would have their hands in their pockets or their purses out, but it wasn't too far inside the car park, so it didn't feel too dark or gloomy. She had an open paperback beside her, a Minette Walters psychological thriller, *The Sculptress.*

As they walked away from the car park and crossed the road to get to the apartment block, Karen turned to Rick. 'You do know she's not planning to put that money towards a safe bed for the night?'

'Of course,' Rick said. 'I know what she'll be using the money for, but I find it impossible to walk by and not give her anything.'

Karen couldn't argue. But she'd seen signs of addiction on the girl, and suspected heroin. The sight of that young woman made her feel frustrated and angry. It was such a waste. Where were her family and friends? How had she ended up sitting in a car park, begging just so she could get her next hit?

Just before they reached the apartment building, Karen turned back and saw the girl had picked up the paperback and started to read.

Karen put her hands in her pockets and looked up at the building looming above them. There were two balconies on each floor. She counted up to the eighth floor and then shuddered. It was a hell of a drop. She looked down at the grey pavement and wondered where he would have fallen. Six months had passed, and there was no sign a tragic death had occurred in the vicinity. The area had been cleaned up and life had moved on.

There was no lock on the main door, so they walked straight into the lobby and stopped at the lift.

'I hope she's home,' Rick said. 'I'm surprised she still lives here. I wouldn't have wanted to stick around after what happened.'

'She's still on the electoral roll, so if she has moved, she hasn't told anybody.'

They travelled up to the eighth floor and stepped out into a hallway. There were wooden doors with brass numbers to each of the four apartments. Karen rang the bell of number 81.

They waited, but there was no answer. She rang the bell again and turned to Rick. 'I hate to say it, but it looks like we've had a wasted journey.'

As they turned to head back to the lift, the door to apartment 84 opened, and a woman carrying an infant looked out. 'Are you looking for Diana? Or are you here to view the flat?'

'We wanted to have a word with Diana,' Karen said. 'Do you know when she'll be back?'

The woman shuffled the baby on her hip to the other side, and it began to cry. 'I'm afraid not. She's not here much at the moment. She's got the flat up for sale, and they've had a lot of viewings. I think she might be staying with her sister.'

That made sense. It was understandable that Diana wouldn't want to stay in the apartment after what had happened to James.

'Do you have a contact telephone number for her?' Rick asked hopefully.

The woman shook her head. 'No, sorry. We're not all that close. I just say hello whenever we run into each other.'

'I'll leave you my card,' Karen said, reaching into her jacket pocket. 'If you do see Diana, can you ask her to give me a ring? She's not in any trouble,' Karen added, seeing the woman's eyes widen when she saw Karen's card had *Lincolnshire Police* stamped on top of it.

'Is this to do with what happened to her husband?'

Karen gave a tight smile, not wanting to discuss Diana's private business with a neighbour. But she didn't want to put the woman off talking, either. If she'd seen or heard anything that night, it could be useful.

'Were you here when it happened?' Karen asked.

The woman nodded solemnly. 'Yes, it was awful. Sirens everywhere, and police running up and down the corridor. I couldn't believe it. He just didn't seem the type.'

Karen had to wonder what the 'type' was. That was the problem when people were depressed. They didn't show it to others until it was too late.

'Did you hear anything before the emergency service vehicles got here?' Rick asked.

'No, nothing. I'm just glad I wasn't outside at the time. It must have been awful for the person who found his body.'

Karen knew from skimming the report that one of the neighbours had heard a shout and found James soon after he fell. 'Did James have any visitors that evening?'

'I don't think so, but I'm on the other side of the building, and fortunately the walls are quite thick here. This little one screams at the top of her lungs, so we need a bit of soundproofing.' She smiled as she jiggled the baby in her arms.

Karen thanked her, and the neighbour closed her door.

Walking back to the lift, Karen sighed. Hopefully, Sophie had had more luck contacting Stuart Bennett and Michael Simpson.

As the lift doors opened, Karen and Rick stood back, seeing it was occupied. A short, blonde woman carrying a bunch of flowers stepped out of the lift and gave them a short, curt smile before striding towards the door of number 81.

'Diana Hunter?' Karen asked.

The woman turned with her keys in her hand. 'Yes?' Her gaze flickered between Karen and Rick.

'I'm DS Hart, and this is my colleague, DC Cooper.' Karen held out her warrant card. 'We'd like a quick chat if that's possible?'

Diana turned back to open the door. 'Come in.'

She carried the bouquet of chrysanthemums out in front of her as she led the way into the apartment. Inside, the furnishings were neutral and warm. The main living area was all open-plan, and on the counter between the kitchen and the dining area sat a vase of flowers that had seen better days.

Diana dropped her handbag on the counter, tutted at the flowers and threw them in the bin.

She gestured at the new chrysanthemums. 'I'm trying to sell the flat,' she said. 'It's silly, I'm sure fresh flowers don't make a difference.' She shrugged off her coat and then gestured to the sofa. 'Please, sit down. Can I get you a drink?'

Both Karen and Rick refused her offer, but went to sit on the sofa.

Diana pulled out a chair next to the dining table and sat down. 'How can I help you?'

'It's about your husband,' Karen began.

Diana gave a sad smile. 'I thought it might be.' She wrapped her arms around herself and shivered. 'I'm sorry it's cold in here. I haven't had the heating on. I've moved in with my sister for a bit. I can't stay here. Not now. I can't wait to get rid of the place, to be honest.'

Karen didn't blame her. 'It can't be easy.'

'No.' Diana's gaze drifted over to a framed photograph of her and her husband on their wedding day.

'It's just a follow-up visit,' Karen said, not wanting to get into the whys and wherefores of Oliver Fox's death. 'What can you tell us about James's state of mind before it happened?'

Diana's lips tightened into a firm line, and she shook her head. 'I'm perfectly aware that your report said he killed himself, but there's absolutely no way.'

Karen leaned forward, resting her elbows on her knees. 'What do you think happened?'

Diana blinked away tears. 'It must have been an accident. He couldn't have meant to do it. James was a practising Catholic, and he considered suicide a sin. He was drunk . . . He'd had a problem with drink for a long time, but he'd been sober for two years. He went to his AA meetings like clockwork, and he was fine when I left for London. Don't get me wrong, he had his dark days. Sometimes he would go for weeks, barely talking to me. I suggested counselling, but he told me that wasn't how he dealt with things.'

'So you think he got drunk and fell?' Rick asked.

'That has to be it. There's no way he would have deliberately tried to kill himself. We had plans. There were so many things we wanted to do. Just the week before, we'd booked a holiday to Prague . . .'

They asked Diana some more questions, but no matter how they pressed her, she still insisted James hadn't been suicidal. She knew the signs, she told them. She knew when he was getting into one of his dark periods, and it hadn't been like that. He simply must have been so drunk he'd done something stupid and leaned over the balcony railings too far.

It was an uncomfortable conversation. Nobody enjoyed questioning a distraught relative, but Karen felt the widow's point of view was extremely valuable.

Perhaps something had happened after Diana left for London which prompted James to commit suicide. Maybe he'd received the same letter as Albert Johnson and William Grant. Either that, or something far worse had happened . . .

Maybe he hadn't jumped or fallen. Maybe he'd been pushed.

CHAPTER TWENTY-SEVEN

After leaving Diana Hunter, they sat in the car and checked their messages. DI Morgan had sent Karen a text to say he'd spoken to Elizabeth and was now heading to Stephen Fox's estate agency offices on Mint Street. So far, he'd been unable to track down Martin Fox.

Karen typed out a quick reply. Either of Oliver's sons could have sent the letters to Albert Johnson and William Grant. Had they found out what had happened to their father and decided to send threatening notes as payback?

Karen slipped her phone back in her pocket as Rick said, 'Sophie has confirmed home and work addresses for Stuart Bennett and Michael Simpson.'

She smiled. 'Excellent. Where are they?'

Rick scrolled through the message on his phone. 'Stuart Bennett works near Hykeham at a car showroom. Sophie called him and said we needed to speak to him, but she hasn't told him why. And Michael Simpson works at Pennells, which is also in Hykeham.'

'Good,' Karen said. Her first instinct was to bring both men in for questioning, but there was no need to rush. They needed to take their time and do this properly. It wasn't as if they had enough information to charge the men for the thirty-year-old crime, and Bennett and Simpson weren't any risk to the public, as far as Karen could tell. However, she did want to speak to them as soon as possible.

'Right, we'll speak to Stuart Bennett first,' Karen said as she began to reverse out of the parking space. 'We won't bring him in yet. Let's see what he has to say for himself.'

Fifteen minutes later, they turned left off the A46 at Damon's restaurant.

'There it is, just up ahead,' Rick said, pointing out the large Volvo sign.

Outside the car showroom were dozens of used vehicles, polished and buffed with signs on their windscreens. Karen picked an empty parking spot beside an XC60. They got out of the car and strode quickly towards the glass building as it began to rain.

Inside, it was quiet. A young woman sat behind a computer at the reception desk, and five members of the public were milling around looking at the cars on display indoors. Karen identified two salesmen by their navy-blue suits and carefully combed hair.

As she walked towards the receptionist, Karen flashed her warrant card. 'We'd like to speak to Stuart Bennett, please.'

The woman's eyes widened and she put down her pen. 'Oh, what's he done?'

Some people had odd reactions when they saw the police, assumed they were either there to arrest somebody or to bring bad news. But, in reality, they usually just wanted to ask some questions.

When Karen didn't give her an answer, the girl half-stood behind the desk and pointed towards a black Volvo V40 and a blond-haired man standing next to it. 'That's him,' she said.

'Thank you,' Karen said, and she and Rick started to walk over to Bennett.

He spotted them coming towards him from about ten feet away. He paled and put one hand on the bonnet of the car beside him to steady himself.

Sophie had phoned ahead, so he'd known they were coming, but Karen hadn't expected a reaction this strong. Unless he knew *why* they were there.

'Mr Bennett?' Rick asked as they reached his side.

'Yes?'

'I'm DC Cooper, and this is DS Hart. Have you got time for a few questions? It's quite important.'

Stuart blinked. 'Of course . . . We can talk over here.' He led the way to a small alcove, and then opened the door to a tiny room that Karen guessed they used as some kind of break room. It smelled of air freshener and stale coffee. On a bench set back against the wall there was a small coffee machine next to a kettle.

'Would you like a drink?' Stuart asked, pointing at the kettle and then shoving his hands in his pockets when he noticed he was shaking.

'No, thanks,' Karen said, and Rick shook his head.

'Do you know why we're here, Stuart?' Karen asked.

Stuart ran a hand through his fair hair and took a couple of shaky breaths. He shook his head and then nodded, looking confused and scared at the same time. He was leaning heavily on the back of a chair, breathing fast. Karen was worried he was going to hyperventilate.

'Come and sit down, Stuart. Try to relax. We're just going to have a conversation.' She put a hand under his elbow and gently urged him to sit down on the chair.

Karen sat beside him, and Rick sat opposite.

Stuart rested his forearms on the table and tried to slow his breathing. They gave him a moment to recover.

When he finally looked up, he said, 'I think it's about something that happened a very long time ago.' He shot a glance at Karen and then at Rick.

'Yes, we want to speak to you about a man called Oliver Fox,' Karen said.

Stuart had already looked pale, but now his skin developed a greenish tinge, and he clapped a hand over his mouth, standing up rapidly and knocking his chair to the floor. He yanked open the door and ran out.

Rick got to his feet. 'Is he doing a runner?'

Karen sat back in her chair and crossed her legs. 'I think he's gone to the bathroom, probably to throw up.'

Rick righted the fallen chair and went into the corridor. 'Should I go after him?'

Karen shook her head. 'I don't think you need to. He'll be back.'

'You sure?'

She shrugged. 'Where else is he going to go? We know where he lives. He's been trying to hide from this for three decades, but he can't hide anymore.'

Rick kept his gaze on the corridor, looking for Stuart. 'How did he know we'd come about Oliver Fox? Sophie didn't tell him.'

'William Grant and Albert Johnson have been trying to protect Stuart Bennett for the past thirty years. Old habits die hard. I imagine William felt guilty about giving us the names of the three boys, and called Stuart and Michael to warn them.'

'Oh,' Rick said. 'I suppose that makes sense.'

Stuart returned a few minutes later.

'Sorry about that,' he said. He was still shaking, but his breathing was now under control.

'Have a seat, Stuart.' Karen said.

Stuart sat down in the seat he'd vacated in a rush.

Rick shut the door firmly and sat opposite him. 'Can you tell us what happened to Oliver Fox, Stuart?'

Stuart stared down at the table. 'We found him. He was lying on the floor in the boys' changing room.'

'Who was with you when you found him?' Karen asked.

'James and Michael.'

'Do you remember their full names?' Rick asked.

Stuart nodded. 'James Hunter and Michael Simpson.'

'And you were all together when you found him?'

Stuart's face crumpled. 'He said we had to meet him there after school. We didn't want to go. He said he would hurt my little sister if I told anyone.'

He began to tremble.

Karen took a deep breath. She wanted answers, but watching Stuart's expression as he relived the experience that must have haunted him for thirty years made her pause. It wasn't hard to picture him as a scared thirteen-year-old boy. 'So you were supposed to be meeting Oliver Fox in the changing room. All three of you?'

Stuart nodded.

'And when you went into the changing room, you found him on the floor?' Karen asked after a moment when Stuart didn't elaborate.

He took a deep breath and looked up at the ceiling. His voice was tight and strained as he spoke. 'There was a lot of blood. He was lying on his front, and when James pulled him over to see what was wrong, he got blood all over his hands and clothes. He stood up quickly but slipped. There was blood on the floor. We went to help him up and I got it all over my hands.' Stuart stared down at his hands as though he could see the blood there now.

'We went running out of there as fast as we could. We were going to go to the headmaster's office because we knew he always worked late, but then we passed Mr Grant's classroom and saw he was there.'

Karen leaned forward. 'So you told Mr Grant what you'd found?'

Stuart raked a hand through his hair. 'Yes, he took control and went to get the headmaster. Then they told us to get in the shower and clean up and gave us some clothes to wear. I don't know what they did with the body. I didn't ask. They told us never to talk about it, and we didn't.'

'You never told anyone about this?' Karen asked. 'Not even your parents?'

Stuart shook his head firmly. 'No, I didn't want anyone to know because then I would have to talk about what he did. I was just glad he was gone.'

'Did he do something that afternoon to make you uncomfortable?' Rick asked. 'If he did, and you or James or Michael got upset and pushed him . . .'

Stuart's head jerked upwards. 'We didn't kill him! We just found him like that. We didn't do anything.'

'All right,' Karen said, suspecting Stuart was close to losing control. They'd need him to come to the station to make a statement, but she didn't think he was going to be in any fit state to do that today.

'What did you suspect Mr Johnson and Mr Grant did with Oliver Fox's body?'

He shrugged. 'I don't know. They were trying to help us. I think they must have hidden it somewhere.'

Stuart rested his head in his hands. He seemed genuine. He had carried this trauma with him for thirty years, and it was still raw and painful.

'Have you kept in touch with James or Michael?' Karen asked.

Stuart leaned back and stared up at the ceiling again. 'I still see Michael from time to time. James moved away, went to university and built a life for himself. But six months ago I heard he'd killed himself. We went to the funeral.'

'I'm sorry,' Karen said. 'I need to ask you if you received an anonymous letter about that time.'

'We all did, I think. Mr Grant and Mr Johnson got them too. They all said: *It's time to pay for your crime.*'

'Did James get a letter?' Karen asked, watching Stuart carefully.

He shrugged. 'I'm not sure. We didn't keep in touch. I hadn't spoken to him in years. The letter came just after he died. I got mine a day or two before the funeral.'

Karen held back on further questions, sensing Stuart was finding this very difficult. She checked she had his correct home address and contact details, and asked him to come in to the station to make a statement the following day.

'But I have to work,' he said.

'If you like, you can come in and make your statement early, before you start work,' Karen said. 'What time is best for you?'

'I don't know.' He was losing the ability to make even simple decisions. Shock and anxiety could do that to people.

'As long as you make a statement tomorrow, we're very flexible on time, okay?' Karen said, trying to sound reassuring. It was hard to watch Bennett falling apart, knowing her questions were upsetting him.

'Would you like to go home now, Stuart?' Rick asked. 'We could give you a lift.'

Stuart shook his head. 'My wife is at home, but I don't want her to see me like this. I'll be fine. I'll just take a few minutes before I go back to work.'

He stood up from the table and shakily made his way out of the room.

Rick looked at Karen. 'Poor bloke. Sometimes I wish we didn't have to deal with cases like this. How could anyone do that to a young kid? After all this time, he's still hurting.'

Karen put her hand on Rick's shoulder. 'It's not the easiest part of the job, but someone's got to deal with it. It's a travesty that this didn't get picked up thirty years ago.'

CHAPTER TWENTY-EIGHT

Karen and Rick's next stop was Pennells, a garden centre in Hykeham not far from the Volvo showroom. They parked out the front by the hot tub section, and walked in through the sliding doors. It was a massive place filled with clothing, furniture and homeware, as well as the plants you'd expect to find in a garden centre.

They stopped beside the customer service section and asked where they could find Michael Simpson. They were pointed in the direction of the furniture department and followed the signs, walking slowly behind an elderly man pushing his wife in a wheelchair.

When they reached the furniture section, they stopped and scanned the area. On the right-hand side of the walkway, a tall, balding man was arranging smaller items on a shelf. He wore green trousers and a khaki shirt with a thin green tie. When he turned, Karen saw the name badge on his chest – *Michael*.

'Michael Simpson?'

He offered a nervous smile. There was a knowing look in his eyes that told Karen he'd been expecting them. He knew what this was about. A police visit to a big store like this could have been due to shoplifting, or perhaps an outdated trading licence, but he knew exactly why they were here.

Karen strongly suspected that he'd recently spoken to Stuart Bennett.

'That's me,' he said with false joviality. 'How can I help?'

They introduced themselves and asked for a quiet word.

'We can talk here,' Michael said. 'I'm not supposed to leave my section.' He gestured to the line of carved wooden ornaments he'd been setting out, a selection of cute little ducks and hedgehogs. He saw Karen looking at them and said, 'They're all handmade.'

'They're lovely,' Karen said. 'As you probably know, we're here to ask you some questions about Oliver Fox.'

The smile slid from Michael's face. 'I see. In that case, sod staying in my section, I need a cigarette. Can we talk outside? My cigarettes are in my car.'

Karen and Rick followed Michael out of the store. He stopped beside a metallic-blue Astra, rummaged inside the glove compartment and grabbed a packet of Marlboro cigarettes.

He pulled one out, lit it and leaned back against the car as he took a long drag.

'Sorry, terrible habit, but in times of stress . . .'

'We've spoken to Stuart Bennett,' Karen said.

Michael shrugged as though he'd expected as much. 'I suppose he's told you everything. There's not much I can add.'

'Did you hear about James Hunter's passing?' Karen asked.

He looked down at the cigarette pinched between his fingers and watched the curling smoke for a moment. 'Yes, it was very sad.'

'Perhaps you can tell us in your own words what happened to Oliver Fox.'

Michael turned, putting both hands on the roof of the car and staring down at the ground as though he didn't want to look them in the eye while he was talking. 'We found his body in the changing rooms. Then we told a couple of the teachers. They dealt with it. That's all.'

Karen could tell from the man's body language that was far from all. The way his eyes had clouded over and the way he was leaning against the car told her he was reliving the incident, picturing the blood and experiencing the fear, just as Stuart had done.

'Did you receive an anonymous letter a few months ago?' Rick asked, already knowing the answer.

'Yes, a cowardly bit of nonsense. It came in the post a few days after James died.'

'What did it say?' Rick asked.

'Can't remember. I burned it. If someone wants to say something to me, they can say it to my face.'

'We'd like you to make a statement, Michael. It might be a bit much for you today, but we'd appreciate it if you could come down to the station tomorrow.'

He nodded stiffly. 'Yes, I can do that.'

'In the course of our investigation, there have been various allegations against Oliver Fox,' Rick said. 'Namely that he abused his position as a teacher to take advantage of the children in his care. Would you say that was accurate?'

Michael let out a long breath. 'Yes, I'd say that was accurate. I'd go further than that and say that he was a dirty, nasty man and he deserved everything that happened to him.'

He dropped his cigarette on the ground and stamped on it, grinding it beneath his heel.

Rick and Karen were both feeling drained by the time they got back to Nettleham station. It was hard to find the motivation to put Michael Simpson and Stuart Bennett through rigorous questioning when it was obvious they were still tormented by what had happened all those years ago.

Before she'd spoken to them, Karen had wondered if either of them could have sent the notes. The team needed to be open to all possibilities, but she couldn't see a strong motive for either man hurting Albert Johnson, who'd tried to cover up what happened in order to protect them. Still, they'd both been under tremendous psychological stress, and that could trigger unexpected behaviour. She intended to keep an eye on them.

The job was easier when they had a clear-cut 'good guys versus bad guys' situation. Life was simpler when they had right on their side and the criminals were clearly defined. In this case, their main suspects were also victims, which added a whole layer of complications.

Karen had a long day ahead of her tomorrow. They had to conclude William Grant's questioning and take Michael Simpson and Stuart Bennett's statements.

Looking thoroughly worn out, Rick sat down beside Sophie's desk and brought her up to speed. Despite the fact Sophie seemed to be back on an even keel and had re-found her passion for the job, Karen was glad she'd had Rick by her side when she'd spoken to Michael and Stuart. She had a feeling that Sophie, who tended to see things in black and white, would very much be on the side of the two men who'd been abused.

Karen chased up the phone company who were supposed to be providing records for Albert Johnson. She was hoping they could find out who had made the anonymous calls to the retired head teacher. Having no luck, and feeling like she was going around in circles as she was placed on hold for the third time, Karen opened up the booking schedule on the system to reserve an interview room for William Grant the following morning.

She was just saying goodbye to the woman manning the phone company's unhelpful helpdesk as DI Morgan walked towards her, shrugging off his coat.

'How did you get on?' he asked, draping it over one arm.

'It wasn't easy,' Karen said. 'Both men were very upset by the news we were looking into Oliver Fox's death. They've been keeping this secret for a long time.'

Bennett's reaction had been more visceral and immediate, whereas Simpson had attempted to mask his emotions beneath a tough exterior. But while the two men were handling things in different ways, there was no doubt in Karen's mind they were both carrying a lot of pain.

'Did they confess to killing Oliver Fox?' DI Morgan asked.

Karen shook her head. 'Nothing as simple as that, I'm afraid. Both Simpson and Bennett were consistent in their stories. They said they found the body in the boys' changing room and deny killing him or even witnessing what happened. They're coming in to make formal statements tomorrow.'

DI Morgan wheeled over a chair from DC Shah's empty desk and sat down. 'I've spoken to Stephen Fox. But I can't track his brother down and he isn't answering the phone. Both Elizabeth and Stephen say they have no idea where Martin is, but there's something odd going on. It's like they're protecting him.'

Rick had overheard their conversation and strolled over. 'I suppose the Fox brothers are top of our list of suspects as to who sent the anonymous letters?'

Karen shrugged. 'I can't think of anyone else who'd send them. Except maybe Elizabeth or Laura, but . . .'

'I know what you mean,' DI Morgan said as Sophie joined them. 'I can't picture Laura or Elizabeth sending those notes.'

'Do we work on the assumption the letters came from one of Oliver Fox's sons, then?' Sophie asked, tapping her pen against her hand.

'I don't think we can assume anything for sure, but they do have a motive,' Karen replied. 'The letters may have been the start of a campaign to clear their father's name.'

Sophie leaned against the desk, looking pleased with herself. 'While you were gone, I was working on the family trees. I discovered James Hunter was Albert Johnson's nephew. Albert had a younger sister called Daisy, who was James's mother.'

'Interesting,' Rick said. 'So that gives Albert another reason for protecting James. Maybe he found out his nephew was being abused by Oliver Fox . . . That may have driven him to a confrontation where Oliver was fatally injured.'

'Good theory,' Karen said. 'Although if there was as much blood as Michael and Stuart described, would Albert have been able to clean himself up in time? When the three boys went to him for help, they would have noticed if his clothes were bloodstained, wouldn't they?'

All four of them fell quiet, mulling things over. Karen's thoughts kept returning to the letters. The anonymous letters had all been received soon after James Hunter's death. Karen wished they knew whether James himself had received a letter. Had that driven him to suicide?

As if reading her mind, DI Morgan said, 'So, do we think James was pushed over the edge by the letter? Maybe it was all too much for him.'

'That could be it,' Karen said. 'What confuses me is why, after thirty years, someone would send those letters.'

Sophie said, 'Oliver Fox's remains were only found because Albert Johnson was trying to move the body. The letter must have scared him into thinking it was about to be discovered.'

'It wasn't the letter,' Karen pointed out. 'They didn't act until after Albert started to get nuisance phone calls. It was only then that Albert and William decided to move the body.'

Rick puffed out his cheeks as he exhaled. 'This case is confusing the heck out of me.'

Karen could see his point. She sat back in her chair, crossing her legs. She was missing a connection. It was infuriating. She needed to step back and look at the case objectively. She checked her watch. It was almost five.

There was no point staying here and getting nowhere. She needed to do something proactive. She stood up and grabbed her jacket. 'I'm going out for a while. I won't be long.'

Stuart Bennett couldn't stop shaking. He'd forgotten to put his jacket on when he went outside, so he was shivering from the cold as well as trembling from fear. He raked a hand through his blond hair and scrolled through the contacts on his mobile phone. He paused at the one he was looking for, and hesitated with his thumb over the screen.

How had it come to this? It wasn't fair. All he'd ever wanted was to be normal. He didn't want to be singled out. He hadn't wanted to be one of Oliver Fox's *special* students. He hadn't wanted any of this.

He pressed dial and held the phone up to his ear, looking around to make sure nobody could overhear him.

'Hello?'

'It's me. Did you tell them anything?'

'No, of course not, I stuck to what we planned. You?'

'Yeah, the same, but I'm really freaking out.'

There was a pause. Stuart closed his eyes and looked up at the cloudy sky. 'We need to meet,' he said.

Another pause, and then, 'Same place as last time?'

'All right. I'll be there in half an hour.'

Stuart hung up and looked at his phone. The screensaver was a picture of his wife and daughter. Somehow he was going to have to hold it all together for them. Would he go to prison? He didn't know. Maybe. He'd been a minor at the time. Surely they'd take that into account.

He tried to imagine what the expression on his wife's face would look like if he explained what had happened all those years ago. She'd be angry. Furious. Not because of what had happened in the past, but because he'd never told her.

But how could he?

Some secrets were better buried deep.

CHAPTER TWENTY-NINE

Karen sat in the car park at Pennells, drumming her fingers on the steering wheel. It was almost five thirty, but Michael Simpson's car was still in the car park. She'd pulled into a space beside a large 4 x 4 some distance away, so he wouldn't spot her waiting for him to leave work.

She was being overly cautious. He was unlikely to notice she was there, and he hadn't seen her car when they'd visited earlier. She could be wasting her time, which was why Karen hadn't told the rest of the team what she was planning. This way, if nothing came of her following Michael, she wouldn't look like an idiot.

She kept her eyes trained on the exit as she reached over to turn up the radio. Lincs FM was playing 'Killer Queen'. He should be out by now. Perhaps he'd got a lift home, Karen thought. Was he already having a nice cup of tea with his family while she was sitting alone in her car? She sighed. Was she doing this so she had a good excuse not to go out on the date her sister had set up for tonight?

Then she spotted him, striding through the sliding doors and jogging down the steps.

Karen smiled and leaned forward, turning on the engine.

He could be going straight home. If that was the case, she would follow him there and then go back to the station. No harm done.

She could be reading too much into things, but she couldn't shake the feeling they'd only scratched the surface of this investigation. It wasn't that she thought Michael or Stuart had been lying to them, but there was still so much she didn't understand. Michael had known they were coming to talk about Oliver Fox, and that meant either Stuart or William Grant had given him a heads-up. Perhaps the men were still very close. Maybe they'd agreed on a story and were sticking to it.

As she left the car park she allowed another car to pull in front of her, so he was less likely to notice her tailing him. Then she indicated left just after he did and pulled out on to the A46. He hadn't travelled far when he turned right. Karen slowed and pulled into the filter lane, hoping he wasn't paying attention to who was behind him.

He'd turned on to a country lane, and Karen followed, but kept well back to avoid being seen. She continued on the long, winding road, swearing under her breath when a tractor pulled out in front of her, causing her to brake.

She edged sideways, looking past the tractor, checking Michael was still in front.

At least the tractor was good camouflage, she thought with a wry smile, before braking again as she saw Stuart turn off and park outside The Fox and Hounds pub. She drove around to the back of the pub, then waited a minute or two before following him in.

The pub was quiet. A few locals were gathered around the bar, and a couple of tables were occupied by families taking advantage of the early-bird special. Karen walked up to the bar, scanning the area for Michael. It only took a moment to find him. He was sitting on the other side in the restaurant section. Opposite him was Stuart Bennett.

They were deep in conversation and didn't notice her. She walked up to them slowly and paused by their table.

Stuart looked up and did a double take.

'Hello, gentlemen. You don't mind if I join you, do you?'

They both looked horrified.

Karen didn't wait for an invitation and slid into the seat beside Stuart. 'Are you getting your stories straight for tomorrow?'

They looked at each other rather than at Karen, and then Stuart groaned.

Michael turned to her. 'It's not like that. We just needed someone to talk to. Someone who understood.'

'You've stayed close friends all this time?'

Michael nodded. 'Yes, we did. James went off to university, so it was never really the same with him, but we kept in touch.'

Karen could understand their need to turn to each other for support. Guilt weighed heavily on her as she thought about her next question. Was finding out the truth really worth digging all this up? If these boys got charged for the murder of Oliver Fox, would that be justice?

'I know this is a horrible time for you. It must be awful to be reminded of everything that happened, but it's better to be honest now. You were both minors. That will be taken into consideration. If you killed him because of what he was doing to you—'

'Honestly,' Michael said, looking at Karen earnestly, 'we told you the truth. We found him like that . . . covered with blood. We have no idea what happened to him.' He turned to his friend. 'Do we . . .'

Stuart shook his head. 'No, we don't know what happened.'

Were they covering for each other? Or covering for James? Karen couldn't tell.

'You mentioned you kept in touch with James?' she said.

They both nodded.

'Do you think he committed suicide?'

Michael swallowed. 'Well, yes, that was the verdict, wasn't it? We went to his funeral. They said it was suicide.'

'If he'd received the same letter as you, could that have driven him to suicide?'

'Honestly, if you'd asked me that a few years ago, I would have said no. But *something* must have driven him to it.'

She talked to them for a little longer, trying to worm the truth out of them, but they stuck to their story. Neither of them admitted to hiding anything.

Were they lying? Karen wished there was some kind of litmus test to find out. She never held much stock in lie detector tests, but right now she wouldn't turn one down.

Karen left Simpson and Bennett at the pub after reiterating how important it was to be completely honest when they made their statements tomorrow. She travelled back to Nettleham HQ thinking how odd this case had been so far. It was nothing like any of her previous investigations. So much time had passed since Oliver Fox's death. The suspects were now forty-three years old, but at the time they'd only been thirteen. There wasn't the urgency there would usually be in a murder case, and despite the fact the top brass liked to say they treated every murder case equally, no matter how historical, it wasn't true. Karen wouldn't have left two murder suspects chatting in a pub in any other case. She'd be bringing them in.

She glanced at the clock on the dashboard. She still had time to go back to the station, file some paperwork and then go home and get ready for this date, although she was tempted to cancel.

She flicked the indicator and turned right on to Deepdale Lane, and sighed. Her sister was right. She needed to start living again. Besides, it was just a date. How bad could it be?

Sophie was working hard. It felt good to have the wind back in her sails. They now had a puzzle to solve, and that was the part of the job Sophie loved and excelled at. Karen was right. She just needed to give herself time. Impatience wasn't a good trait in a police officer. The job involved lots of methodical work and required reports and forms to be filled in for nearly every task. It wasn't all action and chasing criminals down the street. At the end of the day, she loved her job.

Sophie's trouble was, she wanted everything yesterday and couldn't help measuring herself against other people's career trajectories.

Who needed Monaco and swanky parties with glamorous guests when she could be here, working on a case and strategising with the rest of the team? She was doing something that really made a difference, and she should be proud of that.

She was transferring files into a designated folder on her computer when Karen came striding into the office.

'Any luck, Sarge?' She wasn't sure where Karen had rushed off to earlier and was intrigued.

Karen paused by her desk. 'I waited outside Pennells and followed Michael Simpson. He met up with Stuart Bennett after work.'

Sophie raised an eyebrow. 'Were they discussing the case? Getting their stories straight?'

Karen shrugged. 'That was my first thought, but I think they're just scared and needed some support. They still insist they didn't kill him.'

Sophie found that very hard to believe. She thought the best option for the men was to tell the truth. They'd only been young at the time, and the courts would take that into account and be very sympathetic. By lying about it, they would only make the police dig further into the past and unearth more secrets, causing their families more pain.

She supposed there was still a slim chance they hadn't done it. She tapped her pen on the desk. Theoretically, the person who'd attacked Oliver Fox could be any one of a hundred other students, or an outraged parent . . .

She watched as Karen stuffed some paperwork into the drawers beneath her desk and then switched off her computer.

'Are you going home, Sarge?' Sophie asked, surprised. Karen was usually one of the last to leave when they were working on a big case.

'I'm going on that date tonight. I have to be there at seven thirty.' Karen grimaced, making it quite clear she wasn't looking forward to it. 'I've told DI Morgan, but if I'm needed, I can come back in.'

Sophie brightened. 'Oh yes, I forgot about that. Have fun. And if you do need to make a quick getaway, send me a text and I'll ring you.'

'Thanks.' Karen picked up her handbag and keys. 'Are you doing okay, Sophie?' she asked, pausing by her desk on the way out.

'Much better now, thanks,' Sophie said. 'I'm just going to organise the information I collected on the old students of Greenhill Academy. Hopefully it won't be needed, but it's good to be prepared.'

Karen smiled. 'It is. But don't work too hard. I have a feeling tomorrow is going to be a very long day.'

CHAPTER THIRTY

Karen made it back home in record time. She was getting out of the car when her neighbour, Christine, waved to her over the fence. 'I'm just off to the pub for dinner with Pam and wondered if you fancied coming along?'

'I can't tonight, I'm afraid,' Karen said, grabbing her handbag from the passenger seat and then shutting the door.

'Is work keeping you busy?' Christine asked.

Karen wished it *was* work. She would rather face a lock-up full of drunks tonight than go on this date. Why had she ever agreed?

She locked the car and said, 'No, it's not work. I'm going on a date.'

The look of surprise on Christine's face made Karen feel even worse. Was the fact she was going on a date really such shocking news?

'You look a little startled,' Karen said with a laugh.

'Ignore me, Karen. I'm pleased for you. You go out and have fun. You don't want to be stuck in the local with us oldies.'

Christine gave a cheerful wave, opened the gate and walked off along the pavement.

Despite the fact she was running late, Karen paused to watch her go. Right now, she'd give anything for a night in the local with a bunch of oldies, as Christine called them.

Her phone beeped, and she yanked it out of her pocket and saw that it was a message from her sister.

What are you wearing for your date?

Oh, she hadn't even thought about that yet.

She raced inside and called for a taxi before heading upstairs. She was in and out of the shower within five minutes, feeling grateful her short hair didn't require much attention. She selected a pair of straight-cut trousers and a black blouse from her wardrobe.

After looking at her reflection in the mirror, she worried that the top might be a bit too low-cut. No time to change now, though. She grabbed a necklace from the jewellery box on top of her dresser and then paused.

She swallowed the lump in her throat and fought back tears. It was a simple chain with a star-shaped pendant. Josh had bought it for her when they'd visited Switzerland before Tilly was born. With a shaking hand, she put the necklace back in the box and shut the lid. She'd do without jewellery tonight.

She turned around, looking for her perfume. A quick spritz of Chanel Allure and she was almost good to go.

Shoes . . . She looked at the bottom of the wardrobe, her gaze lingering on a strappy pair of heels and then an elegant pair of court shoes with a high heel, but finally she decided to opt for boots. They had a small heel and were relatively smart, but far more comfortable than the others. She wasn't sure how much walking she was going to do, and in Lincoln it was best to be prepared.

A beep from outside told her the taxi had arrived, so she grabbed her jacket, shoved her feet into the boots and rushed downstairs, grabbing her handbag on the way out. Her hair was still damp, but it should dry on the drive to Lincoln.

The traffic was bad, due to a lorry that had double-parked on Lindum Hill, so Karen asked the driver to drop her outside the bingo hall. She passed the library and the Drill Hall, and made her way towards the alleyway that ran down the side of Pizza Express and would bring her out at the bottom of Steep Hill.

As she walked, she pulled out her mobile and called DI Morgan.

'Have you been running?' he asked after Karen breathlessly filled him in on her conversation with Michael Simpson and Stuart Bennett at the pub.

'No, I'm walking uphill, and I haven't even got to the really steep part yet. Anyway, what are you doing tonight?'

'I'm doing some more unpacking and then getting a takeaway,' he said.

'Sounds good to me,' Karen said, doing up her coat as she walked. And it did sound good. A nice takeaway with someone she knew sounded far more appealing than sharing drinks with someone she'd never met.

'Well, if the date goes badly, you can always join me later. I could do with some more help, so long as you hold back the comments on my music collection.'

Karen laughed. 'I'll let you know.'

God, she was shattered. This hill seemed to get steeper and steeper every time she came to Lincoln.

'You all right? You sound like you've run a marathon.'

Karen pulled a face at the phone. 'It's *really* steep.'

'Yes, well, you better hang up before you run out of oxygen.'

'Ha ha, speak to you later.'

She put her mobile back in her bag and moved out of the way for a couple walking past her, arm in arm.

Why was she being so negative? All she had to do was stay for a couple of drinks. The White Hart did excellent cocktails, so that was a bonus. Even if the date was terrible, at least the drinks would be good.

◆ ◆ ◆

After his conversation with Karen, DI Morgan spent a moment staring down at the screen of his phone. He felt bad lying to her, but it couldn't be helped. He couldn't explain what he was doing right now without getting into a whole load of background information that he wasn't ready to share.

He turned back to look at the house he'd been watching. Louise Jackson's house.

It was dark now, but the curtains were still open, and the lights were on downstairs.

She'd been home for over half an hour, and DI Morgan had been watching and waiting.

He'd seen a man he didn't recognise let himself into the house, but still he did nothing but watch.

A few minutes later, when his phone buzzed in his pocket, DI Morgan thought it might be Karen calling to tell him about her disastrous date already, but it wasn't.

Rob Miller's name flashed up on the screen.

As Karen approached the White Hart, her footsteps slowed. Did most people feel like this before they went on a date? Karen couldn't honestly remember. She'd met Josh when she was nineteen, and hadn't dated much before she met him.

She took a deep breath and walked into the pub.

She recognised Tom Prentice from her sister's description, and it seemed he recognised her. He was standing close to the bar, nursing a pint.

He walked towards her. 'Karen?'

She nodded and tried to produce a friendly smile.

'I'm Tom.' He held out his hand.

'Nice to meet you.'

'Likewise. Emma's told me a lot about you. I went to their house for a dinner party last week. Lovely couple.'

'Yes – yes they are.' She glanced at the bar. 'Shall we get a drink?'

'Oh, of course, let me.' He managed to find a space at the bar, and Karen asked for a margarita.

They chatted for a while as the barman prepared Karen's drink. The conversation seemed to flow easily, thanks to Tom. He obviously liked to talk, but that was better than sitting there in an awkward silence.

Ten minutes later, Karen was starting to consider whether it was too early to text Sophie for help. They were standing a little distance from the bar because there were no seats left. Tom had an amazing ability to keep up a monologue about himself with no input from Karen at all. Karen wondered if he'd even notice if she wasn't there.

Plus, the music was too loud.

Now she sounded like her mother. She was getting old.

Boredom had made her drink quickly, and she was rapidly getting to the end of her first margarita. She suspected Tom noticed, because suddenly he excused himself to visit the little boys' room. His loss, Karen thought. It was her round.

As soon as he left her side, Karen headed to the bar to order another cocktail. The barman was a young man with floppy hair and a goatee, and Karen thought he might be a student at the university.

When he set the margarita down on a small paper mat, she slid a ten-pound note across the bar.

He took the money, and then leaned forward so Karen could hear him above the music. 'First date tonight?'

Karen picked up her drink. 'How did you guess?'

He glanced to the side of the bar, presumably to make sure Tom wasn't coming back yet. 'Well, don't tell him I told you, but he was in here last week with another woman.'

Karen was a little surprised. Not that there was anything wrong with Tom Prentice going on other dates, but he didn't really seem to be the type to have great success with women.

'Thanks,' Karen said, turning away from the bar.

Dates were boring. She'd finish this drink and then make her excuses. There was no need to get Sophie involved.

Tom took a while getting back from the gents, and Karen thought there must be a queue. Men's toilets didn't usually have queues. It was always the ladies' bathroom that had a line. One of life's great mysteries. She waited a little longer, taking another few sips of her margarita, and gritted her teeth when somebody seemed to turn the music up even louder.

When Karen had almost finished her drink, she cut across the group of people in front of her and walked towards the toilets. They were in a long corridor behind the bar.

Tom was standing with his back to her, on the phone, and she couldn't resist getting a little closer to hear what he was saying. Her mother had always said she was too curious for her own good.

Tom was pretty predictable really.

'Sweetheart, I'm so sorry,' he crooned into the phone. 'Give the girls a kiss goodnight for me . . . I know, Linda, but it can't be helped. I'm the only one who knows the system . . . I'm only putting in these hours for you and the girls . . . Of course I'd rather be at home with you, darling.'

Karen had heard enough. She tapped him on the shoulder.

When he turned around, he jumped and almost dropped the phone.

Karen handed him her empty glass. 'I'm going home now, Tom, and I really think you should, too.'

CHAPTER THIRTY-ONE

DI Morgan tapped the red icon to ignore Rob Miller's call and stared at the house. From where he sat in his parked car, he could see into the living room and the dining area through his rain-splattered window. They were preparing dinner and drinking wine, but he wasn't close enough to see their expressions. He imagined the couple looked happy and relaxed. They wouldn't be so relaxed if they knew what Rob was up to.

He waited as they moved from room to room, disappearing from the dining area and then appearing again at the kitchen window. The window was partially clouded over with condensation from whatever it was they were cooking for dinner.

DI Morgan's phone rang again, but he muted it and reached for the door handle. He climbed out of the car, turning his collar up and hunching his shoulders against the rain. Slowly, he walked towards the house, then rang the doorbell and waited.

The door was opened by Louise's new man. Rob wouldn't be happy with that.

'I'd like to talk to Louise, please,' DI Morgan said.

The man looked surprised and reluctant to invite him in. He narrowed his eyes. 'We're just about to eat.'

'It won't take a moment.' He moved forward, so the man had no choice other than to step back or try to physically bar him from the house. The man chose to move aside. In the brief moment they stood there watching each other in the hall, DI Morgan weighed him up. He was tall and slim and wore a sulky expression. Most people's sense of hospitality would lead them to greet a visitor pleasantly, even if it was dinnertime. For all this man knew, DI Morgan could be a close friend of Louise.

Louise Jackson came out from the kitchen, holding a tea towel. She was wearing a white apron, which had *Keep Calm and Drink Prosecco* printed on it in red letters.

'I know you, don't I?' She looked embarrassed. 'Sorry, I've got a terrible memory.'

'I work out of Nettleham station.'

Louise's face cleared, and her concern evaporated. 'Ah, that makes sense. I must have seen you there.'

They stood awkwardly in the hallway, as the couple didn't invite him any further into the house. He reached for his wallet and pulled out his card, handing it to Louise.

She frowned and looked down at it, confused.

'You know DI Rob Miller,' DI Morgan said. It was a statement rather than a question.

Louise tensed, and her eyes widened slightly as she looked up at him. 'What is this all about?'

'I thought I should let you know Rob could cause you problems.'

'Problems?' the man repeated, folding his arms across his chest and taking a step away from Louise.

The happy expression on her face had completely evaporated now. She looked tense and frightened as she ran her hands through her hair and tucked the stray strands behind her ears. 'I left him. I moved away from the area to get away. What does it take to get the message through to him?'

'If anything happens or if he turns up here, you can call me. If I were you, I'd gather every piece of evidence you have and get a restraining order.'

She put a hand against the wall to steady herself and then stepped backwards, connecting with the stairs and sitting down with a bump. 'He was so controlling. I had to move away. He just didn't listen when I told him it was over. He's clever about it, though. He sends notes and flowers, but there's always a threatening overtone to them.'

DI Morgan listened to the woman explain how her six-month relationship with Rob Miller had ended. She described his obsession and his unhealthy appetite for directing her every move.

'I thought moving away would mean an end to it, but it isn't over, is it?'

'Perhaps I should leave you to it,' the man said, slipping past DI Morgan and reaching for his jacket on the hook by the door.

DI Morgan looked at him and said sharply, 'There's no need for you to go. In fact, I'm sure Louise could probably do with your support.'

The man offered up a weak smile and let go of the jacket. 'I don't want to get in the middle of anything. The last thing I want to do is get in the way.'

Both DI Morgan and Louise ignored him.

'He wants to know what you're doing and where you're living,' DI Morgan said. 'That doesn't seem healthy to me, and I thought you had a right to know.'

She nodded. 'I did get in touch with a solicitor, but I haven't bothered to follow up since the move.'

'Well, I suggest you try for that restraining order.'

She took a deep breath, reached for the bannister and hauled herself to her feet. 'I will. Thanks.'

'If you need help, you can call me,' DI Morgan said again, before turning and walking back to the front door.

He stepped outside into the soft rain, feeling guilty about ruining their evening. But she needed to know that Rob Miller was still sniffing around. When he got to his car, he looked back and saw both of them staring out of the kitchen window.

They didn't look happy, but at least she was on her guard. Rob Miller had picked the wrong man to blackmail this time. Yes, this would probably cost him. He'd enjoyed working in an environment where he was judged on his skills rather than his past. But if he wanted to build professional relationships with the people on his team, he couldn't keep secrets. Maybe he'd be shunned, but that was a chance he had to take.

There was only one way to deal with people like Rob, and that was to neutralise their power. The only way he could do that was to come clean to the people that mattered.

When Rick got home, he could hear his mother's laughter coming from the living room. He took off his shoes, hung his coat on the rack and then stuck his head into the kitchen.

'You sound like you're having fun,' he said.

Both Priya and his mother were sitting at the kitchen table, heads bent over what looked like children's books.

Rick frowned. 'Are you colouring?'

Priya looked up and smiled. 'Yes, and don't turn your nose up at it. Lots of adults do it now, myself included. It's relaxing.'

Rick raised his eyebrows, but he had to admit his mother seemed very happy. She reached for a pink pencil and began colouring in the tail of a unicorn.

On closer inspection, he could tell they weren't children's colouring books. They were far too intricate.

His mum looked up and smiled at him. 'Put the kettle on, Ricky, love.'

Rick did as he was asked, filling the kettle with water and then switching it on before turning to Priya.

'Thanks for this,' he said. 'It's lovely to see you both getting on so well. I don't mind telling you I was a bit worried about having a carer in the house.'

'We get on like a house on fire, don't we, love?' his mum said, grinning at Priya.

'Yes, we do,' Priya said as she put down the bright-green colouring pencil.

Rick got on with making the tea, thinking he'd lucked out when they'd had Priya assigned to them from the care agency. He was sure Sophie had had a hand in that, and he would always be thankful.

He filled the teapot and watched his mother shading in the leaves of a tree behind the unicorn.

Colouring, Rick smiled and shook his head. Who'd have thought it? She seemed perfectly content, though, and that was what mattered.

He'd found it very hard yesterday when his mother's friends had visited, but that wasn't Priya's fault. She was doing what was best for his mum. Keeping her entertained, but at the same time sticking to a routine. Every time he'd come home, they'd been doing different things – playing cards, chequers and now colouring.

It was strange, but he hadn't really thought about games. He knew his mother loved cards, but he hadn't wanted her getting upset when she forgot the rules or couldn't play properly. So instead of trying, he'd just stopped getting the cards out.

No doubt, there would come a time when she wasn't able to do things like this, but right now she was coping incredibly well.

He finished making the tea and placed the cups on the table. 'I'll take over now, Priya. If you want to get off home early.'

She flipped the colouring book closed and put the pencil she'd been using in a pile with the others. 'Thanks.'

'Unless you want to stay for dinner,' Rick offered. 'We're not having anything fancy, probably just pasta.'

'Thanks, but I have a date tonight.'

'Oh, well, have fun,' Rick said, and began to flick through the colouring book Priya had been using.

'You should have a go, Ricky,' his mum said.

Rick pulled a face. 'Me? Colouring? I haven't done that since I was about five.'

'Try it, you might like it,' Priya said, then leaned over to give Rick's mum a quick hug. 'I'll see you tomorrow, Mrs Cooper.'

Rick waited until he heard the front door close and then opened the colouring book again. Feeling a little self-conscious, he picked up the yellow pencil and began to colour in the sun.

Stephen Fox jogged up the steps and jabbed his thumb repeatedly at the doorbell. He could really do without this. As the elder brother, he'd always been expected to look after Martin, to stick up for him in school when he got bullied, to help him with his maths homework when he struggled, and, these days, to force the medication down his neck when he refused to take his pills.

He'd received a panicked call twenty minutes ago from Martin's ex-girlfriend. She hadn't seen him in over a year, but she'd come home from work to find him in her living room. She'd been almost hysterical on the phone, but Stephen was thankful she had called him rather than the police. He'd liked the woman on the few occasions he'd met her. Her name was Matilda, though everyone called her Matty. They'd met when Martin was on an even keel. His disease had peaked and troughed over the years, and he could be charming when the tablets were working.

A pale-faced Matty yanked open the front door. 'Thank God. He's in there.' She pointed to a door along the hallway.

'Everything is going to be fine, Matty,' Stephen said, trying to reassure her as he walked down the hall.

Martin had caused various problems over the years, and Stephen had assumed he was beyond being shocked by his brother's actions, but what he saw in the room made him stop and stare.

Martin was sitting cross-legged on the floor. He wore a polo shirt and jeans and had covered his arms and face with Biro scribblings. He reminded Stephen of a tattooed tribal warrior he'd once seen on the Discovery Channel.

He stepped into the room and turned in a slow circle. Scribbles defaced two of the walls. Matty's shiny ivory wallpaper with a circular pattern had been completely ruined.

'I'll pay to have it redecorated,' Stephen said, turning to look over his shoulder at Matty. 'I'm sorry.'

Her eyes were wide, and she was trembling as she asked, 'What's the matter with him?'

'He's not been taking his tablets. It happens sometimes.' He shrugged, trying to make it look like it wasn't a big deal.

'How did he get in?' she asked.

That was a good point. 'Does he still have a key?'

She shrugged. 'He shouldn't. Why don't you ask him?'

That was easier said than done. Trying to communicate with Martin when he was in this state was a gamble.

Stephen knelt beside him and lowered his head to make eye contact. He looked into his brother's dark eyes and put a hand on his shoulder. 'We need to go now, Martin. You're going to come with me, okay?'

Martin didn't respond. His dark eyes gazed into the distance. After collecting him from their mother's house the day before, Stephen had made sure Martin took his medication, but usually a few doses were needed before it really kicked in properly. He grabbed his brother's hand and lightly tugged on it. It took a little while, but Martin finally stood up. He allowed Stephen to pat down his pockets.

Stephen produced a key from the back pocket of Martin's jeans. 'I think this was how he got in.'

Matty's jaw dropped open and she snatched it back from Stephen. 'He must have made a copy!'

Stephen had no idea why Martin would have done that, but he had long ago stopped trying to work out how his brother's mind worked.

'I'll make sure he doesn't come back,' Stephen said.

'You'd better, or next time I'm calling the police.'

Stephen's eyes narrowed. Did she have no empathy or concern for Martin, a man she'd shared her life with for months? He understood it must have been a shock to find Martin in her house, but his brother had never been violent, and he'd assured her he would pay for the damage. Some people had no compassion.

'Come on, mate,' Stephen said, putting his arm around his brother's shoulders and leading him out of the room and to the front door.

They'd made it down the front steps and were almost at Stephen's car when Martin finally spoke. 'Where are we going?'

Stephen swallowed hard at the blank, lost look on his brother's face. 'We're going somewhere safe.'

CHAPTER THIRTY-TWO

Karen called DI Morgan as she walked away from the White Hart. He answered on the third ring, but his voice sounded distant, as though he was talking on a hands-free device.

'How did the date go?' he asked. 'I take it your evening wasn't great if you're calling me at eight thirty?'

'It was awful. *Horrible*. And that's all I'm saying on the matter. I'm starving, so I'm going to grab some food. Do you still fancy getting a takeaway, or have you already eaten?'

'Where are you now?'

'Lincoln. I'm walking downhill this time.'

'I gathered that. You're not out of breath.'

'Have you even walked up Steep Hill yet?'

'No.'

'Well, until you do, you shouldn't comment. Steep Hill would have Mo Farah panting for breath.'

DI Morgan laughed. 'I'll tell you what, I'm in the car at the moment so I'll come and meet you there. We can eat out.'

'Fine by me,' Karen said and then frowned, wondering about the change of plan. She'd thought DI Morgan was spending this evening unpacking.

'I'll be there in about fifteen minutes,' he said.

Karen saw she was approaching the Jews House Restaurant and slowed down. It was a cold evening, and the warm light through the mullioned windows looked welcoming. 'If you haven't walked up Steep Hill yet, I guess you haven't eaten at the Jews House?'

'I haven't, but I've heard of the restaurant. Someone recommended it a while ago.'

'It's nice,' Karen said. 'I haven't been for a while, but it's one of the oldest buildings in Lincoln. I'll see if I can get a table.'

'All right, I'll meet you there.'

The restaurant was constructed from the local limestone, and the building was so old it looked like it had sunken and settled into the street. It was part of the scenery.

Inside, it was warm and cosy, and although it was busy she did manage to get a table for two. She sat down and looked at the wine list. She'd already had two margaritas, and hesitated, wondering if she should order a bottle or just a glass. In the end, she opted for the bottle. It had been a long day and a frustrating evening.

Maybe there was something wrong with her, but she was almost glad the date had ended abruptly. It was a relief to get out of there. She wasn't ready. Perhaps she never would be. Anyway, growing old alone wasn't the end of the world.

After all, it could be worse. She could be married to someone like Tom!

No one would ever come close to Josh, and she'd just have to accept it.

Her mobile buzzed in her handbag, and when she pulled it out, she saw she had a text from her sister.

How's the date going?

It's not.

What do you mean???

It didn't work out.

:-(I'm sorry. I thought he seemed really nice.

First impressions can be deceptive.

Was he that bad?

I caught him on the phone to his wife or partner telling her to give the kids a kiss good night from him.

Seriously? He said he was single! He didn't mention kids either!

I get the impression he does this sort of thing a lot.

I'm so sorry!

I'll let you off if you promise to stop nagging me about dates.

:-(You can't just give up.

Yes, I can.

We just need to find you someone nice. One of Mallory's teachers is single . . .

NO.

Maybe just think about it.

NO.

He's really lovely. You'd like him, and he's definitely not married.

I'm putting my phone back in my bag now, Emma.

Are we still on for the weekend?

Yes. You're buying me lunch to make up for my awful evening.

Fair enough. See you Saturday xx

As she waited for DI Morgan, Karen occupied herself by people-watching and creating backstories for the diners sitting close by. There were a group of men on her right, and she guessed they were out for some kind of work-related evening.

The waiter brought the wine, an Australian Shiraz – one of the cheapest on the menu, as a detective sergeant's salary didn't go that far. She tasted it, and then nodded at the waiter to continue to fill her glass. She'd already looked at the menu and decided on the sea bass by the time DI Morgan entered the restaurant.

He saw Karen straightaway and walked over to join her. Turning down the offer of wine, the waiter poured him some water.

'Right,' he said, turning to Karen after the waiter had left. 'Are you going to tell me how the date went?'

Karen frowned and put down her wine glass. 'No, and I told you not to ask. I thought you were spending the evening unpacking.'

'So did I, but something came up.'

Karen topped up her glass. 'Work?'

'Not exactly,' DI Morgan said, reaching for his water. 'Although I did contact Superintendent Murray for permission to bring Martin and Stephen Fox in for questioning tomorrow, but she was dead set against it. After my visit with Elizabeth Fox, the superintendent received a phone call from Robert Fox, crying harassment.'

'That's ridiculous.'

DI Morgan sipped his water. 'Yes, I agree. She's trying to handle him with kid gloves, but it won't work. He'll never be satisfied with the way we're handling the investigation. Right now all we have is a series of letters, and the only strong suspects we have for sending them are Oliver Fox's sons. It has to be either Martin or Stephen.'

'It's possible they went further than sending letters,' Karen said. 'If Albert Johnson really was pushed down the stairs, that's attempted murder at the very least.'

DI Morgan lifted his shoulders and shrugged. 'But can we trust what he said? It wasn't an official statement. Just a few mumbled words to Rick before he died. Plus, there was no evidence there was anyone else at the scene.' He sighed. 'I really think we need to question Stephen and Martin.'

The conversation paused as the waiter came back to take their orders. Karen requested the sea bass, and DI Morgan asked for rib of beef.

When they were alone again, Karen leaned forward. 'I have to agree. It makes sense that it's one of the sons sending the letters. Somehow they found out how their father died, and this is some kind of weird revenge.'

'It's the only thing that makes sense to me. I'm tempted to go and talk to them tomorrow anyway. Even if I can't bring them in, it might help to put some pressure on.'

Karen smiled.

'What?'

'It's just you're normally very by the book. It's strange to hear you say that you're going to go against the superintendent's instructions.'

DI Morgan thought for a moment. 'I know you think I'm a little . . . controlled, but I wasn't always so careful.'

Karen rested an elbow on the table, interested. 'Really? I can't imagine you taking any risks.'

'I wouldn't say I was a risk-taker, but I wasn't quite as careful then as I am now.'

'So what happened to make you risk-averse?' Karen asked, trying to keep the tone light. She didn't want to seem like she was prying, but she'd been curious about DI Morgan's past and his reason for moving to Lincolnshire.

'I messed up on a case back at Thames Valley,' DI Morgan said. 'It's no big secret. There was an internal investigation, and I was placed on gardening leave for a while.'

Karen didn't dare say anything. This was the closest DI Morgan had come to confiding in her since he'd arrived in Lincolnshire.

He sighed. 'I nearly lost my job over it. By rights, I should have. Our team had been tracking a young man called Jason Starkness. He was a joyrider and had been in trouble for years. His mother was an alcoholic, and he had a younger brother, Harry, who was living with a foster family.

'We'd had a tip-off that Jason was in a residential estate. If we'd have gone to the right address, we would have picked him up. He would have spent the night in lock-up and then probably been given a suspended sentence. But I screwed up. I gave the wrong address. Instead of 13 McCarthy Way, I said 30 St Andrews Close. I hadn't written it down, and our logbook wasn't up to date.

'I couldn't believe I'd screwed up at first, but three other team members confirmed I'd said the wrong address.'

Karen waited. It didn't sound too bad to her. She'd done worse on many occasions. It was drummed into them during training to make detailed notes because sometimes things that didn't seem very important at the time could have far-reaching consequences.

DI Morgan took another sip of water and continued. 'We went to the wrong address, so Jason wasn't arrested. Instead, he stole another car and decided to pick up his ten-year-old brother, Harry.'

His grip tightened around the glass, and Karen sensed what was coming.

Her mouth was dry, but she didn't reach for her wine.

'Jason lost control of the car, and Harry died at the scene. He was ten years old, and he died because I gave the team the wrong address.'

'I'm sorry,' Karen said. It sounded completely inadequate, but she just didn't know what else to say.

'You're probably thinking I should have lost my job, and you'd be right. My notes weren't written up. We were busy that evening and everything else seemed more important than catching up on the logs. I put it off, intending to do it later when we had more time.'

He finally raised his gaze to meet Karen's.

She shook her head. 'It wasn't your fault. You weren't driving the car.'

'No, but if we'd gone to the right address, if I hadn't screwed up, Harry would still be alive.'

It was hard to argue with that logic, and Karen sensed he didn't want her to. He didn't want reassurance or to be consoled. She reached for her wine and took a long gulp.

It seemed once he'd started to talk, he wanted to tell her everything. 'After the investigation, I stayed at Thames Valley. I'm not a quitter. But then my marriage broke down. I was paying maintenance, and houses are so much more expensive down there, so I figured it was time for a transfer, a fresh start. There was nothing but stubbornness keeping me down there.'

But there was something else. Something Karen couldn't quite put her finger on.

'Scott,' she said. It felt strange calling him anything other than 'sir' or 'DI Morgan'. 'Is there something else you're not telling me?'

He smiled. 'Can't get anything past you, can I, Karen?'

'I don't mean to pry.'

'You're not. If you had done some digging, you would have found out about the disciplinary action and the internal enquiry. The records are out there in the open for anyone to find.'

'We've all made mistakes, but I can see that would have been a very difficult one to live with.'

DI Morgan nodded. 'It is, and the reason I'm telling you now is I had a visit last night from my old team leader, a man called Rob Miller. We never got along well. He's not a nice guy.'

'What did he want?'

'He wanted me to keep tabs on his ex-girlfriend and tell him what she was up to. In exchange, he wouldn't mention my past screw-up to my new colleagues.'

'What a complete and utter . . .' Karen trailed off after she noticed her raised voice had made the people at the next table turn.

DI Morgan smiled. 'Yeah, like I said, he's not a nice guy.'

Karen was dreaming when the phone woke her the next morning. It had been a nice dream. She'd been sitting in the garden, watching Tilly splash about in a paddling pool.

But the ringing of her phone caused the dream to fragment and drift away.

She fumbled for her mobile on the nightstand, but still groggy with sleep, she knocked it on to the floor. Cursing under her breath, she leaned over the side of the bed, groping for the phone.

She blinked at the screen. Six thirty a.m. The number was displayed as the control room at Nettleham headquarters. She frowned. She wasn't even on call.

She fell back against the pillows. 'DS Hart,' she answered sleepily.

'DS Hart, this is Sergeant Matthews. I'm calling to report an incident involving a person of interest in one of your current cases.'

Karen sat bolt upright. Now she was wide awake. 'Who?'

'William Grant.'

'What happened?'

'I don't have all the details. I can tell you he's deceased.'

Karen leaned back against the headboard, desperately trying to fit things together. She didn't function well when she'd just woken up.

How could William Grant be dead? They'd spoken to him yesterday . . . But the solicitor had said he was feeling unwell. Had the pressure been too much for him? She kicked back the duvet. *Damn.* Her first thought was pity for the old teacher, followed by a fervent wish they'd questioned him for longer yesterday. Now all his answers would die with him.

'How did he die?' Karen asked.

'Just a second.' There was a pause, and Karen suspected Sergeant Matthews was reading through the report. 'He was attacked at 82 Fallowfield, North Greetwell, last night. His body was found early this morning. Emergency services were called at five fifteen a.m.'

'You said 82 Fallowfield?' Karen tried to focus. William Grant's home address was Westfield Drive, so he must have taken her advice and stayed with family or friends.

'Yes.'

'That's not his primary address. Was he staying with friends or family?'

'According to the information I have here, it's his daughter's house.'

'Thank you. I'll go there straightaway.'

Karen hung up and quickly got out of bed. She didn't bother to shower, and only paused to splash some water on her face and clean her teeth before pulling on a fresh set of clothes.

She reached for her deodorant. What the hell had happened? She'd advised William not to stay at home, just in case Albert Johnson had been telling the truth when he told Rick he'd been pushed, but she hadn't seriously thought he was in danger. None of them had.

Karen's heart was thudding as she grabbed her keys. *She* had advised William to stay with someone else. They should have moved him into protective custody, or assigned officers to watch over him. This was their fault. *Her* fault. She should have seen this coming. Because it was an old case, they'd underestimated the risk.

They'd let their guard down, and William Grant had paid the price.

CHAPTER THIRTY-THREE

It was just after seven when Karen pulled up outside William Grant's daughter's home. Fallowfield was a quiet residential cul-de-sac, or it would have been quiet if it hadn't been full of emergency vehicles. Three marked police cars were lined up outside the residence, as well as an unmarked van. Karen guessed the van belonged to the crime scene officers. There was crime scene tape all along the perimeter of the property.

Karen walked up to the uniformed officer standing guard at the front of the driveway, showed him her warrant card and then signed in. 'Who's in charge?'

'DI Freeman was the duty SIO, ma'am. But due to the victim's involvement in one of DI Morgan's cases, he showed up a little while ago to take charge.'

Karen nodded. 'Is the pathologist here?'

'Yes.'

He lifted the crime scene tape, so Karen could duck beneath it, and she walked towards the semi-detached house. The adrenaline that had flooded her system after the phone call hadn't completely dissipated. She felt light-headed and sick.

In the upstairs windows on the left there were bright-pink curtains with a teddy-bear print, and hanging in the top-right window were blue curtains with what looked like a spaceship pattern.

Karen took a deep breath and hoped the children hadn't witnessed the attack on William Grant.

She paused near the front of the house, and put on some blue shoe protectors from a cardboard box and then a pair of gloves. Blood rushed in her ears as she followed the trail laid out by the crime scene team. Halfway around the side of the house, she saw Raj walking towards her.

'Are you finished already?' Karen asked.

He shook his head. 'Just getting started.'

'Right.' Karen squared her shoulders and prepared to pass Raj to head into the house via the back door, but he put a hand up to stop her.

She looked up and met his steady gaze. 'Brace yourself,' he said. 'It's not good.'

He strode away towards the van, and Karen swallowed hard and continued to move towards the back door. Raj was an experienced pathologist. If he said it was bad, then it really was.

The door to the kitchen was open, but Karen didn't step in straightaway. The first thing that grabbed her attention was the bloody footprints. Adult-sized bare feet. Immediately, her mind went into overdrive, imagining what must have happened. Had William Grant's daughter come downstairs? It would have been dark, perhaps she didn't turn on the light straightaway and then stepped on something sticky . . . maybe still warm . . . and it wouldn't be until she'd switched on the light and looked down that she'd have seen the blood.

Inside, a crime scene officer dressed in a white paper suit was taking photographs.

'Is it all right to come in?' Karen asked.

The crime scene officer looked down, noting her protective footwear, and then said, 'Stick to this side of the kitchen.'

Karen stepped inside and was immediately hit by the coppery smell of blood. But it wasn't only the smell. She could almost taste it in the back of her throat.

The floor was covered with sticky, dark-red smears. The pool of blood near the refrigerator was so dark it looked black. William Grant lay on the floor, a shell, so pale he didn't look human. From the amount of blood splattered, smeared and pooled around the room, Karen guessed there must be no blood left in the elderly man's body. A large gash ran across his throat, and beside him lay a long, thin kitchen knife.

She wasn't sure how long she stood there taking it all in, maybe too long, because the smell finally got to her and her stomach rolled. She moved quickly, staggering outside, and then stood in the garden, hands on her knees, bent over gasping for breath, hoping she wouldn't vomit like some rookie seeing their first body.

He had been sitting across the table from her yesterday. Looking tired, worn out and scared. Why hadn't she seen this coming? Why hadn't she done more to protect him? She'd been so busy with this stupid date business last night, and someone had been plotting and planning to commit this evil act.

She should have paid more attention to the threatening notes. There had been something dark and sinister about this case from the start. Why hadn't she paid attention to her instincts?

'Karen?'

Karen straightened up and turned around to see DI Morgan standing beside the back door.

'Are you all right?'

'Not really,' Karen said. 'How the hell could this have happened?'

He shook his head. 'I didn't see it coming.'

She looked back towards the kitchen and felt her stomach roll again. 'Who found the body?'

'His daughter. Thankfully, she managed to keep the children from seeing their grandfather like that. They're with a neighbour now.'

'That's something, I suppose.'

'Look,' DI Morgan said, 'I can handle things here. You should get back to the station and bring Rick and Sophie up to date. The superintendent will want to be brought up to speed, too. If you get the chance, drive home the point we really need to speak to both of Oliver Fox's sons as soon as possible. It's even more important now.'

Karen nodded and turned away, thankful to get away from the gruesome scene.

When Karen got back to the station, she saw Rick and Sophie huddled around Rick's desk talking quietly. As she approached, they looked up, their expressions sombre.

Sophie was first to speak. 'It's just awful. I can't believe it.'

The way they watched her, expecting her to say something reassuring and inspiring, made Karen's chest feel tight. She didn't feel capable of making the two junior officers in the team feel better about what had happened. She took a moment, trying to gather her thoughts, trying to think of something to say that would console them, but she was coming up blank. All she could think about was how this could have been prevented.

In the end, she decided to be honest.

'It was awful,' Karen said as she wheeled over a chair to sit down beside them. 'His throat had been cut as his family slept upstairs. The scene was one of the most bloody and disturbing I've ever seen.'

Rick looked away, and Sophie raised her hands to her mouth before saying, 'I dread to think what would have happened if his daughter or grandchildren had woken up while the killer was there.'

Karen nodded. The same thought had crossed her mind, too.

'We're going to need to work quickly on this,' she said. 'It's my fault for treating this as a cold case, and not seeing how quickly it could escalate. We need to locate Stephen and Martin Fox as soon as possible. We have to talk to them and find out whether they have alibis for last night.'

It was possible the crime had been committed by an outsider, but Karen thought that was very unlikely. And top of her list of suspects were Oliver Fox's sons. Somehow, they must've found out how their father had died, and the fact that William Grant and Albert Johnson were involved.

'What about DCI Fox?' Rick asked.

'What about him?' Karen snapped, a little more harshly than she'd intended.

'He was Oliver's brother. Maybe he wanted revenge.'

'Possible, but unlikely. He likes to be in control, and I can't see him doing something so risky. As an officer, he knows forensics will find a ton of evidence at the scene. He'd have been more careful, but we should still look into his whereabouts last night.'

'He phoned and left a message a little while ago,' Sophie said. 'What do we tell him?'

'Nothing.' She'd had enough of pandering to the Fox family. She had a strong suspicion that Robert Fox had covered up his brother's crimes back in the eighties, although she couldn't prove it.

Karen leaned back in her chair. 'I should have anticipated this. I should have asked for some protection for William Grant, or kept him in custody overnight.'

She noticed Sophie gazing over her shoulder. Karen turned and saw Superintendent Murray standing behind her.

'It's not your fault, DS Hart. If anyone should take the blame, it's me. I'm in charge of the investigation, but I don't believe we could have seen this coming.'

'But we're going to bring in Stephen and Martin Fox now, right?' Karen said, daring the superintendent to deny her request. She wanted an argument, a confrontation.

But that was unfair. Superintendent Murray didn't suffer fools gladly, but she'd always been supportive, and no one could ever accuse her of being part of the old boys' network.

'Yes, we need to bring them in. I don't care how close retired Detective Superintendent Fox is to the assistant commissioner, Stephen and Martin Fox are our prime suspects for William Grant's murder.'

'What do you want us to say to Detective Superintendent Fox, ma'am?' Sophie asked. 'He's phoned twice already this morning.'

The superintendent narrowed her eyes. 'He must have got a tip-off from someone about William Grant's death.'

'He didn't mention that on the phone, and I'm not sure why he would assume it was related to his brother's death. We haven't kept him in the loop on that,' Sophie said. 'He wanted to know why we were hassling Elizabeth Fox yesterday to find out where her sons were. He was very irate, and said he was going to make a formal complaint about DI Morgan's harassment.'

'Don't worry about it. I'll deal with Robert Fox personally.'

'What do we do about Bennett and Simpson?' Karen asked. 'They could be in danger. They also received those letters.'

The superintendent gave Karen a curt nod. 'Put protective measures in place as you see fit, DS Hart. If you need any authorisation or assistance, come to me directly.' Then she addressed the whole team. 'This is no longer a cold case. We have an active killer, and all leave is cancelled until further notice. Understood?'

They all nodded.

'Good. I'll see about getting some extra manpower. But for now, your top priority is finding Stephen and Martin Fox.'

Karen put security measures in place for Stuart Bennett and Michael Simpson. She organised panic buttons to be installed in their houses and their families to be brought to the station, out of harm's way, until they could organise a safe house. Plain-clothes units had been assigned to sit in unmarked cars outside both men's homes. She'd also requested that they not go to work today, to minimise potential problems.

She couldn't force them to do as she asked, but she made sure they understood the risks.

Both men agreed to stay off work, but refused the advice to accompany their families to the station. Michael Simpson was furious at the suggestion, and said he wouldn't be driven from his home by anyone.

Once her immediate tasks were dealt with, Karen's mind travelled back to the scene at 82 Fallowfield. She had seen other dead bodies during her time on the force, but this was different. Seeing William Grant alive just the day before, and then witnessing the gruesome, sickening scene this morning, had made her mind and stomach rebel.

She pressed a hand to her stomach and rushed to the ladies, along the corridor, barging her way into one of the stalls. Thankfully, the other toilets were empty. She waited, expecting to throw up, but after breathing steadily she slowly regained control. There was nothing in her stomach to throw up anyway. She hadn't even had a cup of coffee this morning.

She exited the cubicle, washed her hands, then splashed water on her face, trying to calm down. Why had everything escalated now, after thirty years of silence?

It had all seemed to start with James Hunter's apparent suicide six months ago. The letters had been received just after his death.

Her hands were shaking, and she felt like she was vibrating with anger. How could anyone do that to a man in his family's home, let alone an elderly, frail man like William Grant? It was sick. She tried to push away the guilt that niggled at her, reminding her she could and should have done something to prevent this.

If only they'd paid more attention when Albert Johnson said he was pushed . . . but then Albert had been involved in Oliver Fox's murder and had hidden his body for over thirty years. It hadn't been beyond the realms of possibility to think he would lie about being pushed to try to disrupt the case against him.

Karen glanced at her make-up-free face in the mirror. She looked terrible. She ran her hands through her hair and blotted her face with a paper towel.

Not much better, she thought. But it was time to get to work.

CHAPTER THIRTY-FOUR

DI Morgan travelled straight from the murder scene in North Greetwell to Elizabeth Fox's house in Skellingthorpe. There had been no answer at the addresses they had for Stephen and Martin Fox, and he'd called Stephen's offices and found he'd not turned up for work today. DI Morgan was tired of being given the runaround, and if Elizabeth Fox knew where her sons were, he was going to get her to tell him.

He jabbed impatiently at the doorbell, and an irritable Elizabeth Fox answered the door.

'This is harassment,' she said, raising her voice, making DI Morgan wonder who she thought was listening. Was her shrill accusation for the neighbours' benefit?

'May I come in, please, Mrs Fox? I have a few questions.'

He wondered if she'd already heard about William Grant's death. The team tended to keep details back so they could judge how an individual reacted to the news, but with Detective Superintendent Fox poking his nose in everywhere and cosying up with the assistant commissioner, DI Morgan had no idea how much she knew.

She stood there guarding the door for a moment, and he wondered if she was about to tell him to leave, but finally she opened the door fully, allowing him to enter.

D. S. Butler

'Do you know where your sons are, Mrs Fox?' DI Morgan asked as soon as he was inside.

'I haven't heard from them,' she said as she plucked at the sleeve of her red jumper nervously.

'Are you sure about that?' he asked, narrowing his eyes. 'Hiding them won't help. It will just delay the inevitable.'

She drew herself up to her full height, which wasn't very tall, and said indignantly, 'Are you threatening me, young man? I'm sure my brother-in-law would be very interested to hear that.'

DI Morgan shook his head. What was wrong with this family? Did they think because retired Detective Superintendent Fox was friends with the assistant commissioner that they were above the law? Still, he hadn't been called a young man for a while. Maybe he should take that as a compliment.

She led the way into the small sitting room, and DI Morgan followed.

'It's better for them if they speak to us now. This situation isn't going to get swept under the rug.' He fought back the urge to add: *this time.*

Elizabeth Fox fiddled with the gold rings on her fingers as she looked at the framed family photograph on the mantelpiece.

'They're good boys. They don't deserve to be hounded like this.'

'They aren't being hounded, Mrs Fox. We want to talk to them.'

She crossed the room to the drinks cabinet, took out a crystal decanter, poured herself a large drink and downed it in one.

She was scared. Why? Did she believe that one of her sons had done something wrong? Did she know about William Grant and believe one of her sons was capable of murder?

He sensed she was weakening.

'I think you should sit down, Mrs Fox,' he said. 'I need to tell you something.'

274

Her gaze flew up to his face and then she did as he asked, slowly lowering herself into one of the high-backed chairs. Her face grew pale as DI Morgan told her about William Grant's murder.

After he'd finished, it was some time before she could formulate a sentence. Her mouth opened and closed a few times before she finally said, 'That couldn't have anything to do with us. Are you saying somebody is murdering old teachers from Greenhill Secondary School?' She frowned and shook her head. 'I don't understand.'

'We think it's related to the death of your husband.'

'But that happened thirty years ago. Why now?'

That was a very good question. 'It's possible someone could be looking for revenge for what happened to Oliver. Is there anything you can tell me about that?'

Her eyes widened. 'You can't possibly think that I had anything to do with it . . .' She trailed off and then shook her head. 'You think it's Stephen and Martin.'

DI Morgan said nothing, waiting to see what Elizabeth Fox would say next. A mother's love went a long way, but would she lie to protect them if they'd committed such a heinous crime?

She clasped her hands and leaned forward, breathing heavily.

'Do you think Stephen and Martin could be involved?' DI Morgan asked softly.

She shook her head.

'If you don't talk to me, Mrs Fox, more people could be in danger.'

'More people?' Her head rose sharply. 'This is unbelievable. There's no way Stephen or Martin could be involved. Martin's had his problems, but he's on medication now. He's much better.'

The words leaving her mouth were delivered in a confident tone, but DI Morgan saw the fear in her eyes.

Sophie and Rick were working hard to track down Stephen and Martin Fox. They had some help from DI Freeman's team, but tracing the brothers was proving difficult. It seemed as though they'd vanished. In Karen's eyes, that only made them look more guilty.

The knife from the murder scene had been rushed through forensics but there were no prints on the handle. It had been wiped clean, and as Karen had suspected, William Grant's daughter identified it as one from her kitchen.

Officers were conducting door-to-door enquiries, asking residents in the immediate vicinity if they'd seen or heard anything unusual last night. So far, they had nothing, which wasn't surprising, as most people would have been tucked up in bed at the time the murder was committed.

Feeling frustrated at their lack of progress, Karen told the team she was going into Lincoln, back to James Hunter's flat. Sophie shot her a confused look but didn't question her motives. It was a good job she didn't, because Karen couldn't really have explained the reason she felt compelled to go back. All she knew was that everything had started six months ago, when James Hunter died.

She parked in the same car park as last time, but rather than heading into the apartment block, she walked into a Costa Coffee, bought a breakfast muffin, hot chocolate and a fruit pot, then walked back towards the car park's pay machine.

The girl they'd seen last time was sitting on a folded-up sleeping bag, her cardboard sign propped up against her leg. She had a different paperback today, Val McDermid's *The Wire in the Blood*.

She looked up when Karen paused next to her, then took the cup of hot chocolate from Karen's outstretched hand.

'Thanks,' she said with a smile, pushing back her tangled hair from her forehead.

Then she took the paper bag and peered inside. 'Appreciate it.' She put the paper cup of hot chocolate down on the ground and unwrapped the muffin.

Karen sat beside her. Without the protection of a sleeping bag, the concrete was bloody freezing, but she put up with it. 'I've seen you around.'

The girl took a bite of the muffin. 'Yeah, it's a good spot,' she said with her mouth full.

'I wanted to ask you a question,' Karen said.

The girl's chewing paused as she waited to hear the catch for her free breakfast.

'Were you in the same spot about six months ago?'

The girl shrugged. 'Might have been.'

Karen pointed up to the eighth-floor balcony of the apartment block in front of them. 'A man jumped off of that balcony. Did you see it?'

To Karen's disappointment, the girl looked away and shook her head.

'All right, thanks for your time,' Karen said, getting to her feet and brushing the dirt from her trousers.

She'd taken a couple of steps when the girl said, 'He didn't jump. He was pushed.'

Karen turned slowly. 'He was pushed? Are you sure?'

The girl put the rest of the muffin back in the brown paper bag. 'Yeah, there was another man with him, and he was thrown over the edge.'

'Could you describe the other man?'

The girl's expression grew guarded, and she didn't reply.

'It's important,' Karen said. 'Anything you tell me could help. Didn't the police ask you questions at the time?'

She looked at Karen as though she were crazy. 'I didn't stick around after it happened. I stayed away from here for at least two months. I was sure he'd seen me . . .' She shivered. 'He walked right past me when he left.'

Karen sat down beside her again. This girl had seen their killer. 'If you were so close, you must be able to remember what he looked like.'

The girl pulled a face. 'It was dark.'

'Please, try,' Karen said.

'He was quite tall and had short hair.' She scrunched up her face as she tried to remember. 'He was wearing a suit.'

Karen smiled at her. 'Great. That's a really good start. Look, why don't you come back to the station with me. It's not safe out here. How old are you?'

'Nineteen.'

'Do you have any family or friends who could help you? I could contact them for you.'

She shook her head firmly.

'What about getting into a programme?'

The girl hesitated, and Karen waited to see if she was going to lie and deny she was an addict, even though Karen could see the swelling on her right arm where a puncture wound had become infected.

'We could get a doctor to look at your arm,' Karen said, flicking through her wallet to pull out a card and then handing it to the girl. 'And I could get you into a programme.'

The girl looked away. 'They never work.'

'What's your name?'

'Sam,' she said.

'Come on, Sam, take my card, at least.'

Reluctantly, Sam took the card from Karen and then shoved it in the top pocket of her shirt.

'Even if you don't want to get into a programme, why don't you come to the station with me? You can use the facilities there. Have a shower. I'll buy you a nice lunch, and all you have to do is give us a statement and description.'

The girl licked her lips and thought it over.

'I know what you're thinking,' Karen said, 'but you'll be back straight after lunch, and you'll have plenty of time to earn some money.'

Karen had forty quid in her wallet. She wanted to help, but she drew the line at giving the girl money to get high.

Finally, the girl grinned and scrambled to her feet. 'Okay. Just wait for me to stash my stuff.'

As they walked back to Karen's car, the girl chatted away as though she'd known Karen for ages. 'I know you probably think I'm horrible for running off and not saying anything. I did think about telling the police what I'd seen, but I told myself they must've caught whoever did it without my help.'

'I understand,' Karen said as she pressed the fob to open the car. 'You were scared.'

'Yeah, I'm unprotected out here. I didn't come back for ages in case he'd seen me, but it's a prime spot, and people always have their wallets and purses out ready to pay for their car parking.'

'Makes sense. You didn't see him again?'

The girl looked horrified. 'No, thank God.'

'And you'd recognise him if you did see him again?' Karen asked, getting into the front seat and putting on her seatbelt.

The girl nodded with conviction. 'Absolutely. I'll never forget his face.'

Back at the station, Karen took a short statement from Sam and then escorted her down to the technical unit to talk to a sketch artist. Though they weren't actually *sketch* artists these days. They used a computer program with composite images to generate a likeness according to the witness's description.

Karen left Sam downstairs and went to get a cup of coffee. She didn't want her presence to affect the outcome of the image. It was too easy to look enthusiastic when a witness was picking out features similar to a suspect's. To avoid any complications, Karen thought she was better off out of the room while they generated the image.

When she got back after twenty minutes, she was disappointed. Apart from the fact the composite image generated had dark hair, it didn't look anything like either Stephen or Martin Fox.

'Did I do all right?' Sam asked, before taking a sip from the can of Coke Karen had brought back with her.

Karen smiled, to cover up her disappointment. 'Yeah, thanks for your help. Why don't I show you where you can grab a shower?'

Karen led her to the changing rooms as she thought about her next step. They could show Sam photographs of Stephen Fox and Martin Fox in the hopes she'd identify them. But that wouldn't stand up well in court later. They'd need a full identification parade for an impartial ID. That wouldn't be possible until they'd found the two Fox brothers, and Karen was unwilling to give up on Sam as a witness. Maybe they could put some photographs of Stephen and Martin in an ID book and try that.

If James Hunter really had been thrown from his balcony as Sam said, surely the other killings were all linked. They had to be. And Sam was the only one who could identify the killer.

After Sam showered, Karen found her some clean clothes and left her in the family room with a pile of magazines while she went to find DI Morgan.

He was sitting in his office with his head in his hands, staring down at a printout.

'How did you get on with Elizabeth Fox?' Karen asked as she took the chair in front of his desk. 'Does she have any idea where they are?'

He looked up and shook his head. 'If she does, she won't tell me.'

Karen slid a copy of the composite image across the table to him. 'I went back to James Hunter's flat and talked to a homeless young woman who says she saw him being pushed off his balcony.'

'That's a game changer. She saw who did it?'

'She said she saw a man push him off the balcony, and then the killer walked past her as he left the apartment building. I was hoping she'd give us an ID, but this isn't good enough to identify Stephen or Martin as our killer.'

DI Morgan stared down at the image. 'There is some similarity.' Then he looked up at Karen. 'We have officers watching Michael and Stuart's houses, don't we?'

Karen nodded. 'Yes, and their families have been temporarily relocated. I want to show our witness photos of Stephen and Martin. I'll put them in an ID book along with some other headshots to see if she can give us an ID.'

'Okay. Do we have good-quality photographs of both brothers?'

'I have photographs from the DVLA. They aren't great quality when blown up, but they'll do.'

'Fine. Has Sophie or Rick had any luck tracking down Stephen or Martin yet?'

Karen stood up and shook her head. 'It's like they've vanished into thin air.'

'They're hiding,' DI Morgan said. 'And that tells me they're guilty.'

CHAPTER THIRTY-FIVE

Stuart Bennett was freaking out. His breathing was ragged, and his heart was thudding in his chest. There were police officers outside now, watching him, watching his house. They'd even installed panic buttons. He didn't understand it. They'd told him he could be in danger, and escorted his family out of the house this morning with barely any warning.

He hadn't had a chance to explain things to his wife, and even if he'd had the time to do so, he had no idea what to say.

They'd mentioned it was related to their investigation into Oliver Fox's death but hadn't given any further details. Liz was going to do her nut. He'd never mentioned a word about Oliver Fox to his wife. Ten years of marriage and two kids, and still she knew nothing about it.

And why should she? It didn't involve her, and Stuart didn't want to contaminate his happy family life with that man's evil. Some people coped better when they talked about things, but Stuart found it easier to compartmentalise. He'd locked the memories in a box inside his head and refused to let them out. It was his way of dealing with it all.

Psychologists and doctors might say it was unhealthy, but it was the only way he'd managed to get through the years that followed. If he'd allowed himself to think about it, he'd have gone crazy.

His parents had known something was wrong. After all, a thirteen-year-old boy didn't start wetting the bed for no reason, but Stuart had remained stubbornly silent when they'd questioned him. That afternoon had put the fear of God into him, and he suspected even if he had been tortured, he would never have revealed the truth about what happened.

He glanced around his living room. Everything looked much the same. The TV was on, a quiz show, with flashing lights and an excitable presenter, but Stuart wasn't paying attention. The children's toys were still scattered on the sofa and floor because they hadn't had a chance to tidy up before the police arrived.

He should put them away now, but he couldn't find the strength to move from his chair. He was frozen, unable to act.

How had it come to this? It wasn't fair. None of it had been their fault. They hadn't asked for the disgusting unwanted attentions of that man.

He'd hated being singled out. The way Oliver Fox looked at him when he asked him to stay behind after class had made his skin crawl. He hated the tone of voice he'd used when he told Stuart he was special.

He hadn't wanted to be special. He'd wanted to be normal and to be left alone to do normal things. He hadn't asked for any of this.

James's death had hurt him deeply. He'd stayed close to Michael as the years passed, but James had drifted away after he went to university. Despite the fact they were linked by their dark secret, time had put distance between them. Though neither he nor Michael or James wanted to talk about what happened in the past, it helped to have somebody who knew how it felt. To know that somebody was there for him if he needed them.

Stuart thought James must have killed himself because he didn't have anyone to turn to, and that made him feel terribly guilty. He'd attended the funeral with Michael and wondered if things would have turned out differently if they'd kept in touch. According to James's wife, he'd been doing well but then had started to drink again.

Stuart reached for the remote control and switched off the television. The house was strangely quiet, with just a slight creaking and gurgling from the central heating.

His thoughts returned to the police visit earlier. They'd told him next to nothing but had checked the windows and doors were secure and made sure the panic buttons worked. They'd installed three: one by the front door, one in the sitting room beside the sofa, and the other in the kitchen.

It was a silver button mounted on a black box. Stewart stared at the one beside the sofa and wondered how long it would take for the police to get here if he pressed it.

There were two officers outside, so they could be here almost immediately. But the panic button and the presence of police officers still didn't make him feel safe. It didn't help that the police hadn't explained exactly why they thought he was in danger. He'd spoken to Michael earlier, and he too had no idea what was going on. There had been no reply when he'd called Mr Grant.

Stuart chewed on a fingernail and nervously looked out of the window, checking the police car was still there.

It was.

He sat back down and shivered. What on earth was going on?

Karen stalked into the office area in a bad mood. She had just spent the last twenty minutes with Sam going through an ID folder. They'd included photos of Martin and Stephen in the book, intermingled with dozens of other headshots. Karen thought they'd struck gold when Sam hesitated over the photograph of Martin.

She'd said nothing, not wanting to influence the girl.

But her spirits soared when Sam smiled widely and said, 'That's him.'

'Are you sure?' Karen asked, needing confirmation before she raced off to tell the team.

'One hundred per cent positive,' Sam said. 'I'll never forget his face.'

Karen stood up and smiled. 'Thank you. You've been a great help. Stick around, and we'll get lunch in a bit.'

Sam grinned, but as Karen stood up and moved the file, the page turned, and Sam said, 'Hang on a minute.' She pulled the file back towards her, staring down at the photograph of Stephen Fox.

Karen frowned.

'I was wrong,' Sam said. 'It wasn't that first man. It was this man.'

Karen sat down again heavily. The brothers were similar in appearance, both dark-haired and dark-eyed, but they weren't *that* similar. It wasn't like they were identical twins.

Sam was too eager to please. Her heart was in the right place, but she wasn't a reliable witness. Flip-flopping between two suspects was not a good start.

Sam caught the look on Karen's face. She bit her lower lip. 'Sorry, maybe I didn't get quite as good a look at him as I thought.'

'It's okay. You did your best,' Karen said, closing the folder.

'I really wanted to help. I feel bad about not coming forward earlier.'

Karen tucked the folder under her arm. 'I've got to get back to the office. You can hang around here for an hour or so if you still want to grab lunch?'

'Yeah, thanks.'

Karen was almost at the door when Sam said, 'You will catch him though, won't you?'

'We will,' Karen said, and she meant it.

Wherever the two brothers were hiding, they'd find them.

Now Karen put the folder down on Sophie's desk.

'I take it the ID didn't go well?' Sophie said, looking up and reading Karen's mood from the expression on her face.

'Unfortunately not. How are you getting on? Have you managed to track down either brother yet?'

Sophie pointed to Rick, who was hunched over the phone on his desk. 'Rick said he's got a lead, but nothing concrete yet. Neither brother has gone home. We have officers waiting outside both residences. And Stephen still hasn't turned up for work, which is very unlike him, apparently.'

'Well, they can't hide forever.'

'How sure are we that it's one of the brothers who killed James?' Sophie asked. 'It could be Elizabeth Fox or her sister, Laura.'

Karen shook her head. 'Doubtful. It's hard to imagine someone of Elizabeth or Laura's stature overpowering a man like James Hunter, even if he was drunk. Plus our witness, Sam, says it was definitely a man who pushed James from the balcony.'

Sophie shrugged. 'Sam's not a reliable witness. She could have been high at the time. Or if Elizabeth was behind it, maybe she hired somebody to dispose of James Hunter or William Grant?'

William's murder was particularly brutal, and Karen found it hard to imagine Elizabeth or Laura carrying it out. The sisters had an odd, competitive relationship, but she thought it was very unlikely Elizabeth or Laura were behind any of the murders. She liked to see Sophie working this way, though. The young officer was playing devil's advocate, bouncing around theories and punching holes in assumptions. Karen smiled at her. It was good to see her back in the game and fully invested in the case.

Karen was about to tell her so when Rick put his hand over the mouthpiece of his phone and called out, 'I've found Martin Fox.'

Karen and Sophie waited for him to finish the call.

After an agonising wait, he hung up and said, 'Got him. Martin Fox is in a secure residential unit. The Peter Hodgkinson Centre at Lincoln County Hospital. He's in inpatient mental health care. His brother admitted him last night.'

'What time last night?' Karen asked.

'Eleven.'

'And he's been under observation all that time? If so, that means Martin couldn't have murdered William Grant.'

Sophie leaned forward, resting her elbows on the desk. 'That doesn't mean it wasn't Martin who pushed James off the balcony, or Albert Johnson down the stairs, leaving him for dead.'

'That's one thing I don't understand,' Rick said with a frown. 'If one of the brothers pushed Albert Johnson down the stairs, why would they leave the body in the suitcase? Surely they would want their father's body to be found and laid to rest.'

'Maybe they attacked Albert without knowing the body was in the house,' Karen said, trying to think through the problem logically. 'According to William, only he and Albert knew where the body was.'

Sophie sat back in her chair with a sigh and looked up at the ceiling. 'The first two victims were killed by falls – James thrown from the balcony and Albert pushed down the stairs – but William Grant's murder was far more violent than that. It doesn't quite fit.'

'If it's the same killer, which we assume it is, it's a dramatic escalation,' Karen said.

'True, but the murder was carried out under very different circumstances,' Rick said. 'Whoever killed William Grant would have wanted to dispatch him as quickly and quietly as possible, so they didn't wake up the rest of the household.'

'Very good point, Rick,' Karen said. 'The differences between the MOs had been bothering me, but that makes sense.' She checked her watch. 'If Martin has an iron-clad alibi, that leaves us with Stephen. I'd prefer to talk to him first, but it looks like he's determined to hide, so let's organise a search. We'll turn his property upside down if we need to.'

'I'll get started on the warrant,' Sophie said.

'Great.'

DI Morgan walked into the office area and caught the last part of the conversation. He stopped at Sophie's desk. 'I've just spoken to the superintendent. We've applied for a warrant already, Sophie. We're just waiting for it to be authorised. If he killed William, there must be evidence. In his car, his house . . . There was so much blood at the scene. No matter how careful he was, there will be forensic proof somewhere.'

CHAPTER THIRTY-SIX

As soon as the warrant was issued, Karen and DI Morgan booked a fleet car and drove to Stephen Fox's house near the Cathedral Quarter.

'What are you planning to do about Rob Miller?' Karen asked as they headed along the A46.

DI Morgan looked surprised. 'The man's a bully, but what can I do? I made a mistake, and I have to hold my hands up to that. I've warned his ex-girlfriend. She's on her guard now, and I advised her to collect evidence for a restraining order.'

'He sounds like a real piece of work. Are you sure it was your screw-up and not his?'

'Believe me, I wish that were the case. But two other members of the team heard me say the wrong address, too. It was my mistake.'

'People like him make my blood boil. He gives police officers a bad name.'

'Agreed.' DI Morgan smiled. 'Thanks for listening, by the way. It's a relief to be able to talk to someone about it.'

'No problem.'

DI Morgan slowed as they drove along Wragby Road, approaching Stephen Fox's house. The crime scene van was already parked at the side of the street, waiting for the go-ahead.

Karen called the crime scene manager, telling him things were in place, and DI Morgan turned left into the driveway.

She ended the call and got her first look at Stephen Fox's home. The house and driveway were surrounded by beech and lime trees, which provided privacy both from the neighbouring houses and from the road. Karen shivered as the car came to a stop. It looked like an average Lincolnshire home. The 1930s detached house, with its bow windows and large chimney, looked perfectly ordinary.

The property was well maintained. Cheerful daffodils bloomed in the carefully weeded flowerbeds either side of the front door. There was nothing about the appearance of the house to suggest the person who lived there had lost their grip on reality.

The rest of the search team arrived shortly afterwards. As expected, no one answered when they knocked at the front door, so DI Morgan issued the order for the door to be opened with force. As if on cue, neighbours and other passers-by appeared at the top of the driveway, craning their necks to get a good look at the commotion. One of the uniformed officers stood guard, holding out his arms and gesturing for them to walk on. Karen heard him tell them to move away and go home. They shuffled backwards, but they didn't leave. One woman held up her mobile phone, no doubt recording footage that would be posted on social media within minutes.

Karen turned her back on the rubberneckers and joined the rest of the team in putting on protective clothing. Although they had no reason to suspect the house was a crime scene, they still couldn't risk contaminating any evidence they found there.

Two officers struggled with the garage door, and when they finally yanked it open, snapping the lock, they found the garage was empty. So Stephen Fox had taken his car. That was a good thing. In Lincolnshire, like many other counties, automatic number-plate recognition technology was used by the police to track vehicles. As soon as Stephen's car passed an NPR device, its registration number would be read and then checked against a database of vehicles of interest. They'd flagged Stephen's number plate already, so presumably it would be only a matter of time before they tracked him down.

DI Morgan stayed outside, issuing the officers with instructions. Karen headed in to get started. It was a large three-bed house and would take some time to search thoroughly. They weren't looking for a murder weapon, which actually made the search harder. At this stage, they didn't know what was relevant and what wasn't, so they were going in blind, hoping to stumble upon something incriminating.

The crime scene team began to swab samples around every drain. They would sample and photograph the washing machine, the sinks, toilets and any other outlets. Nothing would escape their attention. She was expecting the search to take hours. A systematic search of a residence took a whole team of police officers the better part of a day.

They'd been in the house for less than five minutes when an officer called out to inform the team that he'd discovered a black bag filled with bloodstained clothes in the utility room just off the kitchen. Karen was surprised that the evidence was lying around in plain sight. Stephen Fox hadn't even attempted to cover his tracks.

Unlike his brother Martin, Stephen had worked hard to create an elaborate façade. His external appearance was that of a mild-mannered, hard-working man in his forties. He didn't stand out, and that was what made him so dangerous.

The bloodstained clothing was placed in labelled evidence bags and taken back to the lab. The blood would be analysed to see if it matched William Grant's, as a priority.

Stephen Fox's computer was in a downstairs room. Although originally designed as a dining room, with a small hatch through to the kitchen, he'd been using the room as a study. The laptop was in plain view in the centre of the desk, and making their job even easier, the laptop was unlocked. Didn't everybody use password protection these days? Why hadn't Stephen Fox bothered to hide anything? Had he been so confident he wouldn't be caught? Or maybe, Karen thought, he didn't care if the police caught up with him. Maybe he wanted recognition for the crimes he'd committed. Maybe he wanted people to know his father's death had been avenged.

'Have you seen this, Karen?' DI Morgan asked. He was standing beside an oak filing cabinet in the corner of the study.

Karen turned and inhaled sharply when she saw he was holding a blue ring binder.

It reminded her of the folder she'd kept after her husband and daughter died. She'd been searching desperately for answers, looking for any reason to explain their deaths other than it all being a cruel, random accident. She'd gathered everything she could, from copies of witness statements and accident reports to photographs of the road where it happened, all intermingled with her own notes.

'Everything all right?' DI Morgan said, frowning.

Karen nodded and held out a gloved hand to take the folder from him. She flicked through it and felt an unexpected pang of sympathy for Stephen Fox. He'd collected articles, photographs, postcards and other information about his father. In a plastic sleeve there were yellowing newspaper clippings. Karen paused, studying one of the articles, which contained a photograph of Oliver Fox awarding prizes at a school sports day. He was smiling widely at the camera, holding up a small trophy. A group of young boys were lined up behind him. She felt the urge to snap the folder shut, but carried on turning the pages.

There were more photographs, but this time they weren't of Oliver Fox. They were pictures of James Hunter, Michael Simpson and Stuart Bennett. As she turned more pages, she saw details on William Grant and Albert Johnson – addresses, phone numbers and daily schedules. He'd been stalking them.

Karen looked up sharply.

'I think we've found our proof,' DI Morgan said.

They spent more time looking over the folder and Karen noticed an interesting aspect. The photographs and newspaper clippings of Oliver Fox were old, but the photographs of Albert, William, James, Michael and Stuart were all recent. There were dates and times scribbled on a sheet of A4 paper relating to Stuart's daily commute to work, what time his wife took their daughter to school, and the days Stuart came home for lunch.

Karen shook her head. 'How was he able to do this while holding down a full-time job?'

DI Morgan shrugged. 'He managed an estate agents on Mint Street. He was the boss, so I suppose he just took time off when he wanted to.'

'Have you noticed that the dates and times he was following them are all after James Hunter's death, but there's no record of him following James before he killed him? That means James was the trigger. We need to find out why.'

'We need to find Stephen. We've had an alert out for all units. He has his car, and yet nothing's been triggered on the NPR.' DI Morgan shook his head, exasperated.

Karen's mobile began to ring. 'It's Rick,' she said.

After speaking to him, she hung up and turned to DI Morgan. 'Rick has CCTV footage of Stephen leaving the hospital last night, but after that he disappeared. He was in his car, though. It should only be a matter of time before he's picked up.'

Another officer called for DI Morgan from upstairs, and he turned and headed for the staircase.

Karen looked around the study. Everything was perfectly ordered and tidy.

There had to be something personal in the house, something that would reveal more of his character and give them some idea of what had triggered him to behave this way.

She slowly walked around the downstairs of the house, going from room to room. In the kitchen, one of the CSIs was working their way through the cupboards and drawers. The dishwasher had been opened, and inside there were some bowls and mugs but no glasses.

Karen opened all the cupboards in turn. There were a couple of tumblers, but no wine glasses to be seen. That was odd. Even if Stephen didn't drink himself, most people kept glasses for visitors. It's not like wine glasses were that expensive.

She walked out of the kitchen towards the sitting room and looked around for any other cupboards or cabinets that could be hiding more glasses. She came up blank.

She then walked into the living room and looked at the framed photographs above the mantelpiece. There were three. One was a duplicate of the happy family photograph they'd been shown at Elizabeth's house. Another was a photograph of Stephen sitting in his father's lap, and the third was a group of men standing in a line. They wore orange vests, and it looked like they'd taken part in some sort of training day. She looked carefully at all of the faces but saw none she recognised, other than Stephen. All the men were raising their drinks to the camera. Every man held a pint. Except Stephen. He held a small glass of orange juice.

She pulled out her mobile again and called Elizabeth Fox.

The woman let the phone ring for a long time before she answered: 'Hello.' Her voice was tense and strained.

'Mrs Fox, DS Karen Hart of the Lincolnshire Police.'

The woman groaned. 'Haven't you put us through enough already?'

'I'm sorry to trouble you again,' Karen said. 'We have a few follow-up questions for Stephen, and it's rather urgent we speak to him. I just wondered if in the meantime you could answer a question for me. Does Stephen have a drink problem?'

'Not anymore,' Elizabeth said proudly. 'He's attended AA meetings for nearly twenty years and hasn't touched a drop in all that time. So you see, he's not the terrible person you think he is. He's helped countless people break their addictions and is always there to support people in his group when they're struggling.'

'Thank you, Mrs Fox.' Karen said. 'You've been very helpful.'

Karen hung up and made her way upstairs to look for DI Morgan. She found him in the master bedroom going through the wardrobe.

'Sir, I think I know how James and Stephen met and how all this started.'

'How?'

'AA. Stephen attends meetings, too.'

Before DI Morgan could reply, his mobile rang and he snatched it up quickly. 'DI Morgan.'

Karen watched his face harden as he listened to the person on the other end of the line. Then he hung up with a curt 'Thanks.'

He walked towards the bedroom door. 'Let's go,' he said. 'Stephen Fox's car has been found.'

'Where is it?' Karen asked, following him down the stairs.

'Merton Road. Two streets away from Stuart Bennett's house.'

CHAPTER THIRTY-SEVEN

Stephen Fox put his hands in his pocket, making sure he still had his latex gloves. He felt the soft rubbery texture and smiled. Everything was ready. But there was no need to put them on yet. He had plenty of time.

He strolled along the street, smiling at a woman with a toddler in a pushchair, and then turned into the alley that ran along the back of the houses on Turner Road. It was quiet in the alley, peaceful, and he paused for a moment to reflect.

There was no need to rush. Everything was in place. People who rushed made mistakes. That was something his father had been fond of saying. More haste, less speed, he'd say when Stephen was getting frustrated with his Lego or Meccano, or trying to knot his own tie in the morning.

His family had been robbed of so much when his father disappeared.

Stephen patted down his pockets, looking for his old mobile. He'd turned it off in case the police tried to track him. He expected to get caught of course, but didn't want them to find him until he'd finished his duty. After clicking the battery into place and switching it on, he had missed calls from numbers he didn't recognise, as well as from his mother and brother, and even a couple from his Aunt Laura.

It wasn't easy to ignore them. Especially Martin. He needed his elder brother, and Stephen had done everything he could to fill a father's role for Martin. But he hadn't been good enough. Despite his best efforts, Martin had been damaged by the whole experience, and no matter how much support Stephen gave him, he would never be able to live a normal life. He couldn't hold down a job, or even be trusted to take the vital medication that kept him safe.

People always felt sorry for the victims of crimes, but their families were forgotten. Stephen, Martin and their mother had been cast aside and left to cope alone.

He closed his eyes and leaned against the brick wall. The sunlight was filtering through the bushes and trees opposite, and he focused on the sound of a bird singing.

He wasn't looking forward to what he had to do now. But it was his duty. The first two deaths had been easy, but William Grant's had been a horrible, gasping death that had haunted him all day. The man had deserved it, though. He'd had it coming. They all did. They'd killed his father then made him suffer the indignity of not allowing him to rest in peace. They'd had no closure. No memorial to their father. Martin was an emotional wreck, and their mother had been consumed by bitterness because for years she'd believed her husband had walked out and left her.

Stephen shook his head, opened his eyes and began to walk again.

It was odd how things had played out. None of this would have happened if he hadn't received that phone call six months ago. Stephen scowled, remembering James Hunter sobbing down the telephone because things were getting too much for him.

James was weak, nothing like Stephen. He didn't know what it was to really suffer.

Stephen had been sober for twenty years and was willing to support those who felt temptation was getting the better of them. *His* willpower was unbreakable. He could still feel the call of the bottle and practically taste the burning alcohol on his tongue if he allowed himself to think about it, but he never gave up. He was strong and knew he would never falter. He probably didn't need the meetings, but kept attending because those afflicted with the same disease needed to see it was possible to beat it.

For the most part, it was a thankless task. Most of the people he tried to help fell off the wagon multiple times, just like James.

James's drunken revelation had been a reward for Stephen's dedication and unselfishness.

When he'd got to James Hunter's flat that night, the pathetic man had been babbling. He'd said the guilt was eating him up from within. It had taken all his self-control to sit beside James and keep his expression neutral, nodding encouragingly now and again as James related the whole story.

He'd never felt anger like it. He'd wanted to throttle the life out of the other man. But he'd kept calm. Somehow he'd kept his emotions in check. But when they'd both been on the balcony, he'd acted on impulse. His head was crystal clear, in contrast to James's foggy, alcohol-contaminated brain. And it had been easier than he'd expected. One quick lift and push, and James was plummeting to the ground.

Afterwards, he'd felt no remorse. None at all.

After his first kill, Mr Johnson had been easy enough. He'd taken the key from under the flowerpot by the back door. Such a silly place to keep a spare key. Wasn't that the first place a burglar would look if they wanted to break in?

One firm shove and the old man had tumbled down the stairs, hitting the wall on the way down. Stephen had been sure he was dead, so when he heard Mr Johnson had been taken to hospital, it had been a shock. If he'd have known he was hanging on to life, he would have finished him off.

He hadn't made the same mistake with William Grant. There had been so much blood, with Mr Grant. He'd almost lost control, wanting to run away and close his eyes so he didn't have to look at the blood. But now it was over, he could see it had been necessary. The blood was cleansing and had purified the sins of his old teacher. It was an apt end for those who had conspired to kill his father.

He'd been a little surprised at his complete lack of remorse. He wasn't a monster, but they didn't deserve his pity or regret. Mr Johnson and Mr Grant had taught him for years after they'd killed his father. Had they ever shown him kindness? No. Had they shown him compassion? No. The evil men deserved it.

He thought back to James Hunter's pathetic babbling. *We didn't know what to do. We just found him there . . . bleeding. There was so much blood.*

Of course, James had been lying. They'd killed his father between them. Otherwise, why would he feel so guilty? He must've seen the disgust on Stephen's face and decided to modify his story. But it was too late. Stephen had seen the truth in his eyes. The man in front of him had killed his father.

Stephen smiled. Now there were just two left.

Outside, a door slammed, and Stuart jumped.

He gripped the arms of his chair. *Relax*, he told himself, *it's just the neighbours getting home from work.* He sat there for a moment, listening for other noises, but all was quiet. All day he'd been on tenterhooks, waiting for something terrible to happen.

He relaxed back into the chair and glanced at his mobile phone as it lit up with another text message from his wife. Liz wasn't happy, and who could blame her? He hadn't answered the phone since she'd left for the safety of the police station with their daughter.

She wanted answers. But he wasn't ready to give her any.

He had no idea how much the police had told her. She'd left the house in a mad panic, stuffing belongings into bags and then rushing out to a waiting unmarked police car.

Stuart had kissed her and his daughter before they left and promised to tell his wife everything later, but he didn't want to. He'd tried so hard to keep Oliver Fox from contaminating his new life. His way of coping was to pretend that it had all happened to someone else, not him. He was a happy, family man. A good husband and a good dad who held down a steady job and provided for his family.

He didn't want her to know what had happened to him when he was only a boy.

The police officers who'd come to the house had looked at him curiously, trying to work out whether he was reckless or brave for refusing to leave his house and go with his family to the safety of the police station. But he was neither reckless nor brave. He was a coward. He was afraid to tell his wife what had happened. Afraid it would make her look at him differently. And he was absolutely terrified that the next time he looked in her eyes, he wouldn't see love or amusement as he delivered his ridiculous jokes, or even mild irritation when he'd forgotten to take the bin out again . . . He would see pity, and he couldn't bear that.

He reached for the remote control, flicking through the channels before settling on an episode of *Homes under the Hammer*. Stuart felt chatter from the programme wash over him and tried to concentrate. But it was no good. Flickering images from the past flooded over him. Things he'd kept locked away and out of mind for so long were now pushing their way back to the front of his brain. Why did this have to happen? Things had been going so well. He'd been holding everything together. So why . . .

Stuart froze when he heard the doorbell.

He waited. Had he imagined it? He switched off the television and almost jumped out of his chair when the doorbell sounded again.

The police officers were still outside, weren't they? Or had they been called away?

He switched off the TV, got to his feet slowly and walked out of the living room into the hallway. Through the opaque glass in the front door he could see a shadow.

Why was he so scared? Should he press the panic button?

He wanted to be brave, to arm himself, but instead he walked towards the door like a lamb to the slaughter, too tired to fight.

He paused at the door, took a deep breath and then reached up to unlock it.

CHAPTER THIRTY-EIGHT

Stuart sagged against the door frame when he saw Karen, DI Morgan and three uniformed officers at his door. He brought a shaky hand up to his forehead to wipe away the sweat.

'I thought . . .' he started to say, but didn't finish his sentence. He didn't need to. Karen understood he was scared. She felt they should have been upfront with him, but the superintendent had wanted to keep developments quiet until they collected the evidence they needed. 'Can we come in, Stuart?'

She looked over her shoulder to check the street was empty. There were a few cars parked along the road, including an unmarked fleet vehicle containing plain-clothed officers watching the house. A curtain twitched at a downstairs window in the house opposite. Apart from that, it was quiet. There was no sign of Stephen Fox yet.

He could be watching them right now.

Stuart walked into the living room. Karen, DI Morgan and the other officers followed, closing the front door behind them. Once inside the living room, Karen pulled the curtains shut.

'What's happened? Liz and my daughter are all right, aren't they?' Stuart asked. He stood in the middle of the room looking dazed.

'They're fine,' DI Morgan said.

The uniformed officers checked the doors and windows as DI Morgan explained the situation. So far, they had told Stuart and Michael the bare minimum. It was a delicate balance. They didn't want to terrify the men, but they were owed an explanation. Now they had the evidence they needed against Stephen Fox, the men could be told the truth.

'We believe Oliver Fox's son, Stephen, is responsible for the deaths of James Hunter, Albert Johnson and William Grant. We're trying to locate him,' DI Morgan said.

'Mr Grant's dead?' Stuart's face crumpled. 'I thought Mr Johnson had a fall? And James committed suicide.'

'I'm sorry. Mr Grant was murdered in the early hours. We think Mr Johnson and James were pushed to their deaths.' DI Morgan paused for a moment to let the words sink in.

Stuart, who looked pale and shaky, took a couple of steps backwards and practically fell into an armchair.

'We've just found Stephen Fox's car. It's parked just a few streets away,' DI Morgan added.

'You mean he's coming for me . . .'

'We think he *could* come here, Stuart,' Karen said. There was no reason to lie to the man. If she'd been in his shoes, she would have appreciated the truth.

'But why would he show up here after all this time?'

'We think James Hunter must have told him the circumstances of his father's death and he's trying to exact some kind of payback.'

'Am I in danger?'

Karen didn't have an answer for that.

There was a chance Stephen Fox could have seen them arrive at the property or noticed the officers outside in the car and decided not to approach the house. But based on everything they now knew about him, Karen guessed he was on a mission and wouldn't easily be dissuaded from his task.

They had an armed unit on standby, but no guns would be used in a residential area unless it was absolutely unavoidable. The uniformed officers who'd escorted them there were part of a special squad armed with CS gas, batons and stun guns.

If Stephen Fox did turn up here, Karen could only hope the element of surprise was still on their side. They'd decided not to sweep the area, because if he was nearby that would definitely alert him to their presence. For all Karen knew, he could be holed up in one of the neighbouring houses or gardens watching them.

A unit had been stationed in an unmarked car near Merton Road, close to Stephen's vehicle, in case he opted to return to his car. Other officers were watching Simpson's house and were on high alert.

Everything was in place. All they had to do now was wait.

There were two doors into Stuart Bennett's living room. One led to the kitchen and the other to the hall. Karen closed both doors. If Stephen Fox broke in, she didn't want him to see the officers until the last moment.

'Should I put the TV on?' Stuart asked after they'd been sitting in silence for ten minutes.

Karen shook her head. 'No. We need to be able to hear him if he tries to break in.'

She wished Stuart had gone to the station with his family, but after he'd kicked up such a fuss, they'd allowed him to stay here. She wondered if he realised he was acting as bait. It wasn't a very nice thought, and one that Karen pushed out of her mind.

Two of the uniformed officers stood either side of the sofa, and the other officer stood by the television. DI Morgan sat in an armchair and Karen perched on the edge of the sofa as the minutes ticked by.

They had been there for about fifteen minutes when the sound of breaking glass made Karen jump. Everyone heard it.

She held her breath. The noise had come from the kitchen at the back of the house. She and DI Morgan both stood up, and the uniformed officers removed their batons from their belts and moved silently into position.

Karen kept her gaze locked on the kitchen door as the door handle turned.

Stuart shrank back and pushed himself against the wall. He let out a low whimper, and Karen held a finger to her lips to warn him to keep quiet.

The door opened slowly at first, and then was yanked open by one of the officers.

Stephen Fox was pulled into the room. For a moment, his face looked a picture of confusion, then frustration, and then finally when his gaze found Stuart, his face morphed into a grimace of hatred.

'It's him,' DI Morgan said unnecessarily. 'Move.'

Suddenly, there was an explosion of movement, batons raised, shouting.

'Down on the ground, police!' Every officer was shouting out orders, but still Stephen resisted, struggling against them.

It was three against one, but Stephen jerked and lashed out, throwing off one officer, who crashed into the glass coffee table, shattering it into a thousand pieces.

Somehow, Stephen Fox found the strength to make a dive for Stuart despite officers pulling at his arms.

Stuart was struck motionless with terror. He stood there, eyes wide, petrified, unable to move out of the way.

Karen shoved him and he fell against the sofa.

DI Morgan helped the other officers, gripping Stephen's shoulders to force him back.

Stephen bared his teeth as he fell to his knees, looking feral and out of control. His normally carefully combed hair fell forward over his eyes, which were now narrowed to slits.

One of the officers forced his hands into cuffs and then hauled him to his feet. Karen's heartbeat slowed as he was led away by two officers, who read him his rights.

She knelt down beside the officer who'd fallen on to the glass table. 'Are you hurt?'

He was patting himself all over, but there was no sign of any blood. 'No,' he said in amazement. 'I'm fine.'

Karen breathed a sigh of relief and held out a hand to help him to his feet.

From the hallway, Stephen Fox screamed, 'Murderer! You'll pay for this.'

Stuart cowered behind the sofa, trembling. He looked up, his lower lip quivering. 'But I didn't kill him. It wasn't me.'

Outside Stuart Bennett's house, DI Morgan and Karen watched Stephen Fox as he was bundled into a police car.

'That was a little hairy,' DI Morgan said. 'Are you okay?'

Karen nodded. 'Yes. Did you see the look on his face? I've never seen so much anger and hatred.'

They stood there for a while longer until the police car drove away.

'He was unhinged,' DI Morgan said as they turned to walk inside. 'But at least Stuart and Michael will be safe now.'

Inside, they found Stuart sitting on the sofa. He couldn't stop trembling, and although he was physically unhurt, Karen knew he would find today very difficult to get over. It wasn't just the trauma of Stephen Fox breaking into his home, but all the memories it had brought back.

'We'll get all this stuff cleared up in no time,' Karen said, trying to sound reassuring. 'Forensics will need to come in first, and then we'll make sure the back door is secured. He smashed a pane of glass to get into the kitchen.'

'Right,' Stuart said, staring blankly straight ahead.

Looking around the room, Karen found it hard to stop thinking about the violent murder that could have taken place in this cosy, domestic scene. Among the shattered glass were children's toys. A weekly gossip magazine rested over the arm of a chair, and a Roald Dahl book was stuffed down the side of one of the sofa cushions.

She took a deep breath and turned back to Stuart. 'We've arranged accommodation for you and your family tonight. If you'd like to come with us, we'll take you to Nettleham, and then someone will drive you to a safe place to stay.'

Stuart still stared blankly ahead.

'Tomorrow night, your family will be back home, asleep in their own beds, and everything will be back to normal.' But even as she said the words, Karen knew Stuart would never feel normal again.

Back at the station, Karen updated Rick and Sophie, who'd been waiting anxiously for news, and DI Morgan went down to the custody suite to see Stephen Fox booked in.

Karen rolled her shoulders, still feeling tense from the encounter.

'I expect we'll be summoned by the superintendent soon,' Karen said. 'She'll want to know the full story.'

'I wouldn't go up there yet, Sarge,' Rick said. 'Robert Fox turned up a few minutes ago. No doubt someone tipped him off about his nephew's arrest. I imagine he's not a happy bunny at the moment.'

Karen shook her head. It amazed her how quickly news could spread. She didn't really fancy a run-in with Robert Fox today.

'Maybe I'll leave it until she summons me then,' Karen said, sitting down.

She felt exhausted. All the adrenaline that had been running through her veins half an hour ago had left her system. All she wanted to do now was curl up on her sofa with a glass of red wine, and a series to binge-watch on Netflix.

'Just so I have this clear, we think Stephen killed James Hunter, then pushed Albert Johnson down the stairs and then slit William Grant's throat?' Sophie asked, looking up from her monitor. 'Martin wasn't involved at all?'

'It looks that way,' Karen said, gratefully accepting a mug of coffee from Rick. 'He was ranting away during the car journey here. I don't think we have to worry about him talking. They couldn't get him to shut up. He's proud of everything he did. He said he found out about James Hunter's involvement after James got drunk one night and confessed. He told Stephen who was involved in his father's death, and then Stephen methodically planned his revenge against everyone involved.'

'But they said they didn't kill him. They said they just stumbled on the body in the changing rooms.'

Karen raised an eyebrow. 'Yes, that's what they *said*.'

Sophie's jaw dropped open, and for a moment she was speechless. She soon recovered, though. 'If they killed Oliver Fox because he abused them like he did Mark Bell, then he got what he deserved. We won't charge them for Oliver Fox's death, will we? That would be inhuman!'

Karen sipped her coffee and then sighed. 'Remember that chat we had, Sophie? You can't be idealistic in this job. It's not a perfect world, and most of the time things aren't fair. Our job is to solve the case. No one appointed us judge and jury.'

Sophie shook her head, her light-brown curls bobbing furiously. 'But it isn't fair. It's just not right, Sarge.'

CHAPTER THIRTY-NINE

Sophie turned away on the pretext of settling down at her computer to do some work, but she stared blankly at the screen. Just when she thought she could really make a go of this job, the rug was pulled from beneath her again. It was so unfair.

If Oliver Fox had abused those boys . . . Sophie's mind ran through the possibilities. What could she do to help them? Surely there had to be something.

She shot a sideways glance at Karen and Rick, and saw that they were still deep in conversation and weren't paying any attention to her.

She could try to talk to Michael and Stuart. Maybe she could tip them off.

Perhaps she could convince them to pin all the blame on James Hunter.

That idea didn't sit easily with Sophie. It wasn't a decent thing to do, and it would be an insult to James Hunter's memory, but on the other hand, the CPS couldn't prosecute a dead man. And at least neither Michael nor Stuart would go to prison. Wasn't that the most important thing?

She looked again at Rick and Karen to make sure they weren't watching, and then pressed a few keys on her keyboard to bring up

Michael Simpson and Stuart Bennett's addresses and contact details. She hesitated. Ideally, she'd need to find a way to speak to them in person. If she called them, there would be a record of her getting in touch, and it could come back to bite her – she could maybe even lose her job over it.

Was it really the right thing to do? She felt torn. Karen had a point. It wasn't her place to see that justice was done, but at the same time, she couldn't stand the thought of those men being punished after everything they'd been through.

Before she could decide what to do, there was a commotion on the far side of the office, and Sophie turned to look, as did everyone else in the vicinity.

Retired Detective Superintendent Robert Fox stormed in, striding towards them, followed by Superintendent Murray. His face was puce, and his jowls wobbled as he began to berate everyone.

'This is ridiculous! You can't possibly have the right man. This investigation was bungled from start to finish. Don't you dare think about questioning Stephen without a lawyer. I swear, I'll throw the book at you.' He jabbed his finger in Karen's direction.

Karen slid her chair backwards and stood up slowly to look Robert Fox in the eye. He was such a nasty man. How could he be so indignant, knowing what his brother had done, and now knowing that his nephew had murdered three people in cold blood?

Sophie believed he must have used his influence to cover up his brother's crimes, and that was why the original investigation into Oliver Fox had been buried before it really started. In her book, that made him complicit. Worse than that, it made him evil.

She stood up beside Karen in a gesture of solidarity and glared at Robert Fox.

How the man had the gall to shout at them was beyond her comprehension. After all, it was his shoddy police work that had led them to this. If Oliver Fox had been investigated and prosecuted when the rumours of abuse had first surfaced, then William Grant, Albert Johnson and James Hunter would still be alive. It was also possible that Mark Bell would not have committed suicide if he believed his abuser would be punished.

But Robert Fox continued to rant and rave at them, spittle gathering at the corners of his mouth as he yelled.

Once or twice, Superintendent Murray tried to interrupt, but she couldn't get a word in edgeways. Sophie looked at Rick and shook her head. It beggared belief.

Unfortunately, Robert Fox caught the look between them and turned on Sophie. 'You, young lady, are everything that's wrong with the police force today. You have no respect for your senior officers.'

Sophie was tempted to snipe back that they called it the police service these days because it was less threatening than using the word 'force', but she thought that would just set him off on another tirade.

'If you spent more time doing actual police work, and less time rolling your eyes, you might catch a clue now and again.'

That hit a nerve. She swallowed hard and tried not to show him she was upset.

Karen put a hand on her shoulder. 'That's uncalled for, *Mr* Fox. You don't know DC Jones, and I can vouch for the fact she's an excellent officer.'

Karen's use of 'Mr' rather than the respectful use of his rank was deliberate, and it only riled the horrible man even more.

Sophie glanced at Superintendent Murray and wondered why she was letting him shout at them like this, making a spectacle of himself. Usually, the superintendent was very quick to deal out a scathing comment and put people in their place. Sophie admired that quality in her boss. Was she holding back because she was worried she might lose her job? It was true the man was friendly with the assistant commissioner, but Superintendent Murray couldn't get in trouble over this surely. She hadn't done anything wrong.

But Superintendent Murray was watching Robert Fox closely, so closely it almost seemed as though she was egging him on. A trace of a smile played on her lips.

Why was she just watching him? His obnoxious temper tantrum was now drawing a crowd, as other officers shifted a little closer and circled around them.

Sophie was getting a little tired of the ranting now, but Robert Fox showed no signs of slowing down.

'This incompetent police work will never stand up in a court of law. Even with all this technology, you're far worse than this force was in the eighties. Things have gone backwards. His murder should have been solved years ago. There must have been so much blood and evidence everywhere. All they had to do was examine the boys' changing room for blood, and the case would have been solved. And another thing . . .'

Robert Fox trailed off as he realised what he'd said.

For a moment, everyone was silent.

Then Karen said, 'We didn't tell Detective Superintendent Fox where his brother's body was found, ma'am, did we?'

Superintendent Murray gave Robert Fox an ice-cold smile. 'No, DS Hart. We did not.'

Robert Fox looked horrified. He began to stammer. 'Well . . . I just . . . I just assumed it must have happened at the school . . . It was where he worked.'

'True,' Karen said slowly. 'But the changing room is a very specific location. And, of course, you're right. We *will* look for trace evidence. I promise you, we'll scour every last inch of the changing room, and I'm willing to bet we'll find something linking you to the scene of the crime.'

The look on his face was pure panic. Sophie held her breath.

He muttered something about the assistant commissioner mentioning it, but Sophie knew that wasn't true. The assistant commissioner may have been perfectly happy to put a little pressure on his junior officers, but he wouldn't leak details of the case and risk losing his comfortable pension.

She watched Robert Fox floundering, trying desperately to correct his mistake, but of course, he couldn't. He'd given the game away. If he'd known Oliver Fox was murdered in the boys' changing room at Greenhill Secondary School that could only mean one thing. He'd killed his own brother.

She wanted to high-five Karen and do a little victory dance, but she had a feeling Superintendent Murray would disapprove, so instead she settled for grinning at Rick.

CHAPTER FORTY

Two days later, Karen, DI Morgan and Superintendent Murray stood in the viewing suite next to interview room three. None of the monitors were on yet, because Robert Fox was in there, conferring with his solicitor.

Superintendent Murray pulled out a chair and sat behind the largest monitor. She didn't often come down to observe interviews, and it seemed strange to see her in this setting.

'I'll be watching,' she said, looking at DI Morgan and then Karen. 'Robert Fox did not make my job easy during this case. Make sure you get him to talk.'

'No pressure, then,' Karen murmured as she followed DI Morgan out of the viewing suite and into the interview room. DI Morgan said nothing, but looked determined.

Robert Fox sat at the table next to his solicitor. His shoulders were slumped. With dark circles under his eyes and hair hanging limply over his forehead, he didn't look so suave and in control now.

Since Robert Fox's unwitting confession, a forensics team had been swarming over Greenhill Academy, focusing on the boys' changing room. But, to their chagrin, the changing room had been remodelled ten years ago, and they'd found nothing to help their case against Robert Fox.

A small amount of blood had been detected under the new flooring, but it had deteriorated to such an extent they couldn't extract any DNA. Karen didn't know whether it was cleaning fluids or sunlight that had destroyed the DNA over the years. All she knew was they'd reached a dead end.

They needed him to confess. Without physical evidence, they had no chance of bringing a strong case against him.

But Robert Fox didn't know that. Karen slid into the seat opposite him. She intended to make the ex-detective superintendent believe they had stacks of evidence against him.

When DI Morgan sat down, they ran through the formalities, then Karen said, 'We've had some good news, Detective Superintendent Fox.'

He blinked at her but said nothing.

'The evidence is still being processed, but it's amazing what can still be detected after thirty years. But then, you know how advanced DNA techniques are these days.'

He frowned and licked his lips before shooting a nervous glance at his solicitor.

His solicitor was a tall woman with dark curly hair and sharp green eyes. She didn't look ruffled in the slightest.

'We know you killed your brother, Robert. But what I'd like to know is, what was your motive? Did you get fed up covering for him? I can't blame you for being sick of his disgusting transgressions. They must have been affecting your career. It can't have been easy for you to constantly be expected to clean up after him, again and again. Did you just snap? Was it one time too many?' Karen leaned forward, meeting his gaze. 'Or did you drop by and see something that made you realise your brother was a monster and you were protecting him?'

Robert Fox's face crumpled, and he closed his eyes, scrunching them shut.

'You don't need to answer that, Robert,' the solicitor said coolly.

DI Morgan took over the questioning. 'You've three other men's deaths on your conscience, too. James Hunter, William Grant and Albert Johnson.' Slowly, he laid out their photographs out on the table, facing Robert Fox.

The detective superintendent's gaze flickered over the photographs before looking away again.

'Your nephew killed them because he believed they'd murdered his father. It wasn't true, though, was it? The boys only found the body, and their teachers helped them cover it up, but they didn't kill him. *You* did that.'

'You have no evidence to support that claim. My client will not be making a comment at this time,' the solicitor said, sounding bored.

'And while we're talking about your nephew, it's your fault Stephen will be going away for a very long time. What sort of man are you, Detective Superintendent Fox? You held a position of trust. You were a police officer. Did that mean nothing to you? You had a responsibility to protect those boys. Or did you not care about the job? Was it all about power to you? Maybe you took the job for its perks, so you could cover up for your brother. You really are a disgrace to your profession.'

Robert Fox buried his face in his hands and then shook his head. 'I'm not a bad man. I made a mistake, but I didn't mean to kill him.'

The solicitor sat up sharply and put a hand on Robert's forearm, saying, 'I'd like to pause the interview so I can speak with my client.'

But Robert Fox sagged back in his chair. 'There's no need. The truth will come out. It always does eventually. I'll tell you what you want to know.'

Karen and DI Morgan stayed silent, waiting for him to continue.

Robert Fox picked up the glass of water in front of him and gulped it down. When he put the glass back down on the table, he met Karen's eye. 'We argued. He disgusted me. You have to believe that. When the allegations involving Mark Bell came out, I didn't believe them. I thought the boy had to be lying. There was no way my brother could have done something like that, but then more stories started to surface and I couldn't ignore it. I went to confront him, and we got into a fight. We struggled, and I threw a punch. Just one . . .' He looked at Karen beseechingly. 'I only hit him once, but he fell and hit his head on the bench. I didn't think he was badly hurt and tried to rouse him, but there was a lot of blood coming from his head wound.'

He broke off, reaching for his glass again and then realising it was empty. 'I panicked and ran when I couldn't feel a pulse.'

Karen picked up the bottle of mineral water and refilled the glass.

Robert Fox grabbed it with shaking hands and took another large gulp.

'I waited for it to catch up with me, waited for the knock at the door, but it never came. Eventually I realised someone had covered it up and removed his body, but I didn't know who. I did consider coming forward, but then I thought, why should I let him ruin my life? He betrayed me. I covered for him, I believed in him, but when the rumours started up again, and I confronted him, he laughed at me.'

He drew in a long breath. 'He was a stain on our family, an embarrassment. I couldn't let it go on. I was planning on reporting him, doing it all officially, but I lost my temper.'

Robert Fox looked down at the desk and began to sob.

The solicitor insisted on a break to confer with her client, but Karen didn't mind. They had him now, and there was no way he was going to get away with it.

Karen drove along Station Road towards Heighington, heading to DI Morgan's housewarming party. She was looking forward to it. An evening away from the job and her thoughts was just what she needed.

She'd invited Christine along, and her neighbour sat in the passenger seat, trying to type out a text message.

'This blasted thing!' Christine exclaimed. She'd recently upgraded her mobile phone and was struggling to get to grips with the new model.

With Christine occupied, muttering curses at her phone, Karen let her mind wander back to the case.

Tying up loose ends had taken longer than expected. Robert Fox would be prosecuted for manslaughter, but it was hard to feel pleased with the outcome of the case after so many unnecessary deaths. In the end, Albert Johnson and William Grant had paid the ultimate price for covering up the death of Oliver Fox. They'd acted on the rumours concerning him and his sick predilection for young boys, and assumed the boys had killed their teacher after he'd abused them.

The sad fact was the three boys had been telling the truth. They really did just stumble on the body after the altercation between the two Fox brothers.

Karen sighed as she veered left after the railway bridge. If Oliver's death had been reported to the police at the time, much of the tragedy that followed could have been averted.

Stephen Fox was currently being assessed in a mental hospital to see if he was fit to stand trial. His brother, Martin, had been discharged from inpatient care and was recovering at home with his mother.

Elizabeth Fox was making it her life's work to send letters complaining about the police to newspapers and journalists around the country. Karen dreaded to think how much the woman's bill for printer ink had been this month. She'd been threatening to sue the officers involved in the case against her son, but so far it had come to nothing. She still refused to believe the allegations of abuse against her husband, and was adamant that her son had been used as a scapegoat. Sometimes, believing a lie was easier than accepting the truth.

Karen slowed as she entered Heighington, keeping to the speed limit of twenty miles an hour as she passed the first set of houses.

The case had involved so many deaths, but at least Michael and Stuart were now safe and could try to put this behind them and enjoy happy lives with their families. That was something to be thankful for, she supposed.

She had to park around the corner from DI Morgan's house as the driveway was full. She and Christine carried their housewarming gifts to the house. Karen had bought a bottle of red from the Co-op, and Christine's gift was a homemade bottle of elderberry wine.

The front door had been left open, and DI Morgan looked up and waved as he saw them enter. Rick and Sophie were already there, along with a few other faces from the station Karen recognised.

She took the elderberry wine from Christine and headed to the kitchen, placing both bottles on the counter.

'Thanks, you didn't need to bring anything,' DI Morgan said as he entered the kitchen behind her.

'I couldn't come empty-handed. Besides, Christine insisted on bringing you a bottle of her elderberry wine.'

He frowned at the bottle. 'I've never had it before. Is it nice?'

Karen leaned forward, lowered her voice, and said with a wink, 'It's lethal.'

DI Morgan grinned. 'Thanks for the warning.'

Someone called for him, and they walked out of the kitchen. Mary Dixon from across the street had arrived with a large tray piled high with freshly baked scones, and DI Morgan went over to thank her.

Christine was talking to Marjorie Wentworth, who worked at the village shop.

'Hi!' Sophie appeared at Karen's side holding a bottle of Prosecco. 'Fancy a glass?'

'Just a small one,' Karen said. 'I'm driving home.'

Sophie grabbed a clean flute from the sideboard and poured Karen half a glass. 'There you go, Sarge.'

'Thanks.'

Sophie's cheeks were flushed and dimpled as she chinked her glass against Karen's and then pulled her in for a hug.

'What was that for?' Karen asked.

'You helped me when I was feeling down, and it means a lot that you believe I'll have a good career.'

'Oh, I see. This isn't your first glass of Prosecco?' Karen teased.

Sophie tottered and leaned against the wall. 'I've had a few,' she confided. 'But I mean it. Thank you.'

Karen raised her own glass. 'Don't mention it.'

'Anyway, you never told me about that date you went on.' Sophie leaned in, eager to get all the gossip.

Karen pulled a face. 'Let's just say I'm not going to be going on any more dates for the foreseeable future.'

'That bad?'

Karen nodded. 'That bad. How's the house-hunting been going?'

Sophie smiled. 'I'm looking at some places this weekend that are a bit more realistic with my budget. Start small and build on a solid foundation, right?'

'Exactly. I'll drink to that.'

'I keep thinking back to the look on Robert Fox's face when he realised he'd given the game away,' Sophie said with a grin. 'It was price-less. Better than a swanky job in Monaco any day.'

Karen frowned. 'Monaco?'

'Oh, it's nothing. A friend of mine from school has been living the high life, jetting off to Monaco to host parties, and I got a bit frustrated with myself and my prospects. I was comparing myself to her, I suppose.'

'That's never a good idea.'

'I know,' Sophie said. 'Besides, no other job could beat the buzz of solving a case.'

DI Morgan walked back into the living room, encouraging some of the guests to try the home-baked scones.

Sophie tilted her head to whisper in Karen's ear. 'Sarge, have you found out why DI Morgan moved to Lincoln? I've always wanted to ask, but thought it seemed a bit nosy to bring it up.'

Karen shrugged. 'I'm sure it's nothing interesting. Maybe property prices.'

Sophie seemed content with that answer, and clinked her glass against Karen's again.

Karen took a sip of her Prosecco. Maybe DI Morgan would tell the rest of the team in time, but as far as she was concerned, it wasn't her secret to tell.

ACKNOWLEDGMENTS

I am very grateful to all the people who have worked hard to produce the books in the DS Karen Hart series. Many thanks to Jack Butler and the team at APub. It's been a pleasure to work with you.

A huge thanks to my family and friends. I'm very lucky to have such a fabulous group of people around me who are my biggest supporters. They encourage me to follow my dreams, cheer me on and make life fun.

And a special thanks to all the amazing readers who have shown me so much support over the past few years. The messages and emails I get from people who have enjoyed the stories mean the world to me – thank you all so very much!

ABOUT THE AUTHOR

Born in Kent, D. S. Butler grew up as an avid reader, with a love for crime fiction and mysteries. She has worked as a scientific officer in a hospital pathology laboratory and as a research scientist.

After obtaining a PhD in biochemistry, she worked at the University of Oxford for four years before moving to the Middle East. While living in Bahrain, she wrote her first novel and hasn't stopped writing since.

She now lives in Lincolnshire with her husband.